I0644684

## Praise for *The Wondrous Springs of Balmorhea*

"Gretchen McCullough, in her heart-breaking and deeply-empathetic novel, *The Wondrous Springs of Balmorhea,* utilizes the Civilian Conservation Corps' 1936 construction of the Balmorhea, Texas, pool to reveal a diverse, fascinating cast of characters. The exotic project brings together people with traumatic and provincial pasts, and their isolation leads to loneliness, the toll of keeping secrets, and complications from misogyny, racism, illicit activity, and the demands of leadership. On top of all that, there's the danger of digging a pit from hard dirt in west Texas heat, sealing it with adobe bricks, and diverting spring water to fill it. McCullough employs her comic madcap, but this book is primarily a deep investigation of people, the frailty of their bodies and minds, and the vicissitudes of responsibility. They all pay a price to bring to life something stunning, beautiful, and lasting."

**Tim Parrish,** Author of ***The Jumper, Red Stick Men: Stories and Fear What Follows: The Violent Education of a Christian Racist.***

"The Civilian Conservation Corps, a key pillar of President Roosevelt's New Deal, played a pivotal role in developing not only Balmorhea State Park but also hundreds of parks across the country. The countless CCC-built structures have created a lasting legacy that connects people to the natural landscapes within and around these parks. Nearly 100 years later, the CCC's impact continues to shape and inspire future generations."

**Tara Fattouh, Assistant Park Superintendent, Balmorhea State Park**

THE WONDROUS SPRINGS OF BALMORHEA

# The Wondrous Springs of BALMORHEA

## A Literary Chronicle of New Deal Days

GRETCHEN MCCULLOUGH

TCU PRESS
Fort Worth, Texas

Library of Congress Cataloging-in-Publication Data

Names: McCullough, Gretchen author
Title: The wondrous springs of Balmorhea : a literary chronicle of New Deal days / Gretchen McCullough.
Description: Fort Worth : TCU Press, [2026] | Includes bibliographical references.
Identifiers: LCCN 2026028715 (print) | LCCN 2026028716 (ebook) | ISBN 9780875659848 paperback | ISBN 9780875659855 ebook
Subjects: LCSH: Civilian Conservation Corps (U.S.). Company 1856 (Balmorhea,Tex.) | New Deal, 1933-1939 | Balmorhea (Tex.) | LCGFT: Novels | Historical fiction | Fiction
Classification: LCC PS3613.C3864496 W66 2026 (print) | LCC PS3613.C3864496 (ebook)
LC record available at https://lccn.loc.gov/2026028715
LC ebook record available at https://lccn.loc.gov/2026028716

Cover design by Adrienne Martinez
Cover illustration by Karina Rodriguez-Alcorta

TCU PRESS

TCU Box 298300
Fort Worth, Texas 76129
www.tcupress.com

To the memory of my grandfather, Gene Frederick McCullough (1910–1980), who quietly fought against the many injustices of this world

CONTENTS

## PART I: Dreams of West Texas

CHAPTER 1 Arroyo Drive, Harlingen, South Texas, 1976 3

CHAPTER 2 Roll Call, Balmorhea, June 1935 5

CHAPTER 3 Rattlesnakes, July 1935 17

CHAPTER 4 Chueco 27

CHAPTER 5 Vim and Vigor, August 1935 37

CHAPTER 6 Devilfish, late August 1935 45

CHAPTER 7 Blue Moon 49

CHAPTER 8 The Infirmary 63

CHAPTER 9 Healing 75

CHAPTER 10 Heat Wave 81

CHAPTER 11 Charlotte, September 1935 91

## PART II: VISITORS

CHAPTER 12 The Attic, Arroyo Drive, Harlingen, Texas, 1976 99

CHAPTER 13 The Camping Trip in the Davis Mountains, October 1935 105

CHAPTER 14 Darlene's Diary, October 8, 1935 127

CHAPTER 15 Arroyo Drive, Harlingen, Texas, 1976 131

CHAPTER 16 Return to Balmorhea, 1935 137

CHAPTER 17 Captain Bell 143

CHAPTER 18 Wonder Cure 151

CHAPTER 19 A Journalist on a Motorcycle with a Sidecar 161

CHAPTER 20 A Lengthy Row over Medical Experimentation 167

CHAPTER 21 Darlene's Diary, October 15, 1935 177
CHAPTER 22 Opium Eaters 179
CHAPTER 23 Captain of the Ship 183
CHAPTER 24 The Lost Dog 187
CHAPTER 25 Thanksgiving, November 24th, 1935 193
CHAPTER 26 Howard Perry 201
CHAPTER 27 Darlene's Diary, November 24, 1935 207
CHAPTER 28 Sam, Arroyo Drive, Thanksgiving, 1976 211

PART III: CLEAN LIVING

CHAPTER 29 Ho, Ho, Ho: Christmas, 1935 219
CHAPTER 30 Darlene's Diary, Christmas, 1935 225
CHAPTER 31 Captain Bell 229
CHAPTER 32 The Brig 233
CHAPTER 33 Jack and the Brig 241
CHAPTER 34 Captain Bell 247
CHAPTER 35 Sam 257
CHAPTER 36 Darlene's Diary, December 31, 1935 261
CHAPTER 37 A Dry New Year's Eve, Almost, 1936 267
CHAPTER 38 Local Olympics, and One Afar, February 1936 279
CHAPTER 39 A Reckoning 285
CHAPTER 40 The Loot 289
CHAPTER 41 Punishment in the Pit, March 1936 293
CHAPTER 42 The Disappearance of Doc Walker's Gold Pocket Watch, Early May 1936 297

## PART IV: The Pool


CHAPTER 43 Sam, Arroyo Drive, Harlingen, Texas, 1980 303

CHAPTER 44 A Midnight Dip, Captain Bell, May 1936 309

CHAPTER 45 Cracks 315

CHAPTER 46 Darlene's Diary, Last Week of May 1936 321

CHAPTER 47 Just Like Sam Spade, Dashiell Hammett's Detective 325

CHAPTER 48 Submerged 329

CHAPTER 49 The Report 335

CHAPTER 50 Captain Bell, The Balmorhea Celebrations Committee 339

CHAPTER 51 Sabah el-Ward, A Morning Full of Roses, June 26, 1936 347

CHAPTER 52 The Lost Letter, Arroyo Drive, Harlingen, Texas, 1980 361

CHAPTER 53 Buoyancy, November 1980 367

ACKNOWLEDGMENTS 371

BIBLIOGRAPHY 374

ENDNOTES 377

# PART I:

# Dreams of West Texas

CHAPTER 1.

# Arroyo Drive, Harlingen, South Texas, 1976

## Samuel McCabe:

He didn't have long. A tumor had wrapped itself around the nerves of his shoulder, and the doctors had taken the arm. They were now telling him that the ol' snake might still be lurking around. Shortly after he and Maggie had gotten married in the thirties, the doctors discovered he had a rare form of melanoma—they'd blasted it out of his body with the new lightning: radiation. That wondrous cure had prolonged his life for forty-three years.

He had rigged up a rope in the lush, green front yard so he could walk back and forth for exercise. A mother armadillo, followed by tiny babies, appeared by the ebony tree, as if they knew. They kept him company when Maggie was in the house. His eye followed a swallow, dipping in the blue sky with such abandon and freedom that he envied her. But even this fierce, determined effort to walk daily could not roll back the force of the nasty vine. He clenched the rope and prayed, but he was quickly losing his balance. Memories from the past also cut loose, buoyed to the surface, making him feel disoriented, as if he was floating in the cool water of the Balmorhea spring, baby minnows tickling his feet. He didn't know why, but he had started dreaming about Darlene, the nurse he had fallen in love with at Balmorhea when he was in his twenties—boy, he had been charmed. What had happened to her? Were any of those rumors at the camp true? He loved his feisty wife, Maggie, and had never told her about Darlene because he wanted to spare her feelings. It had been an early infatuation when he was a hot-blooded young man. Wasn't his diary from Balmorhea in the attic?

There were other dreams, too. When he was a little fella, riding across the stark West Texas plain on a Mustang named Keno, he found his way to school with a rusty compass. When he opened the door to the one-room schoolhouse—there she was, dressed for the dance at Balmorhea in a pale blue dress with a scoop neck that enhanced her cleavage. "Yoo hoo, anybody home? Why, aren't I lucky? To have you all to myself." But he was only five, not a grown man with ardent desires. In another dream, his folks were moving in covered wagons from one ranch to another in Texas and New Mexico because his pa was managing livestock. He was a little older, maybe ten. Those infernal horses ran amuck in Lamesa, close to Lubbock, through the manicured pink rose beds in a lady's yard. The door was flung open: this time, Darlene was dressed in a starched white uniform, a cape over her shoulders, carrying a tiny brown suitcase. He heard her say, "I couldn't tell you. You were just so earnest. So young. And what he did to those men was criminal."

Had she departed this earth?

CHAPTER 2.

# Roll Call, Balmorhea, June 1935

**Sam remembered now.** The smell of lavender—when Darlene had come into the office that day. That was the same day the boy Chueco had arrived at Balmorhea. The heat was oppressive, and he had wished for even the tiniest breeze. The vast, blue West Texas sky was swallowed in puffy white clouds. Behind them, the Davis Mountains rose in the distance, from this flat, barren desert that went on for miles and miles, without even the shade of a single tree. That's what he had loved when he had arrived in the Rio Grande Valley in 1944, the lush orange groves, the smell of citrus. But one blessing between Fort Stockton and Fort Davis was an artesian spring that gushed cold, pure water. The Mexican farmers had called it Mescalero Springs and had funneled off the water through canals to irrigate their crops as early as 1849. But by 1935, folks in this area were calling it the San Solomon spring.

He was lucky. And maybe, he was blessed, too, although sometimes he felt a little sorry for himself, especially when he overheard someone snicker that he was "Bell's errand boy." But he didn't have to work outside so much like the other boys, who dug in the hot sun, wrestled with rattlesnakes, and baked the adobe bricks for the swimming pool. Things were dire before he had come to Balmorhea—his family were mostly eating pickled peas and corn from the garden and the occasional chicken, even prairie dogs. Once, a canned goat, which was the gamiest, foulest thing he had ever eaten. His mama had shown him the foreclosure on the farm near Lubbock. Papa clammed right up and went off to check the tomato vines in the garden. Later, they huddled around the radio, listening to the president speak: "Let me assert my firm belief that the only thing we have to fear is fear itself—nameless, unreasoning, unjustified terror . . . We are stricken by no plague of locusts."

Captain Bell, a veteran from the Great War, stood next to him, as if a steel rod was going through his back. The government was assigning leftover uniforms from the Great War. Not that Sam was complaining. Bell was wearing light brown khakis—creased with a hot iron. The brown tie was knotted tightly, tucked into the shirt. The left sleeve, where his arm should have been, drooped. Just how long did it take for him to get dressed? He had never complained. Bell had tucked his pants into leather boots so the pants billowed slightly above the knee. He wasn't that tall, but his quiet authority and discipline made him seem like a giant.

Word had gotten out about the opportunity for work on the president's Civilian Conservation Corps (CCC) projects. Two full lines of Mexican boys in the front; four Black boys stood next to them off to one side. And four rows deep stood Anglo boys from El Paso or one of those forlorn little towns anywhere near those parts. Ready to work in the sun, they all wore hats—some flat caps and others traditional cowboy hats. The blue jean overalls were baggy and just hung on them, as if they were scarecrows. Dr. Walker shook his head, staring down at the scale, one hundred and fifteen pounds. But come five o'clock, the boys burst into the mess hall, pulling back the wooden benches like hungry wolves who ate everything in sight, licking their dishes and going back for seconds and thirds.

"Welcome to Balmorhea, boys. As our great President Franklin Delano Roosevelt said, 'The forests are the lungs of our land which purify the air and give strength to our people.'"

Sam wished Captain Bell would skip the poetic flourishes and pontification and get these men on their way to the construction site. But as he had learned, Captain Bell couldn't be hurried. He had made it clear to him that he was the one calling the shots. Not that Sam said much—why he figured later Captain Bell had appointed him to be his assistant. He knew all the secrets of the camp. Sam was Captain Bell's right-hand man, or, in military terms, a role a little less elevated: company clerk. A graduate of Sul Ross, he could read and write and had a decent command of Spanish. He clutched the clipboard. As he would learn later, some would call him something more damning than "errand boy." Sam was short and had a baby face—his nickname was "Baby Red" since he had carrot-red hair.

"Son, those britches are too big for you. Look like you've joined Barnum and Bailey Circus, not the Tree Army," Captain Bell said. The shoes were also three sizes too big for him. The kid was wearing a flat cap, which was pulled way down over his eyes.

The other boys hooted: "Go back to your mama! Mama! Mama! Well, shoot, ain't he a mama's boy." Someone else shouted, "Get on back over the river. Go back to Mexico! Greaser!"

"That was not meant as a joke," Captain Bell said sharply. "At attention." The men stood straight: no one wanted to be sent home. Everyone was tired of being hungry.

Sam looked down at his clipboard, scanning through the Mexican names. They all said the "legal" age allowed for the CCC camp—eighteen. He felt sorry for the kid among them, not more than fifteen. He knew that most of them had forged their birth certificates. Once in the office, Captain Bell had said, "If we send 'em back, they'll starve. No one is going to starve or die under my watch, so help me God."

Captain Bell's eyes burned with a certain intensity. What had Captain Bell seen during the Great War? Besides the missing arm, the left side of his cheek was badly burned, and his face was slightly disfigured. Sam never had the courage to ask him directly. After lights-out, someone had whispered that Captain Bell's wife and baby daughter had died in the Spanish flu epidemic of 1918.

"Just so y'all know, all are American citizens here, and we won't have any of that. I do not condone that kind of attitude," Captain Bell said, clearing his throat.

The hat was pulled so far down over the boy's eyes that you couldn't see them. Probably holding back his tears.

"What is your name, son?" Captain Bell asked. When the boy kept saying, "*¿Qué.? ¿Qué.?*" Sam jumped in, "*¿Cómo se llama?*"

"Adrian Gonzalez," he said. Then he added, "Chueco." He was bowlegged, and his face was so thin, it was almost skeletal.

Sam scanned the long list of names again. "He's from Terlingua, Captain. There's a quicksilver mine there. Mercury."

Captain Bell frowned. "Draconian place. Hell, it is. Blazing hot. Old man Perry workin' them to death, like slaves. Thinks he's a Roman emperor. Anyhow," he sighed. "Get him something better. Something that fits. Assign him to the kitchen. Put him in an English class."

Sam licked the pencil and put a check by Adrian's name, and in parentheses (Chueco). What did "draconian" mean? Terlingua was a hundred and forty miles from Balmorhea, might as well be

Antarctica, or even Mars. He must have hitchhiked the whole way. Big Bend State Park was closer.

"Well, boys, we are building a swimming pool for the nation," Captain Bell continued, gesturing to the enormous construction site, the size of a football field, behind them. Small creeks of water were dammed up so the spring wouldn't flow into the site. A few dump trucks were parked smack in the middle. A cluster of men were already gathered there—and were bent over, digging with their shovels. Mounds of dirt like mushrooms dotted the field. In the distance, not far from the site, were the rows of barracks.

"Using the San Solomon spring, we are going to build one of the biggest freshwater swimming pools in the world. This will be an architectural wonder!"

With his right hand, Captain Bell wiped the sweat from his forehead with a pressed white hanky.

Sam felt sweat sticking to his drawers and resisted the need to scratch—that would be right embarrassing. The boys would think that was hilarious.

"Just so you boys know, we're not gonna have any gamblin', chasin' girls. Drinkin'."

Some man shouted, "You runnin' a Catholic monastery, yaaah?"

"*Pendejo*," a Mexican American boy next to Chueco muttered.

Sam put his finger to his lips. Captain Bell might appear cool as a cucumber, but you had to stand out of the way when his temper blew, like a Spindletop gusher.

"This is like the army. And we will have discipline. Who's the smart aleck? Please come forward," Captain Bell said.

A blond giant loped to the front of the line and stood in front of Captain Bell. His hair was shaved close to his scalp. His cheeks were pitted from pimples.

"What's your name, son?" Captain Bell asked.

"Otto Kloss." His brown eyes gleamed with insolence. He towered over Captain Bell, but Bell didn't flinch or show the slightest bit of surprise. Sam hoped this jackass was not in his barracks—feeling his stomach gurgle. Would be just his luck.

"Sam, please could you make sure that Mr. Kloss cleans the latrines for the first two weeks?"

No one laughed this time. Sam circled Otto's name and wrote: LATRINE DUTY.

Otto narrowed his eyes and gave him a spiteful look. Sam kept studying the names on his clipboard.

Captain Bell continued. "Where was I? Clean living. Clean work for the nation. I am not against having a little fun, but it's going to be clean. We'll draw up the lists for baseball teams soon. Or other activities. You'll be over there, digging."

"I'm going back to the office, sir," Sam said. "Have a lot of paperwork. Got to wait for the mail."

"You do that, McCabe," Captain Bell said. "Follow me, men," he gestured, heading toward the construction site.

A tiny, emerald hummingbird with a royal blue breast fluttered near Captain Bell's head. Then, like a rainbow, it disappeared.

• • •

Sam ambled back to the little makeshift office made from plywood, with the one window. Four desks were crammed in there—and Captain Bell had his desk behind a wood partition. Needless to say, there wasn't a lot of privacy. If the captain was on the phone, you could hear every word. A potbellied stove was in the center of the room and provided the only heat in the winter—and it got chilly. Had to even wear long johns in winter.

The first thing he did when he entered the office was raise the window and prop it open with a board. The room was stuffy and had the cheesy smell of dirty socks. He propped open the door with an adobe brick—dust blew in.

He plopped down in the wooden chair and stared at his desk. The pigeonholes were full of papers that needed to be typed. After the postman came, he would have to sort the mail. He stared at the typewriter—a letter unfinished to the general store in Fort Davis. Items requested: Shoe Polish, Smoking Tobacco, Beer, Cigarettes, Soap Flakes, Candy. Vim Cola. Some new drink? And Wonder Cure.

He looked at the business name on the address: *The Kafouri Brothers, Proprietors of General Dry Goods*. Was that an American name? Never heard of it. Was he from around these parts or a foreign country?

Delaying the inevitable, he got up and picked up the pitcher full of water on the potbellied stove. Took a long swig.

"Yoo-hoo," a voice called out. "Anybody home?" Darlene popped her head in the door. "Why, aren't I lucky? To have you all to myself?"

She was wearing a plain white nurse's uniform, but her ample bosom stretched through the material. Sam choked on the water—unable to stop staring at her chest, rather than her face. He hoped she didn't notice.

"Sure is hot," Sam said, setting the pitcher down. "Was just having a drink. Would you like some?"

He could have sworn he was looking at Mae West, instead of Darlene—but Darlene had jet-black hair. She had pulled her curly hair back in a knot. He had sneaked a look at her personnel file so he knew for a fact that she was thirty-one years old—an older woman. In those days, he thought thirty-one was old! The box ticked: UNMARRIED. A few had seen Mae West in *I'm No Angel* with Cary

Grant at the picture show. Many speculated that "unmarried" was a big fib.

"It's good not to get dehydrated," Darlene said. She looked at him directly. "How you been keepin' yourself?"

Before Balmorhea, Sam had kissed a girl or two in a barn, but he had almost no experience with the opposite sex. Darlene probably didn't mean to be provocative when she was just being frank. He was probably misreading her—he speculated she was after bigger fish, like Captain Bell. Or maybe the owner of the grocery, Kafouri.

"Oh, fine," Sam said. "Got a lot of work to do," he said, nodding toward his desk, piled high with letters, documents, and papers. "How can I help you?"

She folded her arms. "I need to see Captain Bell." All business now.

"He's out at the pool with the new enrollees. I don't know when he'll be back. You could leave a message."

"Can't fool with going out there," Darlene said. "Let's just put it this way, McCabe."

So she didn't really consider him a candidate for her affections—she wasn't even calling him by his first name.

"We have a shortage of antivenom at the camp," she said. Her eyes were a light blue. What would she do if he brushed lightly against her?

He breathed in her smell—something floral. Delicate.

"What?" If only he could nuzzle those bosoms. He kept a photograph of Mae West in his wallet for his private adventures after lights-out. He felt stiff in the groin area.

"McCabe, I'm talking to you. Get that dreamy look out of your eyes. We don't have enough antivenom. That's a problem if someone gets bit."

He moved behind another desk so she wouldn't see the bulge in his pants. He pretended to be looking for a paper. He heard himself saying, "I never received any requests from Dr. Walker. I'm the one who sends these supply requests off to the Feds."

"That's why I need to talk to the captain," she said, sighing, exasperated, as if she were talking to her younger brother.

There was a confident rap at the open door. Jack didn't wait for permission to enter.

"Well, if it ain't Jack Huley," she said, hands on her fulsome hips. To Sam's consternation, she looked delighted to see him. "You haven't been over to see me in the clinic lately."

Jack ran his hand through his thick black hair. If Darlene looked like Mae West, Jack looked like Cary Grant. Sam couldn't help being a tad jealous; at Sul Ross, all the girls clustered 'round him. He was known as a "ladies' man."

"Howdy," he said, nodding at her, "Miss Robinson." He was holding a straw hat in his hand. "Of course, if it hadn't been for your nursing care, I would be long dead and gone. You see, Mac, I am allergic to wasps. And Miss Robinson, she knew exactly what to do."

Unlike Sam, Jack could talk your ear off. Didn't know that there needed to be space between people, some discretion.

Darlene winked at Jack. "You've recovered from that wasp sting."

"I have," Jack said, nodding his head. "I am much obliged for the treatment. You are just an angel of mercy. We're lucky to have you at the camp. In fact, we could just dispense with Dr. Walker, altogether."

"Well, I have all sorts of tricks to help a man heal," Darlene said, arranging a black curl behind her ear.

Sam was not imagining anything now: She carried a torch for Jack. He didn't have a chance. Not only was there Bell and Kafouri, but also Huley!

Sam felt himself grow a little officious. "Do you need to see Captain Bell?"

"As a matter of fact, I do. We need more books for the library. Supplies for the correspondence courses. More chalk," Jack said. Where did he get all of that confidence?

Sam was a little sore that Darlene fancied Jack. She was smiling at Jack—that little gap between the teeth now prominent. He was not imagining it; Jack was smiling.

Sam picked up the clipboard on his desk. If he couldn't have Darlene, he could strut his stuff. "Oh, by the way, Jack. Captain Bell wants you to teach a boy named Chueco English. He's from Terlingua. There are probably a lot of boys who'll need English lessons."

Darlene sighed. "Well, I declare. This place is a hot box. Doesn't it make you want to strip off?" She started fanning herself with one of the papers on his desk. The intoxicating smell of roses swirled around the room.

"I know who you're talkin' about. That boy practically walked the entire way to Balmorhea. You shoulda seen his feet when he rolled up here. Lord. Had homemade shoes made from car tires. I made him soak his feet with Epsom salts in a tub."

Sam felt annoyed. "That's how we got here from Alpine."

Jack laughed, as if he didn't have a care in the world. "We hitched after the first twenty miles. Some truck driver felt sorry for us and let us ride in the back. Tell 'em a good story, and they'll carry you for miles."

"If you're gabbing about that around the camp, don't mention the shoes made of tires," Sam said. "Don't think that boy would appreciate it." He felt protective of Chueco, even though he didn't know the kid.

Sam's family was poorer than Jack's—and he was prickly about not having anything. On the other hand, Sam didn't think Darlene was being malicious.

Jack laughed again. "Oh, Sam, no need to get your nose out of joint. None of us have got a penny here. If it weren't for this government pool, you'd still be in Alpine, washing greasy dishes at Mrs. Lockhart's boarding house."

Darlene laughed and touched his arm. "Well, I didn't mean to offend Sam McCabe. I better get back to my post in case I'm needed."

"Sure."

As soon as she sailed out of the office, Sam rushed over to the window and stuck his head out. As if she knew he was staring at her bottom, she turned around and blew him a kiss.

"She's sweet on you," Jack said, watching her until she disappeared.

"Naw," Sam said. "She likes you."

"Don't be a lug," Jack said. "You don't know the first thing about gals. You know, I flirt with anyone wearing a skirt. Besides, I've got my heart set on Ruby. Saving up to propose."

Sam nursed a tiny hope. For some reason, he was reminded of the emerald hummingbird. Maybe, just maybe . . .

But suddenly, he became formal with Jack. "This isn't the time to get carried away. I'm not in a position to start a family."

Jack elbowed him. "Eeee doggie! I didn't say anything about marriage. Mae West is flirtin' with you and all you can think about is *the future.*"

"That's right, Jack," Sam said. "I don't want to be lassoing horses and working on land ventures that don't pan out for the rest of my life, like my pa."

Jack clapped him on the shoulder. "Lighten up just a little, cowboy. We always landed on our feet in Alpine. Moonshine. Milking cows. Waiting tables."

"As far as I can see, neither one of us showed much talent with the cows," Sam said, suddenly feeling blue. The memory of being broke depressed him. He had to get to work before Captain Bell showed up.

Better to keep his feelings about Darlene to himself since Jack couldn't keep a secret.

CHAPTER 3.

# Rattlesnakes, July 1935

**July was hotter than June, and the diggers started tying bandanas around their necks.** Every once in a while, someone got heatstroke and had to be carried off to the clinic. If they were digging deep, nests of rattlesnakes slithered out into the scorching sun. The men caught them on rakes and tossed them into huge gunny sacks. The gunny sacks were tied up, and the snakes were released in the Davis mountains far from the site. Captain Bell forbade the use of pistols to kill the snakes. Sam understood now that Captain Bell was forward in his thinking about a good many things.

One morning in July, Sam was typing up *The Round-Up*, the company newsletter, with the following headline: DANCE PLANNED. LIVE MUSIC.

The phone rang. "Balmorhea," he said. He had been hunting for the "C" on the keyboard.

A voice said, "Otto got bit. Real bad."

"Where?" Sam asked. Most dreaded the rattlers, except for a few of the boys who had taken to hunting them for fun in their spare time. It made Captain Bell furious, and he had commented, "We'll have to come up with more leisure activities, Sam. Any ideas?"

The voice drawled. "Mess hall. That giant got bit by a snake, and it don't look good. Better come quick."

Captain Bell was expecting a phone call from Washington. He popped his head around the wood partition. "McCabe! I told you to answer the phone more formally. What happened to Balmorhea, CCC Camp Headquarters?"

"Sir," Sam said, holding out the black receiver. "It's not Washington. Someone's been bitten by a rattler."

"For crying out loud! Those dern snakes," Captain Bell said. "Scourge of the earth. Call the infirmary."

Sam let it ring twenty times. "No answer. Maybe they stepped out?"

Captain Bell picked up the hard ranger hat that hung on the peg behind the potbellied stove. "We better have a look. Come on, McCabe. Answer the phone, E.O., if anybody calls."

"Sir," E.O. said. He stared at them with his wire-rim glasses that made him look like an owl. He was slogging through an enormous pile of receipts. His real name was Elijah, and no one ever knew what the O stood for. As a member of the Church of Christ, he believed music and dancing were sinful. He didn't partake, either.

"Take a message," Captain Bell said. "You heard me?"

"Yes, sir," E.O. said. E.O. was so reserved the joke around the camp was that he either said "yes" or "sir." The third word he knew in the English language was "sin." He made Sam McCabe look like a wild raconteur.

It was after twelve noon and the sun was bright. Captain Bell was running—he must have been a track star in his other life. His loose sleeve flapped as he ran.

"You run track?" Sam said, jogging alongside him.

"Somethin' like that," he said. "You didn't run like a jackrabbit, you'd get mowed down by bullets."

Sam gulped. And he thought he had suffered in his life just because he had eaten pickled corn! Earned his keep through washing a few greasy dishes in Alpine.

"No romance in war, son." Then he ruffled Sam's hair.

Devilfish,[1] the cook, was singing, "Ooh yaah, Shugah pie, let me put my duffin' in your muffin . . ."[2]

Captain Bell yanked the screen door open with his right arm; Sam followed close behind. The kitchen was boiling. Three black industrial-sized ovens jutted out from the wall on the right. In the middle of the room was a shiny silver counter where Devilfish was rolling out dough with a wooden pin. Two other Mexican boys were in a far corner, perched next to a tub full of fresh peaches. One was peeling off the yellow skins. The other was dicing them. Their foreheads were beaded in sweat. All of them were clad in starched white aprons and puffy chef hats.

Otto leaned against the back wall. He was sitting on a wooden bench, but his color wasn't good. Chueco was dabbing the snake bite with a gingham kitchen towel.

"Let me see," Captain Bell said, taking Otto's hand. There were two tiny marks, where the snake had bitten him. "No blood."

Chueco rushed to the sink and started filling up a kettle with water. Sam had not seen him since the first roll call. His face had filled out a little, and he still reminded Sam a little of an elf, but a healthier one. He rifled through a drawer, searching for something.

Dr. Walker was wearing a suit, rather than the company uniform. His fedora was plopped on the silver counter, next to the mounds of dough that Devilfish was rolling. He was fooling around with his silver wire-rim glasses and put them on, as if he were about to read the *Alpine Avalanche*.

He read aloud the directions to the snake suction kit to no one in particular: "Well, let's see here. Place cup tightly over incision and apply suction by pressing and releasing plunger. Continue suction for twenty minutes before loosening the tourniquet."

"Doc, those are useless!" Captain Bell said, clearly panicked. "Why did you waste federal money on that? Who is the fraud who sold you that suction kit?"

"The gentleman's name was Joseph Kafouri, as I recall," Dr. Walker said. "Owns the dry grocery in Fort Davis. Family immigrated to Mexico during the disintegration of the Ottoman Empire and eventually crossed at El Paso. They started selling trinkets and spools of thread. Ribbons and such."

What had happened during the Ottoman Empire? Sam felt woefully ignorant. But this was the man that the boys had said was courting Darlene. He had no chance if Joseph was handsome and rich.

"This is an emergency!" Captain Bell said. "We don't need a long-winded speech on immigration."

Devilfish waved the roller at Dr. Walker. "How much that cat charged for that kit? You've been had."

"Boy, why ain't you pickin' cotton?" Otto asked. His brown eyes gleamed. His hand had started to swell.

"That's enough!" Captain Bell said. "You're not gonna talk like that around here. I won't have it!"

"Brother, that is why I am here, making peach pies," Devilfish said. He was slapping and kneading the dough on the silver counter. He was thin and wiry, but his muscles bulged. He twirled the flattened dough in the air, as if he were going to make a pizza. He now sang,

"Swing low, sweet chariot, Coming for to carry me home. I looked over Jordan, and what did I see . . ."[3]

Dr. Walker said, "Rattlesnake bites are rarely fatal, although of course, they can cause paralysis if not treated. The internal organs can stop functioning."

"Sam, find Darlene! Where is she?" Captain Bell asked.

"I don't know, sir," Sam said.

"Find her!" he roared. His face contorted strangely where the skin had been grafted when he was angry.

Dr. Walker was saying, "The boy should lie down and put his feet up."

Sam peeled out of the kitchen door and skidded on the dry dirt as he ran back to the clinic, which was seven barracks away—no one in sight, just the occasional lizard. A few vultures circled above. The rays of the sun were so bright you couldn't even see the Davis mountains in the distance, as if the mountains were a mirage.

He opened the door to the clinic and raced in. Darlene's back was to him. She was measuring out some liquid and filling it in plastic bottles. Her long curly hair had been disciplined into tight Native American–styled braids.

A row of starched white single beds—not a single patient. Usually, there would be a goldbrick or two trying to weasel out of work in the hot sun. But Darlene was wise to their tricks and knew that they tried to raise their temperature by putting a bar of soap under their arms.

He was out of breath and almost crashed into her. Was that lavender?

She held his arm. He felt himself quiver from her touch. "Easy does it, Red. Here's your hat, what's your hurry."

But Sam lost his balance and fell over backward onto one of the beds with starched white sheets.

She flipped her braids behind her and laughed heartily.

"Otto's been bit by a rattler," he said, panting, looking up at her. "Come quick. Bring the antivenom."

"He out huntin' snakes again?" she asked, as if she wasn't surprised. "That boy doesn't have a noggin." She looked at him directly with her baby blue eyes—there was no escaping them. But there was a sardonic glint in them that he had not seen before.

"I don't know how he got bit," Sam said. "Anyhow, Dr. Walker is there with a suction kit. He acts like he's out for a Sunday stroll."

"Oh poo," Darlene said, frowning. "They ought to fire him. I have never seen such a fraud except for . . ."

Sam was a little shocked. How could Dr. Walker keep his job if he wasn't qualified?

"Captain Bell is calling for you."

"We gotta move. No time to waste. Can't be lollygagging around," she said, grabbing her purse and a white first-aid box. She thrust the first-aid box at him. "Be a trouper. Carry that."

They ran all the way to the kitchen. When they came in, breathless, Dr. Walker had placed the suction kit on the silver counter next to the flattened dough. Devilfish was still singing, "I looked over to Jordan, and what did I see—coming for to carry me home. A band of angels coming after me."

Dr. Walker was saying, "We cannot underestimate the magnitude of the task before us. If the poison reaches the heart, it can be fatal. He shouldn't raise his arm above the level of his heart."

A small tear rolled slowly down Otto's cheek. "Vere is the poison now?"

Captain Bell was pacing back and forth across the kitchen. His empty left sleeve flapped. "Darlene! You brought the antivenom?"

"Chueco, kid, you got any Sotol?"[4] Otto called out.

But Chueco was at the counter next to the sink, grinding something, using a mortar and pestle. He poured the mixture into a cup and added some boiling water. Then, he spread it onto a cheesecloth.

"Could I have a word with you, Captain Bell?" Darlene said. "Outside."

Their voices were murmurs at first, but then everyone could hear the shouting through the screen window. "For crying out loud! Why isn't there any antivenom?"

"Medicine doesn't grow on trees in West Texas, if you haven't noticed! Somebody we know couldn't be bothered to get the paperwork in. Too busy reading a novel."

"Give me your hand," Dr. Walker said to Otto. Otto was a big fella, but now his hand had ballooned to twice the size.

What was Dr. Walker going to do? He didn't know how to use the snake suction kit. Sam prayed he never got sick at Balmorhea. Darlene's comment about Dr. Walker had not inspired any confidence.

"*¡Yo creo que no!*" Chueco shouted, rushing from the counter to where Otto was sitting. "Hand down," he said, placing a poultice directly onto the snake bite. He recited, "*De las doce verdades del mundo, decimos una: una es la Santa Casa de Jerusalén.*"

Dr. Walker said, "There is no more serious task before us than to save this man's life. Son, do you think you are more qualified to deal with the crisis at hand?"

But Chueco was focused on Otto's swollen hand and had placed the poultice over the wound.

Captain Bell summoned Sam and whispered in his ear, "You go on out to the site and get a truck. My orders. We have to get him to a hospital."

Otto looked up at Sam. "Is zis the end of the road? I don't even have a girl."

"I don't think any of us have a sweetheart," Sam said. "If that is any consolation?"

Otto grunted. "Funny, yaah, Baby Red."

Dr. Walker sighed and sat down on the bench next to Otto. "The fort will be held, even though we are encircled by enemies, decidedly at every turn."

Darlene was standing there with her hands on her hips. "Why, Dr. Walker, you act as if you are waiting for Apaches on the range! This is a rattlesnake bite."

Devilfish waved the wooden pin at Dr. Walker. "With all due respect, Dr. Walker. It's just that Chueco is from Terlingua. Rattlesnakes are as plentiful as the locusts in the Good Book there. As a matter of fact, his uncle lost his right forefinger to one of those rattlers."

Otto looked scared, now, as if he were a small kid. "Vat is on my hand?"

"Flower dried," Chueco said. He swallowed. "I mean, dried flower."

"Why?" Otto asked.

Chueco shrugged, as if it were obvious. "To take out the *malo*."

"Yaah, what's the *malo*?" Otto said.

Sam said, "He's talkin' about the poison. Trying to neutralize it."

But Dr. Walker talked on, "Mr. Shines, perhaps it has slipped your mind, or your consciousness, that I am a graduate of one of the most esteemed, illustrious medical schools in our beloved South, Tulane University. And in the Great War, I was a surgeon in the army. Of course, soldiers had a difficult time afterward, with the phantom arms and legs."

Otto gulped, his Adam's apple bulged. Tears swelled in his brown eyes.

Captain Bell said, "Why don't we talk about something other than the Great War?"

Darlene nodded. "I wholeheartedly agree with the captain."

Dr. Walker said, "Miss Robinson, are you denying my education and qualifications? My experience in the Great War?"

Darlene shook her head, tossing her braids. When she wore her hair this way, she looked like a country girl. And you expected her to say, "Aw shucks, cowboy." But she said simply, "This kind of talk won't do."

Captain Bell said, "No one is disputing your experience, Dr. Walker. You forget that I was in the battle of the Argonne Forest."

Otto pulled a long face. "Will they have to . . . ?"

Captain Bell scribbled a note on a piece of paper and handed it to Sam. "Go on. That is, if anyone doubts my orders."

Devilfish was saying, "Chueco is lightin' the house on fire on the guitar. Never seen such natural talent. Soon, he'll be playing at all the dances."

Sam sprinted down to the pool site and told them they needed a truck to go to Alpine. The only truck he found was a dump truck. But Saul, the driver, said it had gas. The truck rumbled up to the kitchen, and he jumped down off the high step too soon, almost falling in the dirt. He scrambled up and flung open the door.

"Got a truck," Sam shouted. The cooks were laying out strips of dough on the pies to finish up the latticework on top of cut peaches.

Devilfish kept humming and singing, "Swing low, sweet chariot."

Captain Bell, Darlene, and Dr. Walker were hovering around Otto.

Otto stood up, but he was a little shaky.

"Boys, can you give me a hand?" Captain Bell gestured with his right hand. With Chueco on one side and Sam on the other, they helped Otto out to the truck.

Darlene followed behind, her purse tucked under her arm. "Hold your horses." Very gingerly, she took off the poultice and examined the wound. "Looks like the swelling has already gone down some. We'll keep it on."

"We call it the purple flower,"[5] Chueco said. "Takes out the *malo* from the snake." In only a month, he had improved his English greatly with Jack's teaching and encouragement.

Then Chueco and Sam lifted Otto up into the cab—he was tall and very heavy. It was strange to see him so weak.

There was just enough room for Otto, Darlene, and the driver to squeeze into the cab. Captain Bell slapped the side of the truck, as if it were a horse. "Go!"

The dust from the badly rutted dirt road kicked up in their faces.

Captain Bell sighed as he watched the dump truck rumble off. "Fifty-seven miles to Alpine. And the road is bad."

Then he scrutinized Chueco with his kind eyes, and patted him on the back. "You just might have saved that man's life. *Muchas gracias*."

Chueco gave them a hopeful, expectant smile. Then he gestured to the sky, as if it were in God's hands.

Captain Bell turned to him. "Sam, we have work to do. We better get back to the office."

In the distance, Sam could see the building site of the swimming pool. Trucks were going back and forth on the road, carrying away earth. He imagined the cool, clear spring water of Balmorhea. He dreamed of floating in the pool, his arms and legs spread out like a star, looking up at the far-reaching blue sky of West Texas, which seemed to go on forever.

## CHAPTER 4.
# Chueco

**A few days later, Darlene showed up at the office.** Sam was still working on *The Round-Up* newspaper. Besides writing the copy, he also drew cartoons, and added jokes and riddles. Not surprisingly, he preferred this work to typing out requisition forms and letters. *The Round-Up* was a cheerful bulletin that put a positive spin on events in the camp—he recorded all his honest observations, notes, and character sketches in a little black diary that he hid in a trunk in the barracks. Captain Bell usually looked over *The Round-Up* before they distributed it. He wasn't a censor exactly, but he commented, "It's not a real newspaper. It's for company morale." On occasion, he made Sam delete articles that he thought might stir up tensions or cause bad blood in the camp.

He was drawing: an idealized woman with long, flowing hair who was administering medicine to a giant. A nest of rattlesnakes slithered past her. The cartoon had a fairy-tale quality to it.

"You've exaggerated my beauty a little," Darlene said, standing close to him. "But I don't mind basking in the glory. Even nurses are not completely selfless."

Her black hair was swept up in a knot on the top of her head, and she looked like a woman from the eighteenth century about to go to a ball. A few wisps of curly black hair had escaped from the bun.

"Naaw," Sam said, trying out a wink on her. He felt bold. "What can we do for the Angel on this fine hot morning without a breeze?" It was a little out of character for him to flirt so obviously.

E.O. looked up briefly from the adding machine and stared. Then he burrowed back into himself, as if he were a prairie dog going back into his hole, and returned to the numbers. He pulled back the crank when he hit the total.

"As much as I am flattered by the cartoon," Darlene said, "I do believe you have to give credit where credit is due. It was Chueco's poultice. The herbs."

"He didn't get any antivenom at the hospital?"

"The swelling had disappeared by the time we got to Alpine," Darlene said. "He was out of danger."

"Well, shoot," Sam said, yanking the drawing off the clipboard. He had spent the last hour on it and was quite pleased with it.

"Besides," Darlene said. "Don't believe the Giant would be too happy about seeing himself saved by either a woman or a Mexican boy. You might make yourself an enemy."

He wondered if he should even bother with a drawing at all. Maybe a straight news article would be best? Just the facts . . . Which were?

"Oh," he said. "I hadn't thought of it that way." He felt naïve and a little stupid. This made him mad—and he became businesslike. "Do you need to see Captain Bell about something? Or is this visit about a requisition order?"

Darlene smiled at him with those light blue eyes, a little indulgently, as if to say, "you'll learn, kiddo." But she said, "You've got talent. But don't always show your hand, Red."

She was patronizing him now. Who did she think she was? The older, wiser woman who knew it all. "Thanks." He wadded up the drawing and threw it in the trash. "Please don't call me Red. My name is Samuel."

She bent over and fished the ball out of the trash. "Can I have it? For a souvenir?"

"Go ahead," Sam said. "For all I care." His pride was a little hurt.

E.O. looked up again from his numbers—he might not speak, but he was Big Ears. Sam referred to him as B.E., instead of E.O., in his diary. Occasionally, he would speak, and it would be a one-line stunner. He was known for his precision and honesty—why he was in charge of the accounts and payroll at the camp. The heavy metal safe was right next to him. No one else, except for Captain Bell, knew the combination.

Darlene said, smiling again, "You misunderstand, honey. Anyway, I take it Captain Bell is not here? Is he down at the construction site?"

"Yeah," Sam said. He shoved *The Round-Up* into a cubbyhole and pulled out a sheaf of papers from another cubbyhole. One was a telegram from Washington: FIRST LADY SLATED TO VISIT BALMORHEA AND TEXAS CCC CAMPS IN OCTOBER STOP CONFIRM DATES STOP ARRANGE VISIT TO DAVIS MOUNTAINS AND CULTURAL PROGRAM STOP SMALL ENTOURAGE WITH PRESS STOP.

Just as she turned to leave, Captain Bell walked through the door.

Captain Bell took off his ranger hat. "What a pleasure, Darlene," he said. "Otto has recovered?"

"Fit as a fiddle," she said. "Will be in a few days, anyway. I was just telling Sam . . ."

"We can rely on you," Captain Bell said. "It's just that Dr. Walker . . ." his voice trailed off.

The First Lady was coming to Balmorhea? Did Captain Bell already know?

Darlene sighed. "Do you have a minute, Captain Bell? I would like to talk to you."

They disappeared behind the wooden partition.

E.O. was staring at Sam through those round coke-bottle glasses.

"What?"

E.O. just shook his head. "Ain't you the prince."

"Thanks," Sam said. "For your pearls of wisdom, Elijah."

He grunted, yanking a total, which made that annoying clicking, like a salamander.

Darlene had raised her voice. "How do you expect me to work with that quack? I don't give a fiddle if he's got a medical degree from some fancy school. He's useless. Useless."

Captain Bell said, "My hands are tied."

"Why? Can't you write to somebody? Can't you get him transferred to the Big Bend?"

"We have to have proof," Captain Bell said. "He does have a big reputation. I can't just go around accusing without—"

"So you're telling me that I just have to put up and shut up . . . in other words? He gets to lord it over on me? While I am the one who is plugging the hole in this dam about to burst? So we have to wait until someone dies? What if Chueco hadn't been in the kitchen?"

Captain Bell said, "That was awfully lucky."

"No," Darlene said. "It wasn't luck. It was Chueco's herbs. The boy has a gift. He can help me."

"But Darlene," Captain Bell said, "the poultice might have been one factor. And he doesn't have any formal qualifications."

"So we defer to the man with official qualifications who is completely ineffectual?" Darlene said.

Captain Bell said, "I am not saying that."

"Plain as the day is long, that is what you are tellin' me," Darlene said. "I am proposing that he help me in the clinic."

Sam couldn't focus on the letter he was supposed to be typing.

There was a long silence. E.O.'s adding machine made an insistent clicking sound.

"Don't tell me you are protecting Dr. Walker's ego?" Darlene finally asked.

"Well," Captain Bell said. "The news will have to be broken with some delicacy. Some finesse."

"This is for the good of the camp," Darlene said. "You can't play games with the health of the men."

Captain Bell sighed. "'Believe you are right."

Darlene stormed out of the office without saying goodbye. After she had gone, Captain Bell appeared from behind the plywood partition.

"Boys," he said, giving them both a stern look. "That conversation goes no further than this office."

• • •

The next day, Captain Bell suggested Sam place an announcement about Otto's recovery in *The Round-Up*. The announcement didn't acknowledge anyone's heroism in particular—it merely said: "Balmorhea Saves Otto. Community Effort Saved One of Our Own: Rattlesnake Bite Has Happy Ending."

Sam didn't think much of Otto since he qualified as a rattlesnake, himself, but Captain Bell was careful about the messages in *The Round-Up*.

"It's all well and good to want to express yourself, McCabe. But we need an article educating the camp about how to deal with snakes.

Something neutral."

"What about Chueco?" Sam said. "He's the hero. Darlene even said so."

"This has to be done diplomatically," Captain Bell said. "We don't want to imply that our medical team is not—"

"So we don't say what happened?"

"Just the announcement and tips on dealing with snakes," Captain Bell said, "will be enough."

"It doesn't seem right," Sam said. "It isn't fair. When he—"

"Chueco's day will come," Captain Bell said, sighing. "You will find that many things in life are not fair."

Sam had grown up listening to Pa talk about Eugene Debs at the dinner table. Debs believed in the rights of workers and had founded the Industrial Workers of the World. He had even organized a railway strike in 1894 so that workers could get fair wages. Pa had supported the Socialist Party of America, but had said, "Now, don't you go tellin' anyone, because they'll say I'm a Commie, and I'll never get hired on." Debs had only denounced World War I and was arrested in 1918. Pa had said, "This is supposed to be the land of the free."

But here they were at Balmorhea, dealing with a plague of rattlesnakes. Bound by the natural world.

"Not even a drawing?" Sam ventured. He had drawn a cartoon with Chueco putting the poultice on the Giant.

"Thank you, McCabe," Captain Bell said. His disfigured cheek contorted. Sam was trying his patience. Sam tried to imagine what he looked like before the War.

"It's common sense," Sam said. "You don't provoke them. Any fool knows that."

"That's what is needed," Captain Bell said. "I have it on good authority that Otto was hunting snakes for fun. Like a hobby. We want to discourage that kind of behavior at Balmorhea."

Sam wadded up his most recent cartoon and threw it into the wire basket under his desk. Then, he thought better of it—maybe someday he'd want a record of everything Captain Bell had forced him to cut out of the newsletter. It was hard to imagine anything other than the present when he was twenty-two, although he loved history and had done well in it at Sul Ross. He ducked under the desk and retrieved the cartoon, folded up the crinkled drawing, and put it in his front pocket.

As he was typing TIPS ON SNAKE SAFETY, Dr. Walker ambled into the office, wearing his double-breasted suit. As suffocating as it was, Sam could not understand for the life of him why he wore that hot suit unless he wanted to lord it over others that he came from an old family in Tyler. Or maybe he didn't have to wear a uniform since he was a contract physician? If you didn't work at the pool, you had to wear khakis.

Dr. Walker took off his fedora and set it on top of Sam's cluttered desk. He was balding. And he had droopy cheeks that made him look like a hound dog. At the time, Sam thought he was ancient, but looking back, he was probably only in his late forties or early fifties.

"Son, at your liberty, would you please tell Captain Bell I am here on an urgent matter?"

He patted his forehead with a monogrammed white handkerchief. He took off his coat and handed it to Sam. Squeezing past the other desks, Sam hung his coat on a wooden peg on the wall.

"Of course," Sam said. "Would you like a glass of water? It's from the spring."

He sank into an empty chair. "That would be delectable. Most appreciated."

Sam wasn't sure what delectable meant but assumed it meant delicious or refreshing. Why didn't Dr. Walker just say so? Sam picked up the pewter pitcher off the black pot-bellied stove and poured water into a glass.

He was studying the face of a gold pocket watch when Sam handed him the glass. "Dr. Walker?" Sam said, handing the glass to him.

"Hmmm?"

"Your water?"

Dr. Walker snapped the cover back onto the pocket watch. "Given to me by my great-grandfather. A hero of the Confederacy." His hand trembled a little when he took the glass. "Fought at Gettysburg."

Sam spied Captain Bell peeking around the partition. Then, suddenly, there he was, standing in front of Dr. Walker, as if he were seven feet tall. He motioned to Sam. "McCabe, continue with *The Round-Up*."

Sam returned to his article, "Tips on Snakes": 1. WATCH YOUR STEP.

Captain Bell acted surprised to see Dr. Walker and said a little too jauntily, "Well, Dr., it is rare to see you here. You must have something important on your mind."

Dr. Walker frowned. "Indeed, I am most distressed. Darlene has announced that the Mexican boy who was tending Otto will now be working in the clinic. She is most confident and tells me that you have approved of this course of action. We cannot treat patients with cactus and superstition."

2. BE CAREFUL WHEN CLIMBING ROCKS.

"He will be under your supervision. And, of course, Darlene's."

"I refuse this proposition," Dr. Walker said.

3. DO NOT TURN OVER ROCKS OR LOGS.

"Apparently, Chueco's poultice neutralized the poison of the snake," Captain Bell said.

"Medicine is based on facts, Captain Bell," Dr. Walker said. "Science. Logic."

"I talked to the doctor at the hospital in Alpine. He identified the herbs as echinacea. Mexicans use it to treat snake bites."

Sam looked up. He didn't remember any phone call.

"Do you doubt my authority?" Dr. Walker said. He arched one of his bushy brown eyebrows.

"We had no choice," Captain Bell said, his jaw tightening. "Since you dithered about getting the order in for the antivenom."

"I still refuse the proposition," Dr. Walker said. "The boy is ignorant."

Captain Bell switched the topic. "What field hospitals were you assigned to in France in the Great War?"

4. IF YOU HEAR A RATTLE, MOVE AWAY.

"I don't have time for an interrogation of my career in the Army."

5. DO NOT MAKE SUDDEN OR THREATENING MOVEMENTS.

"Just a simple question. I was just curious. Since you mentioned amputations . . . thought you might give me some advice on dealing with my phantom arm."

Dr. Walker banged the empty glass on his desk. "Son, can you get my coat?"

Sam ran over and got his white coat. Dr. Walker put on his fedora.

Captain Bell said, "We've come to an agreement, then? Chueco will help out in the clinic?"

Dr. Walker frowned. "If you insist. Darlene will supervise him. Good afternoon, Captain Bell."

Both E.O. and Sam looked up. Captain Bell was putting on his ranger hat.

"I need some fresh air, boys," he said. "Carry on. Paperwork for the U.S. government never ends."

Sam peeked out the window to make sure that Captain Bell wasn't anywhere near the door or within earshot. Then he asked, "What happened?"

E.O. took off his glasses and rubbed his eyes. He was five or six years older than Sam. His glasses were so thick that Sam never could see the expression in his eyes. But here was real mirth. "Dr. Walker got caught in a lie."

CHAPTER 5.

# Vim and Vigor, August 1935

**As if Sam had conjured him, Joe Kafouri popped his head into the office a few days later.** He was just as short as Sam but had wild, curly black hair, squashed under a checkered flat cap. Surprising that he was wearing a wool cap in this heat. He was sporting a Pancho Villa handlebar mustache.

At the time, Sam was the only one in the office. E.O. had gone to the canteen for some Red Hots—he had a sweet tooth. Despite his short height, Joe had big, calloused hands. He stretched out his hand. "It is my great honor and chance. I have come with the Vim Cola and the Wonder Cure. The other supplies."

Sam almost chortled, but this might be rude. The familiar biblical phrase echoed in his mind: "We have come bearing gold, frankincense, and myrrh."

Sam shook his hand firmly. "Pleased to make your acquaintance."

So this was the fella who owned The Kafouri Brothers' Dry

Goods Grocery in Fort Davis. Sam didn't see what all the fuss was about, although he talked a little funny. Could this be the man who Darlene had set her cap for? Where was he from, originally?

"Sure," he said, a little flummoxed. "You probably want to deliver it to the canteen."

Like a magician, Joe produced a bill, as if he were performing a magic trick. "The bill. The manifest for the goods."

"Much obliged," Sam said. "I will put that on E.O.'s desk. I can show you to the canteen."

Joe smiled. "There is no need to guide me. But, whatever your comfort . . ." He pulled a long white handkerchief out of his hip pocket and wiped his forehead. The handkerchief reminded Sam of those used for magic tricks at the medicine shows, except that it had been embroidered.

Sam cleared his throat. "No trouble 'tall. I need to stretch my legs. Maybe I will sample some of that Vim Cola. Everyone is praising it here, thither, and yon."

Joe smiled impishly. "*Shu?* Who can resist the Vim? Don't all men want vim? Vim for the life, the *hayat.* Vim for the ladies. Vim for the manly man. The man who requires a little more verve."

Sam laughed at this little masculine joke. Or was Joe just repeating the slogan for Vim Cola? Granted, Joe was quite a bit older than he was. Why was he so determined to dislike this fella? He closed the logbook for the mail. If no one was in the office, he ought to lock it—Captain Bell was firm on that point.

Sam followed him outside. The truck was painted a sky blue. On the side, "The Kafouri Brothers' Dry Goods Grocery" was painted in white. The sides were covered with dust from the roads. The tires looked firm. The truck had a small bulbous cab just like all the other trucks he'd seen of the same model, but the back had high panels. His papa had bought one used that barely ran into town for the odd bit of lumber—the cursed car was always breaking down. They spent more time tinkering with it than driving it. Would Sam ever own a decent car, like this one? He stifled the envy he felt—envy was a kind of poison that he didn't want to seep into his heart. His ma had drilled that into him.

Joe gestured, opening the door. "*Habibi*, dear heart, compadre, let us deliver the Vim to the canteen."

It would be rude to ask him about his family, but Sam didn't recall the Kafouri brothers—they must have just come to Fort Davis. "Are you from around these parts?" Sam probed.

"El Paso," Joe said, starting up the engine. "Through Mexico. We come from Mount Lebanon, the Land of the Cedars. We came to Mexico after the 1916 Locust Plague."[1]

Sam balked. He would have to go to the library and consult the map. Where was this fella from? His point of reference seemed woefully small, just the plains of West Texas and a fair bit of New Mexico: all hardscrabble land. He knew how to tame a wild horse. He could milk cows, but not particularly well. He could wash dishes. He had managed to learn Spanish, although he wasn't sure it was *that* good. And what language did they speak in the Land of Cedars? If he opened his mouth, he would betray his ignorance. He felt ashamed.

Joe shrugged. "It is a long way from here over the ocean and thousands of miles away, darling."

"My name is Sam," Sam said, suddenly becoming prickly. "Sam McCabe."

Joe smiled. "But of course, Mister Sam," he said. "My sincerest, most profound apologies. It is just that in our language, everyone's darling or sweetheart. I did not mean any offense."

And just what language was that? Turkish? Sam was feeling out of his depth; this was the longest ride ever to the canteen. Joe was singing some song in a strange language and beating time on the steering wheel. He wished he had walked. At the same time, he was curious about Joe Kafouri. What had made Joe leave his country and venture to West Texas, of all places?

As if Joe could read his mind, he said, "The French took over our country. We started fighting with our brothers. *Bayyi* decided we should leave and that was that, *habibi.* It was written."

Sam felt bewildered. Who was *Bayyi?* What was written? How was that inevitable? How did you go from a faraway country with another language and come to a new one? And so quickly build a business that was making money? Everyone else was standing in bread lines, eating pickled corn, or living off their federal checks. Hoboes wandering the country on rail cars, trying to find work or a crust of bread.

Joe backed up the truck to the canteen and turned off the engine. Sam slammed the door to the truck and followed him inside the canteen. He felt a twinge of jealousy when he heard Darlene giggle. She exclaimed, "Joe Kafouri, just look at you! Where have you been, you old dog, you old rascal?"

Joe laughed. "Dogs are not complimentary in our language. But dear hearts, I have brought Vim Cola and Wonder Cure."

She frowned. "Wonder Cure? Is that quack still selling that stuff? Ol' what's-his-name? And you're buying? No tellin' what's in that Wonder Cure."

Joe said, "Sells like *ataayef*—what you say are hot cakes here. The old ladies love it!"

Sam sighed. "No old ladies here." He felt a twinge of homesickness and missed his mother's apple pie; that is, when they had any sugar. He plopped down on a stool. The canteen had a row of stools in front of a crude wooden bar, which did not serve liquor, but Vim Cola. Above the canteen in huge red letters was the ad for Vim Cola.

Behind the bar was stacked a supply of small items for purchase: candy, shaving cream, razors, smoking tobacco, soda pop. The boys paid with coupons, instead of cash—and that was taken out of their monthly check. Jack was in charge of the canteen and taught English.

Joe curled the tip of his mustache with his fingers. "Only manly men with vim and vigor!"

Darlene hooted. "As far as I can see, the camp could use more of a feminine touch. Some Fem Vim!" Sam felt a surge of happiness when she ignored Joe's mustache. He had tried to grow a mustache himself, but only a few whiskers had sprouted above his lip. "Why, it's Sam McCabe, you're out of the lion's lair. The lion won't be too happy to see you lounging around the canteen."

"Captain Bell doesn't mind if we take a break now and then," Sam said. He was a little shocked by Darlene's sarcasm, but played along. If she was sweet on Captain Bell, she wouldn't be talking like that.

E.O. was sitting next to him on a stool, and he oozed cinnamon—he had just eaten a whole packet of Red Hots. "Have to finish up the checks for the month," he said, getting off the stool.

Sam held up the keys to E.O. "Had to lock it," he said.

E.O. adjusted his coke-bottle glasses. "Always have mine." He officiously waved a huge ring of keys back at him.

"Jack," Sam said. "One Vim Cola, please."

Jack was leaning lazily on one elbow on the counter. He had one eye cocked on Darlene. Was he really being honest about his intention to marry Ruby?

Joe waved his hands in front of Jack, to break the stare. "If you will assist me, man with a pure heart, you will have as much Vim Cola as your heart wishes for. My caravan is full of Vim."

Jack laughed. "You lugged all that Vim on camels all the way from Fort Davis?"

"You will not believe me if I tell you that camels were imported to America to help with exploration of this land. Your President of the Southern states, Jefferson Davis, it was his idea," Joe said.[2] "But no one understood them. They got a few from Tunisia, some from Egypt, Syria, and Crimea."

What was Joe talking about? Sam felt this man named Kafouri was throwing him off balance—everything he thought he knew appeared cattywampus. Threw his perspective out of joint.

Sam didn't make a move to help. He would rather sit at the canteen and flirt with Darlene, or what he imagined at the time was flirting.

"I do hope Captain Bell didn't approve any more snake suction kits," Darlene was saying. "Since Otto's accident."

"Don't believe suction kits were on the order," Sam said.

"Well," Darlene said, lightly brushing her fingertips against his arm. "I do believe that my morning break is over. Have fish to fry. Better get back to the clinic before Dr. Walker starts squawking."

Sam felt the electricity of her touch shoot through his entire body. He yearned to touch her, but instead, just stared at her soft blue eyes. "I'm looking forward to the dance," he said, hoping she would take the hint.

She tossed her head back and laughed. She was wearing her hair in braids, like the day of Otto's accident. "Oh, you boys. Stop giving me those moony eyes . . ."

What did she mean? That she wasn't really sweet on him? Or had she just been playing him along?

Jack huffed as he set down three crates behind the bar of the canteen. "We could use a hand, cowboy. We put in a big order for the dance."

Sam got up from the stool and went out to the truck. Joe handed him a crate of Wonder Cure, not Vim Cola. It took them another fifteen minutes to bring and stack the rest of the crates of Vim Cola.

Joe waved goodbye. "Goodbye with peace," he said. He was backing up the truck and sang out, "Vim for the Manly Man." The truck roared off.

Sam sat down on the stool. Sweat was dripping off his forehead. "You reckon he believes all of that malarkey?"

Darlene had disappeared, but a floral smell lingered in the air.

Jack said, "Naw. You still want a Vim Cola? It'll be hot." Sam was surprised he wasn't more talkative.

Sam picked up one of the bottles of Wonder Cure and studied it. "No. Just water from the spring."

What in the Sam Hill was in this Wonder Cure? He took the lid off and sniffed it. Something sweet? And? He couldn't put his finger on the other smells. Wasn't this the elixir they were peddling at medicine shows? Hadn't his ma been suspicious of these elixirs? She had muttered, "He's just playing on people's fears. Takin' advantage."

Jack was serious. "It's none of my business, cowboy, but if I were you, I would give Miss Darlene a wide berth on the rail car of love. I know I told you otherwise, a few months ago. But it's just that . . ."

Sam felt defensive. "You've set your cap for her?"

Jack suddenly became sharp. "Don't be a darn fool. I already told you my heart's set on Ruby."

Sam set down the Wonder Cure on the counter. He felt annoyed but was determined not to lose his temper. "Gotta get back. Sort the mail."

"Let's just say, as bewitched as we all are, I don't think we have the full story," Jack said. He leaned forward, as if he were about to divulge some devastating morsel of gossip. Why didn't Jack tell him? Since he was Mr. Romeo and so experienced with the opposite sex.

Sam walked toward the door. Then he suddenly turned around. "Reckon you could say. Since you always blab everyone's business."

"Catch." Jack threw him a pack of Sugar Babies. "It's just a feeling . . ."

CHAPTER 6.

# Devilfish, late August 1935

**There were a few Black boys at Balmorhea.** Most of them had been assigned to Big Bend and were building a road through the Chisos Mountains, using pickaxes and shovels in the hot desert sun. They were sleeping in flimsy tents and combating all sorts of insects and critters at night—why Devilfish was very familiar with rattlesnakes: "Rattlesnakes are as plentiful as the locusts in the Good Book." When there was a shortage of cooks at Balmorhea, Captain Bell had requested more men from the camp at Big Bend. Devilfish laughed and said, "Balmorhea is just better than heaven, sho' is. Better than working in the Chisos, sho' is. Better than pickin' cotton, sho' is." It was the government's policy to keep them separate from everyone else if there were a large company of Black folks, but in some cases, it didn't make much sense, especially if there weren't enough to make a camp. Captain Bell didn't enforce this policy in the mess hall or the barracks or the rec hall. Anyway, the cooks ate in the kitchen after the boys had eaten—there were no Anglo cooks, so it was just the Black boys with the Mexican boys. They didn't get along, although Devilfish and Chueco became friends. Devilfish was teaching Chueco how to play the guitar. Most of them groused that the Mexican boys only spoke in Spanish.

One day, Sam was sorting through the mail. The ones from Washington always took priority: CCC Director, Robert Fechner.[1]

Sam handed the letter to Captain Bell. Bell read it to himself and then said aloud, "There should be complete segregation of Black and white enrollees."

Sam wondered if Captain Bell was expecting him to comment.

Captain Bell cursed under his breath, "Damn it." He threw the letter down on his desk. Then he looked Sam in the eye. "You didn't hear that."

"Sir," Sam said, "of course not."

"This is another load of hooey. I saw this in the Great War. Tell 'em you can die for us, but then treat 'em like dirt. There's got to be a way around this."

Captain Bell tapped his pencil, up and down.

"We have a few empty barracks. There's one where we keep extra uniforms," Sam said, standing near the captain's desk.

The captain leaned back in his chair and put his one arm behind his head. The left sleeve flapped, uselessly. He looked up at the ceiling, as if it were the infinite, blue sky. "You are so right."

Then, he straightened up. "Sit," he ordered Sam, as if he were an equal. Sam was flattered by this, and it made him feel like an adult in the know, but it also meant that he had to be even more reserved with the other boys than usual. It wasn't that he was a chatterbox, but he had to be extremely careful about what he said to his pals, even Jack. Sometimes he felt lonesome, and felt like he wasn't one of the boys.

"Did you line up The Texas Boys for the dance?"

"Playing in Alpine," Sam said. "Can't get anybody local that I think will be any good. That's within our budget."

"What about Devilfish? He's pretty good," Captain Bell said. "I heard him one night when I was out looking at the moon."

"Devilfish?" Sam asked, surprised.

"Just because the government says it, doesn't mean it's fair," Bell said. "As you recall, slavery was the law of the land." Was Bell planning to go against the policy? Sam had always thought he played by the book.

"Sir," Sam said. "It's just that the locals might not show up if they know a Black boy is playing."

Captain Bell laughed. "Oh, they'll show. They're so bored, and we're the only game in town for miles. Music and food on the government's nickel."

"Oh," Sam said, feeling a little stupid. Was he missing something? Was Captain Bell trying to stir up trouble?

"We'll give them the barracks so that they can practice for the dance. All other directives on segregation will be ignored," Captain Bell said. "Let's see if we have enough in our budget to give them an extra month's salary for playing at the dance."

Devilfish was talented: no doubt about it. He played on a little banjo, and he strummed the guitar with ease. Once, Sam had heard the melancholy pining of the saxophone outside of the barracks after lights-out. But did they play dance music? Devilfish was delighted with the separate barracks and said, "Now, we have our own juke joint. Better than Deep Ellum."

Of course, much, much later, Sam learned that Devilfish had

cut an album, but he did not know if he was still alive. What was his family name? Wasn't Devilfish his nickname? Did he live in Dallas, or had he moved?

CHAPTER 7.

# Blue Moon

**The plan for the dance went forward.** Devilfish and his band would play. Captain Bell had sent a letter to all the neighboring towns, Balmorhea, Toyahvale, Fort Davis, Pecos, Fort Stockton, inviting "the fairer sex" to a dance in the mess hall. The girls would be provided with transportation to and from the dance in Army trucks. Families were assured that the dance would be heavily chaperoned—and it would end at ten o'clock. Refreshments provided: soda pop and lemonade, watermelon and apple pie. Occasionally there would be dances organized by the Baptist church in Fort Davis. Unless you went to church, there wasn't much chance of meeting a nice girl. Many guys hitched into town and hung around the local watering hole and picked fights with farmers or cowboys. A few came back late Saturday night, the drunk skunks, and were put in the "brig"—the camp jail. Or their weekend passes were suspended for the following week. One reason for Sam's unpopularity was that he issued or withheld weekend passes. If boys caused too much trouble, they were simply discharged. Captain Bell made the decisions, but Sam drew up the paperwork.

When Sam was typing up the letter, he asked Captain Bell, "It's a dry party?"

"I am not against having a beer or two. But we can't be having brawls out here. We'll never get the pool done."

"The boys are not going to be happy. There's going to be a lot of moaning and groaning."

Captain Bell was firm. He held up his right hand. "I said, 'No booze. Just Vim Cola. Or lemonade.'"

There was a lot of grumbling about the beer and when the boys complained, Sam said, "Take it up with Captain Bell. I am not against cold beer."

Still, on the night of the dance, there was an excited buzz in the air. Jack was at the canteen all afternoon, selling shaving cream, toothpaste, tobacco, candy, and shoe polish. You would have thought the dance was a wedding—everyone showered after they came in from working at the construction site of the pool. In the bathroom, there were hoots of laughter and a few boys popped each other with towels.

Sam bunked in the officers' barracks—Captain Bell was standing at the mirror on the wall, lathering his face with a shaving brush. He was too old for any of the girls who would be coming to the dance. Was he secretly hoping some widow might show?

E.O. had the bunk above Sam. He was polishing and buffing his black shoes with a brush. Sam was underneath him and punched the mattress. "Might be your lucky night."

"Yes, sir," he said.

"You might have to talk," Sam said, teasing him. "Say more than yes or no!"

"Speak for yerself," E.O. said.

"Cut it out," Sam said. He lay on his back, pummeling the mattress with his feet.

E.O. hung over the side, mimicking Darlene's voice. "Why I do declare, Sam, you have whiskers now."

"That's enough," Sam said. He didn't want to lose his temper. "Have to check on the preparations."

E.O. had gotten his goat. Sam was starting to feel that everyone was older and more experienced than he was. To make himself feel important and masculine, he got dressed quickly and marched over to the mess hall. He heard Joe Kafouri's voice in his head: "Vim is for the manly man!" The cooks had already moved all the wooden tables and benches out of the center of the room. Instead of the usual drab brown, the place looked cheerful with red, white, and blue streamers hanging from the lamp in the ceiling and draped around the windows. A few tables were set against the wall for the refreshments. They had covered the wooden tables with red tablecloths. In the adjoining kitchen, the cooks who were not playing in the band were cutting up watermelons into wedges.

A platform had been erected at the other end of the mess hall for the band. Devilfish was already there, strumming his banjo. A cowboy hat was cocked on the back of his head, instead of the puffy chef hat. The entire band consisted of the other Black boys, except for Chueco. Chueco was tuning a guitar. Another was on the fiddle. They all wore cowboy hats, except Chueco, who was wearing a black sombrero, decorated with a gold braid around the rim. He waved at Sam and smiled, shrugging good-naturedly, as if to say, "What to do? Now I find myself playing music." They all wore the day denims with the leftover World War I trench boots that they had been assigned—no one could afford cowboy boots with real leather.

Some of the boys had already started trickling into the mess hall, waiting for the trucks of girls to arrive. Even though it was hot, all the boys were wearing the spruce-green dress uniform that made them look like soldiers. Otto towered above all the Anglo boys, but he was standing by himself. The Mexican boys were milling about in a group next to the Anglos—they were laughing and talking among themselves in Spanish. One of them pointed at Otto and said, "*¡Qué cabrón! ¡Puta madre!*"

The Army trucks rumbled off of the main highway. Sam opened the screen door. Captain Bell was standing next to the flagpole. He called out, "Come on out. We need to help them out of those big ol' trucks."

Captain Bell took off his ranger hat and handed it to Sam—he couldn't hold his arm out and his ranger hat at the same time. Girls tittered as they jumped out of the trucks—all dolled up in freshly ironed dresses in bright colors. One said, "I wish we didn't have to come back so early. They treat us like we're little kids." Another giggled. "Cinderella turns into a pumpkin at ten o'clock!" Many of them had done up their hair—luxuriant wavy curls—he was tempted to reach out and touch. They wore high heels. One or two wore stockings, the dark seam prominent on their calves.

"Hello! Hello! Welcome to Balmorhea," Captain Bell said, cheerful. "Good evening."

"Welcome to Balmorhea," Sam said, holding out his arm. "Watch your step." He tried, but not very hard, not to ogle them. So many pretty girls: lips a glossy red. They smelled like soap and starch. Where were they all hiding? He only saw matronly looking women with tired faces at the general store when he went into Fort Davis. A blonde in a blue sailor dress caught his eye. Maybe it was not realistic to set his hopes on Darlene.

When the Anglo girls entered the mess hall, the Mexican boys looked disappointed. And there weren't really very many girls—only about forty. While there were easily a hundred or more men in the mess hall.

"Not a single Mexican girl," Captain Bell whispered. He was right behind Sam. "We didn't send any letters in Spanish, did we?"

"No," Sam said. "Maybe their families are stricter?" Why hadn't they thought of this? The Mexican boys would feel left out.

"Devilfish and his band are playing, but I dropped the ball for the Mexican boys," Captain Bell said. He looked rueful. "Too many details running this place."

Sam was gazing at the blonde, her hair in soft waves, framing her round face, parted down the middle. She was so petite that she looked like a doll.

The band had already started to play. Devilfish was singing, "Heaven."

"What did you say, Captain?" Sam said, still mesmerized by the blonde. If he didn't screw up his courage to ask her to dance, it might be too late.

But Captain Bell was already working the crowd, shaking hands with the mothers and older women who had come as chaperones. "Welcome to Balmorhea!" Some lady in a shapeless gingham dress was exclaiming, "We are obliged to you for this delightful invitation. We are usually next to the radio on Friday nights. This is better than Bob Wills and His Texas Playboys . . ." But then, she gasped, "You have a Negra band?"

Captain Bell said, "Devilfish is destined for greatness."

She fluttered, "Well, nobody told us . . . It's bad enough that we have so many Latins."

Just as Sam was about to cross the dance floor and ask the blonde doll to dance, Jack elbowed him. He had a dab of shaving cream behind his ear. His thick black hair was parted and combed neatly to one side.

"Hey, Jack, I thought your heart was taken," Sam said, elbowing him back. "Haven't seen you since . . ."

Jack was a LEM—a local experienced man—and he was staying in another barracks.

"Shoot. I sold out at the canteen. Barely had time to shave and shower," Jack said.

"Have to move right quick, someone is going to ask that cute girl to dance," Sam said.

Just as Sam was halfway across the crowded dance floor, Otto had pulled her out. She was short and came up to his waist. How could Sam wrangle her away from Otto? He had as much charm as a plank.

Sam searched the crowd for Jack, but he had disappeared from the line of men who were leaning against the wall, looking wistfully at the boys who were already dancing with girls. Oh, there he was over by the refreshment table, talking to a woman with black hair. Her raven black hair was loose and set in waves. She was wearing feminine earrings—looked like sapphires—that matched her light blue eyes. Lordy, that was Darlene—hardly recognized her out of her pressed white uniform. She was wearing a blue sleeveless dress with a scoop neck. She had thrown her head back and was laughing. Had she had a few drinks? But where did she get the booze? Sam thought Jack had set his cap for Ruby.

The cooks were bringing in the apple pies and setting them on the refreshment tables. Some of the men who were just watching the dance moved over to graze. A few of the Mexican boys took slices of watermelon and slipped out the door. Should Sam try with another girl? Even E.O. had found a girl—another girl with thick eyeglasses. Or maybe he had met her at church? Otto was trying to pull the blonde doll back onto the dance floor, but she was shaking her head.

Sam cut in. "May I have this dance?"

Otto towered over him. "Nein."

She smiled. And when she smiled, a dimple appeared in her right cheek. How unusual to have brown eyes and blonde hair, but she did. Her nose was very small, very delicate.

"But I am . . ." Sam said, reaching for her hand. "Sam."

"Charlotte," the girl said. She giggled.

"Would you . . . ?"

"Yes," Charlotte said. "Oh, yes."

But Otto was tugging at her other arm. "Aaaw," she said, "you're hurting me. Let me go."

"Look, fella," Sam said. "She danced with you. Let someone else have a turn."

"You don't tell Otto what to do, Baby Red." Sam's ear burned where Otto had cuffed it.

"My name is Sam McCabe," Sam said.

"She dances with me," Otto said, still clutching her arm. "Mine, yaah."

"No, I'm not," Charlotte said, defiantly.

They couldn't split the girl in two. He suddenly remembered the biblical story of the two mothers fighting over a baby. Solomon had ruled the baby should be split in two with a sword.

Captain Bell stood before them, smiling, with his one arm behind his back. "What seems to be the trouble?"

Otto frowned. "Sam is taking her."

"No," Charlotte said, shaking her head. "It's not like that. I've already danced a few times with you."

Captain Bell said, "Well, Otto, it looks to me like it might be someone else's turn. Why don't you take a break from dancing? Have some pie. Vim Cola. There's plenty."

Otto withdrew, muttering, "Just wait, yaah, Baby Sam."

Sam had finally won the doll, and they twirled around a few times, but he kept stepping on her feet. He was happy to finally be dancing, but he was sore that Jack was flirting with Darlene. She giggled. The band was playing Billie Holiday's "Summertime." Devilfish crooned.

Sam whispered, "Does your papa own a farm?" He couldn't think of anything else to say.

Charlotte giggled. "He's the postman and Ma raises chickens. And your ma and pa?"

Sam shook his head and they kept twirling around the dance floor. "Flat broke. We lost the farm."

Charlotte whispered, "Doesn't matter. Glad you turned up when you did. I don't like him. He's rough."

The band had an inexhaustible repertoire of popular songs. They played on and on: "Pennies from Heaven," "Good night, Irene," "It's a Sin to Tell a Lie," "San Antonio Rose." Having a young lady on his arm gave Sam some confidence—they kept dancing, even though he was suffocating in the spruce-green uniform. Somehow, Sam lost track of time. He laughed a few times. He couldn't remember the last time he had laughed. Charlotte was teaching him how to do the jitterbug—she didn't seem to mind that he was an awkward dancer. In a corner out of the way of most of the dancers, she was teaching him the moves. "Like this," she said, pulling him by the hand. "And then, this . . ."

Suddenly, the music stopped. Devilfish mopped his brow with a handkerchief. "Ladies and gentlemen, we will play one last song for the evening. 'Blue Moon.'"

The boys hooted and hollered. Some whistled. The audience clapped.

"Aren't you thirsty?" he asked Charlotte. He was winded from dancing. Sweat was dripping into his eyes.

Charlotte nodded. He pulled her by the hand to the refreshment table.

Captain Bell said, "I also have an announcement. I'd like to invite y'all to have apple pie and Vim Cola before the end of the dance. The trucks will be leaving at 10:30."

A few boys booed. However, the party had already thinned out. Most of the Mexican boys had disappeared.

"That was our agreement," Captain Bell said.

Sam handed Charlotte a plate with apple pie. She shook her head. "Not hungry. Just a drink." He gave her a Vim soda pop. He admired her smooth, slender neck as she tilted her head back to take a swig. But wasn't his heart set on Darlene? He was a little confused about his feelings now that there was another pretty girl on the scene.

The dance floor was empty now except for a few couples. Jack and Darlene sashayed in front of them on the dance floor—they were doing the foxtrot, and boy, they danced with such ease. Sam felt a twinge of jealousy. Jack was a fine dancer. He twirled her this way and that—as if he were Fred Astaire. Sam had never seen Darlene smile so much or look so radiant. She had swept her long black hair onto a knot on the top of her head—with the dangly earrings, she looked royal. Was it really true that she had never been married?

Charlotte was gazing at Darlene. "Who's she?"

"Darlene," Sam said. "She's our nurse."

"Oh," Charlotte said.

"Why?"

"You can't take your eyes off of her," Charlotte said.

He shook his head. "I have only eyes for one girl at this dance."

Charlotte giggled. "She looks like Mae West, and he looks like Cary Grant. Right out of Hollywood."

"Maybe a tad," Sam said. "A tad," he repeated. It was true: they did. He tried to stifle the slight burning he felt inside.

Charlotte smiled. "I've been thinking. Maybe you could come to my house next weekend for ice cream."

"I look forward to that," Sam said. Did she notice that he sounded so stiff? He felt he might hurt her feelings if he refused the invitation. But what was the harm in going for ice cream?

Captain Bell was standing at the door and motioned to him. "If you will pardon me for a minute," Sam said.

"Help me with goodbyes," Captain Bell said. "The trucks are outside."

Sam rushed back to the refreshment table where Charlotte was standing. He whispered, "Do you have a telephone at your house?"

"No," she said. "We sure don't. But you can call the post office and leave a message with my pa."

Sam dreaded that—that meant everyone in Fort Davis would know their business. Sam pulled a pen out of his pocket and grabbed a napkin from the table. "Write the number."

Devilfish's band were packing up their instruments. The chaperones were gathering up their belongings and ushering the young ladies out the door. The black sky was dotted with stars and seemed to twinkle with promise. Sam gazed up at the moon, so far away, so luminous.

"Goodbye! Goodbye!" the women called out. A girl tittered, "Look, there's a full moon. How romantic!" The trucks rumbled away. "Good night! Good night!"

Soon after, the boys made their way back to the barracks, some of them grumbling.

Captain Bell took Sam aside. "One more thing, Sam," he said. "I forgot to mention it to you today in the office."

"Sure," Sam said. "Whatever you need, Captain Bell."

"You're the night watchman," he said, handing him an Aladdin Lantern. "Just filled it with kerosene."

"But . . ."

"Wake me up if the camp's on fire," Captain Bell said. "Make the rounds. Don't forget to check Devilfish's barracks. No gambling."

"But, Captain, I—"

"I'm counting on you," Captain Bell said, yawning. "It's been a long day." Before Sam could object again, Captain Bell strode off into the darkness.

• • •

Thirty minutes after lights out, the lights blinked back on. Most of the boys were having a second party in their barracks: booze had been smuggled into the camp. Captain Bell was strict. Who had managed that? Sam kept circling back through the barracks with his lantern. Sure as the day was long (or maybe sure as the night was long), he couldn't make one hundred and fifty men go to sleep if they didn't want to. If they didn't have passes to go into town and they didn't get to dance, they wanted to have a little fun. He couldn't blame them. The Mexican boys had certainly gotten the short end of the stick since there were no Mexican girls—and the Anglo girls wouldn't have anything to do with them. All of the Black boys were playing in the band.

The best after-hours party, though, was in the Black boys' barracks. Devilfish invited everybody—Anglos, Mexicans, and his band. His mama had sent him a package from Dallas, and he was sharing sardines, white crackers, a ring of baloney, liverwurst, and graham crackers. He had also pilfered a few leftover apple pies from the dance. The big draw for the boys, though, was two cases of beer and five or six bottles of Sotol.

Devilfish was blowing on his harmonica, sitting on a beer crate when Sam came in. He played the harmonica, too? "I don't give a lick about rules. We all just wanna have a good time, Sam. Have yerself a little hooch."

The other boys booed. He supposed they thought he was going to break up the party. And he should have. Maybe there should have been more than one night watchman? He hated to admit it, but he had very little authority.

Sam set his lantern down and sat down on the bed. Someone thrust a glass at him. One of the other Black boys from the band was fingering his banjo.

Devilfish blew on the harmonica again. "You found yerself a sweet patootie at the dance? She have a name? Wish I could find a chippie." He blew again on the harmonica, and it squealed.

Sam took a generous swig out of the glass and then started choking. It tasted like grass. "Charlotte," he said.

Devilfish laughed. "You never had any of that juice? Boy, we gotta make a man out of you before it's all over."

Sam set the glass down on the floor. "Don't like the taste." Didn't think Sotol would aid him in his duties as night watchman—he'd better cool it.

Devilfish shrugged. "It's cheap. Some cats don't care much about the taste. Just want to get stewed. You ever been stewed?"

Sam didn't answer. He had seen his pa stewed, and he didn't like it. Could make folks mean.

While Devilfish and some of his band were still playing, on the other side of the room, a few boys were sitting on a bed, shooting dice. Devilfish set down the harmonica and started to sing. "Now listen up boys. Y'all singalong. And a one and a two and a three. Shugah, Ooh shugah, let me put my big duffin' in your lil' ole muffin."

Some of the other boys were singing along at the top of their lungs. "Now boys, I can't hear you." They shouted, "Shugah, let me put my big duffin' in your lil' ole muffin."

Devilfish took a swig of Budweiser. "Think I'll take a little break. Sam, you're not embarrassed by my little song, are ya?" He smiled at Sam; he had a mischievous look in his brown eyes.

Sam shook his head, but he felt he was turning red. Compared to Devilfish, he felt wet behind the ears. He probably had had a lot of girlfriends—Sam reckoned he was in his mid-twenties. Or maybe he just knew more because he was from the big city. He was wearing a white undershirt, and he was thin, but his muscles bulged.

"Who taught you to play?" Sam asked.

"Taught myself," he said. He was now rolling a cigarette with tobacco. "First instrument was a cigar box with chicken wire. After that, hung out with a few fellas—Blind Lemon Jefferson and Texas Alexander."

"You're good," Sam said. He had only heard of Bob Wills and His Texas Playboys—Blind Lemon Jefferson and Texas Alexander were not musicians he knew. He had never even visited most of the big cities in Texas. The biggest city he had visited was Lubbock. This conversation reminded him of the conversation with Joe Kafouri, except here was a world he didn't know about in his own country. He felt a little guilty about doubting that Devilfish could play for the dance.

Devilfish laughed. He lit his cigarette and inhaled. "Naawww. Played a few juke joints in Deep Ellum. A few house parties for white folks. That's all."

Suddenly, a nasty fight erupted at the dice game at the other end of the barracks. A few men were shouting in Spanish. *"¡Mierda! ¡Hijo de puta! ¡Puta madre!"* Otto was pushing one of the Mexican boys against a locker, pummeling him with his fist. The other boys were trying to restrain him, but he was like a mad bull. This was a situation that was about to get out of control—Sam better go get Captain Bell. But maybe there was no time for that. "Come on," Devilfish said, gesturing with one of his taut, muscular arms. They ran over to the other end of the barracks and tried to pull Otto off of the Mexican boy, Chuey. Otto was outnumbered so they managed to pull him off the boy, but then he lunged toward Devilfish.

"Get your hands off of me, boy!"

Otto took a slug at Devilfish, but he ducked. Otto was big, but he wasn't quick. Devilfish immediately put up his fists, as if he were an experienced boxer.

Otto roared, "You took my girl, Baby Sam."

Sam was caught off guard when a burst of pain came straight through his nose.

CHAPTER 8.

# The Infirmary

When Sam woke up, E.O. was sitting in a rocking chair next to the bed, reading the *Alpine Avalanche*. Sam moaned. He looked around at the rows of starched white beds. Hadn't he hoped the other day that he didn't get sick? Ma's voice echoed in his head: "Be careful what you wish for." It wasn't a wish, but a fear. If you feared something too much, did that make it happen?

"What happened?"

"Otto broke your nose," E.O. said, adjusting his glasses. "He's locked up. Captain Bell is spittin'."

Sam felt woozy. He touched his face—there was a bandage over his nose. "Owww. Where's Darlene?"

E.O. said, "They're having a meetin'. To decide what to do with 'em. Whether they get a discharge or another chance."

"Who?"

"Devilfish's also in the brig. Smuggling booze," E.O. said. "Against camp regulations."

Sam sighed. "Shoot." What had happened? It hurt to smile. He felt dizzy, as if he were still twirling at the dance. "I met a girl."

"Me, too," E.O. said, suddenly smiling. He had a gap between his two front teeth. "Her name is Loretta." He was usually deadpan and flat. Sam wondered if he was happy to have escaped from the adding machine.

"I thought dancing was a sin," Sam said. "Aren't ya Church of Christ?"

E.O. shrugged. "That's the only way you'll meet a girl around here." Sam had misjudged E.O.—he was selective about his literalism.

Although Sam shouldn't be talking since his ma believed in Christian Science. Pa didn't. Pa was a free thinker: he said he wasn't sure if he believed or not. He said there probably was a Creator, but he didn't have much use for church.

"Speak when the Bible speaks, silent when the Bible is silent," E.O. said. "But if you ask me, drinkin' is worse than dancin' and doesn't bring anything but trouble. That's the way I see it."

Sam wasn't against cold beer, but too much of the hard stuff wasn't good. But he decided he didn't feel like another one of those moralistic discussions that had plagued them all during Prohibition, so he remained silent.

"Anyone else get hurt in the brawl?"

"No," E.O. said.

"Nothing more, E.O?" Sam said, trying to sit up in bed. When he talked, his jaw ached. E.O. was always a fount of information. What would he talk about with his new girl?

"Take it easy," E.O. said. "Nurse's orders." He poured Sam a glass of water from the jug on the table.

"Thanks," Sam said, taking a drink of the spring water.

"Captain Bell's got his tail up," E.O. said.

"At me?" Sam asked.

"Middle of the night, Darlene wasn't in her room. Dr. Walker had been nipping at his flask. Out cold."

"Where was Darlene?"

E.O. leaned forward and whispered, "Think she was off smooching with Jack." Sam had always thought that E.O. was above gossip. "You jealous?"

Sam lied. "What Jack does is his own business."

E.O. switched the topic. "Chueco cleaned your wound."

"Where is he?"

"English class. Was here an hour ago."

As if he had heard the gossip, Jack strode into the clinic and waved. Was it just Sam's imagination or was he walking with more confidence? But then, wasn't Jack always confident about the girls? He ran his hand through his thick, black hair. If he had been up all night carousing, he didn't show it—his khakis were creased. He had shaved, and he looked fresh, as if he had gotten a full eight hours of sleep. He wondered about E.O.'s story—wishful thinking?

"I've come to check on the hero," Jack said. "Word around camp is that you saved Chuey, Chueco's best friend. Anyway, that's what the boys are saying in my English class."

"Naaw," Sam said. "It was Devilfish."

Jack smiled at him, as if he were wiser—that annoyed Sam since they were the same age. Based on the recommendations of Dr. Horton, the English professor at Sul Ross College, Captain Bell had given Jack a lot of responsibility as educational advisor at the camp: he was ordering books for the library, supervising all the correspondence courses, and teaching the Mexican boys English, even though he was a recent graduate. And he was running the canteen, which turned out to be a bigger job than anyone imagined.

"Maybe Devilfish could teach us boxing," Sam said. He had never thought of that before, but Captain Bell had mentioned that they needed more recreation activities.

"I could help," Jack said. He had been a star athlete at Sul Ross and had played almost every single sport at the school: baseball, football, and track—in addition to managing the school yearbook. Was there anything he couldn't do? Why was Sam feeling competitive with him now? Must be miffed about Darlene. But now there was Charlotte. Did he want both? This didn't make any logical sense: he couldn't have two girls.

"Most boys just want to play ball," Sam said. "Otto is fixated on catching those nasty rattlers."

"Sure, I reckon we'll have to get ready for the away games."

E.O. was gazing at Jack with admiration and a little envy. "You could teach us to dance."

"She's not here," Sam said. He sounded like a tom, peeing in his territory.

The twinkle disappeared from Jack's eyes. Had something gone wrong last night? He played with the edges of his frayed straw hat.

"Did you ask her about her church?" E.O. said. "When's the wedding?"

"Elijah," Jack said, frowning. "I wouldn't plow too close to the cotton if I were you."

Jack might not be talking now, but he would eventually. If Sam knew Jack, he would spill the beans about whatever had happened with Darlene last night—if anything had happened. And how Sam had misjudged E.O.—he pretended to be reserved in the office, but was he leaking gossip from the office in the camp?

Suddenly, they heard a loud sneeze. Darlene casually strolled into the clinic, adjusting her ponytail.

How much had she heard?

She just stood there in front of Sam's bed, with her arms folded.

Unlike Jack, she looked tired. Her face was pale, and her eyes were bloodshot. She had pulled her curly hair back into a quick ponytail with a simple rubber band. She was not wearing earrings of any kind. Her uniform was wrinkled, and there was a grease stain near the collar. Had she been up all night?

Jack said, "He'll be all right. Once the swelling goes down. It's like getting kicked in the face by a horse."

Darlene winked at Sam. Her blue eyes always took his breath away. "Buster, you had us worried." She patted his hand in a maternal way. But who had carried him to the infirmary if she and Doc Walker were AWOL?

E.O. said, "If the meeting's over, I better get back to the office. Payroll."

"I've got to be goin' too," Jack said, putting his straw hat on. He headed for the door. "Got to check our inventory at the canteen."

"Wait!" Darlene said, running after him. She stood directly in front of him, close, and straightened his tie. "Now, that's better."

"Darlene, please," Jack said, as if he were exasperated. Sam felt his heart leap, since Jack was not mooning all over her.

She giggled. "See you later? Meet for a Vim Cola at the canteen?"

But Jack was unenthusiastic. "Clean out of Vim Cola," he said. "Have to order some more from Joe Kafouri." So Jack was not that interested in Darlene? Had he told her about Ruby? Or was this a little escapade in his mind?

Darlene giggled again, staring at all of them. "Boys, did y'all have a ball last night? Wasn't it just sweeter than stolen honey?"

E.O. gave Sam a meaningful look, as if to say: "See, I told you." He waved as he walked toward the door. Jack just gave her a formal nod.

"Sure," Sam said. "Until Otto put his fist through my face. Is my nose broken?"

She moved toward the sink and washed her hands. "Dr. Walker will have to examine you. He should be along right soon."

"E.O. said my nose was broken," Sam said.

"That will be determined by an X-ray," Darlene said. "What were you thinking? Gambling with Otto? You know he's a tough customer."

"I wasn't gambling," Sam said. "Or drinkin'. Was supposed to be the night watchman."

She rolled her eyes, as if she didn't believe him.

"Well, not much," Sam said. "A swig of Sotol. Don't think anyone will ask me to be night watchman again."

"The whole barracks was plowed. Captain Bell found eight cases of beer. And ten bottles of Sotol. No dances for a while. He's on the warpath."

"No more nights of stolen honey?" Sam said. He felt like goading her. But even if she had smooched or done the deed with Jack, he doubted she would tell him.

"Don't be a sourpuss," she said, smiling. "You got yerself a girl."

Sam picked up a copy of the *Alpine Avalanche* that E.O. had left on the bed: FIRST LADY TO VISIT CCC CAMPS IN WEST TEXAS. DAVIS MOUNTAINS AND BALMORHEA.[1] He flipped through the paper—an advertisement for Wonder Cure: Are you a Manly Man, Full of Vigor? But he thought that was the slogan for Vim Cola? RUSSIAN DOCTOR DIMITRI VOLKOV VISITS EL PASO: PROMISES REJUVENATION AND PERPETUAL YOUTH. One hundred acres for sale in Davis Mountains. R. T. Wiley, Cattle for Sale.

"So Mrs. Roosevelt's coming to Balmorhea," Sam said. Of course, he already knew.

"Sure is," Darlene said, putting alcohol on a cotton swab. She stopped for a minute, glancing down at the headlines. "Well," she said, taking a deep breath. "I'll be damned."

"Maybe we'll get to meet the First Lady," Sam said. Captain Bell had not shared his ideas with him about the "Cultural Program."

"What?" she asked, taking the bandage off. She was suddenly serious and was thinking about something else.

"I said, maybe we'll get to meet the First Lady," Sam said. "Owww! That hurts." She was dabbing his face with alcohol.

The earlier gaiety and happiness had vanished from her face. Her lips had curled downward into a frown. Maybe Sam had been wrong about her age—maybe she was more like mid-thirties, rather than thirty. Many people lied on their applications to the CCC camps. But why should she lie about her age? E.O. had the keys to the cabinet where the personnel files were kept.

"My ma loves the First Lady," Sam said. "Thinks she is better than freshly churned butter."

She became strictly professional now. "It might just be badly bruised. Will have to wait for Dr. Walker's humble assessment," she said.

"I have indeed arrived," Dr. Walker said, ambling into the infirmary as if he were going to sit on the front porch and sip a gin and tonic. Instead of wearing the double-breasted suit, he was wearing a white lab coat. He was wearing expensive wing-tipped shoes, not the World War I trench boots that everyone else wore at the camp.

He sat on a stool with wheels and scooted toward the bed. He studied Sam with his brown eyes. "Well, son," he said. "It appears upon the first examination that you got snookered. These things do happen when libation is abundant. I remember when I was a whippersnapper at Tulane in Sigma Chi—poker and bourbon was a recipe for a fracas."

Darlene had taken the newspaper and was reading it with great interest. She pulled up a chair and sat down beside the bed.

"Tried to pull Otto off of a kid," Sam said, looking to see if Darlene was listening. "But he was bigger . . ." But she was completely engrossed in the article. She hadn't been interested when he tried to talk to her about the First Lady. What was she reading, then?

Dr. Walker probed his face, very gently. "The bleeding has stopped, Nurse Robinson."

"Hmmm?" Darlene said, looking up at both of them.

"No more bleeding?" Dr. Walker said.

"Not this morning, no," Darlene said. "Looks like it's just swollen."

Dr. Walker sighed. "I do wish you would pay attention to the matter at hand. The patient in our care at present, Nurse Robinson."

"It appears that you have the matter under control," Darlene said, throwing down the newspaper. She couldn't stand him—it was so obvious.

Dr. Walker kept touching Sam's face. "The nose is not crooked. So it is unclear whether there has been a fracture, in fact. The diagnosis at present requires that we wait a few days until the swelling has subsided. At that point in time, we will determine whether an X-ray is needed. At that juncture, we will arrange transportation to the nearest hospital if need be to determine whether a break has occurred."

Darlene crossed her arms and looked at Sam. She looked tired, but still, her blue eyes tempted him. He had to stop pining after her—he didn't have the experience to deal with such a feisty, moody woman. One moment she was laughing; the next, she was cranky—her behavior seemed inexplicable. Anyway, she was clearly enamored with Jack, and he didn't have a chance, not even as a bench player. And now, there was Charlotte. Of course, he didn't want to see Charlotte until his face looked better.

"Stated plainly, Sam, we'll have to wait until the swelling goes down," Darlene said.

Dr. Walker scooted back from the bed on the swivel stool. "The doctor recommends bed rest and consistent cleaning of the wound so as to avoid infection. In the meantime, my boy, stay out of trouble."

"Can I go back to the barracks? Go back to work?" Sam asked. He was eager to get back to the office and his duties. Find out what was happening in the camp.

Dr. Walker took off his wire-rim glasses and rubbed his eyes. "I don't advise it. I would prefer if we monitor you for a few days. Perhaps one of the boys could bring you paper and pen and you could draw. Work on your newsletter. The swelling needs to subside and then we can determine the next course of action. Maybe Chueco can bring him his supper, Nurse Robinson."

"That will be arranged, Dr. Walker," Darlene said. "I have an errand, anyway, and am going over to the office."

Dr. Walker got up from the swivel stool and washed his hands at the sink. "I will be in my office if I am needed, Nurse Robinson."

As soon as the door slammed, Darlene mimicked him. "Perhaps at a particular juncture, we will be able to determine what the next course of action should be in this situation, that we note is one that is distressing. The patient cannot decipher the sentences and should ask for a rendering of the idea in simple words."

Sam laughed. "Owww, it hurts to laugh. He isn't mean." Suddenly, Sam wondered if Darlene could be mean. He had seen a nasty, malicious streak in her that he was not sure he liked.

"He's an old fool," she said. "Wishes he were a writer." With her finger, she twirled a little curl that had escaped from her ponytail.

He sank back on the bed. He suddenly felt very tired. Darlene put a pillow behind his head. "Sleep. Get some rest." Then she whispered, "Baby Sam."

So she thought of him as a baby? Jack was the man. The absurd slogan from the Wonder Cure popped into his mind: "Vim for the Manly Man."

But when he woke later in the afternoon, Captain Bell was sitting beside his bed. The infirmary was empty.

"Where is everybody?"

Captain Bell smiled. When he smiled, his face contorted in a grotesque way because of his injury. Two deep sutures creased the middle of his cheek—his injury must have been severe. "I thought we might have a private chat. Man to man. How are you feeling?" His eyes were bluer than Darlene's, and there was only sympathy there—no sardonic glints.

"Terrible," Sam said. "As if my face has been pummeled by a bear."

"Avoid the mirror," Captain Bell said. "For now." He pointed to his cheek.

Sam chuckled. Then he said, "I am sorry. I didn't mean . . ."

"Nobody tells you when you sign up that you might come back without a face. Or an arm. A lot of hoopla about heroism in the beginning. Then, you get . . ." He gazed off into the distance, as if he were somewhere else. "When I was at the Queen's hospital, Dr. Gillies[2] banned mirrors until he felt we were ready."

"Oh," Sam said. He was afraid he might say something clumsy, but he wanted to hear more.

"At first, I didn't even have a nose! Old Dr. Gillies would say, 'Now, don't you worry, sonny, everything will be all right.'"

Sam remembered that his pa was staunchly antiwar. Besides being a committed socialist, he was also a pacifist. He hadn't had much formal schooling, but he read everything. He was a rarity on ranches, and he didn't share his views with the other men herding cattle and livestock.

"No, I meant I'm sorry I let you down," Sam said. But now he had put his foot in it. "I mean, I am sorry about what happened to you."

"Awww," he said. "I was just a kid when it happened. I've learned to live with it. I may never get married again . . ." he said. "The injuries were devastating." Did that mean he had other injuries besides his face and arm that were too private to mention? Or that women were repulsed by his face?

Sam was a little embarrassed. Although Captain Bell was kind and shared secrets of the office with him, that was as far as it went.

"I just thought . . ."

Captain Bell waved his one remaining hand. "My wife and daughter died from the Spanish flu in 1918. When I was in France."[3]

"Oh," Sam said. "Gosh, I'm sorry." Sam decided to keep quiet so he wouldn't look like a smart aleck. That he already knew that his wife and daughter were dead. You had to be careful about rumors: some were just half-true.

Captain Bell cleared his throat. "Darlene and Dr. Walker think you'll be all right once the swelling goes down. No disfigurement." He put a large writing tablet and a few colored pencils on the bed. "If you feel like drawing."

"I let you down as night watchman," Sam said. But wasn't it also unrealistic for one twenty-two-year-old kid to be watching over two hundred men who were hot to trot?

"I got to the bottom of what happened," Captain Bell said. "Too much booze. If there is a next time, we'll have more men on duty. I don't know what I was thinking."

“We’re not gonna have any more dances?” Would he see Charlotte again? He dreaded ice cream at her family’s house. He imagined how her ma would stick to them, like Wrigley’s chewing gum.

“We’ll take it under advisement,” Captain Bell said. “I’ve got to get back to the office. Rest for now, my boy.”

CHAPTER 9.

# Healing

**After Captain Bell left, Sam sank back into the fluffy pillow and slept.** When he woke up a few hours later, Chueco was sitting next to his bed with a tray of food from the cafeteria on his lap.

He motioned with his hands. "*¿Quiere algo de comer?*"

"*Muchas gracias,*" Sam said. Spanish had been his major at Sul Ross. He was ambitious—wanted to better himself—thought he might do graduate work in Spanish if he could get a scholarship. He dreamed of going to University of Texas, or one of the bigger state schools.

Chueco shrugged and then smiled. His brown eyes were curious and sympathetic. He wasn't very big physically, with a short torso and bowlegs, even shorter than Sam. They had never figured out how old he was, but he couldn't be more than fifteen or sixteen. Captain Bell had said, "We'll ignore the forged birth certificate. I am not sending him back to that town. Come hell or high water."

His stomach rumbled.

They both laughed at the same time. Chueco put the tray of food on Sam's lap. "Eat," he said, "Señor Sam."

"Chueco," he said, "just call me Sam."

"Sam," he said, repeating the name, as if he were trying it out. "Sam. Sam."

Sam sat up and put the tray on his lap. How he hated his nickname at the camp—Snitch Sam.

Chueco's eyes suddenly became sad. "Juan," he said. "*Mi padre se llamaba Juan*. Died."

"Oh," Sam said. "*Murió*." Sam stared at the glistening corn on the cob, generous portion of green beans, and hunk of baked chicken. He was ravenous. He felt a little guilty since Chueco was telling him about his dead father.

He pulled the leg off from the thigh. In between bites, he said in English, "I am sorry."

It had been two weeks since Sam had received a letter from his folks. His ma wrote in precise loopy handwriting very simple short letters that focused on daily life: Sold a dozen eggs today. Your father is fit as a fiddle. Lost one cow to black leg. Your loving mother, she signed. P.S. We received the check and it makes all the difference. We are proud of you. Other than that, she never mentioned her feelings. He doubted he would mention the fight with Otto or his nose in his next letter—why burden her further? Was Pa really fit as a fiddle? Or was he hitting the corn whiskey?

Chueco genuflected. He prayed in Spanish, "*Dios te salve, Maria* . . ."

Sam felt embarrassed and did not know what to say so he focused on the ear of corn. It seemed insensitive to say how good the food was when Chueco was sad.

"He fell in the mine and broke his head," he said, shaking his head. "You know Chisos?"

"I've heard of it," Sam said. To be honest, that was only because Captain Bell knew about the place. What had he said about it? "Infernal place." He was learning at this camp how much he didn't know: battles in World War I, the Ottoman Empire, Dallas nightlife. And he had no experience with women.

"Everyone works for Señor Perry. Digging the quicksilver,"[1] Chueco said. "But I ran away from Chisos. Some people call Señor Perry El Perro. *Debemos mostrar lo que somos y no ser moscas muertas.* We stand for ourselves and don't let him treat us like dead flies."

"You saved Otto," Sam said.

He shook his head and brushed his bangs out of his eyes. "No," he said. He pointed to the sky. "*Dios y plantas*. We thank God."

"You are too modest," Sam said. "Have a good heart."

Darlene had changed into a fresh white uniform and tamed her hair into two tight braids. She stood a little too close to Chueco and patted him on his shoulder. "Well, how is our patient? It looks like you are on the mend. Have a hearty appetite at least."

Sam speared two or three green beans and ate. His jaw was sore, and it hurt to chew.

Chueco gazed at Darlene, as if he adored her. "Good," he said. "He is good, Señora." Did he have a crush on her?

"Captain Bell wants you to sleep here, Chueco," Darlene said, patting him again on the shoulder.

Why did she keep touching him? He would surely misunderstand. But maybe these pats were maternal—and could not be misconstrued as anything other than that. She was at least fifteen years older. Old enough to be his mother.

"*¿Dormiré aquí?*"

Darlene smiled and said, "You will sleep here tonight."

Chueco looked puzzled and confused.

"Where is your bedroom?" Sam asked.

Darlene gave him a piercing look with her blue eyes. "What does that have to do with the price of bananas, Mister?"

"Bananas?" Chueco asked.

"Well," Sam said. "A misunderstanding might be brewing."

"Oh," she said. To his surprise, she snickered. "You're not serious. A little ol' broom closet off of Dr. Walker's office. That's all Captain Bell could spare. A nun's cell."

Was that where she and Jack had disappeared to last night? He imagined them necking and petting on her single bed—this made him seethe with jealousy.

"Bananas?" Chueco asked again. "You want bananas?"

"Can you help me out?" Darlene said, turning to Sam. "I didn't study Spanish at nursing school in Galveston. Although Lord knows it would come in handy 'round here."

Sam handed Chueco his plate. "No bananas. You will sleep here," he said, gesturing to the bed next to him. "*Dormirán aquí.*"

Chueco's face lit up with joy—he felt as if he had made a new friend. He took Sam's plate and returned with his guitar, a rosary, and a pair of pajamas. Every night after he put a salve on his face and played his guitar, he told Sam a story about his life in Chisos. How he laughed when Sam sang, "*Ay, ay, ay, ay, canta y no llores, porque cantando se alegren* . . ." Was it his accent? Or the fact that he was an Anglo singing in Spanish?

A few nights later, Chueco told him more about the death of his father. "Daddy died about four or five in the afternoon. Fell in the shaft. The next day you have to bury. Have to put an iron on the stomach to keep it from going up . . ."

He had learned some English at the school at Chisos and was improving his English right along.

"When did your papa die?" Sam asked.

"One year," he said. "El Perro refused to pay. He said Daddy was drunk. Too much Sotol."

Before the accident, Chueco's mother was working as a *curandera* if someone didn't want to go to Señor Perry's doctor.[2] And sometimes they were embarrassed, if it were a case of "*susto*" or "*bilis*." Chueco explained this as if it were the most natural thing in the world—she cures "anger illnesses." His mother, Magdalena—sometimes, she used the herbs, but other times, she used lemons or eggs or cleansed the body with holy water. She always said the Apostle's Creed—she listened when people came knocking on her door.

Then she started ironing at night. "Sometimes, she ironed all night until three or four o'clock in the morning. She used to iron everything, underwear, sheets . . ." Always, she was singing "Cielito lindo" or "Mal hombre." Everyone worked. He told Sam how his sisters were frying *nopales* and carrying water, even Feliciana who was six. Sometimes, they took the burro.

Of course, Sam had not had an easy ride, either. Sam remembered his papa's support of Eugene Debs and the working man. The president had all of these folks in mind.

"It's not all sad," Chueco said. "Sometimes, on Saturdays we dance." He held out the guitar to Sam and sang, "*Aaay, aaay, canta y no llores, porque cantando se alegran.*" They laughed. Then he became serious again. "I give the money from playing at the dance to Mama."

"I thought Devilfish taught you how to play?"

Chueco shook his head. "I knew before. But he taught me many new things. New songs."

He had planted a few herbs in pots at the far end of the infirmary in a very unobtrusive corner of the barracks. Every night, he taught Sam the name of the plant in Spanish and explained to him how it was used. Of course, Sam knew the prickly pear, which he called *nopal*. Could identify sunflowers. Sam sniffed another plant—and guessed it was mint since it smelled like Wrigley's spearmint gum. Jack was selling Wrigley's at the canteen. "*Hierba buena*," Sam repeated after him. "For a bad stomach." Aloe vera was *sábila.* Chueco peeled off the skin with a paring knife and showed him the green gel. Magdalena says: "We must respect the plants and the nature. With God's help, they can save us." But even *sábila* couldn't save his Uncle Carlos. Señor Perry said that Uncle Carlos was stealing gasoline from the compressor. His pants were wet with gasoline and when he tried to light his lamp, his clothes caught on fire. Chueco did not hide his rage: "They said he was a robber and that's why they didn't pay." It was after this latest accident that Chueco decided to leave Chisos. But now he was homesick and missed his youngest sister, Feliciana—and he missed the fried *nopales* and *cabrito* and *salsa*—and he missed Consuela, Violeta, and Carmela, his other sisters. And he missed his mama, Magdalena—"the plants remind me of her." But most of all, he missed his pet burro, Lazaro Cardenas.

"Why'd you call him that?"

"He's the president of Mexico. Against the haciendas. He's for the people."

Why did folks suffer so much? Sam didn't find comfort even in the story of Job. Something he had never shared with anyone—it would displease his mama to hear this.

By the end of the week, the swelling had gone down. Sam almost told Dr. Walker about Chueco's salve, but then decided against it. He hadn't been happy about the salve Chueco had put on Otto's snake bite. Why would he rejoice about the yucca salve?

Dr. Walker examined his face and nose. He touched Sam's face very gingerly with his long fingers. "Does that hurt?"

"Just a little bruised," Sam said.

He scooted back on the little stool with wheels. "To the best of my knowledge, your nose doesn't appear to be broken. I don't think an X-ray is, in fact, required or needed. But I do want you to stay here another day to rest."

CHAPTER 10.

# Heat Wave

**The day Sam was supposed to leave the infirmary, the weather got even hotter–and for August it was unbearable.** The temperature pushed toward a hundred degrees. It was high noon. He had started packing up his things and hoped to spend the night back in the officers' barracks. He had only sketched one drawing in that week—and it was Chueco in pencil, playing his guitar under the moon. What had happened to that sketch? He could not remember if it was in the attic—or had he given it to Chueco?

One of the boys called out, "Water."

Captain Bell couldn't walk straight, as if he were dizzy. At first, Sam thought he had been bitten by a snake. He was leaning on two boys—his face was red, and he wasn't wearing his ranger hat.

Chueco was tending his plants and rushed over. "*Insolación.*"

"What?" Sam asked, following him.

"Sick from the sun," Chueco said. "Too much."

Darlene rushed over with a thermometer. She shook it and then tucked it under Captain Bell's tongue. "We have to get it down. Boys, put him right there," she said, pointing to a bed.

Captain Bell was mumbling, "Now, don't you die on me, Private. We're gonna get you outta here."

The boys helped him onto the bed and he lay down. She plumped a pillow and put it under his head.

She dabbed the sweat off his forehead with a wet towel. "Well, Captain, you're not in France. And you're gonna be fit as a fiddle soon."

Sam just stood there, staring. It had never occurred to him that something could happen to Captain Bell—he was like a rock. What horrible things had happened to him in France?

Darlene placed a damp towel around Captain Bell's neck. "Don't just stand there gawking, Sam. Go fetch Dr. Walker."

Sam ran to Dr. Walker's office. He kept rapping on the door and then rattled the handle—locked, tight as a drum. A note was pinned to the door: "An opportunity for professional edification has presented itself and I have absented myself from the office for the afternoon. Should there be any emergency, I am confident Nurse Robinson can treat whatever that may be, should it occur. In any event, I will be back later this evening. Dr. Walker."

When Sam returned with the note, Darlene was sprinkling Captain Bell with water. "Well?" she asked.

"Gone to town," Sam said.

She snorted. "Figures. Help me get him out of these clothes," she said. "We've got to get his temperature down. Get him cooled off."

"Where's Chueco?"

"Gone for ice."

Captain Bell was delirious, as if he were staring into a tunnel. His face was still beet red. "Get the medics. For crying out loud. We have to get him to a field hospital!"

"Sam, get his pants off. Quit lollygagging around. This isn't a damned picnic."

Sam felt a little embarrassed about taking Captain Bell's pants off for him. "Oh, all right," she said, yanking his pants off. Stripped, except for his starched white underwear. Sam avoided looking at his private area. Of course, he was curious, but he couldn't tell anything about his size. Darlene wasn't embarrassed a bit, but she was a nurse. Why had she checked the box "single" on the application form? What was she hiding? She unbuttoned his khaki shirt as well. Captain Bell had tufts of curly brown hair all over his chest.

But Chueco didn't return with ice, but with a stone mortar and pestle, like the kind they sold in Mexican markets. He began crushing seeds and mixing them with some kind of oil.

Darlene was trying to get Captain Bell to drink water. "Easy does it, Captain. You've got to drink now. Where's the ice?"

Captain Bell gulped the water. Then wiped his hand on his mouth, as if he were on the battlefield.

Chueco shrugged. "*No hay hielo.*" Then he added, "No ice."

"Never have what we need around here in terms of supplies," she railed. "Can't even get something as simple as ice. Did you ask in the kitchen?"

Chueco shook his head. "Better," he said, pointing to the leaf of the elephant ear. He spread the paste on the leaf.

"Well," she sighed. "You saved Otto. Reckon you know what you're doing."

She did not know he was putting a yucca paste on Sam's face every night.

Chueco placed the leaf on Captain Bell's forehead and temples. Captain Bell closed his eyes. Chueco held his hand. He was praying.

He waited thirty minutes and then repeated the treatment.

Darlene shook the thermometer again and took Captain Bell's temperature. "Down four degrees already. A miracle."

While Captain Bell was lying with elephant leaves on his head, Chueco ran off again. When he returned, he was carrying a green, gooey mixture in a jar.

"What's that?" Sam asked. He couldn't restrain his curiosity.

"Red," Darlene said, tossing her braids back. "Sweetheart, you're in the way."

"Stop treating me like a little kid." Sam wanted her to treat him like she treated Captain Bell—and that wasn't possible, because he didn't have his life experience or maturity.

"Don't get all huffy," Darlene said, teasing him with her blue eyes. Was she flirting with him? But why now?

Chueco went and got one of the plants from the other side of the room. He pointed to the sunflower. "We cook the flower."

Chueco took off the damp towel and put a dry towel on Captain Bell's shoulders. Then he massaged his hair with the green mixture two times.[1] Captain Bell's hair was thinning on the top, but he had brown curls at the back.

By the time he had had two treatments of the shampoo, his temperature had gone down to 99 degrees, and he was no longer delirious. Darlene shook the thermometer again and put it under Captain Bell's tongue. "Now, that's more like it."

"Forgot my hat in the office. Wasn't out in the sun that long . . ." Captain Bell said.

Darlene stood with her hands on her fulsome hips and threw him his pants. "You're in Balmorhea, Captain. Not the Argonne Forest. Put your pants on."

Captain Bell smiled. "You're not flirtin' with me, Miss Robinson?"

"Wouldn't dream of it," Darlene said. "Captain."

Captain Bell slept the rest of the afternoon.

Darlene apologized. "I am sorry, Sam. Sometimes, you say things when you're under pressure. We just had to get Captain Bell's body temperature down. It could have been dangerous for him."

"Should I leave?" Sam asked, setting his kit on the bed. "Am I still in the way?"

She put her hand on his shoulder. Her touch was electric. Chueco was on the other side of the room, but he heard her. Chueco looked displeased and was shaking his head.

"Here's your hat. Where's your hurry?" she said. "Stick around and see if the captain needs anything. I have got to catch up on my paperwork."

Sam sat on his bed, cross-legged, the rest of the afternoon, drawing Chueco's little garden in his notebook. Under each plant, he wrote the name in Spanish. Chueco crossed out the words if they were misspelled and wrote them correctly in Spanish. Sam also sketched Captain Bell, asleep.

Later that evening when it was cooler and the vast West Texas sky was turning orange, they took Captain Bell outside for the third treatment under the shade of an ash tree. The landscape was bare, except for the seedlings of new trees, little scarecrows, except for this one full tree, which had shot up next to the clinic. The leaves provided a fair amount of shade.

While Chueco was pouring the green goo on Captain Bell's head, Dr. Walker rolled up in his shiny Model A Ford coupe. The big round lights made the car look like a yellow doodlebug. Dr. Walker easily had the nicest car of any Local Experienced Men of the camp. Just how rich was his family from Tyler? Did they own a big plantation?

Dr. Walker slammed the car door. He was carrying his black bag.

"What in the Sam Hill is going on here? Looks like you are having your hair done."

"Hardly," Captain Bell said. He laughed. When he laughed, his sutured cheek caved in, like a giant dimple. Sam wondered if he had been shot at close range—or what ammunition had caused such an injury. Would Captain Bell tell him, if he asked?

"Well, then," Dr. Walker said. "Why is Chueco shampooing your hair with that dastardly green lubricant? Looks like fluid for my automobile."

"I got heatstroke," Captain Bell said.

Dr. Walker raised his thick brown eyebrows, as if he were skeptical. "That is not the prescribed treatment for such a malady. Nurse Robinson, you were left in charge of the clinic. You're allowing an uneducated Latin boy to prescribe treatments?"

"The treatment was just as effective as ice," Darlene said, tossing one of her braids. As if to say, "Take that." Those full lips curled into a snarl. "Besides, we didn't have ice. Just like we didn't have antivenom."

Chueco looked angry, but he did not speak. He kept massaging Captain Bell's head with the green shampoo. Then he rinsed out the shampoo with water.

Captain Bell stared at Dr. Walker. "His name is Chueco. The salve was better than ice."

"Pssssaw," Dr. Walker said, taking off his fedora. He brushed a piece of his thinning brown hair on the top of his head with his hand. A small gold ring with an onyx stone glistened on his pinky finger. "You are subscribing to hocus-pocus? Superstition? The boy has no medical training."

"You weren't here, Doctor," Darlene said, handing Chueco another pitcher of water. "We did the best we could. All of us chipped in. If it weren't for Chueco . . ."

"Generally, you report to me if you are leaving the camp, Dr. Walker. That is the protocol," Captain Bell said with more equanimity. "I will follow up on this matter later."

But it was as if Dr. Walker had not heard Captain Bell. He held up a bottle of "Wonder Cure." He bowed with a courtly flourish. "My sincerest apologies, but an opportunity arose that surely could not have been missed. A matter of professional development for the medical field. I attended a lecture at Sul Ross by the eminent Dr. Dimitri Volkov on the topic of rejuvenation. A remarkable theory that could change the whole history of medicine."

Wasn't that the doctor Sam had read about in the *Alpine Avalanche*?

Captain Bell cocked a shrewd eye at Dr. Walker. "Sure that it's not just morphine in that magic elixir? Or even a little brandy?"

Dr. Walker was offended. "Are you suggesting that as a medical practitioner, I would be hoodwinked so easily? Dr. Volkov was educated in Paris and has impeccable qualifications. He has the endorsement of the Texas Medical Association. It was the most edifying lecture."

Chueco finished rinsing Captain Bell's hair and wrapped the towel around his head in a turban.

"Thank you, Chueco," Captain Bell said. Then, turning to Dr. Walker he said, "Edify us."

"Lost youth can be revived with animal glands," Dr. Walker said. "They can be transplanted to the human body and give those who are aging more vigor. More virility."

Chueco whispered to Sam, "*¿Qué?*"

Sam shrugged. "Manliness." It would have been easier to resort to crude language, but he didn't dare in front of Captain Bell. *Cojones*, he thought, but he didn't dare say it in front of Captain Bell.

Captain Bell sighed. "What kind of animal glands?"

Dr. Walker couldn't stop talking. "This is the newest medical advancement of our time. I am a little flummoxed that you are not interested in the future advancements which will ameliorate any suffering that surfaces in regards to the male organ. That could prevent consummation of the sexual act."

Darlene held up her hand. "I don't mean to interrupt this edifying lecture on the prostate," she said. "But I didn't have supper."

Dr. Walker continued, "Even Eugene Debs has had the operation and he is currently recovering in Chicago. To answer your question about the animal glands that are utilized in the transplant, they are goats."[2]

Captain Bell guffawed. His laugh sounded like a donkey. Sam had never seen him so amused. "Ah, Dr. Walker, no one will live forever. If I could bring back all the boys I lost at the battle of the Argonne Forest . . ."

Dr. Walker held up the bottle of Wonder Cure—"The latest innovation in medicine." Didn't they have Wonder Cure in the canteen? Had Dr. Walker ordered it?

Captain Bell got up out of the chair. "Thank you, Dr. Walker, but I am feeling as fit as a goat now and think I will saunter back to my barracks."

"Howdy, fellas," Jack said to the group, taking off his straw hat since he was under the shade of the ash tree. "What's going on here?"

"Just talking about goats and the benefits of their private parts," Captain Bell said.

Jack looked surprised. "Oh," he said. But this time, his eyes were directed at Darlene, and he didn't hide his feelings. "I've been huntin' for you everywhere."

"Captain Bell had a bad case of heatstroke this afternoon," Darlene said. Suddenly, she took out the tight rubber bands in her braids, and her wavy black hair cascaded over her shoulders—that one move changed her look from hillbilly country girl to glamorous movie star. "Ah, that's better," she said, shaking her hair.

Captain Bell looked as if he envied Jack. Or maybe, because of his disfigured face, he just envied any man who was attractive to a woman. It had been longer than a week since Sam had met Charlotte—did he still have her phone number? He had promised to call. But then, of course he had not, since he had been pummeled by Otto.

"May I be excused?" Darlene said. "I'm starvin' and could eat a horse."

"You have done your duty," Captain Bell said. "All of you. I am deeply grateful."

Sam caught Chueco sneaking a look at Darlene's rear end while he was picking up the pitcher and the empty jar of sunflower shampoo. Dr. Walker popped open his gold pocket watch and glanced down at it. Then he looked up. "I wasn't cognizant of the fact that a romance was developing under my nose . . ."

Darlene strolled off with Jack, just as the sky burst into pink, a few minutes before sunset.

CHAPTER 11.

# Charlotte, September 1935

Sam would call Charlotte. He mulled it over for a few days and didn't share his feelings with anyone. If Jack and Darlene were an item, he didn't need to keep waiting around. Of course, much later, he would realize that it wasn't a good idea to court a girl when your feelings were hurt over another one.

That day, no one was in the office, not even E.O. Sam fished out the torn napkin from his wallet and stared at it for a few minutes. What if she said no? But she had seemed eager enough to give him her folks' number. If she wasn't interested, she could have refused to give it out. And then, there was a problem of what to do if she said yes. Captain Bell had ruled out the idea of any more dances. Sam didn't have any extra money to speak of. And there wasn't much to do around here. He couldn't just invite her out to Balmorhea on a weekend, either: female visitors weren't allowed. He stared at the black rotary phone. If he didn't call, he'd never know. And if he didn't dial soon, someone was bound to come into the office—and then he'd have no privacy.

The phone rang a few times. And then a pleasant voice said, "U.S. Post Office, Fort Davis." It must be Charlotte's mama.

"Afternoon, ma'am. I would like to speak with Charlotte."

"Well," the voice said. "Charlotte is running an errand with her pa. You are?"

"Sam McCabe. I'm at the Balmorhea camp," he said, clearing his throat. "We, uh, we met at the dance last month."

"What a nice event! Does Captain Bell have any plans to do it again?"

"Well, uh," Sam said. "I am not right sure about that."

At just that moment, Captain Bell came into the office. Dr. Walker was following him and shaking his cane.

Dr. Walker said in a loud voice, "The boy is not qualified. Not educated. Adhering to all of this hocus-pocus."

The voice carried on. "Captain Bell is such a gentleman. I thought the dance was such a lovely idea for our local girls. Might be a chance . . ."

Captain Bell walked toward the hat rack and put his ranger hat on the peg. "Sam, did Washington call?"

Sam covered the mouthpiece. "No, sir."

It was strictly forbidden to use the phone for private phone calls, so Sam had to get off, gracefully. Captain Bell had explained it to Sam this way: "If I let you do it, then everyone in the camp'll be in here. Phone is reserved for emergencies and Washington."

Charlotte's mama wanted to gab. "I was impressed with the apple pie. You have some good cooks over there?"

So Charlotte's mother had been at the dance?

"You're the young man who danced with her the second part of the night."

"Uh," Sam said. "Yes. Well, if you could relay the message, I would be grateful, ma'am."

Captain Bell's eyes bored into Sam as he headed toward the partition that separated his desk from the rest of the office. Dr. Walker toddled after him.

"I would be delighted, young man," Charlotte's mother said. "You could come to church with us on Sunday and then come for lunch."

He knew it. Going to church would be part of the deal.

"That's a nice idea," Sam said. "Thank you, goodbye."

"Young man. Young man," Charlotte's mother said. "Do you fancy fried chicken? I make the best fried chicken in all of West Texas."

"Thank you," Sam said. "That sounds mighty tasty."

"Is that a yes or a no?" Charlotte's mother asked.

Captain Bell's head bobbed around the partition. "We need to keep the line clear."

"Yes, I am much obliged," Sam said. How could he get off without being rude?

Charlotte's mother's voice hardened. "I need to know so we can slaughter the chicken."

"Chicken is fine."

"Well, then," Charlotte's mother laughed. "That's settled. Pa will pick you up on Sunday at 9:00 for Sunday school and church at the entrance of the Balmorhea camp."

Oh, no! What had he done? Hadn't they talked about ice cream?

E.O. dumped the mail on his desk. "Was in town to double check on supplies. I stopped by the post office, and the postmaster gave me the mail."

At the top of the heap was the *Journal of the American Medical Association*. There was a picture of a billy goat on the cover with the headline: "Goat Gland Doctor Transplants Organs to Rejuvenate Men's Virility: True Medical Experimentation or Hoax?"

Captain Bell was saying, "With all due respect, Doctor, some of Chueco's natural cures really do work. When we didn't have the antivenom, he knew what to do. And the sunflower shampoo helped me recover from heatstroke. Don't you think you're being a bit hard on the boy?"

"The training of a doctor is a long and arduous one," Dr. Walker said. "A young Latin boy cannot be entrusted with such a weighty and ponderous responsibility. I am displeased at this turn of events."

"Well, Dr. Walker," Captain Bell said. "You might be, at that. But I might also remind you that you should have notified me that you were going to a lecture at Alpine. Technically speaking, you are supposed to be on call."

"This is preposterous. I was attending a lecture that will advance the course of medical science. You are implying that I should not have gone to this important lecture by Dr. Volkov?"

"Might I remind you that you are the doctor for the camp," Captain Bell said. "If you are not interested in your regular duties, we might find another local man who is . . ."

E.O. stopped the clicking of his adding machine.

Just as Sam had flipped to the right page about the Goat Gland Doctor in the journal, Dr. Walker suddenly appeared in front of Sam. "Young man," he said. "My hat and my cane."

Sam read the first line: "*Dr. John Brinkley claims that he can cure male impotence by transplanting the goat glands in a two-step operation. Many patients swear by him. However, there are reports . . .*"

Dr. Walker grumbled as he stood at the doorjamb, "A prophet is never recognized in his own country. Never a truer word said."

Sam leaped up from his chair. Dr. Walker was standing just outside the door and squinted in the blinding sunlight. "I trust you have recovered, dear boy, from that rather abominable trouncing of your nose."

As if Dr. Walker were in slow motion, he put his fedora on his head. Wasn't that the wrong hat for this time of year?

"I am fine as cream gravy," Sam said, handing him the journal with the goat on the cover. Sam kicked himself for not keeping it so he could read the article. How could he read it now? Could he ask Darlene to get it for him?

When Sam ducked back into the office, Captain Bell was pouring himself a glass of water with his one hand. After he drank his fill, he set the glass down. He massaged the stub of his left shoulder. He laughed. "Sometimes, I think it's still there. It's what you call a phantom arm. The nerves are still there."

"Does it hurt?" Sam asked.

"Aches," Captain Bell said. "A little like grief." Sam felt out of his depth. Was he also thinking about his wife and daughter? Had he ever fallen in love again?

"Oh," Sam said. "I am sorry, sir."

"We need to be thinkin' about the First Lady's visit," Captain Bell said. "You boys got any ideas on how we are going to entertain the First Lady?"

E.O. perked up. "Joe Kafouri is organizing horse rides in the Davis Mountains. I read the First Lady likes to ride horses."

"Good idea," Captain Bell said. "The only hitch I can see is security detail. But they will probably bring their own. Sam?"

"She loves the natural world. Read somewhere she rides well," Sam said.

Captain Walker said, "I'll need to set up a meeting with Joe Kafouri. Soon."

• • •

Sam enjoyed the crispy fried chicken that Charlotte's mama had prepared, and he ate with a good appetite, but there was a lot of talk about sin and hell at church. It made him realize how encouraging his mother was, and he felt a little homesick. After Ma's last pregnancy, she was healed by one of Mary Baker Eddy's followers and so she came to believe in some of the principles of Christian Science, combining Christ's scriptures with healing practices. His little sister, Augusta, was fifteen years younger than he was.

But Charlotte's mama was a Baptist, and she couldn't stop talking about sin. She had been a member of the temperance movement, and she was perturbed that Prohibition had been repealed in 1933. She gabbed so much about the sin of spirits that no one could get in a word edgewise, not even Charlotte. After that, she zeroed in on the "Latins" at Balmorhea. Wasn't Sam disturbed by them?

He repressed his anger. At the same time, he didn't have to agree with her. "All good fellas, as far as I can see."

"You don't think they're taking over our land?"

Her pa focused on the food and didn't comment. "Delicious, Rita," he said. "You've outdone yerself."

"Young man, is it my imagination or is your nose swollen?"

His fib of running into a door wasn't very convincing, but that was the first thing that came to mind. He supposed he might go to hell for telling a lie.

Sam and Charlotte sat on the front porch swing and had ten minutes alone. But before Sam could say what a good time he had hearing about sin and hell or get acquainted, her mama popped out the door with fresh lemonade.

Charlotte looked miserable, sitting there next to her pa when they dropped him back at the entrance of the camp. He felt sorry for her.

"You will come to church next week?" she asked, smiling.

But he just waved goodbye, as the truck rolled out of sight in a cloud of dust.

# PART II:

# VISITORS

CHAPTER 12.

# The Attic, Arroyo Drive, Harlingen, Texas, 1976

**The doctors had taken not only his left arm, but a good bit of his left shoulder.** Maggie was trying to fit the brace over the lump of what had been his shoulder. He couldn't remember everything about the camp at Balmorhea, but that year had been vital, somehow.

"Just hold on," she said, tying the straps. "Oh poo," she said, reminding him of Darlene. Hadn't Darlene used that expression? "I forgot about that one." She buckled up one more set of straps. "Now you're ready to fly."

He felt guilty about dreaming about Darlene. Maggie wasn't very big, but she was a spitfire. Her eyes were blue, too, but she wasn't gorgeous in the way Darlene had been—she had a feisty cuteness. When she woke up in the morning, her curly hair made her look angelic. But now it was snow-white; she had stopped dyeing it brown. He still couldn't predict what she might do: this was exciting, but also could be irksome, especially when she said something tactless, or even racist. He cringed when she said "Negras." His thesis at Chapel Hill was on the history of Mexico: focusing on Benito Juarez, the Mexican president from 1861 to 1872 who also fought against the French occupation and Emperor Maximilian and sought constitutional reforms to create a democratic republic. Unlike him, Maggie didn't come from a ranch family. Her father worked for the railroad and practically every woman in her family had been to college. He remembered their first meeting at Chapel Hill at a student picnic. When she had started whooping like a Native American, he hadn't thought that very funny. He was having a serious discussion about Cynthia Anne Parker, who had been kidnapped by the Comanches and then rescued in 1860 by the Texas Rangers. The other graduate student said, "Funny thing, though, she didn't want to be rescued. Starved herself and died of influenza." Maggie chimed in, "That's because the Comanches had become her family." Maggie's mother had died when she was a baby, and the girl had been sent off to boarding school when she was little. She had been shuffled between a stepmother and an aunt.

Maggie was studying Latin and Classics—and she liked to play gin rummy and taught him the foxtrot. Things had gone fast, like a runaway train: at first, they pledged a year engagement, whittled it down to six months, and then their resolve evaporated, and they were married at the courthouse after six weeks. He wouldn't recommend this path to youngsters, but the marriage had endured. When he brought her back to West Texas after they graduated, Maggie couldn't stop complaining: "My hair's gone flat and there are no trees!" Subtropical South Texas had made her happier, although he was the gardener. She had very cleverly managed the income from his modest law practice. She always stuck her hand out: "What are you bringing me from the mint?"

He hoped the brace would help him with his balance. He looked down at the yellow, ugly-looking contraption which cupped his left shoulder: it was uncomfortable and hot. He edged out of the seat and stood up. The brace was so heavy he was now being pulled to the left, as if he were becoming Humpty Dumpty. But at least he would have the rope to hang onto as he walked across the yard. The mother armadillo and her babies had disappeared. Instead, a few chachalacas squawked in the ebony tree. Although he loved birds, he didn't much enjoy squawking, and he missed the armadillos. Was there a way of summoning them back from the arroyo?

Maggie scooched to the edge of her porch chair, as if she were about to get up, but then changed her mind. She lit up a cigarette and exhaled the smoke through her nose. He had given up on trying to get her to stop smoking. She just shrugged when he lectured on how bad it was for your health. Gave him some maddening answer, like, "No one knows when they are going to die. Might as well enjoy life." He'd answer, "No need to hurry it along."

He held onto the rope. A dove cooed and settled on one of the electrical wires above. He gazed at a tiny emerald hummingbird, whirring around the feeder, tempted by the red syrup—how majestic she was! But she suddenly disappeared.

A blue Mustang roared into the driveway and stopped abruptly behind the rusty 1930 Chevrolet truck with its small, square cab and bulbous headlights in the carport. He didn't expect restoration would ever happen now, but he couldn't bear to have it towed away. He remembered Joe's shiny blue truck, "The Kafouri Brothers' Dry Goods Grocery" painted on the side. He felt as if he were seeing double; everything now reminded him of Balmorhea. Was it Dr. Volkov's shiny promise of Rejuvenation and Everlasting Youth?

Maggie smiled. "Our precious little lamb."

"It's the lion," Sam said. He had nicknamed their sixteen-year-old granddaughter, Rosemary, "the lion" because her blonde hair fell straight into her eyes. Rosemary was named for her maternal grandmother, although she was just as forthright as Maggie and more like her—one of life's ironies. She went around in torn tee shirts and blue jeans, and she hated frilly clothes. He figured this was a stage, and she would come out of it at some point. She probably didn't like this nickname of "the lion" just as he had detested "Red" and "Baby Sam" at Balmorhea. Rosemary had inherited his green eyes and big ears, but not the red hair. An image of her as a little tyke, tottering toward him with thimble-sized lace-up shoes, rose up in his mind—she was their first grandchild.

"Granddaddy," Rosemary asked. "How are you feeling?"

He felt as if he were swaying, but maybe it was just the brace weighing him down. He suddenly felt exhausted. Was it his own persistence to fight this new condition that was wearing him down? What kind of psychological strength had Captain Bell needed to overcome his facial injuries?

"Why don't you save the walk for later?" said Maggie, who flew off the porch. By the time he looked up, she was standing next to the rope. "Have some iced tea with us?"

It was when they were sitting at the round table in the dining room that he remembered the attic again. The trap door was just above the ceiling in the kitchen. With his balance there was no way he would be able to get up the stairs that folded out from the ceiling, like an accordion. He didn't want to ask Maggie to go prowling around in the attic, but maybe Rosemary would. Maggie was a packrat and it would be hard to find, maybe under piles of Christmas tinsel and the artificial tree. Or was it that he didn't want Maggie reading through his diaries and letters? Maybe Darlene's diary was still there. Once he had swiped a watermelon from a neighbor's patch, and for that, his pa had beaten his hide with a horse whip. "Never, ever, take what's not yours," he said. "We might be cowhands, but you're gonna live yer life fair and square. You understand? Do what's right." He had seemed so strong at that moment. Tired of herding animals and managing livestock, his pa had bought a small patch of land near Lubbock to farm. Unsummoned, a memory flashed in his head of his father howling with rage and impotence after wheat prices had fallen to an all-time low of thirty-two cents in 1932. He didn't know that Sam was in the barn, brushing down one of the horses. They lost the year, completely.

Rosemary plopped down next to him. "How are you feeling, Granddaddy?" she asked again.

He sighed. "Fair." His pa's words, "fair and square," echoed in his head.

Maggie smiled and drank her iced coffee. "How about a sugar cookie?" she said, pushing forward a plate full of freshly baked cookies, lightly dusted with sugar.

But his granddaughter ignored the cookies. "What do the doctors say?"

Maggie jumped in. "Doctors are not always right. Although they saved your grandfather's life the first time in the thirties when he had melanoma. Sometimes, they are just experimenting, especially if it's a new procedure or a new medicine."

He remembered very distinctly that Dr. Volkov had worn a pince-nez, like a European, and sported a mustache and a goatee in the photograph in the newspaper. The word was that he had escaped from the Russian Revolution in 1917 and gone to Paris for his medical education, and after Paris, he had rolled up in West Texas. It all seemed highly unlikely, except that many had believed it. In one of his local law cases in the '70s, a B. S. Goldman had claimed to have patent rights on a uranium upgrader. The pitch was that with this device low-grade uranium could be reproduced and would bring a windfall, a sweetheart deal. He'd conned poor widows and retired schoolteachers into gambling with him on the venture. Folks were too ashamed to admit they had been had, until they had been completely cleaned out.

He didn't want to talk about doctors. He said, "How's the tennis? Any more victories?"

Rosemary smiled. "We're going to the state tournament."

He was now reduced to very short walks in the front yard. He remembered running after horses, leaping over fences, tumbling on the ground. At Sul Ross, he ran track, like the speed of lightning. Although his pal Jack had been a better all-around athlete. Why did he care about that now? He felt as if he were invincible, except of course, when Otto's fist had come through his nose. He had always wanted to learn to box. After the debacle of the boxing match at Balmorhea, Captain Bell had steered everyone to other sports.

"That's wonderful," he said. He wasn't sure the shoulder brace was a good idea. It felt like it was constraining him even more, irritating the wound. Could a part of your body be suffocated, just like your lungs? He couldn't remember which doctor had advised that.

He took a swig from the iced tea. "Rosemary, honey, do you think you could climb up into the attic and look for a box for me?"

"Sure, Granddaddy," Rosemary said. "Is it labeled?"

Maggie giggled. "Everything is up there, even Confederate money. Are you sure, Sam? Did you root out the possums? This could be an all-morning project."

He didn't envision trapping any more possums, ever. But possums or no possums, he wanted that box. He remembered a jackrabbit drive in the Panhandle where farmers had clubbed the rabbits to death with bats.

"It's labeled 'Balmorhea' in blue letters. It's in a legal box."

Maggie looked surprised. "Psssaw. Why, that was years ago. Why do you want to fool with that now?"

But even though the nerves in his arm prickled like needles, he didn't waver. "I am trying to remember something."

CHAPTER 13.

# The Camping Trip in the Davis Mountains, October 1935

**He fished a yellow newspaper clipping out of the box from the attic with his right hand.** Now his only hand. Maggie had gone to the store, and he was alone in the house. He felt compassion for Captain Bell, and he wondered if he were still alive. Could you still have compassion for someone who was now dead? Or was the tragedy that you only had insight too late?

From the *Alpine Avalanche*: October 7, 1935. FIRST LADY'S TEXAS TOUR: DALLAS, LUBBOCK, BALMORHEA, BIG BEND AND EL PASO. *After a speaking tour in some of Texas' biggest cities, First Lady Eleanor Roosevelt and a small entourage will visit some of the Civilian Conservation Camps in West Texas.*

He flipped open the diary, an old composition book: The inside cover said, "'Red' Sam McCabe, Gambler, Rambler, Ace Reporter." He had fancied himself a journalist as a youngster, but he was not hard-boiled enough to make it as a newspaper man. After he completed his graduate work, he and Maggie had gone into public school work. For a time, he ran a school. He read law in the summers, until he sat for the bar in 1944. It was really the law that attracted him—helping ordinary folks protect themselves. Pa had gotten chiseled out of his rights by ol' man Collier on many a land venture because he hadn't gotten a decent contract.

He turned the page of the diary and read:

Sept. 1, 1935: *Captain Bell tells me I will be going on the horse trip with the First Lady in the Davis Mountains. Since I know how to handle horses.* He turned the page. It was blank. He flipped the next page: *The Feds will stay at Balmorhea with Hick and Tommy.*

October 8, 1935: *Met Frank Hamer,[1] the Texas Ranger who caught Bonnie and Clyde, on the trip!!! Kafouri passed Rangers' muster, but they thought he was a "Latin." Made Bell furious. I will set up the pup tents. Ten Rangers to go, all carrying rifles and pistols. Feds think it's okay. Kafouri learned how to ride in New Mexico, he was a horse-trader before he became a peddler. Sold pelts. His food was better than Balmorhea camp kitchen. The First Lady was more interested in Kafouri than Hamer!!!*

That was all? He couldn't believe that was all he had written. He set down the diaries on the table and looked out the window at a green jay that had landed on the branch of an ebony tree. The years rolled back and the memory returned, surprisingly crisp:

They had all convened at Joe Kafouri's dry-goods store. The Texas Rangers were already saddled up and carrying shotguns, as if they were going on a posse to shoot Indians or catch bootleggers. They were impressive, all rigged up with gray felt hats, tilted to one side, impressive boots. Pistols displayed prominently on their hips. With a bedroll on the back of their saddle. Frank Hamer wasn't working with the Rangers anymore, but he'd agreed to go on the camping trip. That had given the Feds the confidence to agree to the trip. In fact, at that time, they were no longer Rangers, but they were called Texas Border Patrol. When he was a graduate student a few years later, he read up on *Los Diablos Tejanos*, The Texan Devils.[2] They had served as a paramilitary force for the state in the early days, restoring order along the Mexican border. A rough bunch, they had conducted summary executions and torture and mostly gotten away with it. On January 28, 1918, they massacred fifteen men at Porvenir, Texas. Texas lawmaker José Canales led an investigation of their abuses and found that they had killed anywhere from three hundred to five thousand people of Hispanic descent in the state of Texas from 1910 to 1919. As a result, the Rangers were disbanded and reduced as a force. A complaints system was instituted.

As Sam recalled, even Frank Hamer was in for a surprise when they returned from the camping trip.

Mrs. R. was standing in front of Joe's store, surrounded by federal agents. She was much taller than many of her security detail. She was wearing a maroon jacket with stretch breeches, tucked into shiny black leather riding boots. They must have cost a fortune. A single headband to keep her hair in place. Sam had only seen her dressed in a dress, wearing gloves, in photographs in the *Alpine Avalanche*. But here she was in the flesh, the First Lady of the United States. He wondered how he would describe this to his mother in a letter.

Joe was bringing two horses around from the back to the front of the store. He could see Joe as if he were standing in front of him now with his curly black hair and his extravagant moustache, which had been carefully groomed and curled.

Joe led the white horse directly toward Mrs. R. "Meet Noor," he said, smiling. "Her name means light in our language. She is suitable for you."

"Thank you, Mr. Kafouri," Mrs. R. said, patting the snout of the horse, who neighed, as if to say hello. "What language is that?"

He seemed pleased to be called by his family name. "We are from Mount Lebanon, but lived in Mexico for a time . . . We speak the ancient, revered language, A-R-A-B-I-C."

Mrs. R. said, "I have never met someone who spoke that language. You speak English, Arabic, and Spanish, then? Very impressive. I only speak French."

Some of the Rangers looked impatient and jealous that Mrs. R. was giving Joe so much attention.

"We speak that, too," Joe said. "The French had designs on our country, as you must know. We left in 1915 after the locust plague. There was a very bad famine."

"But we're in Texas now," one of the Rangers said, as if there were no other place in the world.

Joe laughed lightly. "Who could forget this *vérité*?" He winked at Sam. "For you, *habibi*, you will ride our stallion, Amir. The prince. Proud, but gentle."

Frank Hamer tipped his hat at Mrs. R. "Mrs. Roosevelt, we better head out while we still have daylight."

Once saddled up, the group headed toward the trail, which wound up into the Davis Mountains. Mrs. R. was riding in the middle. Rangers were riding in front of her; some were in the back. Sam was riding at the tail end, tethered to the two supply horses, Buni, a brown horse, and a silvery gray horse called Lulua, meaning pearl. Sam had a good view of Mrs. R. from where he was in the train: she was a confident, experienced rider and kept her back erect and straight. The trail was rocky, and the horses picked their way gingerly through the switchbacks. On either side of the trail, the grass looked yellow. Dry. Little rain this year. The pungent smell of pine made him forget the drought. Sam heard a rustle. When he looked to the right of the trail, he caught a glimpse of a mule deer, darting down the rocky hill. A red-tailed hawk soared above. An expansive sky, blue with clouds that puffed like cotton candy, but in other places trailed off into silky threads. This place wasn't immediately pleasing to the eye with lumpen-shaped small hills, dotted with scrub, yucca, and the occasional pine or mesquite. He passed a trunk of spiked yucca, a single white flower burst from the middle. A rare surprise, since they mostly bloomed in the spring and the summer. "Why, hel-lo, sweetheart," he said to the bloom of the yucca as he passed it.

They hit an overlook where they had a view of the craggy rock faces of these small mountains. They dismounted from their horses, and the First Lady took a few pictures. Then they crossed through the scrubby hills down into a little valley or plateau, where they would camp. The conical-shaped mountain, Mount Mitre, rose in the distance. It was not far from Alpine. He had been over closer to the mountain for picnics with his pals at Sul Ross, where he had lolled around for hours, jumping into that natural spring that hugged the rocky shear of the mountain. Jack was the editor of the Sul Ross annual, *The Brand*, and had taken photographs that day. Was Jack still mooning over Darlene? Sam brushed away the thought. He felt miserable when he thought about his one date with Charlotte. Her mother's talk of sin. Everything, for her, was doom and hell.

Once they had found a clearing with a few mesquite trees, they set up camp. Sam untied the supply bags that Lulua, the silver horse, was carrying. He heaved the flap off the horse's back, and it plopped onto the ground. The pup tents had been neatly folded up. It took him some time, but he set up the pup tents. On either side of Mrs. R's tent, there was a tent for a Ranger.

Before it got dark, one of the Rangers, named Slim Jim, helped him build a fire. He was balding with a few wisps of reddish curls at the back.

"Looks like you could use a hand, sonny. The name's Slim Jim," he said.

Slim Jim had short legs and a tummy shaped like a barrel—he wasn't slim, nor was he fat. He had a jaunty walk with a spring in his step.

"Thank you," Sam said. He hadn't expected a hand from anyone. "Mister . . . ?"

"Just call me Slim Jim," he said, chortling. "Not so slim anymore."

Once it was dark, they settled around the fire. Sam took out the food that the cooks at Balmorhea had prepared and put it into an iron pot near the coals.

Slim Jim sighed. "This reminds me of the old days. Borger. Mexia. Sleeping in the open. All those wildcatters."

One of the other Rangers hooted. "Was that the town where the jails were so full, we had to chain boys to the telephone poles?"

Slim Jim said, "Coulda been. Either Borger or Mexia. Those oil boom towns were full of crooks, moonshiners, gamblers, dancing girls, and wildcatters. You name it. Well, hell, when oil struck, you suddenly had thirty thousand in a town overnight. All of 'em thought they were gonna get rich. Men sleeping in the grass. Believe it was 1922 when we were called in to restore order to Mexia. Martial law. Governor Neff called us in. By God, we did it. The people of Mexia were weeping because we poured out all their moonshine. I do remember water was as scarce as gold. Didn't bathe for a week."

Slim Jim was rolling a cigarette. He licked the paper and folded it over. "Borger was another boom town. We only cleaned it up for a time. King of Bootleggers, 'Shine Popejay,' ruled the roost. And then there was 'Two-Gun Dick,' that mobster. Nickname was Booger Town 'cuz fugitives for miles sought refuge there. There, in the summer of 1927, waddn't it?"

"You sure can strut sitting down, Slim," Captain Hamer said, chuckling to himself. "That's enough of that talk. Would you look at that moon? What were the odds that we'd get a full moon on this trip?"

A dazzling moon dipped a little to the left of the conical-shaped Mount Mitre. A bird was making a sound that sounded like "Uh, Uh, Uh."

"Believe that's a spotted owl," Frank Hamer said.

"But Captain, you could shoot craps with the devil himself," Slim Jim said, smiling. "Why don't you tell Mrs. R. how you led the posse against Bonnie and Clyde? You'll go down in history for that."

Hamer shook his head. "Nope."

There was an awkward silence.

Mrs. R. smiled. "I can understand. It's an experience not to be brandished. He was simply doing his duty."

Frank Hamer tipped his wide-brimmed gray hat. "Mrs. Roosevelt. Ma'am." Then he took a branch from the fire and lit his cigarette. Several of the other Rangers were rolling their tobacco into cigarettes.

Sam couldn't restrain himself. Was that all? Wasn't Captain Hamer going to say more? "We read about you in the papers."

"Extra! Extra! Clyde Barrow and Bonnie Parker Slain by Officers."

Sam had never met a famous person before, so he didn't know what to expect. Hamer didn't want to tell the story of Bonnie and

Clyde and how he had led the posse against them. Maybe Mr. Hamer resisted the role of circus clown? The stories couldn't be told on cue. Or maybe he was sick of being twinned with this story? Hamer didn't look like a lawman: his face was pensive and he looked like a poet. Sam remembered the photograph in the newspaper of Bonnie and Clyde's car, crashed against an embankment, riddled with bullets, their dead bodies splayed like puppets in the front seat.

Even though the First Lady wasn't beautiful like Darlene, there was intelligence and sympathy in her blue eyes, and you forgot about her craggy teeth. Who was he to be throwing stones? He didn't think he was much to gaze at, either. Maybe that's why he hadn't had any luck with Darlene. The Bible verse echoed in his head: "Thou hypocrite, first cast out the beam out of thine own eye, and then shalt thou see clearly to cast out the mote out of thy brother's eye."

Everyone at Balmorhea envied him and wished they could go on this trip. This wasn't what he expected at all. Well, what did he expect? A parade?

Hamer shrugged. "Nothing to tell, son. Bonnie and Clyde killed eleven people. We just shot the devil out of them. A little like those farmers, clubbing jackrabbits."

Sam cringed. Those jackrabbits were a nuisance and ate everything green in sight, even gardens or cattle feed. If they didn't get rid of them, everyone would starve. Come Sunday, there were roundups to club those jackrabbits, who had just gone rampant on the plains. The counties couldn't afford to pay bounties, so they made it an activity after church. They'd had more of those grisly events in the Panhandle than around Lubbock way.

"Young man, where are you from?" Mrs. R. said, gazing at him intently.

He panicked and didn't know what to say. "From a little town outside of Lubbock, called Loop." What did he have to say that would interest anyone? One of the greatest Texas Rangers in history was sitting near the fire, and he refused to say a single word about himself. And why didn't the First Lady talk about herself?

The way she gazed at him so intently, he felt as if he were the most important person in the world.

"Are you building the pool at Balmorhea? That spring in the desert is like a miracle," the First Lady said, enthused.

"Lots of miracles in the desert," Sam said, thinking of the yucca that he had seen in bloom. "I work in the office. I'm helping Captain Bell. He sent me along because I was brought up with horses."

"You were brought up on a farm?" the First Lady said, pressing him.

He felt embarrassed; all the Rangers were listening. Being brought up on a farm wasn't anything special in West Texas. The land was so sparsely populated that most folks lived in the country. He felt thirsty for green: green plants, green trees, birds. No escape from that whirling nasty dust, soil that got into your throat, your ears, your lungs. Scrambling down into the cellar to avoid tornadoes, which could blow your house away before you got down the stairs.

"Pa managed livestock at a few ranches in New Mexico. When there was a chance to settle near Lubbock, he bought land. We were farming a little cotton. Some wheat until . . ."

He suddenly choked up. They would think he was a crybaby. He thought of how hopeless his father was. How he spent his days, moping around the house, drinking moonshine now—a far cry from the man who could break horses and who could lasso a bull.

As if she understood what he was thinking, Mrs. R. said, "You're young and you have your whole life ahead of you. What do you think you'll do after Balmorhea?"

The jingle from Mr. Roosevelt's 1932 Democratic campaign,

"Happy Days Are Here Again," popped into his mind. "Happy days are here again; the skies above are clear again."

"Study," he said, gazing into the flames of the fire. He couldn't see the faces of the Rangers, just their silhouettes in the dim light. "History. Or maybe work in the newspapers?" It was hard to know what direction his life would take. "Depends . . ." Money was the main obstacle as far as he could see. But a tiny hope fluttered in his mind, like the wings of an emerald hummingbird. His mama always said, "Where there's a will, there's a way. It's just a matter of finding it."

Mrs. R. was sitting next to him. The First Lady had a kind smile. "You'll have to talk to Lorena[3] when we get back. She used to work for the AP. She will regale you with stories about working for newspapers. She covered the kidnapping of Charles Lindbergh's baby." Lindbergh's baby! He had read about that in the *Alpine Avalanche*.

Then her mood changed, and she whispered, "What a tragedy for the Lindberghs. I lost my parents when I was a youngster. My brother died of diphtheria."

"Oh," he said. He didn't know what to say. Was it better to say nothing? He added, "That's sad."

"Do you have brothers and sisters?" she asked.

"One sister. She's just a tyke. Her name is Augusta." He had given much thought to Augusta since he was at Balmorhea. His mother had nearly died giving birth to her.

What if Augusta had been kidnapped for a bounty? How would he feel? But that would never happen since they didn't have a nickel to their names. He distinctly remembered reading about the kidnapping of the Lindbergh baby in 1932. In his mind, it was tied up with the hit they took on wheat and his father howling. March? He had followed the case on the radio and in the *Alpine Avalanche*. The case had gone on and on with eleven or twelve ransom notes. The body of the mutilated baby had been found four miles from the Lindberghs' house. Didn't the FBI get involved? Tracked the ransom notes to a German immigrant, a carpenter. Convicted of murder. Was it a fair trial, he suddenly wondered. What if someone like Joe was accused of murder? Would jurors treat him unfairly, like the Rangers, because he was an immigrant?

He had seen Lorena Hickok, the reporter, in Captain Bell's office. Very round, dressed in men's clothes, she was puffing on a cigar. He had never seen a woman like her. He wondered what was happening at Balmorhea. Instinctively, he felt he was missing a bigger party. Why wasn't he happier? He had the privilege of meeting the First Lady, something most folks would love to have.

One of the Texas Rangers said, "Young feller, could you pass me a fried drumstick? Nothing better than fried chicken."

Sam jumped up.

"Do you mind?" the First Lady asked, holding out her crude metal dish to Sam. "But I would like to sample those rolled cabbage leaves again, not the fried chicken."

Joe scrambled up and found the pot at the edge of the fire. "That is our cuisine from Zahle. My wife made them."

"That in India?" Slim Jim said, trying to be funny. Joe had already told them he was from Greater Syria near Mount Lebanon. Sam had read about the heroism of the Rangers but meeting them was a disappointment; most of them were rough as cobs.

"That's enough, boys," Frank Hamer said. "Get some shuteye."

Many of them disappeared and crawled off to their tents, except for a few who would stand guard.

For a time, it was just Mrs. R., Joe, and Sam sitting around the fire. Even Mr. Hamer had gone to his tent.

Mrs. R. turned to Joe and said, "How did you come to this country?"

"It is not an easy story," Joe said, reluctant to talk. "I don't think this is the story before sleep, Mrs. Roosevelt. It is not the story of dreams."

Mrs. R. smiled again. "But don't you see, this is why I've come on this tour. To hear the stories of all Americans."

Sam was astounded. He had never met a person like her. Could she really be this good?

"We came to Mejico on a freighter from Beirut," Joe said. "I was just a kid. About your age," he said, gazing at Sam. "A young man. Not so old. One and twenty."

Were those tears in his eyes? But Joe did not seem ashamed. But the Rangers had also disappeared, and he didn't have to worry about those cowboys.

"We had a bad harvest. No rain. No rain. We prayed for rain, but what came after was worse, and we thought God was punishing us. Those locusts devoured everything—it was like a sea of black. Then, because of the war there were blockades. No grain came to the mountains. We were eating rats. Cats. Scouring the garbage. My grandmother, *Taita,*, said to me, 'Darling, *habibi*, close the window. I can't bear to hear people screaming, "*Jou'aneen! Jou'aneen!* We are hungry."' They sold some land and sent us out, away from Bilad el-Sham."

Sam was speechless. Was there more? Mrs. R. was nodding.

Joe fished out a cloth handkerchief from his pocket and dabbed his eyes. "We stayed in Mejico for a time but crossed at Ciudad Juarez. More chances in Amer-ee-ka. I had a cousin in El Paso. Peddled. Sold ribbons, threads, and cloth to ladies in their homes. I had to carry the pack on my back. And then we got a car," he said. "We sold from the car."

He suddenly laughed, as if he were embarrassed. "My dear lady,

I so hope you enjoyed our oriental cuisine." He jumped up, offering her more cabbage leaves with a bow. "Hosts must serve."

Mrs. R. shook her head. "It was delicious . . . And then?"

He sighed dreamily, staring at the fire. But then he cut the story short. "Now, we have the store in Fort Davis. We have our life and our customers. I am sorry to trouble you with these details."

"No trouble," Mrs. R. said.

Without intending to, Sam yawned. He felt guilty, but he was bushed.

Joe rose. "Ah, you both must be tired. And we must rest before the journey tomorrow. If you will excuse me."

They bid each other good night and crawled into their tents.

• • •

Instinctively, Sam sat up, unzipped his bed roll. The horses were stamping. They had been tied in a line, loosely, between two trees. Not too far away, he heard a bull. No, it was throatier—not a bull. The racket in the brush made it sound like bigger animals. He peeked out of his pup tent. What? Javelina?

Just the dark sky dotted with hundreds of stars and the round moon. The fire had gone out. Wasn't someone supposed to stand guard all night?

An animal crashed through the bushes, very close to the camp. Or was it two?

The whinnying of the horses almost sounded like a high-pitched scream. It sounded like a stampede. They were galloping away. God! What was out there? Where had he put that infernal lantern? Matches! He felt blind. Was this what it was like to be blind? Darn it.

"Damn it," a voice said. Mr. Hamer? "What happened to the fire?"

A single lantern flickered in the dark. It didn't offer much light.

"*Shu hal khara. Wayn el-khayl?*" Joe said, reverting to Arabic. A second lantern was lit.

Another voice said, "What language is that? It ain't Spanish."

"Not that you know a word of Spanish! Knucklehead!"

"A-R-A-B-I-C. You heard him, yerself, ancient language."

"What's out there?" Mrs. R. said.

"Mrs. R., please stay in your tent. Let us handle this."

The crashing sounds in the brush were getting closer. These were large animals. No way it could be a javelina or even a coyote. A Barbary ram? But it didn't bleat like a ram. The growling that he didn't recognize continued. Sam was puzzled.

A single gunshot rang out. Then, silence. The rustling stopped.

Had Hamer killed the creature, whatever it was?

Where were the frickin' matches? For crying out loud. Sam finally found them under his bedroll. How stupid! He crawled out of the tent and lit his lantern. Someone had started the fire again and it crackled and popped. Once his eyes adjusted from the glow of the fire, he could see the ring of Rangers, fully armed with their shotguns.

"Well," Slim Jim said, chuckling. "At least we know it wasn't a human critter. Not a crook, a moonshiner. A cattle thief. A fugitive on the run. Not 'Two-Gun Dick.'"

Frank Hamer said, "You are always all hat and no cattle, Jim. If your life depended on it, you couldn't keep your trap shut."

"I was just saying what we know . . ." Slim Jim said.

"Speculations are not welcome," Frank Hamer said.

But Sam couldn't resist asking even though he thought he might get his knuckles rapped, "Do you think it was a bear, Captain Hamer?"

"Don't know, son. Whatever it was, it's gone now," Frank Hamer said. "You all go back to bed. Lucky and Slim Jim will stand guard.

Stoke the fire."

A lantern glowed. "My horses. They have vanished into the wind," Joe said, turning to Frank.

Someone chortled. Were they laughing at the way Joe spoke English? Or at him?

"It's too dark to search for them now. Let's wait until it's daylight. We're liable to fall in a hole. Off a ledge. Break a leg," Frank Hamer said.

How were they going to get back to Fort Davis without the horses? Sam didn't sleep much after that. He tossed and turned before the first ray of light hit his tent. It was going to be a long walk back, miles and miles, and he dreaded it. Or they could leave the supplies here, and he could come back on his own and get the supplies? That wasn't very practical. The cook, Devilfish, wouldn't be very happy about losing his pots. Or maybe he'd just laugh it off: "It's on the government's nickel."

But most of the horses drifted back to the camp by daylight. Joe was leading Amir and the rest of the other horses back to the camp while Sam was stoking the fire. Sam placed the aluminum coffee pot on the fire—it had been used so much that it had turned black. The cooks at Balmorhea had made thick flapjacks, and he heated them up. He fixed Mrs. R's dish first.

"I am sorry, Mrs. Roosevelt. We are short on butter and syrup," he said, holding out a crude silver camp dish to her. "They taste better with homemade butter."

She chuckled. "Sam, dear, this is not my first camping trip."

Sam then handed a plate to Slim Jim. "Thanks, sonny." After Slim Jim scarfed down a few bites of the pancake, he said, "I saw it with my own eyes. It was one of those feral camels.[4] And darned if he wasn't tussling with a bear."

Mrs. R. laughed. "But how is that possible? There aren't any camels out here."

Frank Hamer said, "You strutting again?"

"Swear on the Bible," Slim Jim said. "That was one of those feral camels left over from Jeff Davis's Camel Experiment in 1856. He got attacked by a black bear."

"Don't swear," Frank Hamer said. "It doesn't become a Ranger. Cleanliness is next to godliness."

Sam was wolfing down a pancake, and he thought he might choke on it. But Hamer's face was deadpan, and he seemed serious.

Joe chimed in. "If we consider the historical details . . . The camels were brought from Turkey, Egypt, and Tunisia in 1856. You see, your Jefferson Davis thought they could transfer supplies for the Army across the desert. Better than mules or horses. The French were doing this in Algeria. Why not?"

Slim Jim said, "There have been camel sightings in these parts. Dead and alive. And that is a fact. A surveyor I know was out yonder in Big Bend, and he found a carcass."

Frank Hamer commented, "Glad there's at least a promise of a fact or two in these tales."

But Joe didn't laugh. Instead, he said, "You have to understand them, like horses. The Americans didn't know how to care for them. Were confused by their habits. The Army brought a Syrian to train the Americans how to care for the camels. He was called 'Haji Ali,' and the people here called him 'Hi Jolly.'"

Slim Jim scratched his head. "Say, I heard of that fella, Hi Jolly. Hadn't heard much about him."

"Haji Ali is an honorable title for a man who has done the pilgrimage in Mecca in our language. But his name was Phillip Tedro, and he was half Greek, half Syrian. He converted to Islam later."

What was Joe talking about? Sam was about to ask him about the religion, Islam. What religion was Joe?

But Slim Jim raced on: "The first herd came in at Indianola in 1856. They used them for a few expeditions. But everything went to hell in a handbasket with the outbreak of the Civil War. Herds were sold off. Scattered. U.S. government had bigger fish to fry."

"That's interesting. I didn't know this tidbit of history," Mrs. R. said. "I always learn a lot on these tours."

Captain Hamer tipped his hat to Mrs. R. "Sorry to interrupt the history lesson, but we better saddle up, ma'am."

A peach glow burst from the horizon. The sky was a shadowy purple, draped with a few low-lying clouds, the mountains in dark silhouette—you couldn't see the scrub—and for a few moments, it seemed like a magical, fantastical place. They left the plateau and ascended back over the grassy, rocky hills, heading back to Fort Davis. A swallow dipped in the wind, freely. Sam envied the swallow's freedom—he just felt gritty, not free. Only wanted to sink into his lumpy bunk bed at Balmorhea. He prayed Captain Bell didn't have anything urgent for him to do: no typing projects or letters that had to go out to Washington.

Just as they were crossing the road to Joe Kafouri's store, a forest-green Deluxe Roadster squealed to a stop, did a U-turn, and abruptly stopped in the middle of the road. Who could afford such a car? Sam pulled the single rein of his horse, Amir, and said, "Whoa. Whoa." The car was a convertible. He felt a wave of envy pass through him. He thought of the old beat-up truck they had on their farm, which limped into town like a hound dog.

"Who in the Sam Hill?" Frank Hamer asked.

The driver of the car leapt out. He was in his fifties, a fedora hat cocked on his head. He was wearing a suit with a vest, a long wool coat, and two-toned, white and black, lace-up shoes. A rig that had cost more than a penny.

Two other men got out of the convertible, but they didn't bother opening the door but simply jumped over it. They were also wearing fedoras, which hid their faces. One of them had a pencil moustache. Not from around these parts. Their clothes didn't look as expensive as the driver of the car, but they wore black suits, with plain black ties. Were they goons? Security? Detectives?

The one with the moustache pulled his coat back so they could see his pistol. They were real hot dogs, show-offs.

Frank Hamer dismounted from his horse and tied it to the post of Joe's store, calmly, as if, gee shucks, he were going inside to buy a lemonade.

All the Rangers put their hands on their hips, as if they might draw their pistols. Texas Rangers were edgy about the First Lady's safety. It hadn't been so long since the assassination attempt on Mr. Roosevelt in 1932, shortly before he was inaugurated. Sam remembered reading the story in the *Avalanche*: "FDR Narrowly Escapes Assassination." An Italian bricklayer had shot six rounds at the president in Miami. He had shouted, "Too many people are starving!" Many people had been hurt, and the mayor of Chicago died from a bad stomach wound.

Hamer was completely unarmed and held up his hand to the Rangers. "Hold your fire."

"Hand him over," the man with the expensive wool coat said.

"Hand who over?" Frank Hamer asked.

The man frowned and made a face. "Volkov."

Hamer scratched his head. "I never heard of that fella. We don't have anyone named Volkov in this party. And could you care to identify yourselves? You a lawman? Have a warrant?"

The man sighed. "I am Howard Perry, owner of the Chisos Mine Company. Most people around here know who I am."[5]

Sam patted Amir's neck. He whinnied. El Perro? The owner of the mine. He remembered how Chueco had recounted how his father had fallen down the shaft of the mine. The image of his uncle on fire suddenly came to his mind.

Hamer was silent. "Heard the name. That's in Terlingua. About a hundred miles from here." Then he nodded at the two men wearing the fedoras. "Can you fellas do me a favor and put away your triggers?"

The two men wearing fedoras and black suits suddenly shrank back from the scene.

"Now you listen here, Mister," Perry said. "If this is a posse and you have got Volkov, he comes with me."

Hamer scratched his head again and smiled. "Believe there has been some kind of misunderstanding, Mr. Perry. Don't have any earthly idea who this Volkov is. But it looks to me like you're a private citizen. Pinkerton detectives don't have any right to arrest folks."

Sam's ears perked up. Dr. Volkov? Hadn't Dr. Walker gone to his lecture at Sul Ross? The one who was transplanting goat testicles to increase male virility.

"I own most of Brewster County," Howard Perry said, fishing into his pocket. He pulled out a fat roll of bills. "If you come across any information on that crook Volkov."

A green bill fluttered to the ground near Frank Hamer's worn, brown boot.

Sam stared. He had never even seen a thousand-dollar bill in his life.

Hamer ignored the bill and extended his hand toward Perry. "The name's Frank Hamer. I used to be with the Texas Rangers. The Federal Secret Service detail asked me to lead this party."

But Perry ignored his hand.

The flatfoot with the moustache called out, "Mr. Perry, sir . . ." The second one, who was chunkier, called out, "Sir . . . Please. Can you just . . .? We better get on down the road . . ."

Mrs. R.'s horse whinnied. She dismounted.

"Please, ma'am, let me handle this," Hamer said, calmly, but there was an edge to his voice. "Believe you've dropped something in the road, Mr. Perry."

No one moved. A few of the horses snorted.

Frank Hamer moved in front of Mrs. Roosevelt, just as she was extending her hand to Perry. "A pleasure to meet you, Mr. Perry."

Howard Perry looked bewildered and picked up the thousand-dollar bill.

"Mrs. Roosevelt?" Perry asked, suddenly losing his bluster. His face turned beet red. "What . . . ?"

Mrs. R. broke into a smile. "I am, the last time I checked."

Someone chortled.

Hamer's wide chest stood between Mrs. Roosevelt and Mr. Perry.

"You see, we are just getting in from a delightful camping trip. We don't know of this man Volkov that you are searching for," Mrs. Roosevelt continued, as if she were chatting with some nice old lady from Joe's store. "I am doing a tour of CCC camps in Texas. Franklin's wonderful program to get people back to work."

Mr. Perry snorted. "This strikes me as leaning toward Communist ideology. The state providing for citizens. They have to know the value of the dollar."

Had Perry just snorted? How rude! Sam felt woozy from lack of sleep.

Mrs. Roosevelt shook her head. "People are in dire straits. And are in need of help in these hard times."

Perry ignored her remark and smiled. But it was a cunning, wolfish smile. He tipped his fedora. "I have a mine to run, if you'll excuse me, Mrs. Roosevelt."

The men in fedoras slunk back to the green roadster, without looking anyone in the eye. Howard Perry fired up the engine, and they roared off down the highway.

Sam stared at the green roadster until it disappeared on the horizon. Who was this jackass?

Mrs. Roosevelt looked puzzled. "What was that about?"

Frank Hamer sighed. "Darned if I know, Mrs. Roosevelt. But we've got to get you back to Balmorhea. Boys . . ."

Sam now knew he had to get his hands on that article in the *Journal of the American Medical Association.*

CHAPTER 14.

# Darlene's Diary, October 8, 1935

**Too much testosterone at Balmorhea, I declare.** *First Lady gone off to Mountains with the Rangers. Don't envy her. Hanging around with those cowboys. Don't love horses much.*

*I am to entertain a lady friend, Hick, and secretary, Tommy. Always chain-smoking. One was a fatso, the other skinny-minnie. Funny looking together. Odd ducks.*

*Thought it would be fun. Having female company. Ha! Be careful what you wish for. Just because someone was a woman, didn't mean you'd have any chemistry. Be pals. Could relate.*

*Never even got close to Jack to tell him when to come. Our code: three quick knocks.*

*Keep out Doc Walker. One night, waiting for Jack. Doc Walker yanked the door open. Sloshed. Wearing some expensive robe. Chicken legs. Not sure if there was anything underneath. "Miss Robinson, would you care to hear me recite 'Song of Hiawatha' by Longfellow? I have my own supply of libations in the office that*

*I would willingly share." Bet your bottom dollar, he had expensive libations. Who? Some tragic love story about two Indians. Starts bawling. Can't be everybody's mama. Got roped into listening to that fool reciting Hiawatha's story. Surprised I feel sorry for Doc, though. Wife died of T.B. Lonesome.*[1]

*Since I am the only "fe-male" round for miles, my job: entertain Mrs. R's pals. Wasn't very nice of me. but I said, "You go on and have them to tea. See for yourself how sweet they are."*

*Not my outgoing personality. Nothing personal. Don't know me at all. They think they are seeing Mae West, even Jack. Just need a roll in the hay. Make 'em feel better. No more dances after the fiasco. Makes it worse for me. Too much testosterone.*

*No way to tell anyone. Terrible burden to keep it all bottled up. Like swimming underwater. When would we ever get to swim in Balmorhea? Look forward to cool water floating.*

*If only I could hug J. No way to go back. Over my dead body.*

*B. will have to answer for the dead bodies. Can't keep fooling people. All those men... Just hoping for same intensity. Not twenty forever. Ponce de Leon didn't find the Fountain of Youth in 1513 in Florida. Long time ago.*

*Bell just stared at me with that face. God in heaven, he must've been handsome before the shrapnel decimated his cheek. Breaks your heart. But the doctor must have worked miracles if that is what he could salvage. What was his name? Dr. Gillies. Much smarter than Walker. Sure, Wilson said, the war to end all wars. Malarkey. But what about losing your face?*

*Bell says, "No tea and pie. Devilfish'll play. Live music."*

*Seemed a good idea. But everyone had already hit the sauce.*

*Hick puffing on her cigar. Drunk as a skunk. Believe she had hit the Scotch.*

*That's when shit hit the fan. Rollin' around on the ground. Like a nasty girls' street fight. Punching. Kicking. Pulling hair. Hick screaming, "You're a fuckin' cunt!" Even Bell, who thought he had seen it all in the Great War, looked shocked. Feds pulled them apart.*

*Party's over, Bell said.*

*Tommy stormed off. "Have to get a press release ready. Don't have time for this nonsense."*

*Hick whined. "Please, Captain, just one more . . . Love the blues. Reminds me of Chicago."*

*Devilfish strummed. "This one's for the boys who must be hankering for a little honey. Oh, yeah! Here we go: Come on baby, come to your dandy, He's gonna lick your candy, oh yeah."*

*Hick sidled over to me. Puffing on her cigar. Gets down my nose, that smell. Reminds me of B. "Was a reporter for the AP. My biggest scoop was the kidnapping of the Lindbergh baby. That was my other life . . . before." Hick waved her chubby fingers at me. Before? She was trailing around with the First Lady. At her beck and call?*

*Would I see J. again? Must have been agony for Lindberghs. Where are J. and B. now? Were they in the state of Texas or on the move? B. peddling cures in Hollywood?*

*Hick smiled at me and put her head on my shoulder. Started weeping. "I get so lonely."*

*Gave Captain Bell a look. Help!*

*"You'll have to put her to bed," he said. "I can't do it," Bell said. Sure. The Feds are all men. Maybe they should think about having some lady Feds on security detail for two women. What planet were they on?*

*Led her to special guest house with Feds trailing behind, like a bunch of ducks. All wearing shoulder harnesses with pistols.*

*Just took off her shoes. Saddle shoes with laces. Got a big picture of her wearing high heels! Sitting down. Then pulled the sheet back and coaxed her to lie down. "There you go. You'll feel better in the morning." Never get a day off in this place. Never! Tugged at me so hard, I plopped down onto her as she fell backwards onto bed. Like a two-hundred-pound boulder. Bed crashed down.*

*Where were the Feds?*

*I rolled off. Leave bed as is. Someone else can clean up mess!*

*She murmured, "Not a maid! Can't treat me like dirt. Get out of Nebraska! What's the deadline? You bet. I got it! Scoop of the century."*

*Suddenly, she started snoring. At first a snort, then a bellowing sound, and then a whistle. Like sound of kettle, whistling.*

*Ran out. Off duty! Enough is enough! Feds outside. Standing around, smoking. One of them smirked. "You get her tucked in?"*

*"You fellas are supposed to be the frickin' babysitters." Started crying. "Get some other nursemaid! I have had it!"*

*Bell caught up with me. Reached for my hand. Shivered. Tingling. Much stronger than Jack. No. I can't. Don't go there.*

*Roy whispered, "Darlene."*

*Walked me back to room. Full moon.*

CHAPTER 15.

# Arroyo Drive, Harlingen, Texas, 1976

**Maggie came in from the store, lugging two paper sacks of groceries.** Just in time, he shoved the two torn-loose pages of Darlene's diary back into the box marked "Balmorhea." Why did he need to hide this from Maggie? She wouldn't give a hoot about an old infatuation with a bosomy nurse from forty years ago.

He did not know what could be gained from remembering the year in Balmorhea. But he felt compulsive about it, the way his son, Griffin, was about collecting baseball cards when he was a kid. The way he had obsessively tracked down his family tree in Ireland, going from one courthouse to another, from one small village to another. He hadn't been able to interest his grandkids, even Rosemary, in the family tree. Was he obsessed with the injustice that Darlene, or whatever her name was, was tangled up with?

They didn't keep secrets from each other in their marriage. How could he still be so naïve after all his experiences with the law? Infernal quarrels about money that went on and on. Or nasty surprises, after the reading of a will.

Even though Maggie blurted out her opinions, she must have her own secrets—private thoughts that she didn't share with anyone, not even the Presbyterian preacher. He remembered how his ma had kept secrets from his pa to save his pride.

"Price of milk has gone up," Maggie called out from the kitchen. "You still foolin' with those old diaries from Balmorhea?"

She was prescient. Maybe she had read the diaries. Then he suddenly felt confident she had not. Maggie knew Latin and Greek history from her studies at the university, but lacked the patience to pore over the details, as he had when they visited museums together. He stopped at every exhibit and read every single caption at the National Museum in Dublin. He was particularly interested in the Irish Famine, which had taken place from 1845 to 1852. A million died in Ireland—and around two million had emigrated. From what he had learned from his genealogical research, the McCabes had emigrated to the United States during this time. Because their landlord was in debt, they had been shipped to America, rather than being provided for at the poor house. The blight of the potato crop meant that people had nothing to eat. It was much worse than what he had witnessed during the Depression. The one exhibit that brought this home to him was a mannequin of a skeletal figure, knocking on the door of a British landlord, who was carving into a succulent, roasted chicken. One could understand how this tragedy had fueled immigration and the nationalist movement for independence. Maggie had been less interested in these exhibits. Or was it that he was interested in every single historical detail? She zipped through the museum and waited for him at the end on a bench, puffing on a cigarette. It frustrated him that she only wanted to read Harlequin Romances now.

He rubbed his left shoulder with the one remaining arm; the nerves tingled as if the arm were still there. "A phantom arm," the doctor had said. "The tingling will go away after two or three years." Did he have that long? When he glanced down, it was just an empty sleeve now. Was the past like this phantom arm? So real at one time and yet when he glanced down, it had vanished.

After the scrub of West Texas, this yard on Arroyo Drive was his paradise, lush with purple crotons, orange-blooming bougainvillea, and date palms. He had even built a little rock waterfall with a small pond on the patio. When his grandkids were young, they lay on their bellies on the red bricks, lingering near the pond, to trap tadpoles or little bitty frogs between their palms. Since his operation, he hadn't nursed his plants or talked to them. He believed plants had spirits, just like animals. He didn't share this sentiment with anyone, but that's what he believed—and he knew this was why the plants flourished under his care. He had learned this from Chueco at Balmorhea. The yellow petunias had flourished, though, without pampering. He knelt down and touched a bloom.

He had no right! No right! But he felt so much passion for her, he couldn't stop himself from rifling in the drawer of her bedside table. He had forgotten about Darlene putting Hick to bed! That had been a raucous night! More raucous than his night in the Davis Mountains.

Sam had never mentioned it to Jack. A shard of jealousy over Jack's confidence with women burst through. Jack was a Don Juan and hadn't married Ruby, anyhow. He didn't want to think about Jack now, or what had happened to him.

Maggie was standing in front of him, her hands on her hips. She was wearing a loose blue dress with a belt. Was he hallucinating or had she gotten shorter? She was too thin. Was she losing weight?

"You're too broody," she said, giving him a toothy smile. "Thought I might fry up some catfish for lunch. Your favorite."

"I'd like that," he said. But he didn't feel like chatting. Was he being unfaithful to Maggie by thinking so much about Darlene?

"Look what Rosemary found in the attic when she was hunting for that box," Maggie said, slapping down an old black-and-white photograph on the round oak table, as if she had the winning suit in a bridge game.

They were sitting together in the window of a stone building, shortly after they had gotten married on their way back to Texas from North Carolina. Maggie looked dreamily into the distance with a white sailor hat cocked on her head. Her hair was brown. She was wearing a striped dress and dangled her crossed legs. To complete the outfit, she was wearing brand-new white shoes. His left arm was not visible, but it was tucked behind her. It looked as if he were missing his left arm. But that couldn't be, just the illusion of a missing arm. He could not know, then, that he would lose the arm some forty years later. He was squinting, looking straight into the camera, a shy smile, wearing a cream-colored suit with a tie. He stared at himself; he resembled, just a tad, a young Spencer Tracy.

The clock chimed.

He blinked back the tears. He had so little money that Maggie's father had bought him the suit. Her father was the station master for the railroad in Wilmington, North Carolina, and they were a different class of people than his folks.

He stared at the mantel grandfather clock. Maggie's father had also given them that, too, for a wedding present. Gold leaf curlicues decorated the round face, which was in Roman numerals. It was framed in oak. At the bottom, a little glass door, which hid the chime. A single tulip had been painted on the glass, but it looked fantastical.

It was German. The image of Captain Bell's badly scarred face came to his mind, the price for fighting the Germans in World War I.

Maggie frowned. "This picture of us has been lost for years. I thought we lost it in the flood in '67. I thought you would be happy."

"I am," he said. Was that true? Was he lying again? Why couldn't he express what he felt? It wasn't that he wished he had married Darlene.

"You've been rooting around in the past while I was gone to Keeners," Maggie said. "That's not going to raise your spirits. Lord! Why don't you just throw out all that junk?"

"No!" he said, sharply. More sharply than he intended. Had she forgotten that he was losing his balance?

Maggie sighed. "Oh, all right."

"I'll tell you if you should throw anything away," he said. "Babe," he added. He never used these sugary endearments with her. It sounded phony when he said it.

She leaned over and pecked him on the cheek. Her blue eyes twinkled with affection. "Fried catfish'll make you feel better, you'll see."

CHAPTER 16.

# Return to Balmorhea, 1935

**But when Sam returned to Balmorhea from the camping trip, no one would talk about the party that he had missed.**

Captain Bell shrugged, rubbing his left shoulder with his right hand, where the arm had been amputated. "The First Lady's speech to the camp was canceled. They're leaving for El Paso today," he said.

Sam looked at E.O. for any kind of signal. But E.O. just shook his head. Behind those coke-bottle glasses that made him look like an owl, Sam detected a knowing look. But, what? Then he returned to the clicking of the adding machine.

There was a tight silence in the office. What had happened? Mrs. R. had planned to give a speech to all the men at the construction site of the swimming pool. How should he write this up for the newsletter, *The Round-Up*? How was he supposed to make this into cheerful news?

He sat at his desk and surveyed the mess. He had only been gone one night, but there was a sheaf of correspondence piled next to his typewriter. Requisitions for Joe's store. Some letters from Washington.

Captain Bell had retreated behind his wooden partition. He appeared to just be sitting there, since Sam didn't even hear the rustling of paper.

"Captain? Sir?"

"What?" Captain Bell asked, more abrupt than he usually was.

"Should I report that in the newsletter?" he asked. "What do I say?"

After all, it wasn't the triumph that they had envisioned when they were planning the entertainment for the First Lady. He remembered vividly the joy they all felt about the First Lady's visit when the news had come through by telegram.

Captain Bell sighed. "Use your noggin, McCabe. Make up some cockamamie story."

Sam felt restless and couldn't settle down to work. Being out in the fresh air had made him dissatisfied with the confines of this tiny office. He missed the smell of pine in the mountains. He suddenly felt claustrophobic. He looked at his watch: only four hours until lunch. He suddenly wished he had a job at the camp that required him to roam around.

He hunted and pecked on his Wander-Werke Continental typewriter: *HEROC RAGER SAVES FIST LADY FROM CHARG OF BLACK BEER IN DAVIS MOUNTAINS.*

His fingers felt rusty. Resistant. As if they didn't want to go for the right keys. Come on, Wanda—what he called the typewriter.

*RANGER REGALS FIST LADY OF HIS CATURE OF CRIMNALS, BONER AND CLYDE.*

Fun Fact: Did you know that in 1856 the Secretary of War,

Jefferson Davis, imported camels from the Middle East for the American frontier army?

Captain Bell was drumming his fingers on his desk. "E.O., go to the kitchen and tell Devilfish he should report to me."

"I'll go," Sam said, eager to escape. Maybe he could pass by the clinic and ask Darlene. She would tell him what had happened. What about that medical journal that Dr. Walker had in his office?

Captain Bell stood up and peeked around the wooden partition. His cheek contorted, as if he were angry. "I asked E.O. to go. Let me see what you came up with."

Sam pulled out the paper from the typewriter and edged past his desk. Put the paper down on Captain Bell's desk. Captain Bell leaned back in his chair, pursing his lips. He didn't like it. "Lots of typos. You've got Boner instead of Bonnie. Beer instead of Bear."

E.O. snorted, as if he were about to laugh then pretended it was a cough.

What did Captain Bell want?

"We don't want to suggest that the First Lady might have been harmed," he said. "The newspapers might pick this up. And if I know Frank Hamer, he wouldn't like this rumor to be perpetrated about him. So, forget the Bonnie and Clyde story. He agreed to be part of security for the camping trip on the QT."

Captain Bell would not be pleased with anything today. Sam could have hung upside down, like a monkey in the circus, and he would have been put out.

"Well?"

"Write about the camels," Captain Bell said. "And," he said, pointing his right forefinger at Sam as if it were a gun, "I want a warning in block letters against smuggling booze into the camp."

"Yes, sir," Sam said. That was a clue. All the boys were drunk?

Or was Captain Bell frustrated about something else, and was kicking the cat?

• • •

Fifteen minutes later, Devilfish walked jauntily into the office, as if he were about to go fishing on a summer afternoon. Sam had not seen Devilfish much since the party in the barracks when Otto had punched him in the nose. He had taken off his tall chef hat, but he was still wearing a long white starched apron, with a string tied tight around his small waist. Sam admired the taut muscles in his arms and thought that maybe he'd have some like that, someday. He envied his street smarts. Was it all those years in the big city?

Devilfish nodded at Sam and gave him a quick wink.

Captain Bell was still drumming his fingers on the desk. "Have a seat, Mister Shines. Do you know why you're here?"

Sam could not see him behind the wooden partition.

Devilfish was silent for a minute. Then he said, "Nawww. No earthly idea. You asked me to pro-vide entertainment."

"Don't play dumb!" Captain Bell shouted. "Did you have to play that song?"

Sam stopped typing. The one about the duffin' in the muffin? Or . . . ?

"Well," Devilfish said. "Wrote it myself, as a matter of fact. White folks liked it well enough at the house parties. Played it at a few juke joints. I am sorry if it offended."

"You are not!" Captain Bell said. "You could have played something a little less obscene. These ladies were part of the entourage of the First Lady. This was a complete embarrassment for me!"

Devilfish sighed. "Well, Captain, from the bottom of my heart,

I am sorry. But it ain't my fault if everyone was stewed. As high as kites."

"What do you mean? Everyone?"

After Sam had his nose punched, Captain Bell had read the riot act to the camp about booze. Any man caught with booze would be kicked out. Sent home. Straight back to the dusty farm. No more three hot meals a day. No more thirty dollars a month. End of story.

Devilfish repeated, "Everyone was stewed."

"This is your final warning," Captain Bell said. "I know you're smuggling Sotol into the camp. One more time, and you're out. Bye-bye. Back to Deep Ellum."

"Nawww," Devilfish said. "I stopped that. While ago after Sam got punched. Don't want to be scratchin' around like a hen for work. Pickin' cotton. Playing on street corners."

"I want names!" Captain Bell pounded his fist against the desk. "Or you're going straight to the brig!"

Sam had never seen Captain Bell like this. He could be tough.

"Why," Devilfish said, "the boys were drinkin' Wonder Cure, Captain."

The silence was deafening. Even E.O. had stopped clicking on his adding machine. Was Joe selling moonshine? Or was there something else in the Wonder Cure? Who was making it?

At last, Captain Bell said, quietly, "You may return to your duties in the kitchen, Mr. Shines."

CHAPTER 17.
# Captain Bell

**Captain Bell did not know what to do.** Should he charge over to the canteen himself, like a mad bull? Call Joe Kafouri on the phone? Chew him out. Stop doing business with him. But wasn't Dr. Volkov the supplier? Or someone else? Just what was in it? Where was Volkov? Kafouri was giving them good prices and sold wholesale.

Easy does it.

He needed to talk. He couldn't confide in these kids in the office—E.O. and Sam. They already knew too many secrets in Balmorhea.

Captain Bell was confused about what had happened with Darlene last night, too. It had been so long, years and years. Since his return to San Antonio after the war, his mother had suggested many debutantes from "good families," but many recoiled because of his face. And he had lost interest in them as well: most were beautiful, spoiled, and shallow. He was not tempted by their beauty and knew the marriages would never last. No one was interested in the war. Yet his whole perspective on living had changed. He woke up, sweating, from nightmares. A sudden loud noise could bring back the memory of perching in the trenches, waiting for incoming bombs. Not that he had been a happy-go-lucky character before, but he found it impossible to bridge the gap now.

He heard himself say, "Now, boys, we need to resist temptation." Soldiers could be court-martialed for frequenting whorehouses during the War. He remembered reading General Pershing's communiqué: "Sexual continence is the plain duty of the members of the AEF . . ." Were the French and British command more realistic about men and their needs? A few had sneaked over to the Maison d'Abbatage, slaughterhouses, waited outside with their numbered tickets for a quickie. He had heard that the whores there serviced sixty to a hundred men a day. Red lantern for privates; blue lantern for officers. The boys could deny it all day and night, but once the chancres broke out on their mouths or rashes covered their bodies, he would have to send them to get treatment. Once, he had gone himself, the day before they had gone to the front, to a blue lantern bordello. Worried about syphilis, he had carried his own condoms. It was rumored that at Chez Christiane the girls whipped you and put you in chains and handcuffs.

Pauline had been gone so long that he was starting to forget what she had looked like. Occasionally, late at night at Balmorhea, he would fish out a small, faded photograph of her that he still kept in his wallet. They had not been married long, just long enough to have Thelma. She was sitting on a settee in his parents' living room in Alamo Heights with her hands folded in her lap. She was wearing long white gloves. A vase of tulips was set on the table next to her. A lacy wedding veil covered her head, yet wisps of her unruly curly blonde hair escaped the sides.

Because of the war, they had not gone to Paris on their honeymoon in 1916 as they had planned. Exasperated, he had said at last,

"Have you read the papers? There's a war on." She had not. She was only twenty and had just finished two years at Goucher Women's College.

He did not know why he had run after Darlene after she stormed out of Hick's room.

"Darlene."

"That's not my name."

"What?"

She gave a half-laugh. "Oh, nothin.' I go by my nickname. What my . . ." Then she stopped. "I'm just fed up with this place. Babysittin' two hundred men. And then this . . ."

He supposed a nurse did not have any illusions. Had to deal with life on the ground.

"Sorry about Hick," he said. "Things got out of hand. What a fiasco!"

"Oh, her. She's just lonely."

He pressed her hand. "Would you look at the moon?" The moon was a stunning orange.

She laughed heartily. "Captain Bell, you gettin' all sentimental on me now?"

They had stopped at the door of the clinic. She smelled so feminine, like lavender or roses, and he couldn't resist. Suddenly, he leaned forward and kissed her on the lips. She giggled. It had been years since he had kissed anyone.

He had not known if a woman would ever want to kiss him. It was only after the last operation that he had received the letter. He was waiting for Dr. Gillies to take off the bandages. He felt like a mummy, and they had fed him broth through a straw. Dr. Gillies's voice whispered in his ear, "Don't you worry, sonny, everything will be all right."

*Dear Roy, I begged Pauline not to visit the sick at Fort Sam Houston, but she wanted to cheer them up. She didn't like how she looked in the mask and refused to wear it. I know this must come as a terrible shock, my dear. Baby Thelma got it, too. Precious thing. This is too much to bear. We ask God to fortify us.*

"Whatta you say you come in for a little nightcap," Darlene said. But he had resisted when she tried to tug him through the door of the clinic. He didn't trust himself.

He cleared his throat. "I am sorry," he said, suddenly becoming officious. "But I've forbidden all alcohol in the camp."

She laughed out loud. "Don't be such a prude, Roy. When are you gonna lighten up? Have a little fun?"

He had given that canned Marine lecture on temptation but hadn't followed it himself. Shortie said, "Hell, Captain, we don't want to die virgins. Cut us some slack." Soon after, he turned over his boys, one by one, their bodies strewn in that muddy wheat field. He couldn't stop cursing. Pershing could rot in hell! General Pershing had ignored the French experience of fighting behind fortified areas, as if he were going to invent the wheel. His strategy was that they would rely on sharpshooters alone in an open field. The occasional pop of a pistol was not enough to counter the rat-a-tat-tat of hundreds of machine guns. Outgunned and without heavier artillery, his boys were sitting ducks: virtual suicide.

It got uglier: hand-to-hand combat. Knives, rifle butts, bayonets. He even killed one German kid with a trench shovel. Every man for himself. After that, mustard gas in bombs. His nostrils were raw. He did not take off his shoes for ten days. If he slept, no more than ten minutes.

Incoming shells splintered the trees and sent wooden splinters and metal shards flying. If there were a hell, this is what it looked like.

A few weeks later, a trench mortar got him, and he was pulled out by a medic shouting, "This one's alive."

They had stopped the Germans.

He didn't have much use for generals. Most of them were pompous. Pershing was old-fashioned and out of touch with reality. When he returned to San Antonio after the War, he had to listen to his father's monologues about the greatness of Pershing.

The word was that one general had gone too far with erotica asphyxia. His widow had been told he had a sudden heart attack. Did she believe it? Maybe. Maybe not. Captain Bell had thought himself experienced because of a few trips to cheap bordellos in Nuevo Laredo. But Paris was an eye-opener, and he realized that his sexual tastes were tame. His pal Charlie had taken him to the Lanterne Verte, the Green Lantern, where there were no rooms, but the nude waitresses did the deed with you on a bench or a chair in a large hall. Two or three men were in the throes of it with a few girls when they arrived. Charlie elbowed him. "Don't tell me you've got cold feet." But he had left immediately, repulsed by the depravity of the scene.

He thought Darlene was carrying on with Jack, anyway. Did Darlene really fancy him or was this just convenient?

He withdrew his hand. "Good night, Miss Robinson."

The camp was quiet. A coyote howled in the distance. He sat outside on the steps, in front of the barracks, looking up at the moon. He took a second photograph out of his wallet. But he could not see it, even in the moonlight, just the two shapes that he knew well. Tiny Thelma was swaddled in white cloth and peeked out at him. Pauline cradled her in her arms and gazed at her in adoration. If his daughter Thelma had lived, she would be nineteen.

After a while, he got up and went into the barracks and undressed in the dark. Many of the men snored.

He lay with his one arm behind his head on the pillow for a long time. He fell asleep at last.

At once, she knelt before him, unzipping his pants, yanking them off, in a hurry. A confident male voice said, "Look for the house with the blue lantern. That's for officers." Then she mounted him, as if she were riding a stallion, much practiced. He cupped one of her fleshy breasts with a sense of wonder, but she didn't notice. *J't'aime*, he whispered. She guffawed, as if this were ridiculous. "*Tas de merde.*" Darlene's laugh. The springs on the cheap mattress squeaked mercilessly, while she rocked up and down on him. Her tousled black hair covered her eyes. She shouted, "Va cowboy! Texas. Bang! Bang!" What? He rolled off of her. But wasn't she riding him? Suddenly, he did not know where he was. Was he in France? It was not Darlene. The pleasure was so intense that for a few moments, he felt as if he wouldn't care if his existence were erased. He woke up, wet and slippery.

In the early morning, the water from the shower beat down on him pleasantly. When he soaped his penis, he became erect again. Would you kiss like that if you were unmarried? She had ticked "unmarried" on her application.

He couldn't have an affair with Darlene Robinson. But another voice whispered, "Why not?"

But here he was now just staring at this wooden partition. He had a duty to run this camp. The ludicrous caption of one of the posters from the war popped into his mind: "You wouldn't use another fellow's toothbrush, so why use his whore?"

"Sam," he said, "type up the requisition for Joe's store. Supplies are the same as last month for the canteen, except for Wonder Cure. And Vim Cola. We're not ordering either."

He tousled the boy's red hair affectionately. Shortie had red hair, too. And his family was from Waco. The boy's glassy eyes stared up at him on that wheat field. He looked as if he were smirking. "Aww,

Captain, cut us some slack," he had said. Captain Bell kept shaking him, as if this would bring him back to life: "Live! Live! Live! You can go to all the whorehouses you want!"

"Vim Cola, too?" Sam said.

"What?" Captain Bell asked.

"Vim Cola, too?" Sam repeated.

"Yes," he said. "ASAP. Before the camel article for the newsletter."

"Sir," Sam said, yanking out the camel article from the typewriter, as if he were annoyed. He rolled another sheet of paper into the typewriter and started to hunt and peck.

"I need some air," Captain Bell said. He put on his hat and opened the door of the small office to a glorious blue sky.

CHAPTER 18.

# Wonder Cure

**Despite his resolve, Captain Bell found himself walking to the clinic.** Maybe Darlene would know what was in Wonder Cure. But if she knew what was in it, why hadn't she said? She was forthright and didn't mince words—what he admired about her.

When he peeked in the door, he thought the clinic was empty, just rows of beds with starched white sheets, tightly tucked into the mattresses. The last time he had been here was when he had heatstroke.

"Darlene!" he called out.

He passed through the clinic to a short passageway, which led to Dr. Walker's office. Inside the office was also an area for the examination of patients, with a white cloth screen that divided the room. Against the wall was a large white cupboard. Next to it, another shelf with bottles of all sizes. A tall scale stood against the wall, like a soldier, to measure height and weight.

She was sitting alone at Dr. Walker's enormous oak desk, reading. She frowned. Her hair had been pulled hurriedly into a ponytail. She was wearing a shapeless white smock.

"Are you still sore about what happened with Miss Hickok?" he asked. He did not know how to approach her after their stroll in the moonlight.

He yearned to see her smile. But she was still frowning. "No one taught you to knock?"

"The door was open," he said. "Where is Dr. Walker?"

"Gone to town."

He sat down in the chair that faced the desk. She folded her arms across her chest, as if she were defending herself. She seemed to be in a foul mood.

She put a single black curl behind her ear. "Water under the bridge. I have already forgotten about Hick and that night."

Did she mean holding hands? She didn't have any feelings for him? She had acted as if she wanted it to go further.

"You seem upset," he said.

Her light blue eyes were somber, and he could see nothing of that playful seductiveness that had attracted him in the moonlight a few days ago. Had she forgotten that she was the one who had suggested that he go to her room?

"My troubles are not your concern," she said. Then she smiled. "I am sorry, Captain. That was just plain rude. But you do have a lot on your plate, and I don't want to burden you anymore."

He sighed. "The First Lady and her entourage have gone on to El Paso. But I never expected the visit to be such a fiasco. Hope it blows over."

She giggled, suddenly. "Who could have predicted that Devilfish would play his candy song?"

He gestured with his one arm. "The press would have had a field day. We will have to keep it under our hats."

She closed the magazine. "Guess I better get to work. See if anyone needs to be rescued."

He got up and edged over to the desk. "What are you reading?"

The Journal of the American Medical Association. The caricature of a billy goat was on the cover. The headline: "Goat Gland Doctor Transplants Organs to Rejuvenate Men's Virility: True Medical Experimentation or Hoax?"

"Professional development, you might say," she said. "Need to know what's going on in the field."

Dr. Walker had been in Alpine, listening to a lecture about virility the day of his heatstroke. Was that the same doctor?

"I do need your help with something," Captain Bell said. "Do you have any idea what's in that Wonder Cure?"

He couldn't be absolutely sure, but she suddenly seemed anxious. "Why, no," she said, taking out the rubber band in her ponytail and shaking out her hair. She put the rubber band in her mouth. She had beautiful black curly hair, and he longed to touch it. He squashed this feeling.

She pulled it back again and made the ponytail tighter. "Why do you ask?"

He was tempted to tell her. Why had her mood changed again? "Well," he said, "I want to get to the bottom of something."

She winked at him. "You can tell me." Only a few minutes ago, she had been sharp with him. Her flirtatiousness seemed disingenuous.

Instinctually, he felt he should keep his own counsel. Instead, he said, "I just want to make sure it's not moonshine."

"Oh, Captain Bell," she said, laughing. "Very well could be. There are a lot of elixirs out there. Burdock's Blood Bitters. Aunt Fanny's Worm Candy. Cure the liver. Constipation. Flatulence. Cure unhappiness. They can even make you live forever!"

"If only it were that simple," Captain Bell said. He thought she would be outraged. He was surprised she was making light of the elixirs. Why was this suddenly a joke for her?

"You better ask Dr. Walker," Darlene said. "He's the one who ordered it."

"Well," he said, "I'll be on my way, then."

She did not call him back, and he felt as if the distance between them had widened, not grown closer.

He would not waste his time talking to Dr. Walker. Anyway, the loquacious old crank wasn't around, so he couldn't ask him if he wanted to. Instead, he patrolled through the whole camp, making spot checks through the kitchen, the barracks, and then on out to the muddy field where the boys were working on the swimming pool, which was now more than just an ugly swatch in the earth. The pit was shaped by brick walls on each side, and one could imagine how it would be transformed into an enormous swimming pool with clear, cool spring water. A number of trucks were parked in the middle of the earth. They had dammed the spring so that it would not flow into the pit. A few boys were digging. One or two leaned on their shovels. Some were setting out adobe bricks in the sun to set. Once they filled it in with water, he would need to set up some kind of program for water safety. Many did not know how to swim. The incident with Otto and the rattler had unnerved him.

"Work's going real well, Captain," Mac said. He was smoking a Lucky Strike. "Still countin' on inviting the former Governor Neff to the opening?" Mac had also been in the Great War and had seen action, but he had not been an officer.

"Let's not put the cart before the horse," Captain Bell said. "I am still smartin' from what happened with the First Lady's visit."

Mac snorted. "Shoot. No one would believe it if we wrote it in a novel. Not that I read any. That Hick was a real cow."

Captain Bell said, "That's enough."

"You ain't sweet on her?" Mac said. "Wouldn't blame you if you were. She is sure purty. Darlene, that is."

"Look, Mac, just focus on the pool."

Mac stamped out his cigarette on the ground with his muddy boot. "Suit yerself, Captain."

"You survived the Great War, and you have even still got a face. Yet you are killin' yourself with those damn cigarettes."

Mac shrugged. "No one ever knows when their time will come." He reached for the pack of Lucky Strikes in his front pocket.

• • •

Captain Bell headed back to the office after his tour of the camp. But his mood had not improved. There were no problems with the pool, but he was sore. Darlene had been curt with him.

When he entered the tiny office, E.O. and Sam had their heads together and were giggling.

"Now, boys," Captain Bell said. "You've got work to do. Sam, did you finish the requisition order for Joe's store?"

"I . . ." Sam said. "Almost . . . Can you give me a few minutes?"

The office was silent, except for the tapping of Sam's typewriter and the clicking of E.O.'s adding machine.

Captain Bell headed for his desk and sat behind the ugly wooden partition. Surprising himself, he said, "Sam, can you bring me Miss Robinson's personnel file?"

In block letters, U.S. DEPARTMENT OF LABOR. He scanned through the form. Place of birth: Texarkana. Marital status: Single. Medical training: John Sealy Hospital Training for Nurses, Galveston, Diploma, 1922. Previous employment: Private-duty nurse, Roy Starr,

Houston, Texas. References available upon request. Address for salary remuneration: Lavinia Wilder, 2302 Mockingbird Lane, Kansas City, Kansas. Relationship: Sister. I, Darlene Robinson, testify that the information I have offered is correct, etc., etc.

He didn't see anything that offered him any insight into her background. Had she worked as a private-duty nurse all those years after she had gotten her diploma? No hospital work? Not listed.

• • •

In the afternoon, he took another break from the office and went over to the canteen.

Joe's truck was backed up to the canteen. He heard Darlene's laughter. He felt a pang of jealousy.

Jack was standing behind the counter, popping the caps off of Vim Colas. Darlene and Joe were seated on the stools. Darlene's white smock was hitched up a little from sitting on the stool, and he noticed her firm legs.

Joe jumped off the stool and offered his hand. "Captain Bell. It is a good chance this afternoon."

What did he mean? This coincidental meeting? Captain Bell shook his hand heartily. Before he could say anything, Joe said, "On our trip, a lonely camel in the mountains was searching for his beloved. Instead, he met up with a lady bear. This is no exaggeration! The First Lady barely escaped with her life."

"Maybe," Captain Bell said. That was not what Frank Hamer had reported to him.

"Oh, poo," Darlene said. "You are spoiling the fun. Let him finish the story." She tipped her long neck back as she took a swig of icy Vim Cola.

Jack piped up, eager to talk. "Captain, did you hear what happened on the trip?"

Darlene gazed at Joe adoringly. Did she know him from before? But he thought she was interested in Jack?

"I heard about it," Captain Bell said. As far as he could see, the camping trip was just marginally more successful than Devilfish's concert, where he was singing about "candy."

"Loosen up," Darlene said, winking at him. There was no trace of the earlier worry he had seen in her face in Dr. Walker's office.

Jack laughed. "This fella sure can tell a tale. Have you ever . . . ?"

Joe pulled an embroidered cloth handkerchief out of his pocket and wiped the sweat off his brow.

"What's that on your hanky?" Darlene said.

"My wife sewed my name in Arabic," Joe said, handing her the handkerchief. "*Itfaddali*. Go ahead, it is yours."

Darlene giggled. "Oh, I couldn't. But it is so beautiful." Darlene touched the embroidery, the loops of blue. Green vines with grapes decorated the edges.

Captain Bell noticed that Jack, whose nickname in the camp was Cary Grant, was starting to look annoyed.

Joe bowed. "I insist. If someone admires something in our culture, you must give it to them."

"I don't know what to say," Darlene said. "I am touched."

Joe laughed.

Captain Bell could see that Jack wasn't having it. "That's some shirt you are wearing," he said, trying to get Joe's attention.

But Joe was charmed by Darlene and didn't give him his shirt. Instead, he twirled his moustache, saying, "In our language, we have poems addressed to a gazelle, instead of the beloved. If I wrote verse instead of selling butter and Vim Cola, I would write a homage to the camel. She is a most misunderstood creature. Like so many animals."

Captain Bell felt himself becoming impatient. He was no closer to finding out what was in the Wonder Cure. "Do you think the camels of 1856 drank Wonder Cure? Lived forever. Even until 1935 . . . ?"

Darlene spewed her Vim Cola all over the counter of the canteen. She couldn't stop laughing. "Don't be ridiculous."

Joe looked puzzled. "Captain, habibi, dear, they can live for a week without water in the desert. They eat grass. *Ay Wallah,*, I swear to God, I saw a camel on the camping trip! A few are left over from that epoch, and they wander wild in the Davis Mountains."

Captain Bell moved in for the kill. "Do you know what else is in the drink? Who is producing it?"

"It is pleasing," Joe said. "It cures the burning in the stomach. Problems with the colon. The air we get in our stomach if we eat cabbage."

Jack guffawed.

"Is that so?" Captain Bell said. "So you mean to say that you don't actually know what is in the drink?"

Joe smiled. "I can assure you that customers are pleased by the taste. It has started to become one of our best-selling items, besides the Vim Cola."

"Captain!" Darlene said. "Go easy on the man."

Jack was wiping down the counter with a sponge where Darlene had spewed the sticky cola. He chimed in, "The boys love Vim Cola."

Captain Bell said, "I am starting to have doubts about that, too."

Joe was astonished. "But Captain, everyone is drinking the Vim Cola. It is popular all over the state."

Captain Bell noticed the four crates of Vim Cola behind the counter. Where was the Wonder Cure?

"We'll pay for this order," Captain Bell said. "But that's it. We won't be ordering any more Wonder Cure or Vim Cola."

Joe flourished the bill. "With your permission, I believe there has been a misunderstanding. Can I—?"

Jack interrupted, "But Captain Bell, the boys love Vim. I see no reason to ban plain soda pop. This is going too far."

Captain Bell felt his anger rising but counted to ten before he answered. "I'm in charge of this outfit. And the safety of the boys here. I have my doubts about both."

Joe smiled. "As you wish," he said. "I must go."

Captain Bell could feel the imprint of the other language in Joe's English. But who was he to judge? He did not speak Spanish well. Or French. "*Je t'aime*," he whispered.

Joe had already hoisted the empty Vim crates on his shoulder and was moving toward the gate.

Darlene called out, "Thanks for the present!"

Soon they heard the roar of Joe's truck as he drove off. The carefree mood in the canteen had vanished.

Darlene slid off the stool. "You sure do know how to pop the balloon! Between you and Dr. Walker . . ."

He was hurt by the remark. Darlene twirled the handkerchief playfully as she sauntered out of the canteen, her hips swaying from side to side. He had a sudden doubt that she was just thirty.

"Jack, let me see a bottle of that Wonder Cure."

"Of course, Captain," Jack said, pulling a bottle of Wonder Cure from the shelves next to the razor blades. "Do you think it might be poisonous?"

"I don't know," Captain Bell said.

It had a fanciful, attractive label, with curlicues in the shape of vines at the top, a rooster embossed in the middle. "Wonder Cure: Purified Extracts for Everlasting Youth, Vim, and Vitality: Cures general malaise, biliousness, and erectile dysfunction. Established 1895." The ingredients were not listed. "Brinkley Pharmaceutical Association."

Captain Bell unscrewed the top and sniffed it. The liquid was a cheerful red color. He took a small sip. Tasted like strawberry. Sugary. But what were the other mysterious ingredients?

"Sold like hotcakes the day Devilfish played. I was surprised. No one had ever bought the stuff before except Dr. Walker," Jack said.

"Lock it up," Captain Bell said. "Until I get to the bottom of this. That's an order."

CHAPTER 19.

# A Journalist on a Motorcycle with a Sidecar

The next day, Sam was struggling to finish *The Round-Up*. He felt unhappy with this issue. He felt as if every sentence he had written was a lie. Captain Bell was out inspecting the construction site of the swimming pool. Sam was mulling over his journalistic ambitions. If he had to write lies and flattery, he was starting to have doubts about a career in the newspapers. Perhaps he shouldn't go in that direction. He wanted to get some advice from Captain Bell about his future, but he had been in a bad mood lately.

E.O. was hunched over, poring over the ledgers.

"Captain Bell sure is mad about something," Sam said. "Do you think it's just the party for Miss Hickock? Mrs. Roosevelt's visit?"

E.O. didn't look up. "Nope."

"Never know when he's going to bite your head off."

"Yep."

"What's eatin' at him?"

"Darlene," E.O. said.

So that was why he had wanted to look at her personnel file. On the other hand, he was the C.O. of the camp, and he could have his reasons for looking at anyone's personnel file. Captain Bell kept his cards close to his chest.

"How do you know?" Sam said, feeling annoyed. Now there was not only Jack, but Captain Bell. He didn't have a chance. His date with Charlotte had failed, too. Her folks couldn't stop gabbing about sin and hell! Dances indefinitely postponed. What chances did he have of meeting another girl?

"Saw them after the party, walking back to her room," E.O said. "Gazing at the moon. Smooching."

"Do you think . . . ?" Sam said. The news kept getting worse and worse.

"I heard they broke her bed," E.O. said, pushing up the glasses on his nose. "Don't tell anybody I told you."

"Just who would I tell?" Sam said, annoyed again that E.O. was suggesting he was a gossip, but he also felt his spirits plummet. He remembered Darlene ripping Captain Bell's pants off when he had heatstroke. How expert her hands were. Why was he mooning over this harlot?

"There's something else. He's worried about Wonder Cure. Looks like it's poison," E.O. said.

"Poison?" Sam asked, astounded. "Has anyone gotten sick?"

"Miss Hickock drank it," E.O. said, speculating now. "Night of the party."

"Poison," Sam repeated. He hadn't paid much attention to that Wonder Cure, but remembered his mama's doubts about such elixirs.

But he had drunk plenty of Vim Cola. He liked the sugary taste with a hint of vanilla. Was the same producer making Wonder Cure and Vim Cola?

E.O. put his head down again. "Look, I gave you the dirt. I gotta finish payroll."

There was an urgent knock at the door. Before Sam could get up out of his seat, a man wearing a motorcycle helmet and huge round goggles strode in. He looked like a pilot.

"Good morning," Sam said, shaking his hand heartily. He had a jolly-looking face, but his brown eyes were intense. He was balding—somewhere in his forties.

"Dr. Morris Fishbein," the man said.[1] "I am doing a series of investigative exclusives for the *Kansas City Star*."

Captain Bell followed behind him. "You missed her. She's gone on to El Paso."

The man took off his goggles. "The person I am investigating is not a woman, but a quack. A seller of nostrums. In short, a medical charlatan. A flimflam man."

Captain Bell laughed. "I thought you were looking for Mrs. Roosevelt."

The man said. "Of course, I am a fan of the Roosevelts. But politics is not my area of expertise. I am a medical doctor. I chase quacks."

Captain Bell laughed again.

The man was offended. "I am perfectly serious. The world needs to be rid of these charlatans. I am serious about chasing quacks."

Captain Bell said, "No offense was meant. Please, would you care to have a seat? Did you come all the way from Kansas on that motorcycle outside?"

Sam opened the door and peered out. An expensive-looking

motorcycle with a shiny maroon sidecar was parked outside of the building. He had always wanted to ride a motorcycle. How long would the journalist be here? Sam wondered if he could ask to ride in the sidecar.

The man wiped the dust off his face with a monogrammed cloth handkerchief. "I am originally from Chicago. Visiting my sister in Dallas. Thought I might explore Texas. It does stretch on for a while."

"You must be thirsty," Captain Bell said. "Water?"

Sam poured him a glass of spring water from the pitcher they kept on top of the wood-burning stove.

"Thank you, son," he said. He took off the motorcycle gloves and stuffed them in his brown leather jacket. His intense brown eyes bulged slightly.

Once he sat down in the seat in front of Captain Bell's desk, Captain Bell said, "How can I help you?"

"You see, in 1930, I wrote an article for the *Kansas City Star* about a man who purports to be a medical doctor. His name is John Brinkley.[2] He's a fraud, and Kansas ran him out of the state and stripped him of his medical license. His medical qualifications are dubious. Concocts all sorts of nostrums. Elixirs. Hundreds of farmers also died from his operations. Promised them greater virility with a goat transplant operation."

For a minute or so, there was silence except for the clicking of E.O.'s adding machine. Then Captain Bell said, "We have heard of someone named Volkov who gave a lecture about goat transplants at Sul Ross Normal College in Alpine. You might talk to Dr. Walker, our physician at the camp. See what he has to say."

So focused on finishing up his newsletter about those infernal camels, why hadn't Sam gotten his hands on that article in the *Journal of the American Medical Association*? He had to ask Darlene about it.

"There are so many of these frauds running around," Dr. Fishbein said. "It enrages me how people are taken in. One man drank radium water from one of these elixirs, and his jaw fell off."

Sam was shocked.

"You might be interested in this," Captain Bell said. "It is being sold at our canteen. Wonder Cure. Brinkley's name is on it."

What was in the Wonder Cure? Had Miss Hickock been poisoned? And that was why Mrs. R. had canceled her speech at Balmorhea? Other than the shenanigans, was this the real reason her speech had been canceled?

"It can't be sold!" Dr. Fishbein said. "That charlatan must be stopped at once! At all costs. There's another case . . ."

"Please, Doctor," Captain Bell said. "I think I have heard enough. Anyway, I have canceled the order."

"The *Kansas City Star* asked me to write a follow-up article on Brinkley. I hear he has a radio station in Mexico, not far from here. That is where he advertises his 'medicines.' Pharmacists can't resist the profits."

"I will arrange a meeting with Dr. Walker," Captain Bell said. "Could you hold off on interviewing any of the boys for now? We don't want to cause panic at the camp."

But wasn't Dr. Walker a fan of Volkov? Sam wondered how useful a meeting with Dr. Walker would be. Why hadn't Captain Bell mentioned Darlene?

• • •

Sam stretched his legs. He peered out the open door as Dr. Fishbein put on his goggles and helmet and launched onto his motorcycle, as if it were about to fly. He envied Dr. Fishbein's freedom.

"Wish I had one of those," Sam said. His typewriter felt like a ball and chain.

Captain Bell snorted. "Be careful what you wish for. They're very dangerous."

"Captain Bell, something strange happened at the end of the camping trip."

Captain Bell moaned. "McCabe, can't you see I am dealing with a bigger crisis right now? Just finish the newsletter with the tall tales about camels! We need happy endings!"

"Mr. Perry was looking for Dr. Volkov at the end of our trip. He even threatened Mr. Hamer. He thought we were a posse and had captured Volkov. Do you think Mr. Perry had one of those goat transplant operations Dr. Fishbein was talking about?"

"Why didn't you tell me this before?" Captain Bell said. "Frank Hamer never mentioned it."

Sam shrugged. "I forgot. Anyhow, Captain Hamer couldn't make sense of it, either."

Captain Bell looked at him thoughtfully. "Perry owns the mine over at Terlingua. He is a wealthy man. He might have paid a lot of money for an operation if he believed it would . . ."

Sam's eyes locked with Captain Bell's. He felt like he was blushing. Sam had never even been with a girl in that way. But he lived in the countryside, and he had watched stallions humping mares. And he had listened to men talk very frankly about their problems in the bedroom.

"You boys need to be discreet. Not a word leaks out about what's going on in this office, you hear?"

CHAPTER 20.

# A Lengthy Row over Medical Experimentation

**Dr. Fishbein roared up on his motorcycle at 9 a.m., and Captain Bell led him over to Dr. Walker's office.** He had decided he would stay for the meeting. He didn't expect that Dr. Fishbein would get much help from Dr. Walker, but maybe he would find out more about Wonder Cure. His tiny office wasn't big enough for all of them, anyway—and it didn't offer any privacy. The boys already knew too many of the secrets of Balmorhea.

As they walked over to the clinic, Dr. Fishbein detailed his expose of the "Escanaba Fever Girl."[1] The *Chicago Daily News* had also asked him to investigate that hoax. It was only through peeking in through a keyhole to her bedroom that he had discovered the trick. The girl, apparently in good health, had convinced doctors that she had a fever of 114 degrees for three weeks. The girl had hidden a hot water bottle in her bed, and when no one was in the room, she had put the thermometer directly onto the hot water bottle. Once he had finished that anecdote, he asked, "Perhaps you have heard of my book *Fads and Quackery in Healing*?"

"Well, uh, no," Captain Bell said. "It's not exactly my field. My father owns a hotel."

"Ah," he said, then plunged on. "In my book, I discuss quackery in great detail. Homeopathy, osteopathy, chiropractic practices, radionics."

"Radionics?"

"By placing radio waves to the body, you can detect cures."

Captain Bell had never heard of such a thing. But then, technology was constantly evolving. His face had almost been obliterated by a trench mortar, yet Dr. Gillies's experimentation had saved it. Or had salvaged it? Yet he was a stranger to himself with this new face.

The door was open.

Dr. Walker was sitting at his desk, deeply engrossed in a book. His eyes were red. Was he drinking again?

"Dr. Walker, this is Dr. Fishbein. He is writing a series of articles about a doctor called Brinkley who is doing goat transplant operations."

Dr. Walker stood up. He was wearing a three-piece suit with a vest. He extended his hand to Dr. Fishbein. "A pleasure on this fine morning in West Texas. I am keeping abreast of the recent work being done on rejuvenation."

"What are you reading?" Dr. Fishbein asked.

"A veritable genius," Dr. Walker held up the novel. "*As I Lay Dying*, by William Faulkner. It follows the woeful travails of a poor family from Mississippi, trying to bury their beloved mother. Of course, the title refers to Homer's *Odyssey*."

Captain Bell had never heard of the writer, but he was mostly a reader of history. He was interested in Abraham Lincoln and his leadership during the Civil War. "The reason why we are here—"

"Of course, Faulkner. Of course," Dr. Fishbein interrupted him. "Sinclair Lewis is a dear friend of mine. In fact, I reviewed his novel *Main Street* for the *Chicago Daily News*. There is a very convincing chapter where a doctor amputates the crushed arm of a farmer."

Captain Bell remembered how shocked he had been when he woke to find his arm was gone. The odd pinging of the nerves, as if it were still there. Worse, the injuries to his face. Even when Dr. Gillies had allowed him to look at his new face in the mirror, he was shocked.

"That was tactless of me," Dr. Fishbein said. "Forgive me, Captain Bell."

Captain Bell just nodded. He was not up to telling the story of his amputation again, as if it were a dog and pony show. He was starting to dislike Dr. Fishbein.

"Aaah," Dr. Walker said, giving Captain Bell a sympathetic look. He launched in another direction. "Of course, no one should underestimate the talent of Lewis, but in my humble opinion, and I am not exaggerating my humility, Faulkner will be hailed as one of the greatest writers in American literature. You have read the novel?"

Dr. Fishbein shook his head. "Unfortunately not. But you are aware that Sinclair recently won the Nobel Prize."

"As for the medical condition described in *As I Lay Dying*, it is the decomposition of the human body over a series of days. Putrefaction."

Captain Bell cleared his throat. "Dr. Fishbein is writing an article on Dr. Brinkley, who is doing goat transplant operations."

Dr. Walker fingered the gold watch chain that hung from his vest. "I am not acquainted with Dr. Brinkley. But most recently, I attended an edifying lecture by the brilliant Dr. Volkov, sponsored by the Texas

Medical Association. It will have grand implications for treatment of erectile dysfunction and impotence."

"I am sorry to inform you that Dr. Brinkley is a charlatan. A flim-flam man! I have never heard of Dr. Volkov, but if he espouses the same ideas, he is a charlatan as well. Hundreds of farmers died from those goat transplant operations."

Dr. Walker huffed. "Are you against the advancement of medical science?"

"Of course not!" Dr. Fishbein said, his face turning red. His eyes bulged.

"Medical science will never advance without experimentation and vision. Of course, no one can deny the greatest recent invention of penicillin by Dr. Alex Fleming in 1928. No one can dispute, either, that some inventions are, in fact, a result of trial and error or sudden illumination, for example when Fleming realized the value of mold in his Petri dish. Or we can point to Dr. Snow, who discovered that cholera was not caused by 'bad air,' but could be traced to a water pump in London."

"Dr. Walker, I am talking about men who are not qualified to practice medicine. Charlatans. Dr. Brinkley bought his degree from some flimsy night school. He was discredited by the Kansas Medical Association."[2]

But Dr. Walker was unconvinced. "Dr. Volkov had degrees from France and Italy. Are you suggesting that the Texas Medical Association can't tell an authentic doctor from a charlatan?"

Dr. Fishbein shook his head. "Yes. He has already been discredited in Kansas and California."

Captain Bell feared they were getting nowhere fast. What about Wonder Cure?

"Are you aware of the research on rejuvenation done by the

Germans? In 1933, the *New York Times* reported on the important work being done on testosterone. Most notably by a Dr. Steinach," Dr. Walker said. "This could have huge implications for the treatment of erectile dysfunction."

"His work is questionable," Dr. Fishbein said.

Dr. Walker snorted. "I suppose you would have classified Leonardo da Vinci, the greatest artist of all time, who had boundless curiosity, as questionable."

"Experimentation cannot take place on live human subjects!" Dr. Fishbein shouted. "The Hippocratic oath stipulates, 'Do no harm.'"

"Do not lecture me on the Hippocratic oath! Of course, I am acquainted with the oath and uphold it in my practice of medicine," Dr. Walker said.

"Please," Captain Bell said. "Gentlemen." He raised his one hand.

Darlene poked her head into the office. "Everything all right?"

Why hadn't he invited her to join the meeting? "Darlene, you should be part of this meeting."

Her hair was swept up into a loose knot on the top of her head; a few unruly curls had escaped the rubber band. She smiled flirtatiously. "Should I?"

Captain Bell said, "Dr. Fishbein is investigating Dr. Brinkley. A charlatan who practiced medicine in Kansas. He believes he is in Texas."

The color drained from Darlene's face. "Dr. Fishbein," she said, shaking his hand. He wouldn't let go of her hand. "Pleased to . . ." Finally, she pulled her hand away.

Dr. Fishbein couldn't stop staring at her, as if he had never seen a woman before.

"I, uh, won't stay because I am dealing with problems on the ground," Darlene said. "We are plumb out of aspirin, and I will need to go into town. It's that time of month, and I have run out of sanitary napkins . . ."

Captain Bell was not sure he believed her.

Dr. Walker seemed embarrassed. "Of course, dear, you are excused. I will inform you of developments later. We are having a most elucidatory discussion on the advancement of medical science and the implications for the treatment of prostate problems."

Since when had Dr. Walker called her "dear"? He thought those two hated each other. Captain Bell followed her out into the corridor, but she had disappeared.

"Can I ask you what Dr. Volkov looked like?"

"As I recall, he was tall. Wore a pince-nez. Spoke with an accent. He has qualifications from France and Italy, as duly noted. Is all of this necessary? Am I the one being accused of this chicanery and these machinations?"

Captain Bell interrupted, "No one is accusing you, Dr. Walker."

"I wouldn't trust the medical experimentation of the Germans, anyway. They have already broken the Treaty of Versailles. And now, I hear from my uncle about their new policies against Jews," Dr. Fishbein said.

Dr. Walker shrugged. "But we have already fought the 'war to end all wars,' Dr. Fishbein. Do you think that you are, in fact, exaggerating the case?"

The door to the clinic slammed shut from the wind. Suddenly, Captain Bell's palms felt sweaty. He felt dizzy. His head was pounding. Trees split, as if they had been struck by lightning. The noise from the explosions was deafening. Splinters and shrapnel rained down upon him. He could not see, damn it. "Boys, run for cover!" he shouted. He crouched behind Dr. Walker's oak desk and curled into a ball, covering his face.

Dr. Fishbein squatted next to him and gently touched his arm. "Captain, it's all right. You're at Balmorhea."

Dr. Walker walked around the edge of his desk and patted him on the back. "My boy."

Captain Bell was embarrassed. He felt shaken. Wobbly. He was shaking. "I never know when . . ."

"Shell shock," Dr. Fishbein said, turning to Dr. Walker. "You have read the work of Charles Meyers in the *Lancet*?"

Dr. Walker shook his head. "I do believe, though, that this condition was addressed, if I am not mistaken, during the Civil War as 'soldier's heart.'"

Captain Bell sat down in the chair and took a deep breath. He hated losing control. And he never knew when the memories of the war would be jarred loose. Surge to the surface. Throw him off balance.

Dr. Walker handed him a glass of cool water from the Balmorhea spring. "That is very kind."

They were all silent for a few minutes until he finished the water.

At least Dr. Fishbein seemed to be a better-informed doctor than Dr. Walker. "So you don't know what is in Dr. Brinkley's Wonder Cure?"

Dr. Fishbein shook his head. "But as I told you, Liver Cure No. 50 almost caused the death of a man in Kansas. Other elixirs contain radium."

"Why have you ordered Wonder Cure for the canteen?" Captain Bell said, looking up at Dr. Walker. "If you don't know what's in it?"

"I was assured profusely of the rejuvenative benefits by a pharmacist," Dr. Walker said. "I assumed—"

"Joe Kafouri is not a pharmacist," Captain Bell said. "He's a dry grocer."

"Of course. Of course," Dr. Walker said. "But I was assured by a pharmacist whom I hold in good esteem that—"

Dr. Fishbein interrupted, "But if you had read my recent article in *JAMA*, you would know that pharmacists are also part of these fraudulent practices. They are making money like there's no tomorrow. Dr. Brinkley's other scheme is the goat transplant operations to 'cure' impotence. Promise everlasting regeneration."

"Don't you have the journal?" Captain Bell asked.

Wasn't that the journal Darlene was reading? Had she taken it?

There were stacks of files and books on Dr. Walker's desk. Dr. Walker lifted up William Faulkner's *The Sound and the Fury*. Collected poems of Alfred, Lord Tennyson.

Dr. Fishbein asked pointedly, "You have read my article?"

"Well, of course it was my sincere intention." Dr. Walker laughed a little nervously. "But I have been rather preoccupied here at the camp with a number of pertinent matters."

Like what? He had not been available when Captain Bell, himself, had heatstroke. If it had not been for Darlene and Chueco . . . He was at Dr. Volkov's lecture in Alpine.

Dr. Fishbein frowned. "I have heard Dr. Brinkley has a radio station near the Texas border in a place called Del Rio."[3]

"That's around two hundred and twenty miles. A long ride, Dr. Fishbein," Captain Bell said. "What will you do if you find him?"

Dr. Fishbein pulled his goggles out of his pocket. "I will not be deterred in my quest to stop such a quack. Dr. Brinkley must be stopped before . . ."

Dr. Walker shuffled more loose papers and medical files around on his desk. "It was here a few days ago. Of course, I had every intention of reading your edifying article, Dr. Fishbein."

"Did you find it?" Captain Bell asked. "We are waiting."

Dr. Walker sighed. "I am confident beyond all doubt that it was here." He stacked novels on his desk. Took a passel of loose papers, and licked each one. The medical files were in another stack.

But the journal had disappeared.

CHAPTER 21.

# Darlene's Diary, October 15, 1935

**I hate pretending.** *It was fun when I was a little girl, but the game is up. Darlene was my aunt's name. Not even on my birth certificate.*

*Some fancy doctor from back East told me Minerva is the Roman goddess of wisdom. Hardly. My parents called me "Minnie." Don't know where I am. Just a farm girl from Texarkana. I did get a diploma at the University of Texas at Galveston in nursing. That's not a lie.*

*Captain Bell thinks I swiped the JAMA journal. Not sure if he believes me or not. Getting suspicious. If he calls Roy Starr, the oilman in Houston, he'll vouch for me. He paid well. Anything, not to be dirt poor.*

*My heart aches to see J., though. Is B. dragging him around from town to town?*

*"If you didn't take it, then who did?" Felt like an interrogation.*

*"Hell if I know," I said. Dr. Walker can be careless and he doesn't always lock his office. Keeps his spirits locked up in a wardrobe in his bedroom. Who would want to steal his fancy novels, anyhow? Longed for a Harlequin Romance.*

*Too much reality!*

*"Dr. Walker keeps the key to his office in Chueco's aloe vera plant," I said.*

*Afraid Fishbein might recognize me. Why was he staring at me like that? Was the black dye too cheap? He must have seen earlier photographs of me. Or was he just a horny old goat? Ha. Ha.*

*I had to know if Fishbein mentioned me in the JAMA article.*

*Suits me just fine if the JAMA article was stolen. Was it that kid, Sam?*

*I hear B.'s bought a mansion in Del Rio. Advertising his elixirs through his "Medicine Box" on his radio station in Mexico.*[1] *The boys at Balmorhea heard about Wonder Cure from the show. Playing some country and western. A little blues.*

*"The ram that I am with every lamb"—his little jingle for those old Kansas farmers down on their luck.*

*"Vim and Vigor for the Manly Man."*

*The goat gonads didn't take to the body. Failed to graft. Just placed inside the testicle sac. $750 an operation.*

*We didn't stay long enough to see the burials. Fled to Texas.*

*Roy Bell wouldn't have me, anyway, if he knew. He's too straightforward for his own good, although no fool. He would turn me in.*

*Can't sue for divorce. Am stuck.*

*The price for all of those poor farmers who met their Maker too soon? Does the universe find a way to make you pay for your deeds?*

*Sally can take care of the Galápagos tortoises, penguins, and monkeys at the mansion at Del Rio. Good for her. Don't miss the big maroon Cadillac. Wouldn't mind another luxury cruise to Italy. But . . .*

*Late at night, B. can chase her around the mansion with a whip when he gets sauced. Bend over.*

*Not jealous a bit.*

CHAPTER 22.

# Opium Eaters

The next morning after breakfast, Sam strolled over to the clinic to ask Darlene about the *JAMA* journal. She was not helpful. He couldn't understand it. She simply shrugged. "You'll have to ask Dr. Walker yourself. He keeps everything under lock and key. Doesn't share information."

He ventured over to Dr. Walker's office and knocked lightly on the door, which was slightly ajar.

Dr. Walker was sitting at his desk. His head was bowed, but he was not praying. He had nodded off, and was snoring slightly. A light whistle emanated from his mouth. It seemed a little early in the morning for a nap. Unless he had been up all night?

Sam tiptoed toward his desk, which was in complete disarray. Besides medical files, there were opened envelopes, bills, prescriptions, and requisition orders from the federal government. Stacks of novels: William Faulkner, Pearl Buck, Robert Graves. A collection of Alfred, Lord Tennyson. Collected poems of Samuel Taylor Coleridge. He had memorized "Kubla Khan" at Sul Ross for literature class.

He couldn't make heads or tails of it, until Miss Burnett, the professor, had explained it in class: "This was written after a hallucination of opium." Reckoned it was a lot stronger than moonshine. He picked up a stethoscope and put it around his neck. He had never fantasized about becoming a doctor, but he wondered what it would be like to be one. He didn't dislike science, but he was more interested in words, history, English, and Spanish. He picked up a metal rose that said TYLER. When he put it back, it made a heavy thud.

Dr. Walker stirred. Then his eyes blinked open.

"My boy," he said. "Come in. Come in. How is the nose? I trust nature has done its work and you have properly healed since the unseemly fracas?"

"It's just fine," Sam said. He gingerly lifted the stethoscope from his neck and put it back on Dr. Walker's desk. He touched his nose to make sure it was still there.

Dr. Walker laughed heartily. "You can't listen to your own heart. I will have to do it. It is, in fact, a physical impossibility. What can I do for you if your nose has healed? If you have cut yourself or have some minor injury, Darlene can assist you. She is quite capable."

"I was just curious to read an article in one of your medical journals, Dr. Walker. I started reading it when it came through the mail. The one about goat transplants. A goat was on the cover. 'Medical Experimentation or Hoax?'"

Dr. Walker frowned. Had he said something wrong? Why was the doctor displeased?

Then he sighed. "I applaud your curiosity to the utmost. And believe me, if I had the journal in my possession, I would not hesitate to lend it to you, my boy. Dr. Volkov's advances will change the history of medicine. I am never against the acquisition of knowledge."

Not what Darlene had said. But then, he remembered how she

had mocked him when he was in the infirmary. She hated his guts.

"You don't have it?" Sam asked.

Dr. Walker's eyes were red. He smiled faintly. "It has been purloined."

If Sam had not read "The Purloined Letter" by Edgar Allen Poe in freshman English, he would not know what Dr. Walker was talking about. "Why?"

"I do not know the answer to your query," Dr. Walker said. "It is a conundrum that we must get to the bottom of."

When Sam returned to the office, the mail had just been delivered. He plopped down in his chair and started sorting. Why would someone steal the journal? Any correspondence from the federal government was a priority. He flipped quickly through the stack of envelopes.

One letter caught his attention: Attn: Captain Bell. Return Address: Dr. Ernest Heatwell, Dept. of Chemistry, Sul Ross College, Alpine. He slit it open with the silver opener.

October 22, 1935

Dear Captain Bell:

I applaud your work with the CCC camps at Balmorhea. The swimming pool will be a most welcome addition to this part of the state. Thank you for supper last week at the Holland Hotel.

I have examined the contents of the two samples which you gave me. The one that is a dark color, which is commonly known as Vim Cola, has these elements: extracts of the kola leaf (which contains caffeine), vanilla extract, caramel flavoring, carbon dioxide (fizz), and sugar. There is nothing harmful in the drink, except excessive amounts of sugar which will rot your teeth. Forgive the levity.

But I must warn you that my examination of the second sample, known as Wonder Cure, contains stronger elements, which could become addictive if ingested in larger doses. The elements are: strawberry extract, sugar, and laudanum with opium alkaloids of morphine and codeine. (This is the tincture of opium.) As per the legislation of 1919 under the Volstead Act, doctors have to register the drugs they prescribe. You were correct to be suspicious of this drug. It should not be sold to the boys at your canteen or to customers anywhere. You should report this to the Texas Medical Association as soon as possible.

Please do not hesitate to contact me again if you need any further assistance.

Sincerely,

Dr. Ernest Heatwell

Professor of Chemistry, Sul Ross College

• • •

"Captain?" Sam called out.

"What is it?" Captain Bell said. "Use your own judgment on articles for the *Round-Up*. I have more important things to think about than camels."

"I think you should see this," Sam said. He scooted around the edge of his desk and squeezed behind Captain Bell's partition.

He handed him the letter.

CHAPTER 23.

# Captain of the Ship

**Captain Bell couldn't sleep.** He felt alone. He doubted Dr. Walker. Was he really unaware that Wonder Cure contained opium? He was a G.P. who had served at Camp Gordon near Atlanta, not in the Great War. Captain Bell had already caught him in one fib. Darlene had been curt with him lately, and he couldn't ask her, either. The boys in the office were too young to know anything about it.

With his one hand, he carried the lantern out into the dark night. Maybe listening to Duke Ellington or Glenn Miller would cheer him up, a little big-band music.

It was past midnight. Most of the boys were fast asleep. He closed the door gently. The lantern made an elongated shadow in front of his body, as if he were a monster, and he followed it to his office. At least he was not looking at himself in the mirror!

The weather was cool at night now. Soon it would be winter. It was not a full moon, like the night he had kissed Darlene. He had to banish her from his mind. He gazed up at a black, almost purplish sky dotted with blinking stars and could see the Big Dipper and the North Star. A few traces of clouds threaded through the sky. A romance with her was as illusory and ephemeral as the clouds above him—besides, he didn't know much about her. With his face, he doubted he would ever find another woman in his life. He had to accept that sad fact.

He took out the key to his office and jiggled the lock. The door popped open. He dragged the big farm radio and put it next to the window so he could look out at the stars while he was listening. He fiddled with the dials. Fred Astaire's familiar voice crooned "Heaven."

No, not that. Too sentimental. He fiddled a little more.

A confident, folksy voice boomed: "Howdy, this is a little homegrown wisdom from a country doctor. Isn't that true, Sally?"[1]

A feminine voice drawled, "It sure is. We welcome y'all, one and all, to our awfully nice home in Del Rio. Everyone in the county is welcome to our fountain nights under the stars. Come for a little fried chicken and Vim Cola and pet the monkeys from the Galápagos. We have our own zoo in the backyard."

"Let's see what we have in the Medical Question Box today, shall we?"

"Everyone needs someone like you, John. A good country doctor who they can trust. Talk about those sensitive problems that can be mighty embarrassing."

"One of our patients has written that he has a question about his prostate. That 'troublesome old cocklebur.' Nothing to be ashamed of, my friend. When we get older, sometimes we aren't as energetic as we used to be. With my cures, romance will be rekindled in the bedroom."

Sally giggled. "Oh, John, how right you are. Right as the day is long. Now, dear, the question."

Dr. Brinkley cleared his throat. "The question is, 'What do I do when my member will not cooperate when I want to have relations with my wife?'"

"Go on and tell them about your cures, John."

"Why, it's easy as pie. My goat gonad operation is the answer for penile dysfunction. Only seven hundred and fifty dollars and your happiness is guaranteed. I have cured millionaires and movie stars, haven't I, dear?"

"They swear by you, they sure do. Remember when we were out in Hollywood? The owner of the *L.A. Times* swore it was the best operation he ever had. A cure made in heaven."

"Yes sirree, there are so many testimonials to this cure. Why, Tobias, the Chancellor of the University of Chicago, even tried it. He said, 'Five days later the headaches disappeared . . . And I grow younger by the day,'" John said.

Sally giggled.

"Besides the operation where I transplant the gonads, I recommend my Wonder Cure. It's available at your nearest pharmacist. And boy, does it work wonders."

Sally simpered and sighed, seductively. "It sure does, dear John."

"I am here to cure people. I am one of the nicest men out there . . ."

Sally echoed. "You sure are. One of the nicest!"

"Always tell the truth. Never tell a lie."

"Never met a more decent man," Sally said.

"Stay with us. You hear? Now, we'll hear from our friends at Miracle Life, the Insurance Company from the Great Lakes:

"Do you want to protect your loved ones from the shock of penury? None of us want to admit that we are mortal. Pay ten dollars a month and your loved one will be secure for life with a handsome settlement of one hundred thousand dollars in the event of your demise . . ."

"And now, some gospel music by the Carter family."

After a few twangs, the singer pined:

"Oh, my loving mother, when the world's on fire/Don't you want God's bosom to be your pillow?/Tide me over in the Rock of Ages/Rock of Ages cleft for me/I'm going to heaven when the world's on fire."

CHAPTER 24.

# The Lost Dog

**The next day in the office, Captain Bell asked the boys about the radio station, XER.**

"Do either of you listen to a station called XER out of Mexico? It plays gospel music," he asked.

Sam shook his head. "No, Captain. I never heard of that station."

E.O. pushed his thick glasses up on his nose. "Yep."

"Did you ever hear them advertising Wonder Cure?" he asked.

"Yep," E.O. said. "Was more interested in hearing the Carter family. Singing is not allowed in our church. Church of Christ. They also play Gene Autry."

"Why didn't you tell me?" Captain Bell said. "You knew that we stopped ordering Wonder Cure."

"You never asked," E.O. said.

"Use your noggin, E.O.," Captain Bell said. He felt E.O.'s extreme reserve was sometimes a liability. On the other hand, he could be trusted with money and the combination to the safe.

Should he tell E.O.? What harm did it do to tell the truth, rather than clouding the whole thing in mystery? He needed to destroy those bottles of Wonder Cure. Right now it was locked up at the canteen. Jack had the key.

"Opium. As addictive as moonshine."

E.O. whistled, then shook his head. His face screwed up with distaste. "Spirits are bad for your health. Cause nothin' but trouble. Better to drink water. What my ma says."

"I wish you had told me," Captain Bell said. "If there's anything related to the safety of the boys, you better inform me. You're like my eyes and ears. You promise?"

They nodded their heads. Were they serious? He hoped so. It wasn't that he was asking them to spy on the others. But he couldn't be everywhere at the camp. How could you keep tabs on so many men?

The door burst open and was flung backward against the opposite wall by the wind. A dog trotted into the office, as if it owned the place. Half of its face was black, and the other half was white. Speckles of black dotted one white ear. The dog was a mongrel, an uncertain mix, but it had a smashed broad nose, as if one of its parents was a boxer. Its ears tipped back, a little like a terrier's. It had brown, eager eyes. Joe followed the dog into the office.

"Another day like a carnation. Good morning!" Joe called out. He radiated cheerfulness.

"What's your dog's name?" Sam asked. The dog nuzzled him. Licked his hands.

"*Habibi*, darling, it's not my dog," Joe said. "She just followed my truck." Then he laughed. "She followed the music."

E.O. got up from his desk. He scratched her behind the ears. "Friendly all right. But she ain't pretty."

"Captain Bell, can we keep her?" Sam asked.

Captain Bell felt as if he were a parent who was about to say no. "Maybe she belongs to someone else?"

"I'll feed her," Sam said. "I promise. I'll take care of her."

The dog barked.

"Call her Delilah," Joe said.

She headed straight for Captain Bell and licked his hand. She barked again. Was there any compelling reason why they shouldn't adopt her?

"The story of Samson and Delilah?" E.O asked. "Delilah's a whore."

"That's enough," Captain Bell said. "We don't want to be calling anyone a whore."

E.O. said, "She convinced Samson to tell him the secret of his power. It was his long hair. And then she betrayed him."

"But maybe we want to compliment her with such a name," Joe said. "Like imagining the beauty of a lover."

E.O. shook his head. "The best name for her from the Bible is Martha."

The dog kept licking Captain Bell's hand. "Maybe she's hungry." Her tail thumped against the floor.

Joe put down a light brown sweet in the shape of a thick sausage. She left Captain Bell and ate it in one bite. Then she barked. Joe held up the sweet high, and she jumped in the air to snatch it.

"What are you feeding her?" Sam asked.

Joe smiled. "My wife has made *balah es-sham* for you, my friends. It is shaped like a date, but is fried. We pour a syrup over it. Please, take one."

Captain Bell took one and bit into it. It was delicious, but too sugary for his taste. It reminded him a little of the sopaipillas that the cooks at the Menger Hotel used to make.

"Like sopaipillas," Captain Bell said.

"Ah, yes," Joe said. He laughed. "We tried them in Mexico. But ours are much better. Less doughy. They are lighter. Boys?"

Sam nodded because his mouth was full. E.O. smiled. His cheeks were so full, he looked like a chipmunk.

"This was very kind of you," Captain Bell said. "Please thank your wife."

Delilah barked. Joe set another piece down in front of her.

"So we'll keep her, then?" Sam asked. He poured a glass of water and offered it to Joe.

Captain Bell didn't have the heart to say no. "If you promise to feed her every day. Get scraps from the kitchen."

"Come on, girl," Sam said. They didn't have a dog now at the farm, but they had in the past. When he was little, they had a boxer named Oliver. Even though he was big, he was a gentle dog.

"Not now," Captain Bell said. "At lunchtime."

Joe took off his checkered flat cap and squeezed behind the wooden partition.

Captain Bell cleared his throat. "We'll be ordering Vim Cola this month."

"Of course," Joe said. "Of course, Captain." He laughed. "Vim is for the manly man. You have all of these manly men at your camp! Ha. Too many Samsons!"

Delilah barked. Captain Bell reached down and stroked her. Wasn't that the slogan for Wonder Cure?

"But," Captain Bell said. He wondered how he could broach Wonder Cure with Joe without accusing him. "I have it on good information that Wonder Cure contains opium."

"Ahhhh!" Joe said, as if he were shocked. "Positive? I was told by a respectable pharmacist who swore that the tincture is harmless. Was mostly a cure for flatulence, if you know what I mean?"

Captain Bell heard the two boys laughing behind the partition. He wished he had a separate room. There was no privacy here!

Captain Bell could not tell if Joe was leading him down a path. Was he a good actor?

"So you don't know Dr. Brinkley?" Captain Bell asked.

Joe shook his head. "The name does not resonate in my mind," he said. Then he smiled. "But we have lots of orders."

"We won't be ordering Wonder Cure," Captain Bell said.

"Aaaah," Joe said. "But of course, I understand your reservations about the tincture."

"You shouldn't be selling it!" Captain Bell said, pounding his one hand on the desk.

Did the man get his drift or not? Or was he just toying with him?

"Aaaah," Joe said. "*Hadir. Hadir*. I will inform my brother."

But Captain Bell forgot he was annoyed when Sam popped his head behind the partition. "Captain, we need to order for Thanksgiving."

"You are so right. It is just around the corner," Captain Bell said. "Turkeys. Potatoes. Corn. Butter. Pumpkins. Raisins. We will be feeding around two hundred boys."

Joe smiled. "*Habibi*, we are waiting. Please send us the number of turkeys. Whatever you desire."

Did he just snap his fingers and twenty turkeys appeared? Why did he have the feeling that Joe could work in a magic show?

"You and your wife will have to come celebrate with us," Captain Bell said. He was feeling generous. It could not be easy to be an Arab immigrant in Texas.

"We must thank God for our life in Amereeka. After what we . . ." Joe said, ruffling Delilah's fur. "*Em-neeha*, Delilah? *Em-neeha*, *Habibti*?

"Delilah will be happy with you," Joe said.

They said their goodbyes. Maybe Delilah would be a less mercurial companion than Darlene. Captain Bell felt his earlier gloom lift. He began to work his way through the stack of paperwork on his desk. From the open window, he heard Joe whistling a tune he had never heard before. Then the oriental melody was lost in the whir of the engine.

CHAPTER 25.

# Thanksgiving, November 24th, 1935

**Sam fed Delilah, but she mostly followed Captain Bell around.** She even slept at the foot of his bed. Sometimes, if Sam was free in the afternoon, he and Chueco would play ball with her. A few boys at the camp called Delilah "Bell's Bitch" behind Captain Bell's back. Sam didn't like it, but he didn't rise to the bait. Nor did he tattle on them. He had too much to do. The entire upcoming issue of the *Round-Up* was devoted to Thanksgiving, the early Pilgrims, and turkeys. E.O. even chose some suitable Bible verses about blessings and thankfulness. By the time Sam finished the bulletin, he felt like squawking. Instead of making him happy, though, he started to feel homesick. This would be his first Thanksgiving away from his folks and Augusta. His mama had written to him: "We'll be all right and don't worry about us. Have enough potatoes and there's a chicken in the barn. Augusta is getting tall." She didn't mention his father.

But he didn't have much time to sulk, since Captain Bell kept giving him assignments. After the bulletin was finished, he was responsible for designing a special card with a menu for the day. He drew a cartoon of a turkey being chased by a cook with a knife. Underneath was a list of the menu: turkey with cornbread dressing, potatoes, canned sweet potatoes, green peas with butter, rolls. For dessert: pecan pie, apple pie, pumpkin pie. Mints, cigarettes, and cigars.

On Thanksgiving Day, he went over early to the mess hall before the guests arrived. Devilfish was standing on a chair, hanging orange streamers from the rafters. "Well, if it ain't the gambler? How's the nose?" Devilfish said, looking down at him. Other cooks were laying out orange tablecloths over the plain wooden tables lined with benches. The drab mess hall had been transformed into a cheerful, attractive place. It reminded Sam of the night of the dance.

"I wouldn't call myself a gambler," Sam said.

"Sho'," Devilfish said. "Anyone who takes on Otto is a gambler. Been thinkin' of inviting him for a little boxing practice, myself. Although rattlers best be left alone."

"I didn't take him on," Sam said. "Remember? He just put his fist through my face."

"Can you hand me that turkey?" Devilfish asked. He was hanging crudely cut-out turkeys from the ceiling. "We got to get you playing *cards* with us again. Or a little dice. Where you been keeping yerself?"

Once the mess hall was decorated, the cooks retreated to the kitchen, where they carved the huge turkeys with huge butcher knives.

It was Sam's job to hand out the cards as guests arrived. Darlene arrived first. Sam was surprised but she had not dressed up for the occasion. Everyone else was dressed to the nines in their formal green uniforms, with the CCC patch over the left breast pocket. She was still a beauty, but her hair was loose and uncombed. She was just wearing her shapeless white uniform, which had not even been pressed. She took the card without speaking. Sam was reminded of how ravishing she had looked at the dance with her low-cut dress, and her hair knotted into a bun on her head, as if she were a queen.

"Happy Thanksgiving!" Sam said, trying to catch her eye. But she shook her head dolefully, as if there was nothing to be happy about.

"What's wrong?"

She smiled ruefully. "Don't worry about me, sweetheart."

He hated when she patronized him. She chose one of the tables close to the kitchen. Dr. Walker followed close behind.

"My boy," Dr. Walker said. "Are you doing the honors on this fine Thanksgiving afternoon? We will feast upon game to commemorate the anomalous survival of those early settlers of the Mayflower after their first winter. If it had not been for Squanto, they would have certainly perished."

Sam was still handing out cards to all the boys, who had suddenly converged upon him. "Have a seat wherever you like, Dr."

Dr. Walker stood next to him, tinkering with his gold pocket watch. "As a matter of fact, many of the early settlers died from exposure, scurvy, and contagious diseases, spread by rats . . ."

What was scurvy? He didn't have time to ask Dr. Walker. One boy hooted, "Would ya look at those mashed potatoes. Can't wait to taste that gravy!" The cooks were bringing in the bowls, the steam rising from the plentiful, hot food, and set them on each table, family-style.

Dr. Walker shifted awkwardly beside him and then made a beeline for Darlene's table.

Darlene rolled her eyes at Sam, as if to say, "Can you believe it?"

No, she was acting as if they were friends. But he didn't dislike Dr. Walker, who had been very kind to him when he was in the infirmary. Sam wondered again about her age. Sometimes, he felt she was just thirty—and other times, he felt she seemed to have seen more of life.

Chueco appeared and embraced him. "Mister Sam," he said. They had rekindled their friendship, playing with Delilah in the afternoons. They took turns feeding her. Chueco missed his pet burro at Terlingua. Sam told him about Mr. Perry's appearance at the end of the camping trip. He said, "You have nothing to worry about." But Chueco had been doubtful. "He is El Perro, not like Delilah."

But before Sam could say another word, Chueco had drifted away. Soon he was chatting happily in Spanish with some of his Mexican pals on the far side of the room.

The boys crowded in and soon the tables were full. The noise from the excitement was deafening. The acoustics were poor in the mess hall. Sam couldn't hear himself think. One boy shouted, "You think they'll let us really smoke cigars?"

Captain Bell had said the blessing, and they sang "Amazing Grace." The boys belted out: "Amazing grace! How sweet the sound That saved a wretch like me! I once was lost, but now am found; Was blind, but now I see." Everyone was off-key, but they sang happily. The boys had already started to spoon out huge helpings of potatoes onto their plates when Joe Kafouri arrived, about twenty minutes late.

"Happy Thanksgiving!" Captain Bell said. His smile was crooked because of the sutures in his cheek. "It was our invitation. You didn't need to bring anything."

Joe smiled. "Ah, but this is my chance! You will taste some of the most delicious dishes of our country. The chicken is stuffed with chestnuts."

He pulled out a few unmarked glass bottles and uncorked one.

"As nourishing as orange juice, *Ay Wallah*, I swear. My grandmother's recipe from Zahle. They are famous for the arak."

Without asking if anyone wanted it, Joe poured a little of the mixture into a glass and then added water to it. It looked a little milky when diluted with water.

Joe was sitting next to Darlene, so he handed her the first glass. Then he handed one to Sam.

"Tastes like licorice," Sam said.

Joe winked at them. "*Dal helou la ilna.* This is our dessert."

Darlene suddenly laughed.

Sam wondered what was so funny. She was doleful when she came into the mess hall. Now she was laughing. He never could figure her out.

Captain Bell said, "Of course, we are grateful for all of this. But you must realize that we are not serving alcohol at the dinner."

Joe said, "But at least have a taste of my grandmother's recipe from Zahle." He smiled again. "There is no danger."

Before Captain Bell could finish, Dr. Walker interjected, "This beverage reminds me of absinthe. A beverage that I partook of in my younger days at Tulane. I do remember being imbibed once with this particular beverage when I attended the class on dissecting corpses. It was an unfortunate coincidence."

Darlene guffawed.

Sam was a little shocked by her crude laugh. She never mentioned her family. Where was she from?

Joe had refilled everyone's glasses at the table with his grandmother's recipe. He taught them the toast, "*Sahtain!*" To your health. It had a sweet, pleasing taste that complemented the nutty taste of the chestnuts in the chicken. Most of them had forgotten about the slabs of dry turkey breast on the table. They were plunging their spoons into the rice with nuts and cutting into Joe's moist chicken.

Captain Walker said, "I think your wife is a better cook than the cooks at the Menger Hotel. Our hotel in San Antonio."

"I was the cook!" Joe said. "It was my pleasure. You have to cook with love or you'll spoil the recipe. *Sahtain*! To your health!"

Sam was astounded. He couldn't imagine his father cooking a meal for the family. He thought that was sissy work. But this man was masculine, and he could make delicious food.

Misunderstanding Darlene's laugh, Dr. Walker continued, "After the absinthe and a fracas-laden night of blackjack and shenanigans, a group of us went down to the French Quarter and feasted on raw oysters. You can imagine that that did not sit well with the digestive system when we were ordered to slice open a cadaver."

But Joe was whispering something in Darlene's ear. He poured more of the milky mixture into Darlene's glass.

Sam could see that this was making Jack hopping mad. Jack elbowed him. "Get a load of that. Who does he think he is?"

Sam enjoyed the taste of Joe's grandmother's drink. He felt a little giddy. "You said yerself you're set on Ruby."

Perhaps he had spoken too plainly. He needed to hold back. But it seemed like he was blurting things out, which went against his nature.

"Think Ruby might have found another fella," Jack whispered. "Her feelings seem to have cooled. Not answering my letters."

Sam said, "Well, shoot. Sorry to hear that. But why don't you just enjoy the food and drink?"

"What happened with Charlotte?"

Sam shrugged. He took another bite of the moist chicken stuffed with chestnuts. "Can't stomach so much talk about sin. Gets up my britches."

Besides the nutty taste, there was the richness of butter and a hint of citrus.

Jack whispered, "Do you think Darlene is doing it with Joe?"

"Are you . . .?" Sam asked. It was none of his business. Was he getting drunk? There was a spice he didn't recognize in the chicken. Maybe the milky drink was stronger than it appeared.

But Jack smiled. "Don't kiss and tell. 'Course, there's a lot to tell."

That got Sam's goat. Jack was always bragging about his sweethearts, as if he were Mr. Romeo. How many he had. How handsome he was. How easy it was to attract them, as if he were the honey pot Cary Grant.

Sam blurted out, "Think she's sweet on Captain Bell."

Captain Bell looked up. Had he heard?

Sam regretted it the moment he said it. Jack looked so devastated. Sam whispered, "I mean, that's just talk. I don't know that for sure." Was E.O. just spreading rumors?

Sam looked at Darlene—she was now animated and tossing back the grandmother drink. Joe was regaling her with a story.

Captain Bell was looking thoughtfully at Dr. Walker, listening to the monologue.

Had he ruined Jack's Thanksgiving? But why were they all mooning over Darlene? She was so unpredictable. If there were other women around, would they care so much about every little thing she said or did? Even Captain Bell, who had years of experience on them . . . how had he fallen under Darlene's spell?

"Come on," Sam said. "Let's get some pie. Before it's gone. The boys will gobble 'em up."

Devilfish was bringing in the pies, which he set on a nearby table: pecan, apple, and pumpkin.

"Boys," Devilfish said, "take your pick of these sweet patooties. Rolled out the dough myself."

Otto was standing at the pie table. Sam should avoid him. He didn't need another busted nose.

Which one to try? They were all tempting. The crusts were a golden brown—just right. Hot out of the oven. Sam was stuffed, and he couldn't really eat another bite. His mother usually made pecan pie. He felt a pang of homesickness. Was his family having their dinner right now? Would his mama be able to afford the sugar for a pie? And it wouldn't be easy to get the pecans.

Otto took one entire pie and plopped it on his plate.

Devilfish wagged his finger at him. "You don't take the whole pie, mister."

Otto loomed in front of them, ominously. He said in a voice barely audible, "Back off, boy."

Devilfish didn't confront him. But he said, "I am going to git him. He won't be quick enough for my left jab."

Sam exchanged a look with Jack. Then they took their plates, piled high with pie, back to the table.

CHAPTER 26.

# Howard Perry

**Captain Bell just wished they could get through one major event at Balmorhea without an incident.** It seemed like they just lurched from crisis to crisis. He wasn't happy that Joe had brought the homemade arak, but he couldn't insult the man. He had met some Greeks in Paris who had introduced him to ouzo—and this arak drink tasted similar. But the two bottles disappeared, and no one was the wiser. He had to admit Joe's food was more delicious than the cooks at the Menger Hotel or the cooks at Balmorhea. And drinking a little arak with his chestnut chicken beat Vim soda pop.

Just as he was about to take a bite of pumpkin pie, a man wearing an expensive wool coat stood up with his two bodyguards, surveying the mess hall.

Captain Bell put his fork down.

Sam whispered in his ear, "Sir, it's Howard Perry. The one who owns Terlingua Quicksilver Mine."

"I know who he is," Captain Bell said. He had heard from some of the locals how he bullied officials in Brewster County. One night when he was restless, he had motored over to Fort Davis and hung out at the Hotel Limpia bar. The court reporter, Billy, was sitting on the next stool. He told him about all the cases against Perry—and all the workers at the mine who had been badly hurt or even died and the families who had brought cases against him.[1] Billy said, "Not all of them sued. But hell, from what you hear. Fallin' down shafts. Cracked skulls. Broken jaws. Severe burns. Legs caught in flywheels. The man might have money, but he'll pay when he meets his Maker! I overheard him as he was leaving the courthouse. Know what he said? 'A dead man isn't worth much, anyway . . . When a plaintiff is dead, the court loses interest . . .'"

Captain Bell pushed the bench back and went over to see them. The two bodyguards were wearing shoulder holsters.

Captain Bell held out his hand, but Mr. Perry didn't shake it. "Happy Thanksgiving, gentlemen. Why don't you put your guns down and have a little turkey with us?"

The chunkier one with the beady eyes said, "We have been on the road all morning, Mr. Perry."

Mr. Perry held up his hand, imperiously, as if he were a Roman emperor, and the chunky man was not supposed to speak.

Captain Bell didn't have time for such a pompous man. He had to put up with officers like this in the Marines during the War, but he wasn't going to stand for it now. What could Perry do to him, anyway? He had lost his face and his arm. He had already faced the threat of death.

"Did you ever find Dr. Volkov?" Captain Bell asked.

"Flat disappeared off of the face of the earth," Perry said. "How do you know about that?"

"I have my sources," Captain Bell said. "What do you want with

Dr. Volkov?"

"None of your business," Mr. Perry snapped. "I am looking for Joe Kafouri."

So maybe he'd had a transplant operation that had gone awry?

"Why?"

"Let's just say I have business with him," Mr. Perry said. "I see him over there at that table."

"He's our guest. As you can see, we are having a party. I'll see if he wants to speak with you."

"He doesn't have a choice," Mr. Perry said.

Captain Bell was dumbfounded by his arrogance, but he didn't lose his cool. Then he looked at the two men accompanying Perry. "You gentlemen work for the law. Have a warrant?"

"Pinkerton Detectives. Chicago," the one with the pencil moustache said. "Don't have a warrant."

"So you don't have any authority to be barging in on our Thanksgiving party? Trying to intimidate people?"

The chunkier one said, sheepishly, "We're just private eyes."

"I own the county," Perry said. "I can get a sheriff to come any time."

"Last time I checked we live in a democracy," Captain Bell said. "There's something called 'rule of law.'"

Joe appeared beside him. "Ah," he said, completely unfazed, twirling his moustache. "It is Mr. Perry. You are a long way from Terlingua. Are you visiting your family? Why aren't you eating the turkey like the other Americans?"

"You and your brother stop selling your wares to my workers!" Howard Perry said. "You hear! They buy from the Chisos store. And Chisos only.[2] If I catch one of your trucks near Terlingua, I will . . ."

Joe smiled. "But is a free country, no? They like our cloth. They like to marvel at the notions we have. How do you say it in Amereeka? Trinkets?"

"You're an A-rab," Mr. Perry said. "Why, you're not even a citizen of our country!"

Captain Bell said, "That's enough. You're not welcome here."

"You're not complying with the law, either," Mr. Perry said. "Black people are supposed to be in their own CCC camps."

"If I have to ask you another time, I am going to call the sheriff. You are trespassing on federal property," Captain Bell said.

He hoped Perry wouldn't call his bluff. What if Perry did contact federal authorities? He would be in the doghouse for disobeying the order to segregate.

The chunky detective intervened. "Mr. Perry, we'd better go."

Mr. Perry put on his fedora. "I do the deciding around here."

Captain Bell escorted them out of the mess hall and watched as they got into a shiny yellow roadster.

Captain Bell apologized to Joe, patting him on the shoulder. "I am sorry. Some of our countrymen are not very friendly to strangers."

But Joe shrugged it off. "We are still happier here. We are not starving." His eyes suddenly filled with tears. "The locusts devoured everything in 1916—why we left. I will not disgust you with the creatures we were forced to eat."

"Well, you are safe now," Captain Bell said.

He was safe from the threat of hunger, at least. But Captain Bell worried about Mr. Perry. What did he have up his sleeve?

Joe dabbed his face with a cloth handkerchief. "I must return. My wife is running the store . . . But thank you, *habibi*, darling." The tears had disappeared and he smiled. "For your *Beit el-Ward.* This house of roses."

Maybe the part of the dinner where he was sipping arak was

rose-like. But it had turned thorny. He breathed a sigh of relief. At last, he could enjoy the rest of his pie.

Most of the boys had cleared out. The cooks were carrying out the empty dishes from the tables.

Perry and his goons had not been gone more than fifteen minutes when Sam rushed into the mess hall, breathless. He had been running.

"For crying out loud, what is it now?" Captain Bell asked.

Sam shook his head. He was out of breath. "Sir."

"Go on, then. Speak up. What is it, son?" Captain Bell said, softening his tone.

"It's Chueco," Sam said. "He's disappeared. I think Mr. Perry must have kidnapped him."

CHAPTER 27.

# Darlene's Diary, November 24, 1935

I am having a hard time feeling thankful. *Thankful that I escaped from B. I had enjoyed the little sadomasochistic games when we first married, but it became tiresome, being tied up. Lying on the poster bed as he licked off the molasses that he smeared on my breasts.*

*As if it weren't bad enough playing nurse in real life, he made me play nurse in the bedroom. Bend over, honey. Or playing a count. And I was the countess. Was so horny, he didn't even wait to take off my clothes. Bend over, Minerva. That's an order.*

*Got hooked on the lifestyle. The easy living. The money. The cruise to Italy.*

*I drew the line when he started chasing me with a whip.*

*How had I been led down the garden path by B.? In the beginning, I had believed all of that malarkey when he had lectured at Galveston. His confidence was intoxicating.*

*Thankful that no one has guessed about me. Or am I underestimating all of these men at Balmorhea?*

*Bell hasn't been quite so friendly. Did he write to the oilman in Houston? If I told him about Wonder Cure, that would blow my cover.*

*Thankful that I finished my nurse's training. Thankful that I enjoy the work, even if Doc Walker is a pompous old fart.*

*Thankful that I still have a job. Have a little money. But for how long?*

*Thankful that I am not milking cows on a dusty old farm in Texarkana.*

*But of course, the worst part of all is being separated from my son. If I sue, then I have to use my real name. Don't think B. ever divorced Sally. Just told me he did. Maybe J. is not legitimate?*

*Named in Fishbein's article.*

*Was it only a matter of time until the victims of the families in Kansas found out where we were? Then what?*

*J. keeps appearing in my dreams. Mama. Mama. Please don't leave me. Impossible to quell the ache. I don't want to be with Daddy. Daddy beats me. Daddy is MEAN.*

*How dare he? How dare he?*

*Underestimated B.'s contacts in Kansas. Thought we were safe in Mrs. Milly's boarding house. But the sheriff yanked the boy straight out of my arms and said, "You're not fit to be a mother. Go on back to Texas. Find yerself a cowboy." Bad scene. J.'s screams curdled in my ears.*

*B. had said, "I swear if you sue for custody, we'll lock you up in the nuthouse. I have friends everywhere in Kansas. Isn't that right, Sheriff?"*

*But he's too small and will only be dragged around from town to town, state to state, like the child of a movie star. Had things gotten worse, really, after they had gone to L.A.? B. had thought he would operate on every famous movie star in Hollywood.*

*California Medical Association didn't buy the act. We regret to inform you that there are multiple discrepancies in your documents. You are hereby . . .*

*Kansas, California, back to Kansas, then Texas.*[1]

*But was I such a paragon of virtue? I cringe when I think of that one old farmer, who looked into my eyes with such trust before he went under. What was his name? Lynch. Lynchwell. No. Lightwell. Mr. Lightwell smiled and said, "So this'll do the trick, you say?" Graft didn't take. Died of septicemia.*

*Feel like I am swimming underwater. Hiding my feelings all the time.*

*Have to keep sending J. letters. Hope and pray he gets them. But Sally, maybe not so inclined…*

*What if I am just writing letters to myself?*

*Is J. having a Thanksgiving lunch in the Del Rio mansion with Sally, B., and the monkeys?*

*We have two hundred hungry monkeys here. Ha! Save a wretch like me.*

*Haven't been in the mood for any more cuddles with Jack. He is pressing me. Can't tell him. It was a mistake to kiss Captain Bell. Leading him on.*

*Best part of Thanksgiving was the licorice drink. Better than Doc Walker's Scotch. Heavy price for the Scotch, listening to Doc's maudlin speeches and fusty poems.*

*At dinner, he kept going on about cutting open cadavers. Am pretty sure no one was interested.*

*Joe made me laugh. The funny way he talks. The food! The pleasurable taste of the licorice with the chestnuts. Put me in a better mood.*

*Lick me, Joe. I wish. But maybe he wouldn't mind a side dish apart from the main course? Have to see what his wife looks like.*

*'Course there was the cruise to Italy. Never thought the Italians would have bought B.'s act. But they fell for it and granted him the honorary doctorate at Pavia.*

*If I could return to Italy . . .*

*Penne pasta with homemade tomato sauce, a hint of spice, with fresh squid. I will take that any day over overcooked green peas, lumpy potatoes and greasy gravy. Huge slabs of turkey.*

*Finally, feeling lighter. A tad more thankful. As if I were floating. Thank you, Joe's grandma, if you are still on this earth!*

*Sam runs into the mess hall and tells us that Chueco has been kidnapped.*

*Bell organized a search party. And we all had to pitch in. Searched high and low for him. For at least three hours.*

*"He's afraid of Mr. Perry. Calls him El Perro."*

*What? The dog. Yes, the dog.*

*"Aloe vera didn't save his Uncle Carlos. Señor Perry said that Uncle Carlos was*

*stealing gasoline from the compressor. His pants were wet with gasoline and when he tried to light his lamp, his clothes caught on fire."*

*Bell said Chueco's family lost the case against Perry.*[2] *Didn't get a cent. How did he know?*

*Doesn't want to go back to Terlingua. Work in the mine.*

*Bless Delilah. She led us to Chueco. A trail of lanterns, flickering in the dark, like lightning bugs.*

*Bell scratched Delilah behind the ears. "Good girl."*

*Then he said, "Thank God."*

*Chueco was curled up in a ball, in the pit of the swimming pool. Sam jumped into the pit. "El Perro is gone. Come on."*

*I was the closest thing to a mama. He rushed into my arms and hugged me. He was crying. "Muy malo. Muy malo." He was trembling. "We become dead muscas."*

*Malo?*

*"Evil," Sam said. "Mr. Perry's evil."*

*I started crying, too.*

*On the way back to the barracks, Bell asked, "Are you all right? We found Chueco. No need to cry."*

*I longed to see my boy, J. One year. Starting first grade soon.*

*Longed to tell. But all I said was, "Had my share of sadness."*

*Captain Bell said, "Know what you mean."*

*Thought of all those old farmers who had perished because of B.'s grand promises. Live forever. Be a bull forever. I had assisted. One night I dreamed of Rita Lightwell, her unwashed hair covered with a red bandana, sitting on her front porch, staring out at an empty field.*

*Lightwell's voice echoed in my head. "Say, will this do the trick?"*

CHAPTER 28.

# Sam, Arroyo Drive, Harlingen, Texas, Thanksgiving, 1976

He was outside, tinkering in his garden in the backyard. The air was muggy. Maggie was inside, cooking up a storm, and he needed to be out of her way. The whole family was coming over for lunch. He couldn't just keep sitting at the dining room table, gazing out the large picture window, feeling sorry for himself. Or rummaging through old diaries and letters from the attic. But he couldn't stop reading about Balmorhea. Although as he reread the diaries, it was clear Darlene hadn't really taken him seriously, or even Jack. A chachalaca squawked and flew after his mate, who was perched in a nearby ash tree. They were gangly, aggressive white and black birds, indigenous to the border—and he had never seen one in

West Texas. He found their squawking cheerful, not annoying. Since he had moved here in 1944, he had become used to their morning squawking.

His foot hit a dip in the yard, and he almost tripped. Steady now. He felt proud of himself, that he recovered his balance. He had given up on the shoulder brace. When he turned around, he noticed that Maggie was watching him from the picture window. She was frowning. But when their eyes met, she smiled and waved. She was his girl.

Passing the ebony tree, he noticed that the hummingbird feeder was empty. Maybe one of his grandkids could help him get it down—he wouldn't trust himself to stay on a ladder. Then they could pour the syrupy red sugar into the feeder.

He yearned to see a ruby-throated hummingbird with shiny emerald feathers.

Since the doctors at Duke were experimenting, they didn't know what they were doing—and it had burned the skin and left red splotches up and down his arm. But the radiation had also caused another kind of cancer that had eventually killed the nerves in his arm. At what juncture did the cure become the poison?

He was delighted by the Mexican blue-wing butterfly that fluttered by him. Dabs of iridescent blue on black. It had white spots. It was heading toward the brick wall covered with creepers; the little orange blooms looked like trumpets. The vivid colors lifted his spirits. They had grown wild and didn't need to be tended.

It was the first time he had been out in his garden since he had lost his arm. The yard looked neglected; it needed to be weeded. Should he start now? Even though it was only late morning, he felt tired. He ignored the weeds and tottered toward the brick patio, shaped like a crescent, in front of his small pond. The water smelled rank. He flipped on the switch, and immediately the water gurgled with life.

In the right corner was a slab of marble, where he potted plants. Where was his trowel? Had someone swiped it? Small orange pots were stacked on the slab. He had intended to plant violet petunias. His cloth gloves were lying next to the pots, where he had left them over a month ago.

He tried to wiggle his fingers into the right glove. It was difficult without the help of his left hand to pull on the glove. Yet it felt as if the arm was still there. But, of course, it wasn't. Then he tried to pull his hand out, but his fingers were stuck in the middle of the glove. He didn't have to plant anything yet. Things that had been easy before were more difficult now. He shook the glove up and down until it became looser. The glove fell onto the red brick, covered with leaves.

"Dammit," he said, reaching down with difficulty to pick up the glove. He tossed the glove back onto the marble slab.

His son had wanted a cutting from one of his Petra Crotons. He loved these plants with their red, orange, and yellow veins. They had almost outgrown the tiled blue pot he had bought in Mexico. All he needed was his pruning shears. But then, suddenly, he lost confidence after his failure to put on the glove. The shears felt heavy in his hand. But why was he giving up so easily?

He snipped a branch off and placed it next to his small red pots. At least that was done.

A bag of birdseed had been torn open and was spilled on the bricks. Looked like the raccoons had gotten into it, or a possum. A broom was leaning against the ebony tree. He swept the seeds into a little pile with his one arm.

When he turned around to find the dustpan, a green jay was pecking at the corn. He was bold, completely unafraid. Sam didn't feel bold. He envied the bird.

"Well, hello, young fella," Sam said.

The green jay had a blue head, rimmed with black around his eyes, as if he were wearing a mask. He had rich green feathers.

Sam had only tried one criminal case in his entire law career. It was a case of negligent homicide: a driver had veered off the road and run over a ten-year-old girl. The client had failed the alcohol test and couldn't remember hitting the girl. The psychologist testified it was a case of regressive amnesia: people who experience traumatic events can't remember what happened. They had caused a doubt in the jury's mind, by casting a doubt on a defective wheel that had somehow caused the car to shear in the wrong direction. He wouldn't say that Darlene was suffering from regressive amnesia. And what about the flimflam con man, Brinkley? But everyone was entitled to a defense, no matter the charge: "Innocent until proven guilty."

He didn't know why Darlene was coming to him in dreams now. He really had been foolish over that bosomy nurse.

Most of his law cases were smaller fish. Bread and butter, domestic and municipal. A picayunish and troublesome divorce case: divide the property down to the last chicken and egg. An optometrist who wanted to spread his ashes on the island of Waikiki, a fair distance from Harlingen, Texas. When you think about it, it was a mighty selfish request, given the distance and the cost. A fractious barber who had filed for divorce four times, then retracted. A Black lady who had sued the bus company when a suitcase had fallen off a rack and injured her spine. Evictions, wills, water rights, land titles. He and Maggie had even delivered a baby to the adoptive parents once the papers were signed. His granddaughter, Rosemary, wanted to go into law. He didn't want to discourage any young person, but just said, "It's not Perry Mason. Why don't you work in the office one summer? See what it's like."

A woodpecker was pecking at the ebony tree. He was delighted. He felt as if these birds were welcoming him back. Could it be? Were they aware of his absence in the garden? He remembered how Delilah had led them to Chueco that day in the swimming pool. They would never have thought to look for him there. Did animals have a greater consciousness and sensitivity than humans gave them credit for?

Initially, he had been attracted to the law because his daddy had been chiseled. He thought of Chueco's Uncle Carlos, who had been badly burned from an accident at the Chisos mine. His family had lost the case against Perry. On the other hand, the big guns didn't always win. He remembered a case with Amoco years ago at a plant in the port of Brownsville where they were converting natural gas into gasoline, which the Germans perfected during World War II. Two workers were badly burned from an explosion. He had represented the widows and gotten them a settlement by proving "gross negligence" on the part of the company.

He admired Captain Bell's courage, his sense of fairness. He supposed he would be in his nineties if he were alive. He should write to him again. Had he ever remarried?

His granddaughter, Rosemary, stood in front of him. He almost blurted out her nickname, "The Lion," but then thought better of it.

"Grandaddy, your cheeks are wet," she said.

"Sweat," he said, wiping his long sleeve on his face. "Weather's muggy even in November. What happened to you?"

Her face was bright red, especially her nose. "Was playing in a tennis tournament."

"You're fair, and you've got to protect your skin," he said. "We'll fix you up with a little aloe vera. Get me the shears."

He was standing next to a cluster of aloe vera. She handed him the shears, and he clipped off a shoot. He sat down on a wrought-iron porch chair and peeled back a piece of the skin with a pocketknife without a problem. Underneath was a green gelatin. He rubbed the gelatin on her nose with his one hand. He heard Chueco's voice. He was talking about his mother. Magdalena says: "We must respect the plants and the nature. With God's help, they can save us."

"You'll be in fine fettle in no time. This will take out the sting. It's like a salve. But make sure next time to put on sunscreen."

But she wasn't paying attention. "We lost."

"Well," he said. "These things happen . . . There'll be another tournament."

His words didn't seem to comfort her. Aloe vera hadn't been enough to save Chueco's Uncle Carlos—it must have been a terrible death. Why was he thinking about this now? What had been the shampoo that had cured Bell's sunstroke? A shampoo made of sunflowers.

"How are you feeling?" Rosemary asked. "Any better?"

"Fair," he said. He didn't want to complain. But was it only his arm that was bothering him?

Maggie was calling from the backsteps. "Y'all come on. Dinner is ready."

He felt as if he were waving back, but it was just the nerves of his arm. His mind seemed disconnected from his body.

"Let's take some flowers for the table," he said. He had to stop moping. He plucked a few red blooms from a hibiscus bush and handed them to Rosemary.

Then they went inside for Thanksgiving dinner.

# PART III:

# CLEAN LIVING

CHAPTER 29.

# Ho, Ho, Ho: Christmas, 1935

**If Sam had been homesick at Thanksgiving, Christmas was worse.** No one had enough money to go home for Christmas. They could be granted a leave, but they would have to pay for their own transportation or hitchhike home.

Sam sat at his desk. He was not in the mood. He didn't want to work on a phony newsletter about Christmas. He pecked one letter at a time.

Captain Bell stood in front of him. His left sleeve was tucked into the side of his pants. "Cheer up."

"What's there to cheer about?" Sam said, looking at the headline, the *Round-Up*. Ho, ho, ho.

"You're in charge of entertainment. We'll put on a play, and Devilfish and his band can play after."

E.O. chimed in, singing in a baritone voice, "We three kings of Orient are."

Sam was surprised. E.O. had a good voice, yet belonged to a church that forbade music and song.

"Write a little play," Captain Bell said. "It doesn't have to be serious."

"I can write whatever I want?" Sam said, bouncing the pencil up and down on his desk. This was tempting. He already felt lighter.

"Yes," Captain Bell said. "I'll act in the play if you need volunteers."

"Really?" Sam said. "Thank you, Captain."

In a few days, Sam had written a short script and had assigned roles for the play. Captain Bell agreed to be Joseph; Darlene would be the Virgin Mary; Delilah would be the "babe" in the manger; E.O. would be the innkeeper; Angel of God, Chueco; Wise Man, Dr. Walker.

They met in the rec hall and practiced a few times. But the day before Christmas, Darlene appeared in the office, her hands on her hips. "You'll have to find another Virgin Mary," she said. "Something came up. I'm not in the mood."

Sam was bewildered. "But you're the only woman at the camp. Are you sure you won't change your mind?"

Things had been going so well. Everyone was enthusiastic about the play, even Dr. Walker. Had Darlene quarreled with him?

"Is it the doctor?" he asked.

Darlene shook her head, her eyes welling with tears. Why was she crying?

The same day, Joe passed by to deliver the supplies for Christmas dinner. He pulled out the receipt and handed it to E.O.: "The manifest for the goods."

"Would you like to be in our play?" Sam asked. He had nothing to lose. He was desperate.

Joe bowed, as if he were a showman in the circus and had just performed an act, instead of delivering the bill for supplies from a dry-goods grocery store.

Sam handed him the script. "You will be the Virgin Mary. We can strap a pillow around you to make you look pregnant."

Joe laughed. "I will be the Virgin! But you have the nurse, Darlene. Is she ailing?"

"I don't know what's wrong," Sam said. Did anyone in the camp know her innermost thoughts? He doubted it.

"The show must go on," Joe said. "Isn't that what they say at the Stanley Graham's World-Famous International Midgets' Circus?"

The next day, a few hours after a hearty Christmas dinner, much like what they had eaten at Thanksgiving, the boys gathered in the rec hall. There was an excited hum from the audience. Captain Bell was draped in a sheet for a robe. He was wearing his swimming trunks underneath. With his one hand, he was holding onto the sheet. Everyone was praising him for being such a good sport.

They had found a green World War I raincoat for Joe and stuffed a pillow inside to make him look pregnant. He was wearing an orange-colored wig, which didn't match his Turkish-style moustache. He was bowlegged, but walked as if he were a ballet dancer.

The boys drummed their hands on the tables and stomped their feet. "More!"

Sam carried in a sign that said THE DREAM.

Then Chueco skipped in. They had fashioned a set of wings from a cardboard box. "My dear girl, I have a surprise for you. You are expecting . . ."

Joe said, "But Lord, I have not done the deed with anyone . . ."

The boys stomped their feet.

Sam carried in the sign for Dream #2: THE SECOND

SURPRISE.

Chueco said: "My dear man, your beloved Mary is in the family way . . ."

The boys shouted, "NOOOOOOOOOOOOOOOOOOOO. Bad boy!"

Joe looked at Captain Bell and said in a falsetto voice, "I have been a good girl. I swear."

The laughter was raucous. The boys were having fun. Someone shouted, "She's been doing it in the barn. Yeah! Eeeee doggie!"

Sam carried in a sign that said: GOD IS LOVE.

E.O. said in a stern voice, "There is no room at the inn." The boys booed. "But there's a stable in the back."

The boys shouted, "Yeah!"

Sam carried Delilah and set her down in a cardboard box. On the side of the box was written: Brinkley Pharmaceutical Company.

Dr. Walker was playing the Wise Man and carried in the leftovers from the Christmas dinner. He knelt down and said to Delilah, "Lord, I come bringing ye great tidings of joy. It is the best we could do since we had no gold. Corn on the cob, a turkey leg, and a piece of pecan pie. We hope such an offering will not insult the babe. As we are offering our profound respect and honor for the babe, who is in fact, the Son of God."

Delilah barked. She jumped out of the box.

Dr. Walker continued, "I hope, Lord, that you are not displeased that I was unable to bring the myrrh and frankincense. Boys, you do know what those two items are, I presume. But you may not know that frankincense comes from the trunk of the Boswellian tree. It kills bacteria . . ."

Sam was afraid of this. Dr. Walker had gone off script.

"Of course, at the time of Jesus, it was used in fragrances."

The boys booed.

Sam carried in the sign, "THE END."

But Dr. Walker continued to speak. "But you should know that the ancient Egyptians used it in their mummification process. They put it in cleansed body cavities."

Joe embraced Captain Bell and said, "Oh, Joseph, I will love you forever." Spontaneously, he sang, "That's Stella by Starlight, and not a dream" by Frank Sinatra.

Just as quickly, the boys' mood changed and they cheered.

The other actors trooped off the stage. Sam was happy that Joe had saved the audience from one of Dr. Walker's ponderous lectures. The play had been a hit. Maybe he would go into writing and journalism, after all.

Soon after, Devilfish and his band started to play. He sang, "Ooh, shugah pie, sho' enough, ding-dong. Ding, ding, ding. It's been so long. Touch my dong, dong, dong . . ."[1]

Devilfish sang, "Sing it to me, boys. That's just like Li'l Johnson."

They stomped their feet and raised bottles of Wonder Cure.

Wonder Cure? Who had distributed that? Sam thought it was forbidden. Had Captain Bell told Jack that Wonder Cure contained opium?

They were shouting at the tops of their lungs: "Ding, ding, ding. It's been so long. Touch my dong, dong, dong."

A few minutes later, Captain Bell had changed out of his costume and was in full uniform now. "Where did they get the Wonder Cure?"

"I don't know," Sam said.

"Where's Jack?" Captain Bell said. "He has the key to the cupboard in the canteen."

"Thought he would be here," Sam said. He searched the crowd. The boys were getting high. Some of them had smuggled food out of the cafeteria and had started a food fight. Others were chasing each other in the melee. Someone shouted, "The ram that I am with every lamb."

But Devilfish kept singing, "It's been so long . . . Baby, come touch my dong."[2]

Captain Bell took the microphone from Devilfish. "Party's over, boys. Leave the bottles here."

Everyone groaned. It took at least fifteen minutes to clear the hall. A few stragglers left reluctantly.

The captain summoned Sam. Sam feared the sternness in his voice. "Find Jack."

CHAPTER 30.

# Darlene's Diary, Christmas, 1935

Thought being in the play would be fun. *But Christmas has been worse than Thanksgiving. Feeling very low. Thinking about J. Wouldn't be there on Christmas day, when he skipped down the marble staircase to open his presents from Santa. Would Sally give him the Blue Comet toy train that I had sent?*

*I had a feeling in the pit of my stomach, she would not.*

*Ached to hear his voice, Mama, Mama.*

*Last Christmas, B. dressed up as Santa Claus and handed me a pink silk lingerie set. A cone-shaped bra with underwear, lace-trimmed on the bottom. You'll get the diamonds later, if you oblige. Do the naughty, instead of the nice, like Santa tells you.*

*Bend over, my little Elf. Drunk as a cootered skunk. Too much bourbon. Wanted to do it in front of the Italian mirror so he could see himself while he was thrusting. On my knees, rubbed raw on the marble floor.*

*But he was too drunk. Even though I loved the cruise to Italy, this was tiresome. Starting to weary of the bargain.*

*Chased me around the rosewood piano with a butcher knife. He had done that once in Milford in front of patients. Afterwards, lost his license.*

*Take your own feckin' Wonder Cure!*

*When I ran outside to the backyard, with the three-hundred-pound tortoises we had stolen from the Galápagos, he had locked me out. Made me sleep outside. With the geese, the peacocks, the flamingos, and the penguins. Del Rio, too swampy for the penguins. Poor things. They need icy weather.*

*Spent all night staring at our swimming pool, glittery with light. His name, dotted in tile behind the pool: Brinkley. Colors of the rainbow. In the living room was a four-foot oil painting of him in an admiral uniform, next to a marlin. "Marlin and Yours Truly." Did he think he was the Duce?*

*Where was Minerva? No oil paintings of me in our house.*

*That's when I decided to apply to the CCC. I could work. Could use another name. It had worked so far. But felt like I was walking a tightrope.*

*Joe had very kindly helped me pick out the train set from the catalog. He didn't have any children. Said they had always wanted them, but . . .*

*He smiled. Charmed by his smile. "But I thought you were . . . ?"*

*I had laughed. It's a sad story. You won't tell Captain Bell. It's our little secret.*

*He shook his head. You'll see that the toy train goes to Del Rio? Copied out the address.*

*Joe's wife said something to him in their language. A-R-A-B-I-C. She didn't like it, whatever she saw. She also had curly hair, like him. Looks like his sister. Surely not. Cousin?*

*Joe winked at me. Then I left the store. Drove on back to the camp.*

*Red was not happy with me. Rather just sulk, alone in my little room.*

*The article in the Alpine Avalanche about B.'s Christmas party put me off. Some reporter had really been taken in. There were reports of B.'s "bountiful Christian generosity."*[1] *Food parcels for the poor. Handsome donations to the Texas Society for the Friendless. A rich friendship with Father Flanagan and the Catholic Church. What a crock! On Christmas Eve, B. had opened the gates. Come one, come all. Fried catfish for the town. Sacks of oranges. Chairs on the lawn, so they could watch the fountains, shooting up water hundreds of feet in the air. A light show, full of color, zigzagged across the sky. Let the children come to the zoo out back. Pet the tortoises . . .*

*Step right up.*

*Knock at the door. I didn't want to see anybody.*

*Another knock.*

*Oh, all right, I said, unlatching the door.*

*Jack!*

*He smiled. "Why aren't you at the Christmas party?"*

*He sat down on the bed. There wasn't room for a chair. Did they have to put me in the broom closet?*

*Held my hand. I pulled away.*

*He frowned. "Darlene, what's wrong?" Tried to kiss me. "No one can figure you out."*

*No. It doesn't feel right. Wiggled free.*

*Couldn't tell him about J. or B.*

*What do you mean? It doesn't feel right. He stroked my arm.*

*It felt good. But I was giving this boy the wrong idea.*

*I was so lonely.*

*But there would be hell to pay. Couldn't get pregnant. Taking too many chances. I had taken a few of the condoms from our supply. Didn't think Doc Walker would notice.*

*He kissed my ear.*

*"Whatta you mean? You never refused before."*

*"What about Ruby? Thought you were sweet on her? Saving for a ring?"*

*"Found some other fella. Now's our chance. They're busy with the play."*

*Think of your future.*

*"We could go away together," Jack said.*

*Did J. get the toy train? Was he getting my letters?*

*Now's not the time. He pulled up my nightgown and sucked one of my nipples.*

*Good boy! Come to Mama.*

*Didn't mind that he was taking liberties. Could forget all my troubles. Would be so easy.*

*He started taking off his pants.*

*I told you.*

*I giggled. His cock was erect as a rod. He was burning up.*

*Had to use my mind for once.*

*No.*

*Girls always say no, when they mean yes.*

*Someone's rapping at the door. Urgently. I put my finger to my lips.*

*"Yes," I said. "Who is it?"*

*"Sam."*

*"Yes? Do you mind? I don't feel well. Is somebody hurt? Can't you get Dr. Walker?"*

*"I'm looking for Jack. Have you seen him?"*

*"For crying out loud," I said. "Why would I know where he is?" Could imagine the kid, scratching his head. Head full of red hair. Naive, but not dumb.*

*Were we really fooling anybody at the camp? Everyone knew we were carrying on . . . but just how much?*

*Jack's about to roar with laughter.*

*"Captain Bell wants him. All right," Sam says, "I'll keep looking."*

*Did he believe me?*

*I called out. "Is it an emergency? Know what it's about?"*

*Jack's frowning.*

*Sam says, "Captain Bell wants to see Jack."*

*I said, "Haven't see hide nor hair of him."*

*Sam says, "I'll keep looking." Heard the door to the clinic slam.*

*Jack pulled on his pants. Lickety-split. "I better go."*

*"Know what it's about?"*

*"No," Jack said.*

CHAPTER 31.

# Captain Bell

**Maybe the bawdy play had been a mistake.** It was hard to find the right balance between discipline and fun. But if he were too strict, that would be cruel, especially at Christmastime. Why had Jack distributed Wonder Cure to the entire camp when he had told him to lock it up? Only E.O. and Sam knew about the opium. Bell blamed himself. He should have destroyed that sorry drink, poured it away. But he had been following up other details and quite simply had forgotten about it. He wasn't omniscient. Not that he thought he was God!

He needed to make an example of Jack so the boys wouldn't think they could get away with breaking the rules, going wild. If they went wild, they'd never finish the pool in time for the official opening set for the summer. Former Governor Neff was slated to come.

"I can't find him," Sam said. "Have looked everywhere."

Captain Bell was sitting in the empty rec hall on one of the benches. The place was littered with Wonder Cure bottles. He picked one up and studied it. A red cock was embossed on the label. Cures malaise, biliousness, and erectile dysfunction. Vim! Everlasting Youth, Vim, and Vitality! Had Dr. Fishbein ever found that Brinkley character? Flimflam man?

Leftover mashed potatoes were smeared on the planks of the floor. Homeless folks were wandering the country on trains, searching for a crust of bread. It made him furious.

"Did you go to Darlene's room?" Captain Bell asked.

"Yes," Sam said. "She said she didn't know where he was."

Captain Bell grunted. He was almost sure that Jack had been with Darlene. He almost said, "She's lying," but he refrained from saying it. Did he wish that he were with her? He repressed his rage.

"Did you go out to the building site?" Captain Bell asked. "The pool?"

"Nobody there," Sam said. "Nothing there but a hawk."

But what would be the attraction of being there for Jack? He wasn't Chueco. He wasn't a solitary character. He fancied himself a ladies' man. If he wasn't at the party, he was likely chasing tail. Darlene or a local girl?

"Did you see Darlene?" he asked.

"No," Sam said. "She didn't open the door."

"Okay," Bell said. But was it?

"Said she didn't feel well," Sam said. "Asked if it were an emergency. She said that Dr. Walker should handle it."

Captain Bell knew she felt just fine. He touched his disfigured cheek. "I imagine there are a good many things we don't know about Darlene."

"Sir," Sam said.

He was sharing too much with Sam, but he couldn't control himself.

"We all have secrets," Captain Bell said. "Anyhow, I'm not running a monastery."

Jack appeared with a broom. "Thought I might help clean up this mess. The cooks told me what happened."

"Where were you?" Captain Bell asked.

"In the barracks. I was drawing in my notebook. Felt the need to be on my own," Jack said.

"Sam, did you check the barracks?"

"Yes, Captain."

"Did you see Jack?"

"No, Sir, I did not."

"You might think you are a smart-aleck," Captain Bell said. "But I know that you were with Darlene."

He ventured a bluff to see what would happen.

Jack ruffled his thick, black hair. "I swear I wasn't."

"I wouldn't lie if I were you," Captain Bell said. "I could send you back home. Expel you from the camp."

Did he want to force the kid to confess about Darlene? But wasn't the main issue the Wonder Cure? Was he flagellating Jack because he felt ugly?

"Please, Captain Bell," Jack said. "My family needs the thirty dollars a month."

"So, you still deny that you were with Darlene?"

"Yes," Jack said. He was a good liar. Never wavered. Was he this way with the girls? *You are the only one! I swear, darlin', just one kiss under the moon. One roll in the hay.*

"But you were in a compromised position when Sam knocked on the door?"

Sam was giving him a queer look. Why was he continuing in this line of questioning? The issue was Wonder Cure.

Captain Bell stood up. "Three days in the brig. For lying to me.

And for selling Wonder Cure."

"What?" Jack asked. "I never sold the Wonder Cure. Captain, it's been under lock and key. Just like you asked."

"How do you explain the fact that all of the boys were drinking Wonder Cure?"

"I don't know, but I swear I never sold it to them," Jack said. "You have to believe me."

"But you've just sworn that you weren't with Darlene. Why should I believe you?"

"Maybe someone stole my key?" Jack said. "Just check. Please."

Captain Bell was unmoved. He had been too soft on the boys. He had to be tough or they would never respect him. The camp would degenerate into chaos without discipline. A little fear wasn't a bad thing, as he had learned with his squad in the Great War.

"Take him to the brig," he said.

CHAPTER 32.

# The Brig

**Sam felt Captain Bell was making a mistake.** He felt he should intercede for Jack.

"Captain Bell, why don't we check to see if the Wonder Cure is still there?"

But Captain Bell had made up his mind. "Three days in the brig," he repeated. He wasn't going to reconsider his decision, or be dissuaded.

Captain Bell handed over the large skeleton key to the brig. Sam and Jack walked over to the brig, which was a small, stark wooden hut with a single latrine next to the camp office. Bell rarely sent anyone to the brig—he usually punished the boys with latrine duty or denial of leaves.

"I'm right sorry," Sam said. "Feel you might've been treated unfairly. Were you with Darlene?"

Jack hung his head. "Nothin' happened. She's sweet on someone else."

What? But who? Was she in love with Captain Bell?

"Why did you lie?"

Jack was angry. "He doesn't get to tell me who I can kiss. Who does he think he is?"

Of course, they were all bucks, eager to rut Darlene! Maybe Darlene got sick of it.

"Did you hand out Wonder Cure to the boys?"

"Of course not!" Jack shouted. "He told me to keep it locked up."

"Did you know that Wonder Cure contains a fair bit of opium?"

Jack, who was usually cool as a cucumber, looked dejected. "No one told me."

Sam felt Jack was telling the truth. Captain Bell had only told Sam and E.O.

"Where do you keep the key?" Sam asked.

They had almost reached the miserable hut. Sam put the skeleton key into the lock and the door popped open.

"Most always in my pocket," Jack said. He handed over the keys to the canteen. "But someone could have taken them when I was asleep."

Sam pocketed the keys. He would check the cupboard himself. Captain Bell had forgotten to ask Jack for the keys to the canteen.

"Is there anything you want? Books? Notebook?" Sam asked.

Jack smiled. He had a malicious glint in his eye. "So now, you're Bell's errand boy?"

"That's not fair," Sam said. "You know I don't feel that way."

Jack slumped on the simple cot and stared down at the concrete floor. "He's actin' like this is the army. The boys won't stand for it."

His defiant words did not match the tone of his voice. Sam couldn't think of anything comforting to say. Most of the time he understood Captain Bell's decisions, but he couldn't defend this one.

This was a real low point. He was beginning to wonder if they should have stayed in Alpine, and stuck with milking cows, washing dishes at Mrs. Lockhart's boarding house.

"I'll be checking on you," Sam said. "The office is a stone's throw away."

Jack was now lying down on the cot with his hands behind his head. He was gazing at the wooden rafters of the ceiling. "Sorry. Just kicking the cat. That was mean."

Sam looked up at the tangled web of cobwebs that hung from the rafters. He honestly could not remember the last boy who had been locked in the brig. Yeah, Devilfish for smuggling in Sotol. One day would have been enough. But Sam didn't think Jack was guilty.

"I'll bring you a broom," Sam said.

Jack snorted, like a pig.

Sam almost wished he was working outside at the swimming pool. Being so close to Captain Bell was rife with intrigue, like being a messenger for the king. He turned the key in the lock until it made an unpleasant click. Then he made a beeline for the canteen before anyone saw him.

• • •

Sam unlocked the heavy wooden door to the canteen first. He would have to find the right cupboard before Captain Bell realized he had the key. Captain Bell would be furious that he had taken it upon himself to search the cupboards without his permission. He did not want to end up in the brig himself.

He stood behind the little snack bar, wondering which was the right cupboard. He should have asked Jack. Too late now. He didn't have time to go back to the brig. Wouldn't it be close to the Vim Cola?

Wasn't that the logical place for it to be stored? Or would Wonder Cure be stored with medicines?

He stood at the small sink. Then he pulled back the checkered curtain. Four crates of Vim Cola were stacked under the sink.

Would he have to keep opening cupboards until he found it? He was certain that Jack had not handed out Wonder Cure to the boys. But who had?

Not all of the cupboards had a lock. Forget those.

Three. Jack had locked up the smoking tobacco. Made sense. Would be an item that someone might pilfer.

Two. A few bottles of aspirin.

Last one. This had to be it. Sam jiggled the lock. He was sure that he would find the Wonder Cure here. But when he opened the cupboard, there was only one bottle of Wonder Cure inside. But Jack swore he had not handed out any Wonder Cure. Further back, though, there were other larger bottles.

Sam studied the label: *El Ron Prohibido, Reserva. Made in Mejico.* Rum! Two bottles. And . . .

Two bottles of Virginia Straight Bourbon Whiskey.

Scarce as hen's teeth! Who would believe it? Not like that foul-tasting Sotol. Who had the cash to buy it? None of the boys . . . Unless they were trading it? Dr. Walker might. Darlene?

Captain Bell would be spitting mad! His tail was already up. He had vowed that anyone selling booze would be thrown out of the camp. Devilfish was treading on thin ice. Had he done this?

It was even risky for Sam to be rooting around here. He didn't really believe washing greasy dishes at Mrs. Lockhart's boarding house and milking cows was better than being at Balmorhea. And his folks needed the money.

Was someone using this cupboard as a temporary hiding place?

There had to be an explanation. This did not necessarily prove Jack's innocence. Sam was not sure what he should do next. If he told Captain Bell, it would prove he was right. But Sam felt sure that someone else had taken the Wonder Cure. But if it wasn't Jack, why would they hide the booze here? It didn't make sense. Unless they knew that Jack wouldn't open the cupboard.

On the other hand, maybe he didn't know Jack as well as he thought he did. He was always carrying on about his adventures with girls. Was he selling this booze? Was this some money-making scheme so he could marry Ruby?

He placed the bottles where he had found them and locked the cupboard. Then he left the canteen, locking the wooden door behind him.

Before he returned to the brig, he went to Jack's barracks. They were deserted. He picked up the novel, *Tortilla Flats*, by John Steinbeck. He had heard of Steinbeck, but hadn't read the novel. He turned over the cover: looked like a gang of womanizers in Monterey, California.

He pulled up the lumpy mattress. Not a very original hiding place. There were a few pin-up photographs of actresses. Marlene Dietrich, scantily clad, covered only in a feathery boa, sitting on a chair, her leg tipped upward. The second one was of Bette Davis, draped over a wrought-iron bed, her lips outlined in a fire-engine red. She was puffing on a cigarette. A sketchbook. Curious, Sam flipped through a few pages. There were a series of pencil sketches of a nude woman, lying sideways on a bed, staring provocatively at the artist, as if to say, "Put down that pencil right now." He traced his thumb along the curve of her breast. The drawings were quite good. Had Darlene posed for them? Or had Jack done them from memory?

Jack would be furious if he knew Sam was nosing through his

stuff. He stuffed the sketchbook back under the mattress.

Lying on the trunk next to his bed was another novel, *The Thin Man*, by Dashiell Hammett. A hot-shot detective named Nick Charles who is a big partier. Then, there's a murder.

He preferred Zane Grey's Westerns. He opened Jack's locker. Took out a few changes of underwear, socks, and a clean shirt. At least he could put on clean clothes.

It seemed a lousy way to spend Christmas, and Sam felt sorry for Jack. He opened up the brig.

Jack scrambled up off the simple cot. His fly was open.

"I brought you a few novels. And some clean clothes," Sam said.

"Thanks," Jack said, hurriedly zipping up his fly. "Did you check the cupboard in the canteen?"

"Yeah," Sam said. Sam looked away, embarrassed, until he got himself arranged. How could Jack be thinking of that now? Was he imagining himself with Darlene?

"Well?" Jack said. "Now you know I'm innocent. You can show Captain Bell and get me out of here."

"There's only one bottle of Wonder Cure there," Sam said.

"What?!!" Jack said. "That can't be. I swear it."

His surprise seemed real. He wasn't putting on a show. Sam didn't go in for swearing, but he wasn't going to lecture Jack now.

"There's something else," Sam said. "Four bottles of booze. Two bottles of rum from Mexico and two bottles of Virginia bourbon."

"You're kiddin' me?" Jack said.

"It's a fact. No joke."

Jack groaned. "But how? I'm buzzard's bait."

"You didn't put it there, did you? You're not buyin' and sellin'?"

"Of course not!" Jack said. "Somebody must've taken my key. Or made a copy. But Captain Bell'll never believe me."

"Sit tight for now," Sam said. "I'll see what I can do."

• • •

The next day, Sam wondered how he might bring up the issue of Wonder Cure with Captain Bell. Would it be better to just tell him the truth? If he told him the truth, then Captain Bell would be furious that Sam had checked the cupboard himself. On the other hand, maybe Captain Bell would soften or realize that someone else had distributed the Wonder Cure to the boys.

The only way to spin a cheerful story out of Christmas for the newsletter was to focus on his play. There had been a lot of grumbling at breakfast about the way the party had ended. Some of the boys were wondering if there would even be a New Year's Eve party. Sam was not hopeful.

Captain Bell was sitting at his desk, reading his mail. Just the occasional rustle behind that partition.

Sam screwed up his courage. "Captain, do you think I could talk to you about something?"

E.O. looked up from his figures.

"Shoot!" Captain Bell said, but he did not move from his desk.

"Jack is innocent."

"How do you know?" Captain Bell asked. "A little bird whispered in your ear?"

E.O. gave him a knowing look, as if to say, maybe you better not go there. Sam didn't like Captain Bell's sarcastic tone, but plunged ahead.

"I checked the cupboard in the canteen," Sam said.

"All accounted for?" Captain Bell asked.

"Not exactly," Sam said. "I think you'd better see for yourself."

"I have got to finish this letter to former Governor Neff. We'll go over after lunch," he said.

• • •

After lunch the two of them walked over to the canteen. But when Sam opened up the cupboard, it was empty.

"It's gone!" Sam said.

"Well, of course it is," Captain Bell said. "That's what you wanted to show me?"

"No. There were two bottles of Mexican rum. Two bottles of Virginia bourbon. And one bottle of Wonder Cure."

"Sure enough?" Captain Bell said.

"Saw them with my own eyes," Sam said.

"So someone made a copy of this key," Captain Bell said.

"Must have," Sam said.

"And someone is smuggling booze in," Captain Bell said.

"So Jack can be let out of the brig," Sam said.

"Not yet," Captain Bell said. "Not until we get to the bottom of this."

What? Why would Captain Bell keep Jack in the brig, if he knew that he wasn't responsible?

"But Captain, that might take some time."

But Captain Bell had made up his mind.

CHAPTER 33.

# Jack and the Brig

**Sam didn't know how he would break the news to Jack.** After breakfast, he took Jack a plate piled high with toast, scrambled eggs, and extra bacon. Maybe the extra bacon would cheer him up.

When Sam unlocked the brig, Jack was wide awake and already dressed.

"What are you bringing that for?" Jack asked. "Surely I am free to go."

"Well, there has been another twist since yesterday," Sam said. "Everything that was in the cupboard has disappeared. One bottle of Wonder Cure and all of the booze."

"So the culprit has changed the hiding place," Jack said. "Surely Captain Bell has realized I had nothing to do with it."

"He wants to make absolutely sure before he releases you," Sam said, putting down the plate on a small wooden stool that could be used as a table.

"So I am stuck here, counting the spiders while you figure it out.

It could be anyone! Does he propose to interview all two hundred men at Balmorhea?" Jack said. He flopped back on the flimsy cot. "Nobody died!"

He had forgotten to bring Jack a broom. He gazed up at the nest of cobwebs intertwined in the rafters. He hoped there were no black widows taking up residence there. He vaguely wondered about scorpions, but decided against mentioning it. That was not likely to improve Jack's mood.

"I don't know why he's being so stubborn. I tried to point this out to the captain."

"I am starting to think we'd be better off milking cows in Alpine!" Jack said. "Is this any way to run a railroad?"

"I brought you extra bacon," Sam said.

"This place smells worse than a skunk," Jack said. "Besides the spiders, there's a latrine!"

Sam sniffed. Smell of ammonia, too much pee. He propped open the door to the brig. A gust of wind blew into the small hut. "Do you want to go AWOL?"

"My folks need the money," Jack said, gloomily. "You know that."

He gave Jack a fork. "I brought you *Tortilla Flats* and *The Thin Man.*"

"Very funny," Jack said. "Already read them. Do you think you're Nick Charles, the detective in *The Thin Man*?"

"Come on, cowboy," Sam said. "Old college friend. Until . . ." He almost blurted out Darlene's name.

"Has she asked about me?" Jack said, his mouth full of bacon. Despite his disdain, he was wolfing down the food.

"Has kept herself scarce," Sam said. "Haven't seen her."

"That's the real reason I'm here," Jack said. "Captain Bell wishes he was doing her."

Sam disapproved of this crude talk, but of course, he was curious to know if Jack had done what he implied. "I reckon the War did terrible things to people. Maybe he'll come to his senses."

"Stop making excuses for Captain Bell!" Jack said. "That's why everyone calls you Bell's errand boy."

"Well," Sam said, "Reckon I better be going. Got to get back to my errands. I'll send E.O. with your lunch."

"No!" Jack said. "I'm sorry. Please. E.O. would bore me to tears. Talking to him is like watching paint dry. Only talk is sin and the Church of Christ."

Day two passed without any clues. The boys were starting to complain about the closure of the canteen. They wanted to buy Vim Cola, tobacco, candy, and toothpaste. Jack's classes had also been canceled. On day three, Sam heard boys openly criticizing Captain Bell at breakfast. "He's acting like one of those dictators we hear about on the radio. You heard of Adolf Hitler in Germany? Or what about that fella in Italy? Mussolini?" Someone snickered. "Maybe we ought to rebel. Jack was trying to get us to read *Mutiny on the Bounty*."

Sam agreed with the boys, but didn't comment. As he was leaving the table, someone whispered, "Go on. Snitch is gone."

"Ssshhhh. You wanna get stuck in the brig?"

On the fourth day, Darlene stormed into the office. Sam was sorting the mail. She skipped the niceties. No good morning, but he smelled the lavender. Her uniform had been pressed, and her bosom was straining against the cloth. He felt a stirring in his groin when he thought about Jack's sketches of her nude, the bold way she had stared at the artist.

"I would like to see Captain Bell," she said.

"Think he's out at the pool," Sam said. "Should be in shortly."

"I will wait," Darlene said. She marched past Sam and took a seat in front of Captain Bell's desk. She crossed her arms. It looked like she was spoiling for a fight.

When Captain Bell strolled in about twenty minutes later, he hung his ranger hat on the peg on the wall.

Sam gestured toward the partition. "Darlene," he said.

Captain Bell took his time, and sat down at his desk. "Good morning, Darlene. What can I do for you? Do we need to order more antivenom? Or anything else for the clinic?"

"This camp is rife with rumors," Darlene said. "I don't like being the center of rumors. Could you give me a good explanation of why Jack has been in the brig for four days!"

"Why are you the center of rumors?" Captain Bell said.

"Don't play the fool!" Darlene said.

"I'm listening," Captain Bell said.

"The boys are saying that you're jealous of Jack. And that's why he's locked in the brig."

Sam was astounded she had the audacity to say what everyone was thinking. She just told it to him straight. Captain Bell had pressed Jack a little too hard about Jack's absence the day of the Christmas party.

Captain Bell cleared his throat. "Well, it might come as a surprise to you Darlene, but I am human."

"If you've locked Jack in the brig because of me, I can resign my position as nurse. I'm aware that romantic relationships are forbidden at the camp."

"No, no," Captain Bell said. "That is not the issue. We learned that Wonder Cure contained the tincture of opium."

"Oh," Darlene said. "I had no idea. I am sorry, Captain. I was out of line."

Sam didn't understand why her tone had changed so drastically.

"Jack was supposed to keep Wonder Cure under lock and key. I didn't want anyone at the camp drinking it. I thought he had distributed it to the boys at the Christmas party."

"Of course," Darlene said. "Now I see your point."

"Do you think Joe might have given it to the boys? Or is somehow involved?"

"Joe?" Darlene said, acting surprised. "Why would he jeopardize his business with you?"

"I don't know," Captain Bell said. "I am just asking. Someone is also smuggling rum and bourbon into the camp. Any ideas?"

Darlene laughed lightly. "Haven't the faintest idea."

Her laughter felt artificial to Sam. She had completely retreated from her aggressive position.

"We do need you here," Captain Bell said, walking her to the door. He opened the door for her with his one arm.

CHAPTER 34.

# Captain Bell

**Maybe he was wrong.** After he saw Darlene out, he went back to his desk and stared at the wooden partition. He had a stack of paperwork on his desk. Each one had an emblem: U.S. government. U.S. Army. U.S. Civilian Conservation Corps. So his feelings for Darlene were obvious. His personal feelings had gotten in the way of his ability to make decisions about Balmorhea. They had no clues about who was smuggling booze into the camp. Darlene was right. He had been married only a year, but long enough to have a few rows. His wife, Pauline, had complained that he never could admit he was wrong. He heard her voice: "Why are you always so certain?"

Damn her. The image of his daughter, Thelma, swaddled in her christening dress, arose before him. His eyes welled up with tears.

He took out the cloth handkerchief he always carried in his pants pocket and wiped his face.

But he heard the tap-tap-tap of Sam's typewriter. When he peeked around the partition, he saw that he was looking down at the keys.

He did not know. He had nightmares. Flashbacks. The shakes. Despite Dr. Gillies's efforts to salvage it, his face was as contorted and grotesque as Frankenstein's monster. He still had trouble looking at himself in the mirror just for a simple shave.

If every woman who met him was repulsed, he would have to accept it.

This was not war, but a civilian camp. He had been outraged when Theo Kauffman from his platoon had deserted the night before the battle of the Argonne Forest. The charge had been desertion and cowardice, "to be shot at dawn." The French and the Brits just blindfolded them, tied them to a pole, and shot them at dawn. When the kid had been brought to him, restrained, Captain Bell had been harsh: "You are a coward." He was not much older than Bell himself. But the kid had just said: "I don't want to kill my cousins." He was from a German family in central Texas, and his family had emigrated in the 1890s.[1] Captain Bell had said, "That's not likely." A lock of blond hair fell across one of his eyes. "They are here." "How do you know that? You are consorting with the enemy. That is treason." But the boy had just shrugged. In the next week, Captain Bell lost almost all of the platoon, *if* their mauled bodies were recovered from that wheat field. The official court-martial took place later in Washington, D.C. President Wilson had commuted all the executions for desertion to prison sentences. It had been humiliating for Kauffman, but as the years passed, everyone had forgotten. He now owned a brewery in Fredericksburg.

"I need the key to the brig," Captain Bell said.

Sam was surprised. "Are you releasing him?"

"Yes," he said. He didn't want to talk about the war.

"I can do it," Sam said.

"I will do it myself," Captain Bell said. "I want to talk to him."

It wasn't far to the brig, only one building over. Jack was surprised when Captain Bell jimmied open the door. The wooden door was a little warped.

"Captain Bell," Jack said.

The boy looked depressed. His hair was tousled into a peak, as if he were a rooster. He was still wearing his pajamas. Captain Bell felt guilty for being so harsh.

"Good morning, Jack," Captain Bell said. "Have you had your breakfast?"

"Sam brought it to me an hour or so ago," he said. "Only ate the bacon."

The plate sat on the stool. Most of the food was untouched. The captain took the plate off the stool and sat down.

"Did something else happen?" Jack asked. "Did you find the rest of the Wonder Cure? Or the booze?"

"No," Captain Bell said. "We are stymied. But I think that I have treated you unfairly. This is not the Marines. And we are not in a war. I didn't want Wonder Cure distributed because I was worried about the safety of the boys. It contains opium."

He didn't mention Darlene, his rage that Jack had been smooching with her during the Christmas dinner.

Jack hung his head. "I swear I didn't hand out Wonder Cure. But I think there is something you should know."

"Oh?"

"There's a gambling ring at the camp. Maybe Wonder Cure or the booze is the currency, instead of money."

"Can you tell me who is involved?"

"E.O." Jack said.

"What?!" Captain Bell said. "Do you have any proof?"

But they were counting on E.O. for his honesty with money. He paid out the salaries, organized the requisitions, dealt with vendors and the bank, balanced the books. Captain Bell would need to look at the accounts. He had been focused on other issues at the camp, so confident that E.O. could handle the money.

"No," Jack said. "It's mostly rumors."

"But I can't be accusing anyone based on rumors," Captain Bell said. It didn't make sense. E.O. was a teetotaler and had convinced everyone that he was religious.

Jack shrugged. "The boys are talking about it."

"Thanks for letting me know," Captain Bell said. "You are free to go. Once you get yourself cleaned up, open up the canteen. We will need to get the locks changed. Maybe Joe Kafouri can help with that."

• • •

Captain Bell did not know where to go. He couldn't go back to that cramped office that smelled of socks. Before Christmas, he would have sought out Darlene for advice. But he discounted that idea now. If E.O. was not trustworthy, he would have to hire another accountant for the camp. On the other hand, maybe it was just a malicious rumor.

The weather was crisp, in the fifties. He had already been out to the building site of the pool, where the men were busily laying out adobe bricks to dry. The pool was enormous, in the shape of two water towers with a bulbous head connected to the long rectangular shapes, like an Olympic-sized swimming pool. They wouldn't fill in the water from the spring until they were sure that the sides of the pool were firm. It looked like they would make the deadline for the grand opening with former Governor Neff in June. Neff had already started sending out invitations to dignitaries. Captain Bell dreaded former Governor Neff's guest list—no telling who he would invite. Anyway, he would cross that bridge when he came to it.

He gazed up at the billowy clouds in the blue sky. It was close to New Year's. The boys would be expecting a party. As he strolled past the long line of bland-looking barracks, Delilah trotted around the corner to meet him.

"Why hello, Miss Delilah," he said, scratching her behind the ears. "You've had your breakfast, have you?"

She barked.

"Would you like to go on a walk with me? Solve the problems of the world?"

She jumped up, licking his hand. "You might be the only one I can talk to in this camp!"

She barked again.

• • •

He peeked into the clinic, but Darlene was not there. Delilah followed him to Dr. Walker's office. He had not seen Darlene since she had come to his office to complain about Jack.

Dr. Walker was staring up, dreamily, at the ceiling when Captain Bell entered his office. He did not look terribly busy.

"My boy," Dr. Walker said. "Are you feeling better? Any more nightmares or flashbacks?"

He didn't think that Dr. Walker was that much older than he was, but obviously he thought of him as a boy.

"No," Captain Bell lied. He had come to Dr. Walker for some kind of reassurance. He had just been thinking about Theo Kauffman's case of desertion, and the commuted death sentence, this morning.

"Of course," Dr. Walker said. "I am not an expert like Dr. Fishbein, but I am aware of the latest developments in medical science. Why, you must have heard that Marie Curie's daughter just won the Nobel Prize for her work in artificial radioactivity."

"No," Captain Bell said. "I had not heard about that. I have been involved with more pedestrian concerns at Balmorhea. Like theft and pilfering."

Dr. Walker did not laugh but plunged on. "Her discoveries could have huge implications for the treatment of cancer, that in fact could be ground-breaking, which, as you know, is quite a worrying, incurable disease that physicians are often flummoxed by. I know I have been flummoxed, myself."

Delilah barked. She was sniffing the wastebasket close to Dr. Walker's desk.

Captain Bell was not sure why he was here. "Have you seen Darlene? She's not in the clinic."

Why was he asking? He had decided he'd better not confide in her, either.

"I allowed her to borrow my automobile," Dr. Walker said. "She was distressed and said she had to post a letter in town. She was going to buy a few things at Joe's store."

Captain Bell felt as if he had become infected with jealousy.

Delilah kept her nose to the ground, going this way and that, until she was about to jump in Dr. Walker's lap.

"Down, Delilah," Bell said. "Do you like dogs?"

"I prefer feline company," Dr. Walker said. "My wife, Eleanor, had a cat named Esmeralda that I became rather fond of . . . when she died of tubercular consumption . . ."

"I am sorry to hear that," Captain Bell said. He couldn't think of anything comforting to say. He knew that Dr. Walker was a widower, but he had never talked to him about his wife.

"We called her Esmie. One side of her face was black, the other was brown. A little like Delilah's markings. The cat wandered off after . . ." Dr. Walker's voice trailed off.

Dr. Walker was scratching Delilah behind the ears.

"She was taking the rest-cure in San Angelo. Rest. Desert air. When the infection became untenable, pneumothorax was recommended. I was wholeheartedly in agreement with this treatment, and we were hopeful at first. But collapsing the lung, in fact, made her weaker. Her condition deteriorated soon after . . ."

Captain Bell was silent. He absolutely refused to utter the platitudes that people offered him about the death of Pauline. "Do you have children?"

"Ah," Dr. Walker said. "One belle of the ball. She's married and lives in Mississippi. A boy she met at Tulane. Rarely see her, if it behooves her to touch base with her Tyler paternal origins. That is, after her mother's passing."

"Oh," Captain Bell said. Captain Bell imagined it wouldn't be easy, having Dr. Walker for a father, although he could be sensitive.

"I never asked you before. Do you have children, Captain Bell?"

"I had a baby daughter. Thelma. She died from the Spanish flu when I was in France. They both did . . ."

Delilah had jumped off Dr. Walker's lap. She was busy sniffing around the room.

"Dear boy," Dr. Walker said, rubbing his red eyes. "That is most unfortunate. A heavy burden, indeed. Besides . . ."

If Captain Bell started talking about it, he thought he might well up. Best to switch the topic. "Have you ever seen any more of Dr. Volkov?"

"The doctor who is proposing rejuvenation with his experimental transplant procedures?" Dr. Walker asked. "Just the one lecture that I attended at Sul Ross. It is peculiar, though. At first, he was ubiquitous. Now, he seems to have vanished. Maybe he is lecturing out in California or at some other university. A most impressive gentleman. He was awarded honorary degrees from France and Italy for his work."

"Do you think he might have operated on anyone locally?" Captain Bell asked. "Would you know?"

"Not to my knowledge," Dr. Walker said. "But I am rather yoked to the camp, as you know."

"Did you ever find the *JAMA* journal? I wanted to read about Dr. Brinkley," Captain Bell said.

Dr. Walker shook his head. "Flat disappeared. Don't know who would have taken it. There's the *Alpine Avalanche*, such that it is. The *New York Times* when it comes in the post and the radio. By the way, the news today was rather pernicious. With the growing power of Italy and Germany, I have been ruminating about the possibility of another war. It appears we might be on the precipice."

Captain Bell had not listened to the radio. He had been focused on Jack and the brig.

"What happened?"

"The Italians bombed a Swedish hospital in Ethiopia. Then the Swedes protested to the League of Nations about the use of chemical weapons. Hitler seems to be consolidating his power in Germany. The Germans reinstated military conscription in September. Plan to break the Treaty of Versailles."

"I hope there won't be another war," Captain Bell said. President Wilson's words, "Make the world safe for democracy," echoed in his head.

Delilah was barking insistently. She turned over the wastebasket.

An empty bottle clanked onto the floor and slowly spun toward the wall, where it rolled to a stop. Delilah sniffed it. Then she put her paw on it, as if she might play with it.

"What is it, Miss Delilah?" Captain Bell said, reaching down to pick it up. "What did you find, Missy?"

Not a ball. He whistled. An empty bottle, which said *El Ron Prohibido, Reserva, Made in Mejico.*

"Rum," Bell said.

"Prohibition was canceled," Dr. Walker said. "I have done nothing felonious. Nothing illegal. As a citizen, I have the right to purchase alcohol."

"Technically, you are right," Captain Bell said. "But hard alcohol is forbidden at the camp. Are you consuming it discreetly?"

Dr. Walker waved his hand. He was wearing an expensive onyx pinky ring. "I share the occasional glass, but it is with staff. Not the boys."

"Well, we don't have a very big staff," Captain Bell said. "May I ask . . . ?"

"Darlene humors me with her company," Dr. Walker said. "Listens to my musings on poetry, Faulkner, and such, which must, in fact, be dull for her. One does yearn for the company of the fairer sex, at times."

Captain Bell almost exclaimed, "Darlene!" But he restrained himself. He thought Darlene hated Dr. Walker, yet they were having cocktails together.

"Fair enough," Captain Bell said. "But I don't want the camp overrun with spirits. It will only lead to fights."

Dr. Walker sighed. "This is one of the few pleasures, Captain Bell, in a life brimming with disgruntlement, frustration, and tribulation."

Captain Bell could sympathize with this sentiment.

"Who sells it to you?" Captain Bell asked.

Dr. Walker laughed. "I take umbrage at such a question. You are acting like the Grand Inquisitor for the Anti-Saloon League. I am not at liberty to say."

"As long as it does not impact your professional duties," Captain Bell said. His mood had turned sour. "Good day, Dr. Walker."

CHAPTER 35.

# Sam

**Sam couldn't understand it.** The next morning, Captain Bell had summoned E.O. and the ledgers and went very carefully through every penny of the budget. He had always delegated this completely to E.O.

Once they had gone through the ledgers of expenses for the camp, they went through all the bank slips and requisition orders from Joe's store. After that, they opened the safe and counted the petty cash.

It was hard for Sam to get any work done because they kept talking. He kept making typos.

Finally, Captain Bell said, "You are very thorough, E.O. You should be commended for your work. I will be changing the combination to the safe, though."

E.O. adjusted his coke-bottle glasses. "Will you be sharing that with me?"

Captain Bell said, "No."

"But Captain, this won't be very practical. Every time we need money for the camp, I will have to ask you. Sometimes you are not around."

"New directives from Washington," Captain Bell said. "About the way money is handled. There have been reports about pilfering in the CCC camps. It's normal to check the books."

Sam didn't remember opening any mail about new directives. Captain Bell must be fibbing.

"You mean, thievery," E.O said. "Has someone spread a rumor about me?"

Captain Bell hesitated slightly and then said, "No."

When Captain Bell left the office to inspect the swimming pool, Sam asked, "What's going on?"

E.O. shrugged. He slumped down in his chair. "There must be talk. You know how the boys love to talk."

"But who?" Sam asked. E.O. was such a low-key character, he couldn't imagine that he would have any enemies. There were jokes in the camp about how lily-white E.O. was: didn't drink, didn't smoke, didn't curse, didn't have sex. (Or, at least, that's what they thought.) He could sing and liked to dance. He had a girlfriend from church, Loretta.

"I have an idea," E.O. said.

"Who?"

"It's just a hunch. Too soon to tell. Better to get back to work."

• • •

The next day, another strange thing happened. Instead of the menu that was pinned up in the mess hall, there was one of the pencil sketches of Darlene. She was nude, lying on a bed, propped on her side, her head leaning on her elbow, her voluptuous breasts exposed.

Her smile was slightly mocking.

A cluster of boys stopped to gaze at it at breakfast. "Wouldn't you like to suck those titties?" Another guffawed. "No sirree, I don't want to suck. I'd rather fuck!"

"Who needs a girl when you fuck cows?"

"Shut your trap or I'll whoop you."

Sam had heard of bestiality, but he had never heard of anyone admitting to it. They continued to hoot as they wolfed down pancakes, eggs, and bacon. Sam took his tray and sat as far away from them as possible. He picked at his eggs. He didn't take any joy in Darlene's humiliation.

Jack cornered Sam after breakfast. "Did you go through my stuff when I was in the brig? You must have found the sketchbook."

Sam shrugged. "Sure, I found it. But I put it back. Did she pose for you?"

"Well, I have seen her in her birthday suit, if that's what you mean," Jack said, ruffling his full head of black hair. He winked at Sam.

Sam felt as if he were teasing him. He still couldn't believe she would have posed for him.

"It was an obvious hiding place," Sam said. "Everyone hides dirty pictures under the mattress."

"Darlene is going to be spitting," Jack said. "I have to find out who is doing this."

"Good luck," Sam said.

By lunch the sketch in the mess hall had disappeared.

But in the afternoon, another sketch was pinned to the canteen door. Darlene's hair was loose, her neck tilted back, as she was eating a cluster of grapes.

And another one was found on the door to the latrine. She was nude, draped over a wrought-iron bed, but only the shape of her protruding fanny could be seen, as if she were waiting for her lover to . . . Sam had taken one art appreciation class at Sul Ross, and it reminded him of nude paintings in the nineteenth century.

The next day, a sketch was pinned to the clinic door. She was nude, except for cowboy boots, astride a stallion.

She threw it down on Captain Bell's desk.

CHAPTER 36.

# Darlene's Diary, December 31, 1935

I want to wring Jack's neck. *If I could find him, I would stab him with a fork. But I am partly to blame. For robbing the cradle. I didn't need to be flirting with these boys. Jack had given me Dashiell Hammett's novel,* The Maltese Falcon. *Safer to dream about the detective, Sam Spade. Only got through half of it.*

*What a fool I had been.*

*Jack had convinced me to pose for him one afternoon after . . .*

*I had no idea that he had a sketchbook. He hadn't hidden it very well. Mr. Smarty Pants Cary Grant.*

*Couldn't go back to Del Rio. Sally's there now. I hope she's not mistreating J.*

*Sure I was the center of a lot of smutty jokes in camp.*

*Told Doc Walker I was going to the main office if anyone needed me. But he just said, "Reading Faulkner, the master, this morning."*

*Besides drinking himself silly. Or guzzling Wonder Cure. All of that phony baloney about curing erectile dysfunction. Could have saved Bell the trouble. But then, he would have known that I'm not Darlene, but Minerva B. Then what? Would open the whole can of worms.*

*Marched over to Bell's office with the sketch and threw it down on his desk. "You have to get to the bottom of this, come hell or high water! You're ineffectual! What kind of leader are you?"*

*Bell gave me a hurt look, like a whipped dog. "But Darlene, don't you know who drew it?"*

*"It has to be Jack."*

*"What do you want me to do?"*

*"Find out who is pinning up these sketches!"*

*"Have you taken this up with Jack?"*

*"Can't find the son of a bitch," I shouted.*

*Bell took his time. Rubbed his shoulder stump while he looked at me. "I doubt Jack pinned up those sketches. Someone found them and decided to do it. Probably a prank."*

*"Why, gosh, you're Perry Mason. I couldn't have figured that out for myself."*

*"Why don't you take the afternoon off? Go into town."*

*Stormed out of the office. Slammed the door as hard as I could. Acted like a thirteen-year-old brat.*

*Took Doc Walker's car without even asking and drove to Joe's store. Drove like a bat out of hell and almost wrecked his coupe.*

*Was counting on Joe to cheer me up with his smile and little jokes, but he just handed me the Blue Comet Train, J.'s Christmas package. His wife was hanging around, like Delilah. As if she wanted to be scratched. They were speaking in their language—whatever it was. Singsongy like I-talian.*

*B. and Sally sent back the train. It was Sally's handwriting. Return to Sender. There was no explanation given.*

*"Was it the right address?"*

*Joe shook his head. "Think so."*

*So J. didn't get a present from me for Christmas. He wouldn't understand. I had always given him lots of presents for Christmas. Spoiled him.*

*What had they told him about me? Had they poisoned the well?*

*But . . .*

*A postcard, from our trip from the Galápagos, of a gigantic turtle: Dear Mama. When will you finish your trip? Since you left, Myrtle the Turtle died. One day she was found floating in the swimming pool. I cried a lot. There was a bad smell. Daddy let me bury her in the backyard. We put a cross over the grave. Do you think she went to heaven?*

*I was on a trip? Is that what they had told J.?*

*Joe shook his head.*

*The postcard didn't mention the train. But why had they let him send me the postcard?*

*How did B. explain Sally? Was she the new wife? Or the old wife he had never divorced? Did Sally enjoy her conjugal duties? Was he making her do it in front of the Italian mirror so he could see himself?*

*Joe was busy selling a shovel to a farmer. His wife was measuring out a bolt of cloth to some woman I had never seen before.*

*Just stood there, lost. Didn't feel like buying anything. Might as well go back to Balmorhea. Took the toy train and headed for the car.*

*Threw the box in the front seat. Sat there, then fired up the motor. Just as I was about to pull out of the lot, Joe comes running out.*

*"Please, stop the car." Stopped in the middle of the road.*

*He leaned into the window. "Did you forget?" He was smiling.*

*"Forget what?"*

*"The supplies. The* hamra.*"*

*In exchange for using his address, I had agreed to sell booze for him. He gave me a cut. If I lost the job at Balmorhea, at least I would have a little cash. But where would I go?*

*Brought out the burlap sack. He put his fingers to his lips. Captain Bell mustn't know. I peeked in the sack. This time, there were four bottles of bourbon and two bottles of Sotol. I wasn't happy. Fewer bottles were easier to hide.*

*"What about Wonder Cure?"*

*Joe shook his head. "No supplies now."*

*Was B. still making it?*

*I couldn't use the canteen anymore. Don't think Jack ever knew that I copied his key. Courtesy of Joe.*

*He put his fingers on my lips. "Just our little deal, habibti, my dear. Let me know when you would like to send another letter to your dear son. Or if you are in need of anything else?" He winked at me.*

*Ignored that. Couldn't get tangled up with this man.*

*How long could we keep fooling Bell? He wasn't born yesterday.*

*Before B. had started the goat-testicle scheme, he was transplanting ovaries for desperate women who wanted to conceive. Never would have dreamed that I would have a son, who would then be taken away from me. It had taken ten years.*

*Then B. threw more money at the Institute. Modeled it on the consumption sanatorium idea. Luxury rooms with bathrooms, chandeliers, oriental carpets. Folks in Milford hadn't seen anything like it. Tiny town, ninety-five miles from Wichita, which was starting to boom. It was like they had struck oil.*

*Hired Happy Harry to pick them up from the train station and drive them to the Institute. Once they came in, they were welcomed in the "herd room." Put them in white gowns and took their temperature, flirted with them a bit to get them primed. Batted my eyelashes a little. Showed some cleavage.*

*B. got greedy and started stealing goats from local farmers. We had to revise the plan and put a stable behind the clinic. If the windows were open, the clinic started to stink like a barn. Went around putting lavender sachets in every room.*

*One group of hot dogs insisted they have the testicles of Angora goats.*

*Knew B. had convinced himself he was Ponce de Leon. He didn't have any qualms. Had started to believe his own lies. "All energy is sexual energy." "A man is as old as his glands."*

*And maybe the testicles were a placebo in some cases. The men started to believe in the cure and that empowered them. Sometimes B. took a sliver of a goat's testicle and transplanted it. Sometimes, he just joined a smaller testicle to a bigger one. Depended on his mood. When he was inebriated, I sewed them up.*

*B. hired an ad man. We had the ordinary Prostate Plan.*[1] *The middle range. The deluxe. B. operated on some highflyers from Chicago, even the chancellor at the University of Chicago law school. The newspapers touted the procedure: "The operations, whereby youth has been restored to the aged patients and vigor was revived, were performed by . . ."*

*How would that be explained to J. later?*

*B. was hard to live with. Surrendered to his rage. Destroyed a neighbor's car with an ax. Chased me through the clinic with a scalpel. Should have left then. But what about J.?*

*Folks in Milford were forgiving because he had practically rebuilt the town. Financed the Little League team named the Brinkley Goats. But they drew the line when he wanted to name the church after himself. Thought he was Christ. Could promise everlasting life.*

*But once the Kansas Medical Association received so many complaints, they started to investigate. He lost his license. And then we fled to Texas.*

*But now I'm not the flavor of the month. And B. has J. And has taken up with Sally again, who he never divorced.*

*If things bottom out at Balmorhea, where do I go?*

CHAPTER 37.

# A Dry New Year's Eve, Almost, 1936

**At the last minute, Captain Bell authorized a New Year's Eve party.** He felt a little mean, forbidding a party, but the main problem was alcohol—even beer led to fights. His popularity had plummeted after Jack's incarceration in the brig. Camp morale was at an all-time low, and the boys were surly at the construction site. Mac had complained. "You gotta loosen the reins, Captain. They're straining at the bit. They need to have a little fun."

It was a little late to order beer, but he supposed Joe wouldn't turn down an order if he called the store. It was chilly in the office even with the pot-bellied stove in the middle. He stood at the stove, warming his one hand over it.

"What if we have a special New Year's Eve party today without the booze?"

E.O. just stared at him through those coke-bottle glasses. "We didn't put it in the budget. Isn't it a little late? We don't have the supplies. Didn't tell the cooks."

"We could have extra pie," Captain Bell said. "Hot chocolate."

Sam laughed. "The boys'll want beer."

"What if Devilfish and his band play?"

"I could ask," Sam said.

But when Sam came back from the kitchen, he was shaking his head.

"Devilfish refused to play."

"Why?" Captain Bell asked.

"Says he has already organized a pool tournament in the rec room," Sam said. "The cooks said they will make extra pies."

"Fair enough," Captain Bell said. "If they already have some entertainment organized. Lights out at midnight instead of ten, then."

Captain Bell strolled over to the rec room a few hours after supper to check on the pool tournament. Devilfish had already beaten many of the cooks and was racking up the table.

It looked as if the Anglo boys were playing ping-pong at a nearby table. Someone shouted, "Sore loser!"

At least it was all in good fun. Captain Bell felt maybe they might get through the evening without a mishap or an altercation.

The final game was between Chueco and Devilfish.

Devilfish showed his muscle. Then he twirled a pool cue, as if he were in the circus. "Chueco, you up to losing to the king? Played in every juke joint in the state."

There were hoots of laughter. "No. No. No pero . . . Chueco!" The Mexican boys clapped and shouted. "Chueco! Chueco!" They stomped their feet.

They pushed him forward. Devilfish laughed wickedly. He sang, "Behind the eight ball, ain't it so?"

"I am no good," Chueco said. "You will beat me."

"Aw, come on, Chueco," Devilfish said, poking him with a cue. "*Amigo.* Nothing to the bear but his curly hair. Ha! Ha!"

Chueo was puzzled. "*¿Qué?*"

Devilfish smiled broadly. "It means that your ass is gonna get whupped by the king of juke joints, *amigo*."

Chueco's friends shouted, "Chueco! Chueco! Chueco!"

Devilfish racked up the balls. He focused and held the cue steady, hitting smack into the middle, scattering the colored balls on the table. He dropped several solids on the break. Someone whistled.

Captain Bell had never regretted assigning Chueco to the clinic, despite Dr. Walker's resistance. It hadn't worked out exactly as he thought, though. Chueco was so uncomfortable with Dr. Walker that he asked to be reassigned to the kitchen. One day, he had come to the office and complained, "Dr. Walker has *bilis. Mi madre dice que es como veneno*." Bell was puzzled and asked, "What is *bilis*?" Chueco said, "Too much anger. Like poison." He had said, "Are you sure?" The boy nodded vigorously. He had never thought of Dr. Walker as angry, but maybe Chueco had greater insight. He admired the boy's intuitive understanding. Perhaps the boy also understood that Captain Bell, himself, suffered from suppressed rage. Chueco still tended his plants in the clinic and helped Darlene occasionally. An unlikely friendship had sprung up between Chueco and Devilfish because they played music together. Captain Bell had managed to evade Washington's directives about segregation.

Sam was standing next to him, watching the game. "Why don't you play?" Captain Bell asked.

"Ran track at Sul Ross. Never tried my hand at pool."

"You know the old saying, 'It's not whether you win or lose, but how you play the game.'"

"Sure, Captain. But the boys wanna win," Sam said.

"Is there a prize?"

"'Course! Why do you think they didn't want to cancel the tournament?" Sam said.

He hadn't signed off on any prizes in the budget. He smelled a rat.

"Really? What's the prize?" he asked, playing dumb.

Sam shrugged. "E.O. says it's a surprise."

Did Sam know? Was he covering for someone? Jack had told him about the gambling ring, yet he had found no evidence of pilfering in the budget. Where was E.O.?

Chueco stood, studying the table. He had gained weight in the few months since he had come to Balmorhea. Captain Bell remembered how scrawny he had been when he arrived, wearing sandals made of car tires. Yet now he was standing up straight and walking with more confidence, no longer curled in on himself, snail-like.

Chueco took the cue and aimed for a striped yellow, a straight shot down the table, like a bullet. It snapped into the pocket.

The boys clapped. "Chueco, *El Diablo*!"

Devilfish was a little surprised. Chueco proceeded to hit two more balls.

Devilfish leaned on the cue, trying to be nonchalant. "Like I was saying before, nothing to the bear but his curly hair." He took his cue and aimed for a combination, which was dangerously close to the eight ball.

Just as he was aiming for the ball, Otto shouted, "Happy New Year, fellow inmates!"

Devilfish looked up. He hit the ball at the wrong angle and the cluster of balls knocked against the eight ball. The black eight ball slipped toward the pocket, teetered slightly on the edge, and dropped in.

"Shit!" Devilfish shouted, pounding his hand on the green velvet of the table. "Just lost the bottle of rum!"

The Mexican boys whooped. Chueco had won the prize. How were they getting it into the camp? E.O., directly?

Otto loomed in the doorway with a cub tucked under his arm. Around the cub's neck was a collar, and a nasty silver chain. Where had he gotten that?

Some of the Mexican boys yelled out, "*El Cabrón*."

"For crying out loud," Captain Bell shouted. "What are you doing? Take him outside! Let him go! Bears can't be pets!"

"The king is gonna get that cracker!" Devilfish said.

First Otto was playing with rattlesnakes, now he was catching bears! Otto didn't have any sense. The cub didn't look very old, and oddly, looked like a cute puppy. His eyes blinked. He was covered with very fine, downy hair.

The cub bawled and moaned, as if he were in real distress. Panicked, he kept squirming until he had escaped from Otto's grasp.

The cub was too young to be taken from its mother—and was probably hungry.

Otto loped after him, but he was too late. The cub crawled under the pool table. The tall German dropped to his knees and peered under the table, yanking the chain. The cub bawled, as if it were calling for its mother.

It made an odd yelping sound as it was dragged out from under the pool table.

Captain Bell said, "Stop that, Otto! You are suffocating him. You'll kill him!"

Just as the cub was pulled out from under the pool table, he swiped Otto in the face with his tiny paw.

Otto screamed in pain and fell back on the floor. He had a bad cut on his forehead, and blood gushed out.

The cub shot through the door, out into the open air, the chain clinking behind him.

Some of the boys wanted to chase him. "Let him go," Captain Bell said. "He needs to find his mama."

Captain Bell knelt beside him. Otto's face was covered in blood. "Where is Darlene? Dr. Walker?" Captain Bell yelled out.

No one seemed to know, not even Sam.

Captain Bell took out a cloth handkerchief from his pocket, and he dabbed some of the blood off Otto's face. This brought back memories of stanching wounds at the Argonne Forest in France. He remembered that boy Willie who had been hit in the aorta. No way to stanch the blood; gone by the time the medics came. And the Brit in the bed next to him in the hospital in London. What was his name? Had a cockney accent. Bad bayonet wound in the genitals. Had he lost his . . . ? Name was Knight. They had joked about his name. And he'd said, "Tex, I'm soon to be brown bread . . . Dead. Ha. Ha."

"Doesn't look that bad," Captain Bell said. "Cut's not that deep."

The other boys had stopped playing pool and ping-pong. A circle of boys were standing behind him.

"I can't see," Otto said, thrashing around on the ground. Blood continued to gush from the cut.

A hush fell over the room.

"Don't touch it," Captain Bell said. "Be still."

Chueco was out of breath. He had returned with alcohol, cotton balls, and something unrecognizable. He knelt beside Otto, and he dabbed the wound with alcohol. Then he took a mass of spider webs and put them directly over the cut.

"Spider webs?" Captain Bell asked. Bell wondered how that might be hygienic. On the other hand, all of Chueco's other cures had worked.

Chueco nodded. And within a minute, the flow of blood was stanched. Then it suddenly stopped.

"I was bitten by a bad dog. Mama made it this way," Chueco said. "Otto has *susto,* a bad fright. He should drink *manzanilla.* Chamomile tea."[1]

Otto moaned. "*Susto wusto.* Hocus pocus. Vere's the doctor?"

Captain Bell said, "You're all right. The cuts are not deep. Stop playing with snakes and bears!"

"The *manzanilla* will help. I'll go to the kitchen," Chueco said.

"Can't you speak English? Don't want no *susto.* No *manzanilla.* Tea," Otto said, grousing.

"The *susto* is fright," Captain Bell said. Then, turning to Chueco, he said, "Forget about the tea."

Chueco said, "But it will help with the *susto.*"

"No *manzanilla* or mannlilla or vatever it is for me," Otto said. "I would take a Vim Cola. Yaah, for the Manly Man."

"The canteen's not open," Captain Bell said. "How about thanking Chueco?"

Otto was folded awkwardly into one of the school chairs, which was too small for him. He said it so softly that it was almost inaudible: "Thank you."

He was unattractive, with heavy pitted cheeks from acne. His eyes were brown, but had no lightness or playfulness in them, just spite. He was tall, but not slim. He was slow and ungainly. He had a broad forehead, and his square jaw reminded Bell of a Viking. He could imagine the boy as a warrior with a club. Why was he acting this way? What kind of family did he have? Why did he torture animals?

The Mexican boys were whispering in Spanish. They hated Otto. He could hear the curses and epithets: "*¡Qué cabrón!*" "*¡Pendejo!*" "*¡Puto!*"

Captain Bell shouted, "Emergency's over. Play pool and ping-pong!"

But the earlier gaiety had disappeared from the tournament and many of the boys drifted back to their barracks.

After midnight, when everyone had gone to bed officially, Captain Bell decided to get dressed and do a final inspection of the barracks himself. He remembered the night Sam had gotten punched in the face at Devilfish's poker party. The real party had started after lights-out.

He lit a lantern and patrolled the camp, burrowed against a cold wind.

Why had he taken this job? Was it really better than running a hotel?

Immediately, he spotted a light on in the rec room. He set the lantern down on the ground, so he could open the door with his one hand. Raucous laughter. "You can see her titties!"

Chairs had been arranged to mimic a movie theater. A black-and-white movie was projected onto the wall.

Captain Bell stood at the back of the room and watched. A nurse, wearing only her white cap. Curvaceous, like Darlene.

He turned on the light. The boys moaned.

"Who turned on the light?" Jack shouted. He was running the projector. But when he turned around, his face turned white.

"Captain, what are you doing here?"

"I might be asking you the same question," Captain Bell said. "Blue Movies are over."

After everyone filed out, Jack stayed behind. "Please don't put me in the brig again. I'll clean the latrines for a month."

He really didn't blame them for watching pornography, as sexually deprived as he felt. On the other hand, he couldn't openly condone it. Wouldn't go over well in Washington or with the locals, if it got out. He remembered the Lanterne Verte in Paris during the War, where the topless waitresses had served you at your table, or against the wall.

"I will take it under advisement," he said.

"Does that mean that I am not going to the brig?"

"Go to bed!" Captain Bell said.

"Yes, sir," Jack said.

• • •

After he had dispersed the blue movie party, Captain Bell left the rec room and headed for the clinic. Why did he have medical staff if they were nowhere to be found? What if they had a *real* emergency on their hands? One that Chueco might not be able to handle. One that could not be solved with herbal salves or spider webs.

He heard Darlene's laughter before he even got to Dr. Walker's office. Surely she wasn't carrying on with him? He guessed she had broken it off with Jack if he was watching blue movies. Or had she cut off the relationship after the episode with the nude sketches? They never had found out who had pinned them up.

Dr. Walker was sitting at his desk, reading. He was wearing a checkered flannel robe, with a matching nightcap, and looked like Ebenezer Scrooge in Dickens's *Christmas Carol.*

He adjusted his glasses on his nose. "Now, Miss Robinson, this is Longfellow, although not a love poem: *'Until we meet again! That is the meaning/Of the familiar words that men repeat/At parting in the street./Ah yes, till then! but when death intervening/Rends us asunder, with what ceaseless pain/We wait for the Again!'"*

Darlene was leaning back in her chair. She was wearing a nightdress with a lacy collar. Her blue robe was pulled tight. If she were interested in a tryst, this was not the attire.

"Why, Doc, that is just the saddest poem you could have chosen on New Year's!" She giggled.

Her back was to Captain Bell. She held out her glass, bending forward toward the desk. "Can you top me up, Doc?"

Captain Bell found her rump tantalizing.

Dr. Walker poured from the bottle into her glass. They had killed half of the bottle. Who was supplying it to the camp? Or was Dr. Walker just buying it from Joe Kafouri?

"The quality of Virginia bourbon is indisputable. It is my favorite, of all libations," Dr. Walker said.

Darlene burst out laughing, mimicking him. "I don't usually partake myself, but since it's New Year's and I am feeling low, I thought we might as well enjoy the spoils."

Why? She had broken it off with Jack? Or was she upset about something else?

Dr. Walker looked up. "Captain Bell, what a serendipitous surprise. We were just about to ring in the New Year. Would you like to join us?"

"It's way past midnight," Captain Bell said.

Dr. Walker popped open his gold pocket watch and glanced at the time. "Ah, you are right. As the Virgil of the Aeneid would say, 'Time flies never to be recalled.'"

Darlene laughed again. "You devil, Roy. Win at pool?"

"Didn't play," Captain Bell said. "Otto got clawed by a cub."

"You don't say," Darlene said. "You're not spinning a tall tale, are you? Where did he find a cub?"

Captain Bell shrugged. "Hell if I know. That boy keeps playing with fire. Snakes. Bears. One day he is going to run out of luck."

Dr. Walker gulped the bourbon. "Our services were not required, I hope?"

"Chueco came to the rescue. Otto had a cut. Not very deep," Captain Bell said. "It does seem that you both make yourself scarce when needed."

Was he supposed to police these two as well?

"We are reading sad poetry to ring in the New Year," Darlene said. "Join the party!"

"I've just broken up a blue movie party in the rec room," Captain Bell said.

He was tempted to tell her that Jack had organized it but felt that would be hurtful.

"Boys will be boys!" Darlene said, raising her glass in a sweeping motion. "Not surprised. Spare us the details."

Dr. Walker reached into a drawer and pulled out an expensive crystal glass. Had he brought this from his family mansion in Tyler, East Texas? He poured the bourbon into the glass and handed it to Captain Bell.

"What were you saying?" Captain Bell asked.

Darlene waved her hand, then hiccupped, slurring her words. "Not imporrrr . . . -tunt."

"I would be most interested in all of the salacious details, if you are ready to divulge any. But maybe this is . . ." Dr. Walker said.

Darlene winked at Captain Bell. Her blue eyes were so alluring.

"I am sure you have seen it all before," Captain Bell said.

Dr. Walker chuckled. "I have been to a stag party or two in my life, there is no denying that! On Bourbon Street, activities of a licentious nature, as you might imagine, are celebrated. At the Old Absinthe House Bar, they had dancers who were scantily clad. Pop-up cakes, and such. But this is not polite conversation in front of a lady."

The glass brimmed with tempting bourbon. Although he was the enforcer of the prohibition policies, he felt a seed of rebellion growing within himself. Why not have a taste?

Dr. Walker's eyes were red. He gave Captain Bell a sad, knowing smile.

"My boy," he said. "You are carrying a weighty burden at this camp. You are in need of a little levity. We won't tell Washington! Or any teetotalers hiding under rocks!"

Darlene giggled. "Let your hair down just a tad." She twirled a curl of her black hair with her index finger. "I don't usually . . ." She hiccupped.

Captain Bell took a small swig. It was divinely smooth. He raised his glass, and they all three clinked together, "Carpe diem!"

Dr. Walker added, "'Take everything in moderation, including moderation.' The great Oscar Wilde."

CHAPTER 38.

# Local Olympics, and One Afar, February 1936

**January was cold.** Most of the time, Captain Bell warmed himself against the potbellied stove in the office, working his way through mounds of federal paperwork. He opened the door of the stove and stuck in another piece of wood. He had not discovered who was smuggling spirits into the camp and had lost appetite for the chase, especially after the New Year's gathering with Darlene and Dr. Walker. Should he let it go? He resented being the one-man teetotaler squad. As long as the camp was peaceful, maybe it didn't matter. He was still scrupulous about the budget but could find no discrepancies in E.O.'s accounts. He had only seen Darlene a few times in passing after the New Year's gathering, and she seemed distant. For company, he took Delilah with him on his inspections around the camp—she trotted jauntily beside him. In the middle of the day, he played ball with her, to get some fresh air and escape from the stuffy, close office. She was an affectionate dog, and eased his loneliness.

A sort of understanding, not exactly friendship, had developed with Dr. Walker. They were both worried about Germany's increasing militarism, yet they disagreed bitterly on the boycott of the 1936 Olympics. Captain Bell could not stomach Dr. Walker's monologues on the position of Avery Brundage, the president of the Olympic Committee, that the U.S. should stay out of the "Jew–Nazi altercation." He also parroted Brundage's paranoid rhetoric that the boycott movement was a "Jewish–Communist conspiracy." Captain Bell himself supported the position of Judge Jeremiah Mahoney, the head of the Amateur Athletic Union, who argued that the Olympics should be boycotted because of the Reich's discrimination against Jews. The 1935 Nuremberg laws had stripped German Jews of their citizenship. The Olympic rules forbade discrimination against any athletes or participants on the basis of race and religion. Yet in December 1935, Brundage had outfoxed Mahoney, in a close vote of the Amateur Athletic Union, to send a team to Berlin. Dr. Walker had gloated over this recent victory, and Captain Bell had declined his invitation for cocktails. The New Year's Eve gathering had not been repeated. Jesse Owens, the runner, had at first supported the boycott, reasoning that it was hypocritical to support the Olympics since it discriminated against Jews, just as Blacks were discriminated against in the United States. But in the end after Brundage's victory, Black newspapers had followed another logic, that victory of Black athletes would cast doubt on the Reich's ideology of the "master race." Captain Bell had seen firsthand how soldiers in the War had been segregated in units. There had been only one unit, nicknamed "The Black Devils" by the Germans, that was commanded by Black officers. And yet this practice seemed calcified as Captain Bell recalled the directives from the Director of the CCC to segregate the CCC camps. How had anything changed in eighteen years?

After supper, Captain Bell returned to his office to listen to the news on the radio. His interest in politics became more feverish and intense and started to feel like an addiction. The results of the Winter Olympics were covered nightly on the radio. On February 6, twenty-eight countries participated in the opening ceremony and marched past Adolf Hitler, who raised his arm in a Nazi salute. Americans did not salute. Some athletes gave the Olympic salute, which was unfortunately close to the Nazi salute. Sports and politics had become intertwined in a pernicious way, but Captain Bell still followed the Olympics with interest. On February 18, Great Britain won the ice hockey tournament. They had tied with the U.S. in the last game, but Great Britain had more points in the aggregate.

But the general mood was isolationist, and Americans did not want to get involved in a war. After Captain Bell's experience in the Great War, he was adamantly opposed to it. But when he brought up the issue with Dr. Walker, he found that Dr. Walker was in favor of war. "But Doctor, you spent the entire war in a camp in Georgia!" Dr. Walker blustered, prevaricated, and waxed lyrical about the honor of General Robert E. Lee during the Civil War. Captain Bell didn't have time for these garrulous monologues, and they infuriated him. The memory of the boys he had lost in his platoon at the Argonne Forest was still poignant for him, after all these years.

• • •

He stayed longer than he usually did at the office on the first day of March. It was a chance to catch up with some paperwork since no one was in the office. He got carried away and before he knew it, it was midnight. Delilah was curled next to his desk, snoring loudly. After he lit a lantern, he nudged her, and she shook herself awake. He rubbed her behind the ears. "Come on, big girl, let's call it a night." He opened the door to the darkness, except for a half-moon. Not like the night with the full moon when he had kissed Darlene. A coyote howled in the distance. No matter how hard it was to banish Darlene from his consciousness, he could not. Did like-minded souls naturally find each other? Or was this his fantasy?

The shadow of the lantern elongated in front of him, and he focused on Delilah's shadow. It distracted him from looking at his own.

Delilah trotted to the mess hall, even though that was not the fastest way back to his barracks.

"No. Not that way, Delilah," he said.

But she insisted on skirting the edge of the mess hall. A light was on inside. He heard raucous shouting. Was this another blue movie night? He either erred too much on the side of strictness or on the side of lenience. Would he ever get it right, this balance of maintaining discipline?

All the tables of the mess hall had been shoved into one corner. An open space had been established in the middle, as if it were a boxing ring. Someone had squared off the room with ropes tied to the beams.

"Get that fucker!"

"Give it to him!"

*"¡El Puto! ¡El Puto! ¡El Puto! ¡Hijo de puta!"*

Boys on each side waved little pieces of paper that looked like the coupons from the canteen. They roared. Even though Otto was not popular, it looked as if the Anglo boys were supporting him. The cooks and the Hispanic boys were supporting Devilfish. He didn't like the looks of this at all. He had just been congratulating himself on his evasion of segregation.

Delilah barked, but no one heard her.

Devilfish bounced up and down, as if he were a professional boxer, dodging Otto's lunges. Otto was much bigger, but he was clumsy. It looked as if he had already been pummeled in the face. Otto lunged forward, and Devilfish dodged. Then he got Otto in the face with a left jab. Otto staggered backward and lost his balance, falling flat on his back.

E.O. jumped forward and started the count, as if it were a professional boxing match. 1–2–3 . . .

He held up Otto's limp hand. Delilah barked again.

E.O. looked toward the door. He stopped counting. The room suddenly went quiet.

"Break it up," Captain Bell said.

CHAPTER 39.

# A Reckoning

**The atmosphere in the office wasn't much better.** Captain Bell was on the warpath. Both Devilfish and Otto had been summoned, each separately.

Devilfish had shrugged. He was unapologetic. "Got tired of being called slave boy, Captain. That's all there was to it. Tired of honkeys misbehavin'."

Sam kept trying to type the *Round-Up*, but found he was making too many typos. E.O. didn't look up once from his ledger.

Otto was summoned after he had been treated in the infirmary. He had a black eye, and his face was bruised. He groused, "I'm gonna get that Black boy."

Captain Bell slammed his fist on the desk. "You will not talk like that! One more altercation—I mean it—and you're out! Discharged. You're a troublemaker."

"Sam!" Captain Bell bellowed, even though he was sitting no farther than two feet away.

"Sir!" Sam said, getting up from his desk.

"Call Devilfish back in," he said.

Captain Bell stood up from his desk. "You will apologize to Devilfish," he said to Otto. "Shake hands."

Devilfish held out his hand. Otto grasped it, but barely shook it. "Ya. Sorry," he mumbled.

"That's not loud enough," Captain Bell said.

"Sorry," Otto said, without much conviction.

Devilfish shrugged, as if this peacemaking was a farce. He did not expect anything from Otto, ever.

"Now," Captain Bell said. "Each of you will be cleaning the latrines for a week."

Sam had thought Captain Bell might put Otto in the brig. But it was against camp rules to fight, so maybe he felt that both should be punished.

"Sam will supervise," Captain Bell said. "He will set up your cleaning schedule."

"But Captain . . ." Sam objected. This was going to make him even more unpopular in the camp. It was bad enough that he issued or denied weekend passes, on Captain Bell's orders.

After the boys had left, Captain Bell went over the accounts with E.O. Once they had finished, he asked nonchalantly, "Were you in charge of the fight?"

E.O. said, "No."

Captain Bell asked, "But you were in charge of the prizes?"

E.O. hesitated.

"It wouldn't be a good idea to lie, son," Captain Bell said. "Lying is going to make it worse."

"Yes," E.O. said. "The prizes were supplies from the canteen. The boys were betting cigarettes or candy or whatever!"

Sam was astounded. He was also unaware of this gambling

ring. And everyone thought E.O. was so pious. Church-of-Christer. Straight as an arrow. Was he getting extra supplies for himself?

"Yes, sir," E.O. said. "How did you know?"

Captain Bell did not answer. "You know that gambling is against the rules. This is a one-time warning. If I *ever* catch you doing something against the rules again, you are out. You are also going to clean the latrine for a week."

E.O. pushed the glasses up on his nose. He looked as if he were about to cry. "I can't lose this job," he said. "My folks . . ."

"Now you are going to show me where you keep the loot," Captain Bell said.

CHAPTER 40.

# The Loot

**Captain Bell had caught pilferers in the kitchen before at his father's hotel, the Menger.** His father had assigned him this task. He had said, "Won't hurt you to get your hands dirty, son. Know the business from the ground up. Gotta know the value of a dollar." His father could never resist a cliché. The accountant had summoned him and shown him how expenses for the kitchen had risen compared to the receipts to the restaurant. Yet the price of food was the same. Before the cooks and waiters left every day, it was his job to search them, not a job he relished. He was only eighteen and had been naive. Shrimp plopped out onto the kitchen floor as a cook emptied his boots. He burst out laughing. But what happened after that wasn't so funny. His father had given Raúl not a single dollar of his monthly pay. He had worked for the hotel for fifteen years and was supporting a large family. His father had been unmoved by the man's pleas for mercy. Captain Bell felt this was harsh. The Menger was serving sumptuous meals, yet the employees ate refried beans in the back. Who wouldn't be tempted?

Captain Bell followed E.O. as they left the office. He thought he had escaped the hotel.

He followed E.O. to a small building behind the kitchen, where they kept other supplies for the camp: linens, pillows, sheets, towels. E.O. pulled out a key and opened up a closet.

A number of boxes were neatly stacked, as if these were legitimate supplies. E.O. pulled them out, one by one.

Captain Bell opened each box: Wonder Cure, cigarettes, shaving cream, a few razors. No candy. A few bottles of Vim Cola.

He should fire the kid. But it wasn't that easy to find someone to do accounts. He had found no reason to believe that he was fiddling with the accounts.

"Wonder Cure is forbidden," he said, as harshly as he could. "It contains opium."

E.O. stared at him. "It's no longer a prize if anyone wins a bet."

"You are the one who handed out Wonder Cure at the Christmas party," Captain Bell said, probing.

"No!" E.O. said. "I have no idea who did that."

"What are the boys betting on, besides the Devilfish and Otto match?"

"Anything," E.O. said. "The boxing match between Baby Arizmandi and Henry Armstrong. That was New Year's Eve. World Series in the fall. Detroit Tigers vs. Chicago Cubs."

"So this has been going on for some time?"

E.O. nodded.

"Right under my nose!" Captain Bell shouted.

"I promise . . ." E.O.'s voice trailed off. A single tear rolled down his pudgy cheek.

"But what's in it for you?" Captain Bell asked. "You don't smoke. Don't drink."

"Bored," E.O. said, pushing his thick glasses back onto his nose.

Captain Bell whistled. "With all of the activities at this camp?"

E.O. shrugged. "Just am. Don't like those kinds of games. Have never been good at sports."

The boy wasn't very athletic, and his vision was weak. Captain Bell wanted to believe him, but he still didn't think he had the full story. A doubt lingered.

"You're in charge of the money. Your honesty has to be above reproach!"

"Please," E.O. said. "I have not touched a cent from the camp budget."

Captain Bell let him sweat for a minute or two.

"Take those boxes back to the canteen," Captain Bell said. "Bring me the Wonder Cure. You have one more chance."

CHAPTER 41.

# Punishment in the Pit, March 1936

**It was a terrible three weeks for Sam since he had to supervise Otto, Devilfish, and E.O.'s cleaning of the latrines.** Sam brought the buckets, the broom, the mop, and the strong disinfectant. He propped open the door with a rock while they worked. That way the breeze would diffuse the odiferous smell as well as the acrid scent of the disinfectant. Once they were finished, Captain Bell came to inspect the job.

He was surprised that Otto was the most talkative of the three. E.O. didn't speak at all and refused to say anything more about the gambling ring. If Sam asked him a question, he answered with one syllable. "Yep." "Nope." Devilfish sang while he worked. They were mostly songs that he had sung to the camp, like "Muffin" or "Dandy." He worked fast. On the other hand, Otto was slow as a hundred-year-old turtle, and he spent most of his time leaning on the mop. To Sam's surprise, he wanted to yack.

Otto said, "Once I threw a cat off the barn roof, ya. See if it could fly. Vater beat me with a lariat rope."

"Snakes aren't mean, unless you provoke them," Sam said. "No sense in that."

"Used to steal eggs from my Mater. Took about six eggs for a box of .22 shorts, about a dime. Got beat for that, too," Otto said. He touched his eye, which was still black. "You like Black people?"

"You gotta treat people right," Sam said.

Otto laughed. "Vater made me go to church every Sunday, yaah. But one Sunday I vent with a peddler in a wagon. He had candy. Vent with him down the road to the Gustafsons'. Spent the night there. Vater kept beating me with that rope. Honor your Mater and Vater."

His folks were going to church. But what happened to Otto? Was he a bad seed from the beginning?

"I stole a watermelon once and I got whipped," Sam said. Sam felt a little sorry for Otto. His cheeks were pitted from acne, and his face was unsightly.

"Ya, you're a sissy boy," Otto said. "Baby Red." He had a meanness in his eyes. Sam remembered that Otto had almost broken his nose.

"I've got work to do. This is taking all day," Sam said. "Think we could speed this up?"

"Yaah, so go tell Mater Bell," Otto said. "Tell him. E.O. is trading goods for booze. If he can't trade it, he sells it to the A-rab. Tell him his whore is selling whiskey for that A-rab."

What? Darlene was selling whiskey for Joe? E.O. was making money off the goods from the canteen?

Otto could not really be trusted, anyhow—mean as a bobcat. But here was the conundrum: If he told Captain Bell, then he would be even more isolated in the camp. He decided against carrying the tales.

"She's not a whore," Sam said. He wasn't sure about Darlene's reputation, but he didn't like hearing her maligned.

Otto leered. "Suck her titties, like your Mater."

Sam closed the door to the latrine and turned the key. He yelled out, "Holler when you're finished." He sat out under the shade of a bristly mesquite tree, a fair distance away so he couldn't hear Otto cursing him. The blue sky was heavy with billowy clouds. It wasn't hot yet, and he figured he could sit here all day if he wanted to. Were Otto's folks exasperated with him and that's why they beat him? He didn't see himself as vengeful, but in this case, a fella like this might reside in the latrine, as far as he was concerned. His mouth was filthy and should be washed out with soap, but even whips hadn't worked with him.

Captain Bell found him sitting under the shade of the lone mesquite tree. Delilah was trotting beside him.

"Otto was being a lout, so I decided to lock him in," Sam said. "He's scrubbing it down now."

Sam scratched Delilah behind the ears. She barked.

Sam thought Captain Bell might scold him, but he did not. Because of the way his skin had been grafted onto his cheeks, he looked a little like a pirate when he smiled. "Let's see if it's clean *enough*," Captain Bell said.

On the second round of cleaning, Devilfish couldn't be found. Sam went to the kitchen, to see if Devilfish were there.

Unkneaded, lonesome balls of dough sat in huge silver bowls, in the middle of the counter. The Black cooks were lolling about, their arms crossed, leaning against the wall. Sam expected to see Devilfish singing a tune. Maybe he had forgotten that he had latrine duty.

A few of the Mexican cooks were still peeling potatoes, and they talked among themselves in another corner.

The atmosphere was funereal.

"Did somebody die?" Sam asked.

"No," Chueco said. "But Devil left this morning." He pulled out a shiny harmonica from the pocket of his long white apron and blew on it, emitting a discordant sound. "*Regalo*. Present."

Sam was surprised. "He's AWOL?"

Chueco said, "*¿Que*? AWOL? What is that?"

Where did he go? He complained about picking cotton, scratching out a living through odd jobs, playing in juke joints. Had he returned to Dallas? Did it have to do with his fight with Otto?

But when Sam reported Devilfish's disappearance to Captain Bell, the latter already knew. "John Lomax[1] has been looking for Devilfish for some time. He's collecting ballads. Devilfish is going to help them find ballads at Texas prison farms. He knows the musician Lead Belly. He knows 'em all."

Sam was baffled. "What?" He had never heard of such a thing.

"He knows many of the boys in jail. They're going to record their songs. They're chasing after the ballads. After Texas, they're headed to Angola, Louisiana. Lead Belly is serving time there, apparently."

"But Devilfish didn't say goodbye."

Captain Bell ruffled his hair. "They were itching to get on the road. Believe me, it's good news."

Sam felt wistful. He had just expected that Devilfish would continue to be around the camp. He loved to hear him sing and play music.

Captain Bell sang, "One for the blackbird, one for the crow, one for the cutworm, and two to grow."

Sam had never heard Captain Bell sing, and he couldn't carry a tune. He suppressed a chuckle.

Captain Bell added, "Once Lomax sang me that song, I released Devilfish from his duties. He'll get an honorable discharge."

CHAPTER 42.

# The Disappearance of Doc Walker's Gold Pocket Watch, Early May 1936

At first, he thought he had misplaced great-granddaddy's timepiece, but then upon further investigation, he realized that it must have been purloined by an unknown culprit. Because he partook liberally of Wonder Cure and bourbon straight or other spirits (thank you for such succor in this forlorn camp, Darlene), he could not correctly recall exactly when the watch had disappeared. Was it shortly after Devilfish's sudden departure? He did not want to admit to himself that the copious doses of Wonder Cure and bourbon had addled his brain. The thought had flitted across his mind like a whirring, bright hummingbird, but he had quickly repressed it before any alarming illumination had occurred.

He worried that he was becoming now like Aunt Loulah, who had developed dementia in her later years. She had constantly inquired about her purse. Perhaps he was also developing the same symptoms, and he would continue to inquire about his pocket watch until the end of his days! Where's my watch? Where's my watch? The irony of such a tragedy was not lost upon him because that meant that he had lost his memory of the historical events in his own life and his rather prominent Southern family.

But now it was early May, and no progress whatsoever had been made in Captain Bell's various attempts at detection throughout April. Perhaps in light of his various injuries, wounds, and trauma in the Great War, the doctor should go easy on the boy. Captain Bell could not stop construction of the swimming pool to search for the antique heirloom.

On the other hand, he thought, why not?

The pocket watch had been passed down from generation to generation and was a reminder of the Walker family's honorable military legacy in the Civil War. Great-grandfather Walker had been the last surviving Confederate officer who had refused to sign the amnesty. He had fought at Antietam, Fredericksburg, Gettysburg, and the siege of Petersburg. At first, Great-grandfather Walker had been imprisoned in the Old Capitol building, but then he was relocated to an officers' prison in Johnson's Island, Lake Erie. Since he refused to take the amnesty oath, he was released three months after the Civil War had ended. How could one compete with such fervent patriotism? Dr. Walker was a little ashamed that he had not gone to fight in the Great War but was assigned to Camp Gordon. In a rare moment of perception, he had speculated that he, in fact, did not have the nerves or talent for dealing with war injuries. Perhaps duty at Camp Gordon was providential? If Captain Bell's injuries and trauma were any indication, he should be praising the Almighty that he had been assigned duty as camp doctor in Georgia, where he had spent an inordinate amount of time weighing boys, looking under their tongues, and listening to their hearts. Before they deployed, he had given lectures on sexual hygiene and prophylactics to prevent venereal disease, since he had been informed by the higher officers that this problem was exacerbated in France.

He was mightily disappointed that Captain Bell had refused to join their cocktail hours after New Year's. Captain Bell became irritable and tight-lipped especially when they discussed world developments and the rise of German military hegemony, especially in what had been the previous Weimar Republic. After all, Brundage, the president of the Olympic Committee, had visited Germany and found that Jewish allegations of discrimination were greatly exaggerated. Darlene's mood had also darkened, and she had declined to join his readings of Longfellow, Coleridge, and Faulkner, but she had continued to provide him with spirits and Wonder Cure. In a moment of candor, he had asked her what was dampening her enthusiasm, but she had not answered. He surmised that she did not greatly concern herself with world affairs. Had he erred in confiding his profound sorrow about the loss of his wife, Eleanor, to consumption? He had also told her about his estrangement from his daughter, the belle of the ball, who now lived in Mississippi. One night, after a lengthy reading of Longfellow, he confided in her his disappointment about his dormant literary ambitions, which had never been realized. Daddy had insisted on Tulane medical school, instead of his literary aspirations, and he had acquiesced. He had passed his medical boards after arduous study, but was indifferent to the actual practice of medicine, which did not interest him as much as reading the *Great Books and Poetry of the Western World*.

It seemed Darlene was not unfamiliar with the notion of sadness and had not resented his confession of loneliness. But their time together, discussing great literature, had not led to increased coquetry and dalliance, as he had secretly hoped. Perhaps he should have worn his three-piece suit with a vest, instead of sleep attire, to their cocktail hours?

Wonder Cure had not worked wonders in that department, but it had made him feel more optimistic. He recalled how impressed he had been with the eminent Dr. Volkov that day at Sul Ross. But if Dr. Volkov was on a lecture tour around the United States, surely he could consult Dr. Brinkley. If he had the opportunity to avail himself of Dr. Brinkley's services, he was not averse to the procedure. He had heard Dr. Brinkley was now living in Del Rio, which was not that great a distance from Balmorhea. He dismissed Dr. Fishbein's doubts about Dr. Brinkley's experiments—he surmised it was pure professional jealousy, that Dr. Brinkley had developed a response to the rather delicate issue of malfunction of the male member. Dr. Brinkley was simply responding to a problem that he had faced in his long medical practice as a G.P. and that he, himself, had known in his marriage on occasion. Eleanor dealt with this problem with great delicacy.

He was ensnared in the delusion that a procedure such as Dr. Brinkley was offering might make him more successful in courtship.

# PART IV:

# The Pool

CHAPTER 43.

# Sam, Arroyo Drive, Harlingen, Texas, 1980

**Four years had passed since he had first dreamed of Darlene.** Sam was sitting in his wheelchair in front of the glass window to the backyard, watching green jays. He could no longer walk out in the yard and putter with his plants on the patio. He remembered how he had felt, trying to pull on the glove with one hand that day shortly after his amputation. Now, even simpler tasks than that required immense effort. The tumor that had curled itself around the nerves of his shoulder had snaked its way to his spine. He and Maggie had spent most of their time at doctor's offices, but the doctors had decided against operating because of the tumor's proximity to his spine. He had gradually lost the use of his legs, even with his discipline of walking the rope every day in the front yard. He suffered many indignities that he would never have dreamed of when he was a youngster, running track for Sul Ross. How could the body fail you so completely?

Maggie was running ragged, and they had a burly Hispanic Goliath named Leo, a nurse's aid, to lift him out of the bed and turn him. They spoke in Spanish, and Sam encouraged the young man to enroll in a local junior college.

He was developing bedsores, which itched more than mosquito bites. The little washing machine in the kitchen chugged away at all hours, cleaning sheets. He felt Maggie was smoking too much, but he refrained from nagging her about it.

She always had a pot of coffee brewing—and the smell of coffee cheered him up, even if he only drank one cup. It was as if Maggie was making up for all those years of rationing. In the forties, coffee had been rationed as well as butter, jam, sugar, and shortening. If you needed a tire changed, you'd have to patch it and make do. Meat was in short supply, and they had eaten a good deal of Spam, about as foul as canned goat! He had planted tomatoes in the backyard for a victory garden, and they had ripened into juicy red tomatoes, until the spider mites got the vines.

His son, Griffin, found it difficult to visit him and didn't stay long, but the grandchildren came almost every day, and he told them stories if he was up to it. The Presbyterian preacher, Luke Goodman, visited them once a week and prayed with them. He thought frequently of his mother's strong faith—and how that had carried her through the Depression. Sometimes Reverend Goodman made Maggie laugh.

Sam had decided to record some of his experiences at Seagraves, and the law, into a tape recorder. He had not decided what he would say about Balmorhea. He still had some use of his right arm, and he could hold the microphone, but he felt that might be going soon. After he and Maggie had finished their master's degrees at Chapel

Hill, they had gone to West Texas. He spoke of teaching in Seagraves, a town of five hundred near Lubbock, which had become an oil boom town in the thirties, overrun by six thousand people camping, tenting, shacking, and squatting in and around. As principal of the school, he had a devil of a time finding classrooms, and they had taught just about everywhere—in the gymnasium, auditorium, shop buildings.

He spoke of the odd case here and there in his law practice. One cotton farmer had scratched his last will and testament on his tractor with a nail, and it had been accepted by the court. The sentence had simply said: "I leave it all to my wife."

This was not far from the will he had dictated to his secretary, Gwyneth, witnessed by his son, who had also become a lawyer. He had done well with his practice.

He did not speak about swiping Darlene's diary, or some of his more private thoughts about Balmorhea. He did not speak about losing the race for Congress in 1964. He had wanted to serve, and this was a great disappointment to him.

Would they have to feed him soon? Sometimes he couldn't get a tight grip on the spoon when he was eating. The last time she made fried chicken, he kept dropping the chicken leg.

Rosemary was going to a small college in Missouri on a tennis scholarship. He was happy for her, but he would miss her regular visits. Shortly after she had accepted the scholarship, he dreamed he was sprinting, almost flying, across the plain, the fifty-yard dash, at Sul Ross, as if he were twenty again. Coach Gladson had clicked the stopwatch. "Best, ever, McCabe." But when he woke, he was stretched out on a single bed, and he could not lift his legs, thick as tree trunks. Did time, itself, streak by just as fast as lightning? Maggie was curled up on a single bed beside him, elf-like, with her hands folded under her head. Her curly white hair sprouted wings on her head. When they had first married, she had been quite amorous. But no question of that now . . . Dr. Brinkley's screwball motto popped into his mind: Vim and Vigor for the Manly Man. Or was it Dr. Volkov? But maybe one day, they would have medicine to cure such a problem. Had the boy Chueco gone on with what he had learned from his mother about healing with plants?

As if she could read his distress, Maggie's intelligent blue eyes popped open. "How about some breaky?"

He tried to put up a brave front, but the spouts opened. "Reckon so."

She inched over to the bed and pecked him on the cheek. She dabbed a cloth handkerchief on his cheeks to dry them.

"Bacon, coming right up," she said, squeezing his hand. "I'll put the coffee on."

He barely felt the sensation of her touch.

He and Maggie had faced all sorts of challenges in their marriage: living off of scrip in an oil boom town, studying for the bar, counting their pennies when he had first started practicing law, raising two sons, running for Congress. When they were out at Seagraves, many teachers had been drafted and had gone to fight in the Second World War. If students were near eighteen, they signed up. Many didn't come back. He had wanted to fight, but the army had rejected him because of the earlier melanoma and flat feet. He thought of Captain Bell, who was probably dead now. Captain Bell would have been too old to be drafted for the Second World War. Perhaps he should get the Balmorhea box out again. Surely Maggie had not lugged it back to the attic.

But there was the legal box, marked "Balmorhea" in blue magic marker, sitting like a fat hen, stuffed with letters, Darlene's diary, and documents, on top of an old wooden cedar chest that Maggie claimed had been made by slaves in North Carolina. Did he think the box would lay golden eggs? Maybe Maggie was right. He shouldn't keep going over that year.

Once Sam had passed the bar, they moved to Harlingen in 1944. His sons weren't very old. His older son, Griffin, was old enough to remember and was curious. They read the newspapers together every morning about the war. He asked a hundred questions about D-Day, June 6, 1944. Many soldiers had drowned or were shot on the Normandy beach during the assault. Griffin was especially interested in the story of one soldier who saved numerous comrades from drowning, wading through the surf, under a barrage of shellfire and mortars. Captain Bell had been right to worry about drowning at Balmorhea, and Sam couldn't bring himself to think of that day. He couldn't answer when his son asked, "But why didn't they know how to swim?"

The other son, William, was a tyke and was too little to remember the War. Maggie had scrimped and saved ration cards so she could buy the sugar for his birthday cake. He had become a fine doctor, a heart specialist, and he practiced in Dallas.

One day in early June 1980, Sam dreamed of Darlene again. Whiskery catfish and silvery minnows darted past her as she dove down through the pristine, cold water of the Balmorhea pool. She was examining the belly of an ancient turtle, flipped upside down, resting on the gravelly bottom. Was it dead? Her white nurse's cap was pinned to her hair, but she was nude. Her hair was blonde. Wasn't it black? He dove down after her, but she pointed to the surface.

As soon as she got her breath, she said, "Why, Red, what in the world are you doing here?"

CHAPTER 44.

# A Midnight Dip, Captain Bell, May 1936

The pool had been filled with water from the spring. It was more like a freshwater lake than a swimming pool, with turtles, catfish, and minnows swirling at the bottom near the gravel. In places, it was very deep. They were ahead of schedule, and he should have been happy, but he couldn't sleep. It was hot, and he was sleeping only in his boxers.

He lit the lantern and nudged Delilah, who was sleeping at the edge of his bed. She shook her head, yawned, and put her head down again.

Captain Bell pulled on a light cotton robe but didn't bother to tie the sash. It would take him forever with his one hand. There were only a few boys in the officers' barracks—and they were sleeping peacefully. He peered at Sam's innocent face. He was snoring slightly, the air whistling through his mouth. Shortie was staring up at him, in that wheat field in the Argonne Forest. But Sam's eyes were green, and he was better-looking. The only resemblance to Sam was the red hair. Would he be forever tormented by memories of the war?

He nudged Delilah again. She lifted her head this time, and he scratched her behind the ears. She got up and followed him out. He closed the door gently so he wouldn't wake the boys.

The light from the lantern bobbed through the dark, as if it were a buoy on the sea. The camp was quiet except for the occasional hooting of an owl.

As he was about to pass the clinic, he saw a lone figure sitting on the wooden steps of the building. Only the red tip of a lit cigarette was visible.

"Here's your hat, what's your hurry?" the voice said. "Take a seat."

"What are you doing up at this hour?" Captain Bell asked. They had not talked much since the New Year's Eve party in Dr. Walker's office.

Delilah barked. Darlene stroked her back.

"Jinx. You owe me a Vim Cola," Darlene said, laughing. "Vim for the Manly Man. Love animals, although I could do without the tortoises. The Manly Man loves ancient tortoises from the Galápagos. Cost us a fortune to lug them back."

What was she talking about? "What turtles from the Galápagos?" Captain Bell asked, setting down the lantern on the ground. He sat next to her on the step. She smelled like lavender.

"My ex-husband," Darlene said, exhaling a plume of smoke. "Is something bothering you?"

"Didn't know you'd been married," Captain Bell said.

"He's a rascal," Darlene said. "The less said, the better."

The light was dim, but Captain Bell could see that she was wearing a light cotton robe, loosely tied. Her cleavage was showing. Like him, had she eschewed pajamas?

He didn't see any harm in confiding in Darlene about the guest list. "Am not too thrilled about former Governor Neff's guest list for the inauguration. Some nasty bigwigs."

"Oh?" Darlene said. "Anyone I know?"

"The fella who owns the Chisos Mine in Terlingua. He keeps turning up. One day he turned up at Thanksgiving, looking for that Dr. Volkov. Always brings his thugs."

Darlene sucked on the cigarette. "Heard of him."

"Neff is using the opening to tout himself. I find it a little strange that he included Dr. Brinkley, that fraud who has made a big splash in Del Rio. Has a radio station. Featured on the cover of *JAMA*. Weren't you reading about him?"

"He's coming?" Darlene asked.

Delilah's ears perked up, as if she had heard something out there in the dark.

"Not sure. We're waiting for RSVPs," Captain Bell said. "What's bothering you?"

Darlene laughed lightly. Didn't she laugh like this when she wanted to evade a question? "Oh, nothin'. I dare you to skinny-dip." She nudged him with her elbow.

He felt sweat dripping between his legs. He couldn't just go breaking all of his own rules in the camp—it would lead to a complete breakdown in discipline. The enchanting moon gleamed in the sky and beckoned him. He remembered the night he had kissed her, months ago.

"Swimming's not allowed at night," he said. His voice sounded gruff. "Have to lead by example."

She giggled. "You sound like the Big Bad Wolf. We'll swim near the edge. Come on . . . who's gonna find out?"

This was a harder temptation to fight than the whiskey at New Year's. He felt his resistance weakening.

She stubbed out her cigarette in the dirt. "Come," she said, pulling him by his one arm. "You never have any fun, Roy."

Because he felt this was true, he followed her order, as if she were the Pied Piper and he had surrendered his will. They carried their lanterns to the cluster of cottonwood saplings that shaded the shallow end of the pool. She slipped off her robe and her black, lacy underwear—she stood before him, completely nude. He vaguely wondered how a nurse could afford such expensive lingerie.

She giggled. "Don't act like you're seeing a mermaid!"

He took off his robe and wiggled off his boxers. Folded them neatly next to the tree.

She held out her hand and he squeezed it. They waded into the refreshing water, until they were waist deep. He felt minnows nipping around his ankles.

"Don't think we should go much farther," he said.

"Just a tad," she said, giggling.

Once they were shoulder deep, she curled herself around his waist, straddled his groin, guiding his penis inside of her, until it was snug. He was a little surprised. She had not bothered with any coy small talk.

"So you've been married," Captain Bell said.

She nibbled his ear and whispered, "Call me Minnie."

He stroked her hair as she moved up and down on him, rhythmically. He had never had sex in the water—he felt buoyant, lighter than he had felt for years. The reflection of the moonlight on the water was silvery and unreal, unlike the transparent blue of the daytime.

She moaned. Who was Minnie? But he ignored the question. At this moment, any curiosity was eclipsed by ecstasy. At the last moment, he shouted, "Darlene."

"Minnie," she said, correcting him. They were silent for a few minutes. He wondered what she was thinking. Then she jumped off of him and dove under the water. Just as quickly, she popped up, shaking her hair.

"Is that your middle name?" he asked.

Delilah barked.

He didn't remember this name from her application. What were her other secrets?

A lantern light winked next to the tree. Delilah barked again.

"Someone's there," Captain Bell said. "We better get out."

"We've been caught with our pants down, Roy," Darlene said. "I swear this is just plain bad luck. My luck seems to go from bad to worse."

Delilah chased whoever it was away.

They waded back toward the edge of the pool. The water now felt heavy against Captain Bell's legs as he moved forward, as if it were an unruly surf rather than a still spring. Once they had dressed, they walked back to the barracks in silence. The earlier joie de vivre he had felt had vanished. He didn't ask Darlene if he would see her again, even for a coffee at the canteen. As mercurial and unpredictable as she was, he shouldn't harbor any fantasies about romance. But no comparison to his timid debutante wife, Pauline, the starfish, splayed on the poster-board bed in Galveston!

Just as Captain Bell was about to open the door to his barracks, the shadow of a giant figure loomed in front of him.

Otto held up the lantern. "Skinny-dipping is *verboten.* Is it not?"

"Go to bed," Captain Bell said, as harshly as he could.

"Let's play the game of *kiss* and *tell*, yaah."

Delilah growled at Otto and tugged at his pants leg. Otto pulled away. "*Die Hundin*. Go!"

Captain Bell shut the door. He would worry about Otto in the morning.

CHAPTER 45.

# Cracks

**The next morning, he felt wonderful.** He was whistling as he worked his way through the mail. E.O. and Sam were quietly working at their desks. He and E.O. would go over the accounts later. He might even take a Vim Cola to Darlene in the clinic, or invite her for one if she wasn't busy. He didn't recoil from his own face in the morning when he shaved.

In the middle of the morning, Sam appeared in front of his desk. He was frowning.

"What is it, son?" he asked.

"Otto is insisting that he see you," Sam said.

He had expected something, but not so soon. Was this the price to pay for his night with Darlene? Or Minnie?

Otto simply flopped down in the chair in front of him. He was too gangly for the small chair.

Captain Bell would have to bluff. He wasn't sure it would work. "You weren't invited to sit down."

Otto shrugged, ignoring the threat. He folded his muscular arms.

"You said yerself that skinny-dipping and swimming at night was verboten. Blue movies are *verboten*, except for you. Animals are *verboten*, except for you."

"Rattlesnakes and bears are different from dogs!" Captain Bell said. He already felt he was losing control of the situation.

Otto's brown eyes burrowed into him, a dangerous challenge. He was in a position of strength, and he was enjoying it.

"The boys would love to hear about what I saw in the moonlight, yaah," Otto said, whistling.

Captain Bell repressed his anger. He had to clear the office before E.O. and Sam heard any more. He couldn't count on their total discretion.

He called out, "Sam, you and E.O. go take a break. Go get a Vim Cola at the canteen."

He could probably weather a scandal at Balmorhea. Most of the boys found Darlene attractive, and he was sure there were all kinds of rumors about her, especially after her relationship with Jack.

"I could discharge you for the fighting," Captain Bell said. "Almost breaking Sam's nose. The rattlesnakes. The bears."

Otto scoffed. "You think you are Jesus, yaah. Let me tell you, ficker. I met a reporter who is writing about the inauguration. He wants to know all the details about the camp. Darlene and her titties in the moonlight with the fotze of Balmorhea will be goot. Better than Governor Neff."

Captain Bell couldn't afford this. This would be very embarrassing. Was Otto bluffing? Could he take the chance?

"What do you want?" Captain Bell asked. He couldn't believe that he was being blackmailed. He regretted throwing caution to the wind last night. Or did he? No! He was just as human as the next man, whatever his aspirations for fairness and discipline.

"A carton of cigarettes. A carton of Wonder Cure. Two bottles of mescal. Two bottles of bourbon."

"No Wonder Cure," Captain Bell said. "I destroyed it." This was a lie. He still had not poured the Wonder Cure down the sink. He fixed his eye on a nail on the wooden partition, rather than looking Otto in the eye. But weren't the mescal and bourbon just as lethal in large doses? Why was he putting his foot down on Wonder Cure, but not mescal and bourbon? Four bottles were too much.

"Cigarettes. Two bottles of mescal," he said, as if he were bargaining for avocados in a Mexican market.

Otto frowned, but he agreed. "Goot," Otto said. "Shake on it."

Could he get rid of this kid after the inauguration? Captain Bell felt as if he was in a dark gunny sack, the kind they used to catch rattlesnakes.

He was shaking Otto's hand just as the boys returned from the canteen. He would have to ask E.O. for some of his gambling stash. Then he would have to explain why or make up some cock-and-bull story.

• • •

"Sam, could you go back to the canteen? Get me a bottle of Vim Cola?" Captain Bell asked.

"But we were just there," Sam said.

"I'm thirsty," Captain Bell said. "Have been preoccupied. I'd appreciate it if you'd get me a cola."

"Sure, Captain. I'll be back in a jiffy."

E.O. sat at his desk. He pushed his coke-bottle glasses up on his nose. "The accounts?"

Captain Bell had to talk to E.O. alone, without Sam around. He didn't want Sam to witness the bargain he was about to make. As soon as Sam was out of earshot, he said, "I need your help with something. And you have to promise to be discreet."

E.O. asked, "Darlene?"

Well, of course, they'd been sitting there when Otto had spilled the beans so anyone with half a brain could figure it out. He didn't need to offer any details.

"A Jezebel," E.O. said. "'A whore is a deep ditch; and a strange woman is a narrow pit.'—Proverbs 23:27."

He had fallen into a cool spring, not a narrow well. Captain Bell didn't comment. What did E.O. know about Darlene? Bell wondered if he would trade the evening in the pool with her for all this tumult. Parched sexually, he decided he would.

"Otto wants two bottles of mescal and a carton of cigarettes," Captain Bell said. "Could you make sure he gets it? He's got me by the tail."

"Mean as a snake," E.O. muttered. "Don't like him."

"We have to get through the inauguration without any bad press," Captain Bell said. "Will you do it?"

"Yep," E.O. said. "Consider it done."

"Don't mention it to Sam," Captain Bell said, leaning on his desk. "Or anyone else. It's our little pact."

"Only if I can keep my stash," E.O. said. "I'm saving up for an engagement ring for Loretta."

Captain Bell agreed. "As long as it's not coming from the camp budget."

"Done," E.O. said. "Yep."

Captain Bell felt as if he was becoming like a politician—making separate deals with different constituents to keep them happy. Everything was not aboveboard. It wasn't the way he wanted to run the camp, and he had always considered himself a straight shooter. But maybe he wasn't being completely honest with himself.

He had just sat down and was looking at E.O.'s ledger when Mac, the foreman, burst into the office.

It was rare that Mac came to the office. Captain Bell usually saw him out by the construction site, and they talked there.

"We've got a big problem," Mac said, puffing away on a cigarette.

"Don't you want to sit down?"

Mac shook his head. "The bricks on the wall surrounding the pool have crumbled. We're going to have to redo it."

"Christ," Captain Bell swore. "How did that happen?"

"Hell if I know," Mac said, lighting up another cigarette. "It looked fine a few weeks ago. Maybe the boys didn't let the bricks set long enough."

"We only have three weeks. Do you think we'll make it? Neff has already sent out the invitations."

Sweat dripped down Mac's forehead into his eyes.

"I don't know, Captain." Mac wiped his forehead with a blue bandanna. "We'll try."

"Trying is not good enough!" Captain Bell said, pounding the desk. "Former Governor Neff is coming!"

CHAPTER 46.

# Darlene's Diary, Last Week of May 1936

**Ma always said I was too flighty.** *Flighty as a barn swallow.*

*Now I'm like a fish, writhing in a net. Was a mistake to seduce Roy Bell. He's so good I just wanted to see if I could: easy as pie. Like a game. No, that's not fair. I always felt an affinity with Bell. He's a grown man, not a boy. Felt for him—that face. Must have suffered a lot after the war.*

*But Bell doesn't know me. Caught up in some fantasy about me. Let my hair down and even told him my real name. A bit risky. He might figure it all out, but by that time . . . He's no dummy. Would probably be repulsed when finds out about the operations—in Milford. Bell's pure. Not as the driven snow, but he's a good man.*

*Jack heard.*

*They all heard. Now all of the boys are giving me sly looks at breakfast. Whistles. Catcalls. Started skipping breakfast. Am losing weight.*

*Don't even know if I dare walk alone in the camp. Stopped going out at night. My ma would say, "You've got yerself to blame, you hussy." Way off of the farm was nursing. I got my looks from my pa.*

*Otto's tracking my every move. He pops up behind every barrack. He hisses, "Can I suck your titties?"*

*Once, Otto pulled out his equipment and waved it at me. Broad daylight. Turned around and walked in the other direction back to the clinic. Went to Bell's office to complain. Wasn't there.*

*All Bell cares about now is the pool. Inauguration. Got to repair it.*

*Is the Manly Man, D.B., really going to show his face at the inauguration? Anything for a buck. He'll get some more clients. More operations. Step right up. The ram that I am with every lamb. Promise one and all eternal rejuvenation. As if he could promise them eternal life.*

*If only I could see the little tyke. But would D. bring him?*

*Is D.B. going to drive up in his big old Cadillac with Sally the Pigeon? Big Man from Del Rio. Don't know if I can stand it.*

*Kidnapping hadn't worked before. Why would it work now? He's probably got everyone in his pocket.*

*Being here, becoming unbearable. Jack cornered me in the canteen. "Is it true you did it with Captain Bell in the pool?"*

*Knocked over my Vim Cola, spilled it on my white uniform. Couldn't really go anywhere without being hounded. Could understand why Jack was hurt.*

*"It's over, Jack."*

*"Because of the sketches?"*

*There was no way to explain without a full confession. And I wasn't prepared to do that, just now. You'll find someone better.*

*Jack, coming to my room again. The three light knocks. Then, banging. Couldn't let him in. "Open up. Are you doing it with Dr. Walker, too?" Kicking the door.*

*Put chest of drawers against the door.*

*Who would have thought it of Cary Grant?*

*Handsome is as handsome does, Ma says, Missy.*

*Joe is giving me peanuts to sell the booze for him. Not enough. Needed more.*

*Feel a little guilty about swiping Doc's watch. He had passed out, flat cold on rum, after reading me Longfellow. Hifalutin' verse that I didn't much like, but he was pleasant enough and didn't harass me. The English teacher made us memorize verses in high school. Always saw the sense in studying biology.*

*Pawning it would get me enough for the trip north and then some. Until I got on my feet again . . .*

CHAPTER 47.

# Just Like Sam Spade, Dashiell Hammett's Detective

**Darlene had disappeared.** And no one seemed to know why, although there were a few hints. Sam thought it had something to do with Otto. Had Otto threatened her? Like everyone else, he had heard the rumor about Captain Bell's night with Darlene, skinny-dipping in the swimming pool. He didn't believe it. If the boys couldn't watch blue movies, they'd spend their time making up stories. He couldn't believe that Captain Bell would compromise himself like that. On the other hand, Sam had also fantasized about Darlene. If he were tempted, he knew he would succumb. So, why not Captain Bell?

He felt as if everyone was keeping secrets from him. Captain Bell had sent him on some phony errand so he could talk to E.O.

When he had pressed E.O., he was not forthcoming. He only said, "Jezebel."

"What about Jezebel?"

"She's a harlot. Just like Jezebel. Have you read the scripture?"

Then went back to his numbers. If Sam persisted, he started quoting the Bible. This would put anyone off.

Jack was distraught and moped around. He wasn't himself. Sam challenged him to a game of pool, but he had refused. Just flopped on the couch in the rec room and stared at the ceiling.

Dr. Walker was beside himself as well. One day he came to the office for a chat and he stayed all morning.

Captain Bell was rarely in the office because he was always at the construction site, supervising the repairs on the sides of the pool. Almost everyone in the camp had been recruited to work on the repairs, even drivers. They were under a tight deadline.

"Aren't you worried about Darlene?" Sam asked. "It seems like she has disappeared from the face of the earth. Shouldn't you call the sheriff? The police?"

Captain Bell's face was implacable, except for a slight, knowing smile. "I reckon she can take care of herself."

"Dr. Walker is worried she might have come to some harm," Sam said. "Maybe she was kidnapped. Or . . . ?"

He was surprised Captain Bell was so blasé about her disappearance. "I have to get the pool ready before the inauguration. That is my priority for now, son."

It was as if Captain Bell wasn't listening.

If Captain Bell wouldn't call the police, then he decided to investigate, like Sam Spade in Dashiell Hammett's thrillers. One evening, after he was sure Dr. Walker was passed out in his office, he found the duplicate key to her room. It was marked: "Key to Nurse's Bedroom, next to Clinic." But the door was slightly ajar when he tried the key.

The room was tiny. Only enough space for a single bed and a chest of drawers. A big suitcase was open on the bed. It looked as if she had left in a hurry of her own will. Had she decided to take a smaller bag?

He rifled through the drawers. Underwear. Bras. He sniffed them. Still smelled of lavender. He wished he were Captain Bell. On the other hand, Captain Bell had witnessed some terrible things during the war. Sam wouldn't trade his face for Captain Bell's marred cheeks. Anyhow, you couldn't live someone else's life. Had she left because of Captain Bell? Or did it have something to do with Jack? Was Jack jealous of Captain Bell?

He felt the bottom of the drawer. A stick of Wrigley's chewing gum. A box of melted Red Hots. His hand kept patting the bottom of the drawer. A notebook.

It looked like a diary.

CHAPTER 48.

# Submerged

**The repairs to the sides of the pool had been completed.** They had remade the adobe bricks and made sure they were dry before they were cemented to the side of the pool. Then the small irrigation canals that led to the San Solomon Spring, which had been dammed, were opened, and the pool brimmed with crisp cool water. Sam had been out to take a look. From afar, it was a sapphire blue and almost looked like a magical lake, two sides oblong, which burgeoned into a round circle. Sam was typing up the next newsletter of the *Round-Up*: "Grand Opening of Balmorhea in Five Days!"

The weather was boiling, not even a light breeze. It was the middle of the afternoon, and Sam felt sweat dripping down his back. He got up from the wooden chair. The chair was wet. If only he could jump into the pool. But Captain Bell had made it clear that that was forbidden. Swimming times would be strictly supervised with a lifeguard. Anyone who swam unsupervised would be punished. The brig? The lessons would take place in the evening after supper. Besides organizing the lessons on water safety, Sam had also typed up a request for a new nurse.

Later that day, as they were all sitting down to supper, Otto loped into the mess hall, clear out of breath. His face was pale, as if he had seen a ghost.

"*Hilfe*!"

Captain Bell asked, "What's happened?"

Otto couldn't speak. He shook his head.

"Speak, man. What is it?"

"*Jemand ist ertrunken.*"

At first, Captain Bell didn't move. "In English, my boy. Take your time."

Otto shook his head. "*Auf die Bibel schwören.* Accident at the pool. It's bad. Mac . . ."

Captain Bell leaped up from his chair and barked orders. In his haste, he knocked over a pitcher of tea. The glass pitcher crashed on the floor.

"Someone clean up that mess!"

He roared, "Chueco." Chueco's small head appeared among a crowd of boys. "Sam," Captain Bell said. "Get Dr. Walker! Don't tarry!"

A group of boys moved like a cluster of bees with Captain Bell as he ran toward the pool.

The door to the mess hall slammed shut.

Sam sprinted through the empty clinic. The beds were resplendent white, the corners of the sheets tucked in tight. Darlene was gone. He remembered that day when Otto had busted his nose.

He kept expecting that Darlene might pop up around the corner. He had tucked her diary under some shoes in his locked trunk. He wouldn't make Jack's mistake, hiding it under the mattress.

Through the clinic, past Darlene's small room, then to Dr.

Walker's office.

Dr. Walker was out cold, his head down on the desk. The only movement a loud bellow of a snore as he breathed in and out. Sam gently shook him. He murmured, "But Darlene, before you go you must listen to this masterful poem by Longfellow extolling the virtues of . . ."

Then he bellowed into a snore.

His head was resting on a book of Longfellow's poems. Sam pulled out the book. They were wasting time! He shook Dr. Walker, but he waved his hand, murmuring, "Forgive your pa, Belle of the Ball."

Sam shook him again, this time more roughly. He giggled. "If you care to be licentious, Antoinette, I will not object."

Who was Antoinette?

Sam picked up a bottle of Wonder Cure on his desk. Looking down the throat of the bottle, he saw it had been drained. The red cock embossed on the bottle seemed to mock him. This was an emergency! He had to sober him up. Dashing to the sink, he opened the tap and poured water into a cup. He counted to three and then poured it over Dr. Walker's head.

He sat up immediately, but his eyes stared ahead, as if he were hypnotized. "Young man, what is the meaning of this infraction? You are not Sigma Chi. I was hazed last week."

Sam shouted. "Wake up! There's an emergency at the pool."

"Darlene is perfectly capable. Had her training in Galveston."

"Darlene left. Remember!" Sam shouted. "Gone. Vamoosed!"

"There's no need to shout in my ear," Dr. Walker said, pulling out a comb. He ran it through his wet hair. Water dripped down his pouchy cheeks. "Before we set off to the scene, I will need my bag."

Sam felt as if Dr. Walker was moving in slow motion. His eyes were bloodshot, and his suit was crumpled. Was he in any shape to deal with an emergency?

"I've got your bag," Sam said, picking up the black bag. "Let's go!"

Dr. Walker got up from his chair slowly. He gripped the edge of the wooden desk for support. "Feel a little woozy. Didn't sleep well last night. Have been worried that Darlene might have been kidnapped. Or something nefarious might have happened to her."

"She left of her own free will," Sam said.

Sam guided him as he lurched back and forth. Then he shook off Sam's hand. "I am not that old," he said.

Sam ran ahead with Dr. Walker's black bag. He hoped they were not too late. Dr. Walker sauntered behind him, as if he was going for an evening stroll in Tyler. Sam raced toward the cluster of boys surrounding someone lying on the ground, next to the pool.

• • •

The boys parted to let Sam through. Delilah barked. Captain Bell was bent over the boy's chest, pressing down with his right hand. Chueco was pressing on his chest with his other hand.

Once Chueco understood what to do, he pressed both of his hands onto Jack's chest. One hand was not enough. They did team tag, continuing to pump Jack's chest.

Sam was stunned. Jack's skin was waxy and pale, as if his confident spirit had already fled. His eyes were closed. His brown hair was wet; a few locks had flopped into his eyes. He had lifted weights and worked hard on his body, as an athlete. His arms were muscular, and he had a trim waist, like one of those paintings you saw on Athenian jars. He was wearing a pair of dark blue swimming trunks, framed by a little belt.

"He knows how to swim," Sam kept saying. "I swear. He knows."

But they had only swum in creeks and ponds. Once in the Rio Grande, near Big Bend, in a canyon. As he recalled, it had not been very deep, not even to their waists. And another time, at the spring that hugged Mount Mitre, on that school picnic. Had his swimming skills ever really been tested? Had he gone out too far?

Sam remembered Mac blabbing. His pants were wet. He was puffing on a cigarette. "Was way out in the middle when I came to check one of the canals. Think he was diving down, trying to find the source of the spring. Kept yelling at him to come back in. His head was bobbing. Didn't see his head anymore. It all happened so fast . . ."

"Mac, please!" Captain Bell said. "Could you just shut up?"

Chueco kept compressing his chest, but Jack lay still as a stone. He repeated, "*Señor, levántame por tus bendiciones hoy. Oro para que me unjas con fortaleza y cuidado personal hoy, mañana y siempre.*"

Sam regretted every inch of resentment he had ever harbored against Jack. It all seemed so foolish and petty now. Who cared if he was so handsome that he got all the girls? Would this ever have happened if they had stayed in Alpine? Maybe it was better to milk cows and work in a boarding house. But they didn't think they could stick that out forever. Balmorhea had been their milk and honey, but the milk had sure curdled.

If Darlene had been here, she would have come, quick as a whistle. Was Jack punishing himself because Darlene had left? He sure had moped around the last few weeks, but Sam thought he would get over it. Did he swim out to the middle of the pool on purpose? Sam swiped this disturbing thought away, like a cat swiping at a bird.

Dr. Walker had dillydallied. How much time had Sam lost, trying to rouse him?

It was only when Dr. Walker knelt down to check Jack that Chueco and Captain Bell stood up.

"Took your sweet time," Captain Bell hissed. "Doctor."

Dr. Walker put two fingers on Jack's windpipe. Then he compressed Jack's chest firmly with his hands. After that, he gave him two breaths. The doctor continued to compress Jack's chest for another thirty minutes, but he did not move. Sam kept expecting him to gurgle up water, cough, and start breathing. They would all say "hallelujah" and go back to their barracks. Swig a Vim Cola at the canteen and thank their lucky stars that Jack had made a narrow escape. But Jack's skin had already started to turn a dark purplish, as if another force had already taken over. Sam had seen plenty of animals die on the farm—and his ma was expert at twisting the neck of chickens. Terrible to put down a horse with a broken leg; couldn't stand that, either. Worse, though, to see the creature suffer. He had even witnessed the death of his granny, who had lived to be in her eighties. He could deny it all day and dream about what they would do tomorrow at the canteen, but the purple skin was an ominous sign.

He looked up at the sky, as if he might find the answer there. He repeated one of his ma's prayers from Mary Baker Eddy. "All is infinite mind and its infinite manifestation for God . . ." The sun seeped into the horizon. Soon it would be dark.

Dr. Walker fished out a stethoscope from his bag and placed the chest piece on Jack's lungs. Then he put it on Jack's heart. He closed his eyes and listened.

Dr. Walker's bloodshot eyes popped open. He shook his head sorrowfully. "No heartbeat. I am truly sorry."

Delilah howled and put her paw on Jack's still hand.

CHAPTER 49.

# The Report

**They had buried him.** He and Captain Bell had driven over to Seagraves. Sam felt wobbly, as if he was about to lose his footing in a slick, muddy field. He had not been able to answer any of Jack's folks' questions. Neither had Captain Bell. No one knew why Jack had swum out to the deepest part of the pool. Sam couldn't think of a sadder moment in his life. The idea arose again that Jack was upset about Darlene's disappearance, but Sam kept that to himself. Besides, it was only a hunch. Captain Bell dealt very kindly with Jack's folks—and Sam wished he could think of something comforting to say, but he only choked out a few words. They had also organized a memorial ceremony at Balmorhea for Jack.

Captain Bell had called former Governor Neff about postponing the inauguration of the pool, and Neff had hemmed and hawed. Sam could even hear the governor's voice booming through the earpiece, "Of course, I'm sorry about the boy. I suppose we could postpone it for a few weeks." A short article appeared in the *Alpine Avalanche*, but it had been shunted to the last page: "Drowning Accident at

Balmorhea."

The days alternated between preparations for the inauguration and the investigation of the accident. Captain Bell's mood zigzagged between fury and sadness. The C.O. from Big Bend had conducted the investigation of the accident, interviewing Mac, Captain Bell, Dr. Walker, and everyone at the scene. Sam's testimony was also taken. The file was to include the C.O.'s report, the testimonies, and the death certificate.

He felt as if he were outside of himself, typing a report about someone far away, not his best friend.

**Accident Report:**[1]
**CCC Camp, Balmorhea. No. 1856. June 6th, 1936.**

*Enrollee* ***Jack Huley****: 7575364 accidentally drowned on* ***June 6th, 1936,*** *and was pronounced dead at* ***8:30 p.m.*** *by* ***Dr. Clyde Walker****, doctor assigned to the camp. The enrollee was spotted by* ***Mac Jones, site supervisor,*** *at* ***6:45 p.m. Jones*** *indicated to the enrollee that he should return to shore. Shortly after,* ***Jones*** *noticed that the enrollee had disappeared. He swam out to offer assistance. Enrollee was dragged to shore. At* ***7:10 the C.O. Captain Roy Bell*** *was notified of the situation and proceeded directly to the scene. (Company nurse, Darlene Robinson, had recently resigned so medical personnel only included Dr. Walker, Local Experienced Man).* ***Enrollee Sam McCabe*** *was dispatched to get the doctor while the C.O. proceeded to the scene. The C.O. arrived at the scene at 7:15. The C.O. was assisted by* ***enrollee Chueco Gonzalez*** *in chest compressions. Enrollee was not breathing. They continued for forty-five minutes with chest compressions until the doctor arrived at* ***8:00 p.m. Dr. Walker*** *continued with compression of the chest, but the* ***enrollee, Jack Huley,*** *did not regain consciousness. No heartbeat was detected. After thirty more minutes of chest compressions, the doctor pronounced the enrollee dead at the scene at* ***8:30 p.m. C.O. Captain Roy Bell*** *imme-*

*diately sent a telegram to War Dept. and notified local authorities* ***at 9 p.m.***

***A Second Urgent Request for a New Nurse.*** *In light of medical personnel Nurse Darlene Robinson's (LEM) resignation on* ***May 28th,*** *the C.O. Captain Roy Bell requests a qualified replacement. An older woman is preferred.*

**Recommendation for a Dishonorable Discharge:**

***C.O. Captain Roy Bell*** *recommends that* ***LEM, Dr. Clyde Walker*** *be discharged from his medical duties at Balmorhea. On several occasions documented, the medical officer was unavailable and did not respond to emergencies in a timely fashion. It has been noted by the C.O. and others who have testified that the medical officer has a problem with addictive substances as well as alcohol. This lack of professionalism deterred the medical officer from responding quickly to the drowning victim,* ***Jack Huley 7575364*** *on* ***June 6th, 1936****. The C.O. will provide testimonies and documents to support his recommendation to authorities investigating the matter. Respectfully submitted, etc. etc.*

After Sam finished, he went out and sat under a mesquite tree for a while, to collect himself. Was Jack already gone by the time Dr. Walker finally sauntered out to the pool? The tree rustled. "Coo-ah, coo, coo," a mourning dove sang.

Delilah put her head in his lap, and he rubbed her behind the ears.

CHAPTER 50.

# Captain Bell, The Balmorhea Celebrations Committee

Captain Bell kept thinking about Jack's mother, who had wrung her hands until they were beet red. A rash had broken out all over her neck. He had visited the parents of many of the soldiers whom he had lost during the Great War—it was a dismal, heart-wrenching task, especially since his own daughter had not survived infancy. Captain Bell never offered any graphic details, even if the parents asked. In all cases, ignorance was more merciful. If only he could wring Dr. Walker's neck. But it very well could be that Jack was beyond help once he had been dragged out of the water. On the other hand, they did not know that for a fact. Captain Bell should have followed up on Dr. Walker's drinking earlier. He felt guilty that he had not.

At least the opening of the pool had been postponed a few weeks. He had bargained for a little time.

Once the investigation of Jack's death was concluded, a steady stream of visitors from the town and the county filed through his office to discuss the opening of the pool. How much beef would they need for the barbecue? Who would provide the mixings? Who would sponsor the bathing girl revue? Boat racing, diving, and swimming events were proposed. The boys at Balmorhea would build a dance platform.

In the middle of these conversations with ranchers and local townspeople, Captain Bell felt his mind drifting. This was not the Great War, and they should not have lost a single boy. He blamed himself. Hadn't he known that both Darlene and Dr. Walker were, in some way, unreliable characters? Why hadn't he done anything about it? The question hung in the air.

A head popped around the wooden partition. His curly black hair was squashed tight under a blue flat cap, even though it was summer and much too hot for this hat.

"May I . . . ?" he said, taking off his blue flat cap. His curly hair stood straight up on his head, as if he were a rooster.

Despite his humorous appearance, his brown eyes were solemn. He patted Captain Bell on the shoulder. "*Allah yerhamu.*"

"What?"

"It means, May God have mercy on his soul," Joe said. "He was such a nice boy. Well raised."

"Yes," Captain Bell said. "I believe he was." Captain Bell did not mention Jack's affair with Darlene. Or any of his own doubts about what had happened.

"In our country, we drink black coffee only when we offer condolences," Joe said. "Nothing sweet. But I find it strange that Americans bring pies and cakes to the home."

Captain Bell sighed. "The family won't feel like cooking."

Joe sat down in the chair facing Captain Bell. "The celebration of the pool will take place before the forty days. I objected to the Balmorhea Celebrations Committee, but no one would listen."

Captain Bell did not know what he was talking about. "Forty days?"

"We pray for the souls of the dead on the fortieth day. As they are waiting for their time of judgment. Of course, we are Catholic now, but when we were Orthodox, this is what we did."

"I tried to get the party postponed," Captain Bell said. "This was the best I could do."

"I am not blaming you, *ya khayyi*, my brother. It just seems too soon."

"I agree."

"But since I did not convince the mayor or the Balmorhea Celebration Committee, I have decided to donate bread from our store."

"That is generous of you," Captain Bell said, feebly. He wasn't donating the most expensive item.

"And," Joe said, "I will sponsor one of the contestants in the bathing girl revue. Charlotte, the daughter of the postmaster. *Ma battelet zann a rasi all day. Nag, Nag, nag. She didn't stop nagging me.*"

"Very good." He felt as if he were choking on the small petty details of the Grand Opening.

Joe popped open a gold pocket watch and looked at the time.

"Can I see that for a minute?" Captain Bell asked.

"*Tabaan*. Of course," Joe said, handing over the gold pocket watch.

"This belongs to Dr. Walker."

Joe's surprise showed on his face. "Darlene said it belonged to her great-grandfather."

Joe set the watch on Captain Bell's desk. "Of course, it should be returned to the doctor. Part of his family's history. When we left Zahle, we left only with the clothes on our backs."

"It looks like Darlene hoodwinked a lot of us," Captain Bell said.

Joe shrugged. Then he smiled. "As the Egyptians would say, 'That who you think was Moses turns out to be a pharaoh. *Eli teftekroh Moussa yetlah Pharoan.*'"

"Did you know her well?" Captain Bell asked.

"No," Joe said, a little too quickly. "She visited the store for womanly supplies."

Captain Bell laughed. Did he mean sanitary napkins?

Joe frowned. "This was not a joke, brother. Is your blood thick?"

Captain Bell sighed. He didn't have the energy to ask about thick blood. He supposed it was something dour. "No, but my patience is wearing thin. Thank you for donating to the Balmorhea Celebrations Committee."

"I apologize if I have offended," Joe said, putting his blue flat cap back on his head. "The main reason I came was for the condolences. For the boy, Jack. *Allah yerhamu.*"

"You have not offended me." Captain Bell stood up to shake his hand. "Thank you."

Joe put his hand on his heart. "*Ay Wallah,* I swear, I didn't know that the watch was robbed. I am sorry about this misunderstanding."

• • •

Before he returned Dr. Walker's watch, Captain Bell called a number of doctors and nurses in the area and asked them if they would volunteer to be medical staff "for the day" as part of the Balmorhea Celebration Committee. "You know, everyone is doing their part," he'd say. If they hesitated, he promised free barbecue plates for the whole family. If he didn't have enough volunteers, he would pay doctors out of his own pocket. He asked them if they would teach classes on water safety to the boys at Balmorhea. Then he directed Sam to set up teams of boys who would be "on watch" at different posts around the pool on the day of the celebration. This took most of the afternoon.

In the evening, after supper, he walked over to Dr. Walker's office for the last talk. He didn't look forward to it, but it had to be done. Ignoring Dr. Walker's flaws had been disastrous.

Dr. Walker was just pouring himself a cocktail as he poked his head into the office.

"Ahh, Captain," Dr. Walker said. "A most auspicious time for a visit. We could take our libations out just in time for the setting of the sun."

Dr. Walker held up a full bottle of bourbon and smiled.

"I have come on business," Captain Bell said. "So I think we will have to have the drink another time."

Or never?

"But I won't take no for an answer," Dr. Walker said. "Since Darlene's departure, I have had no company with which to partake, if you know what I mean. By the way, I wanted to inquire why you aren't more concerned about her whereabouts. Perhaps she has been kidnapped by some nefarious characters? Perhaps a rogue cowboy?"

Captain Bell sighed. This wasn't going to be much fun. He pulled out a chair and sat down, facing Dr. Walker. "Darlene slipped a resignation letter under my door. She said, 'due to unforeseen circumstances, she could no longer continue with her duties.' I should have told you."

"She is part of my medical team," Dr. Walker said, chugging the bourbon. He was drinking it as if it were water on a scorching day. Forever parched, until sozzled to the gills. "And I did have a right to be informed . . . although I find it quizzical that she did not tell me herself before she left. Or did not even have the decency to say goodbye."

Captain Bell sighed again. How was he going to deliver this news?

Dr. Walker took another gulp. "Of course, you have been busy with your overwhelming responsibilities, what with the Celebrations Committee. The bathing suit contest. The boat races. But more importantly, I wanted to inquire about the state of Jack's parents. How are they . . . ?"

"What you would expect," Captain Bell said. "Devastated."

"I do think the boy was already dead by the time he was pulled out of the water," Dr. Walker said. "Had been submerged too long. Lost too much oxygen."

"Maybe," Captain Bell said.

"I want to compliment you on your expeditious response to the situation. You responded correctly to a drowning victim. Did you acquire these first aid skills during the war?"

Captain Bell cut to the chase. "I have good news," he said. "And bad news. I will give you the good news first."

He pulled out Dr. Walker's watch from his pocket and swung it in the air. "Your watch has been found."

He placed the watch in the palm of Dr. Walker's hand.

"But how . . . ? I thought your investigation had been stymied, in light of other developments with regard to—"

"Darlene hocked it," Captain Bell said. "Because she needed the money. The buyer did not know it was stolen."

Dr. Walker stared at him. "You are telling me an untruth. A falsehood. A lie would be incorrect. Surely you have been misled?"

"Afraid not," Captain Bell said.

"But why would she resort to such an action? I believed we were companions of a sort, although you must believe me when I say, nothing untoward occurred between us. She had developed a taste for the Romantic poets . . . Coleridge. Wordsworth."

"I don't know," Captain Bell said.

"But . . ." Dr. Walker raised his glass, and then set it down. "Do you think it was linked to her voracious sexual proclivities?"

Captain Bell almost laughed, but he suppressed it. "I don't know that they were voracious." But did the skinny-dipping evening have anything to do with her departure? There had to be more to the story.

Dr. Walker chortled. "My dear boy, you can't be so naive. As men, we are all susceptible to female charm. I have surmised that Darlene was sweet on you. As a young man, I carried on with many coquettes in the French Quarter (that was before I was married, of course), and so I am more than qualified to judge. I have had a plethora of amorous adventures in my life. Once, I became entangled with a much older woman, Antoinette, when I was only a young man. Antoinette had a talent for . . . Have I told you this story?" He giggled. "Antoinette had the ability to regenerate my member. I started failing my anatomy exams. Consorting with her became like an addiction."

Captain Bell became annoyed. "That is not the only bad news, Clyde."

Dr. Walker's hands trembled when he picked up the expensive crystal glass. "Let me fortify myself."

"I have requested your discharge from Balmorhea," Captain Bell said. "There may be an investigation. It may take a month or two for the paperwork to go through."

Dr. Walker's eyes opened wide. He was shocked. "After all of my consideration for the well-being of the boys . . . You can't be . . . Of course, you have filed an honorable discharge."

"No," Captain Bell said. "I'm afraid not. You were often absent when you were needed. You took too long to get to Jack. Because you were high on Wonder Cure."

"But no one in the history of my eminent family has ever received a dishonorable discharge. Never in the long lineage of the Walker family. Great-grandfather Walker was the last officer to take the amnesty oath for the Confederacy. I must have told you before about *my family*."

"Jack is dead," Captain Bell said. "Those few minutes might have made the difference."

"But I am not to blame for the death of that boy," Dr. Walker said. "Although of course, my heartfelt, profound sympathies are with his parents."

Captain Bell felt he had made the right decision. "You are the camp doctor! You ambled out to the pool as if it were a picnic. You were told it was an emergency!"

"I stake my medical license on my assessment of the situation. Too much oxygen had been lost, and his skin was already turning blue upon my arrival."

"If you want to challenge the discharge, go ahead. We already have the testimony of eyewitnesses."

Dr. Walker was suddenly defiant. "I will be challenging this decision at the War Department, at the highest level. The honor of my family has been maligned. I refuse to report for duty on the day of the grand opening!"

Captain Bell stood up. "Good night, Dr. Walker."

But he did not answer.

CHAPTER 51.

# Sabah el-Ward, A Morning Full of Roses, June 26, 1936

In the morning, Captain Bell inspected the wooden platform where former Governor Neff and other dignitaries would sit. Mac was sucking on a cigarette, holding it between his thumb and forefinger. "Whadda you think?" Captain Bell knocked on the wood, then strode up the steps and sat in one of the chairs. The platform had a view of the pool. At this time of the morning, the sun glistened on the blue water. "Magnificent," Captain Bell said. To hide the plywood in front, the boys had pinned colorful Texas flags on the platform, like a skirt. Captain Bell jumped up and followed Mac. Dotted around the entire perimeter of the pool, the boys had erected Army tents. "As we discussed, some will be for first aid. Others for food," Mac said. Chuck wagons for the barbecue.

"We'll need plenty of water," Captain Bell said. "Don't want anyone getting heatstroke."

All swimming races were to be held in the shallow end of the pool. Ropes and buoys marked the shallow from the area over five feet deep. Anyone in a boat was required to wear a life jacket. After Jack's drowning, no one objected to any of these precautions. He and Sam had drawn up the order of activities for the day so that there would only be one event at a time.

Before the gate was officially opened, he met with the volunteer medical teams who were manning the first aid booths. Even though it was only ten o'clock in the morning, he was already sweating; his formal CCC uniform was wool. As he expected, Dr. Walker had not appeared. He sent Sam to the clinic, but Sam shook his head. "Not there."

He didn't need Dr. Walker. He had the local medical teams of nurses and doctors. Chueco had also volunteered to help them.

Before he could catch his breath, former Governor Neff showed up with a delegation from the State Parks. He had never met Neff, but he kept shaking his hand vigorously. An intellectual-looking man, wearing a three-piece suit with a vest, he said, "This is the culmination of a dream, this astonishing emerald pool. I congratulate you. It is a shame about that young man . . ."

"Yes. It was a tragedy." Why had Jack swum out to the deepest part of the pool? Was he overconfident? "We hope . . ." but his voice trailed off.

Former Governor Neff was already climbing the steps onto the platform.

Captain Bell was introducing Neff now. Sam had written up an introduction, and he read it. He felt emotionally detached from the words he was reading.

It was hot, and former Governor Neff's speech was too long. Captain Bell longed to tear off his hot wool uniform and jump into the cool spring. He wondered what had happened to Darlene. How could she leave just like that?

A row of boys were whispering behind him. He turned around and said, "Cool it." But who could blame them?

Former Governor Neff was saying, "When I established the Texas Park system in 1923, this was exactly the kind of facility I had in mind. Balmorhea is 'back to nature' where the bees hum, the breezes blow, and the flowers bloom. Here, spending your hours at this cool spring in an atmosphere with the perfume of flowers of a thousand hues, the old grow young, the sick regain health, and the weary enjoy a quiet rest."[1]

Was Captain Bell growing young? Could floating in water make you feel younger? He remembered that night, skinny-dipping with Darlene. The sex had made him feel younger. But instead of the perfume of flowers of a thousand hues, there had been lavender. It was as if he could smell it, but when he looked around, he was surrounded only by sweaty boys.

"As I wrote in 1923, the health, welfare, and happiness of the people of Texas are largely enhanced by the number of places within the borders where the people can go for rest, recreation, and leisure. Balmorhea is such a place. I congratulate you on your work here. Made possible by a partnership with our federal government and the vision of our President Franklin Delano Roosevelt."

The boys cheered.

Boat races were first. Captain Bell floated around the grounds, stopping at tents and checking in with his teams. Thumbs up. No problems.

"Hello, hello," he said, nodding to townspeople he knew. "Welcome to Balmorhea." He felt a little like a mayor.

The sun rose higher in the sky. Swimming and diving races were next. He was tempted by the smell of barbecue, but kept circling around the pool. In the end, they had decided food would be free since it had been donated. Captain Bell was adamant that no alcohol should be served, not even beer. Besides bread, Joe had donated a hundred cases of Vim Cola. A woman manning a chuckwagon said cheerfully, "More beef brisket? Coming right up. Captain, did you get a plate?"

"Thank you. Maybe later."

Sam was out of breath. "Captain, I've been looking for you everywhere. Former Governor Neff wants to introduce you to somebody."

"Who is the somebody?"

Sam shook his head. "They're over there." He pointed to a family talking to former Governor Neff.

"Captain Bell, I would like to introduce you to a pioneer in the medical field. He currently resides in Del Rio, but has excellent qualifications and has been recognized for his work on male regeneration. The state is lucky to have him."

Dr. Brinkley stuck out his hand. "Howdy. Governor Neff tells me you have done an outstanding job on this pool. We could interview you on our show on station XER, discussing the benefits of bathing in a spring. We can do it, sure as shootin'."

Captain Bell was staring. He had just noticed the little boy holding the hand of Dr. Brinkley's wife. He was dressed in a purple velvet Lord Fauntleroy outfit, with a frilly lace collar. It was completely archaic as an outfit. Why was Dr. Brinkley forcing the kid to wear such an outfit from the 1890s? The boy had curly blond hair. His face looked exactly like Darlene: light blue eyes, small nose, and fair complexion. The resemblance was uncanny.

"That is my son, John Romulus Brinkley, Junior. Can you shake Captain Bell's hand?"

The boy tentatively stretched out his hand. "Pleased to . . ."

Dr. Brinkley became gruff. "Go on, Johnny boy."

Darlene had a son? Brinkley was her husband? Why, she had been reading that article in *JAMA* so intently in Dr. Walker's office. What had the article said about her?

Dr. Brinkley chuckled. "He is talking about my ex-wife, Minnie. She was declared unfit by a court in Kansas, and I was awarded custody. This is my new wife, Sally."

She kept saying her name was Minnie, not Darlene. Was that the only true thing she had told him?

Sally smiled toothily at him. She had buck teeth. "Pleased to meetcha." Her brown hair was clipped short, and she was wearing granny glasses. Her dress was covered with large purple peonies, which reminded him of the curtains in his mother's living room.

The boy said, "Do you . . . ?"

While she was smiling at Captain Bell, she bopped the boy on his ear. She murmured, "You know the story about curiosity and the cat."

"She used to work here, but she left. I don't know where she is, son. I am sorry," Captain Bell said.

"I always contended that she was unfit to raise a child," Dr. Brinkley said, stroking his beard thoughtfully. "Did she just fly the coop? Must have used an assumed name. Never seen such a dishonest woman, no sirree."

"I'll say," Sally echoed him, like a parrot.

The boy said, "Our turtle died."

Dr. Brinkley said, "We'd best be moving on. I don't want to miss the bathing suit contest. Wouldn't you like to see that, Ma?"

Sally giggled. "Sure would, Pa. Might even put on a swimming suit myself and join."

Dr. Brinkley grinned lewdly, staring at her chest. "Now, Ma. Don't tease me like that. This is not the time nor the place."

Darlene's son stuck out his lip, as if he were about to cry. "She sent me a train for Christmas, but they wouldn't let me keep it."

Dr. Brinkley said, "That's enough! John Romulus, Jr.!" He pulled the boy roughly away from Sally. "Captain Bell is a busy man, and we won't take any more of his precious time."

"Would a little B-B-Q make you feel better, sugar pie? Honey Bunch? How about a Vimmie Cola Wola?" Sally said.

The boy was crying silently.

As if he were handing out flyers to a circus, Dr. Brinkley whipped out a leaflet from his breast pocket. "If you ever feel the need for more vigor, I am just the man to regenerate your love life, if you know what I mean. But I have not even asked you about your wife, er . . ."

"She passed away," Captain Bell said. Should he tell him that Darlene had relit the spark?

Sally fanned herself with one of the leaflets. Then she smiled at him toothily. "It's never too late for romance . . . Why, I met Pa when I was a mature woman."

Dr. Brinkley smiled broadly. "Del Rio's just a stone's throw from Balmorhea. You could have it done in a weekend. Because of your position at the camp, as a patriotic act to the nation, I'd give you a reduced rate. My goat gonad operation is just the answer to penile dysfunction. Just like the New Deal . . ."

Captain Bell turned away. "Hardly . . ."

He caught sight of them in a mob, surging at one of the chuck-wagons. The free food was being wolfed down and soon there wouldn't be anything left. Plates were piled high with barbecue, corn, potatoes, bread, and fresh tomatoes. Some ladies in the booths were already brandishing knives and carving watermelons into huge slices and wedges.

Sam handed him a Vim Cola.

Captain Bell took a long swig. The sugary drink made him thirstier. He needed water, not soda pop.

"The boy looks exactly like Darlene," Sam said.

"He sure does." Captain Bell had to sit down. He was stunned. "You heard all of that?"

"So she was married to Dr. Brinkley?"

"Looks like it," Captain Bell said.

"She never mentioned a son," Sam said.

Captain Bell changed the subject before he spilled the beans. "Is everything going all right? No crises?"

"So far, so good," Sam said. "We got through all the swimming and diving events. Last thing will be the bathing suit contest. I've got all the prizes lined up."

"Good job," Captain Bell said.

"Sure you're not hungry? I'll get you a plate," Sam said. "Best brisket barbecue I have eaten in my whole life."

"It's too hot for meat." Captain Bell tugged at his collar. He rolled up his sleeves. He wished he could plunge into the cool water of the pool.

When he looked up, Sam had disappeared.

He decided to sit in the shade of a tent for a while before the bathing suit revue. He had been on his feet since early morning, and the formal black lace-up shoes he was wearing were too tight. While Captain Bell adjusted his laces, Dr. Walker walked up to him.

"I have a matter of utmost importance to discuss," Dr. Walker said. "It could be construed as a confession of sorts."

"I'm not talking about the investigation today," Captain Bell said. "I will trade clothes with you, though."

Dr. Walker adjusted his Panama hat, even though he was sitting in the shade. "No, it's not about that unfortunate day. But something alarming has come to my attention. I thought you should be apprised of the situation."

"You mean, your refusal to be on call today?"

Dr. Walker said in a low, conspiratorial tone, "I saw you shaking hands with Dr. Brinkley."

"He's a quack," Captain Bell said. "Remember Dr. Fishbein?"

"Do you recall the day that I went to the lecture at Sul Ross? Dr. Volkov's lecture on regeneration? That was the day you got heatstroke."

"Perfectly," Captain Bell said.

"Upon greeting Dr. Brinkley," Doc Walker said. "I had the distinct impression that I had met the man before."

"And . . . ?"

"He had altered his speech slightly that day in Alpine. But upon further inspection, it was clear beyond a doubt that Dr. Brinkley is Volkov. Brinkley denied that he knew Volkov, of course."

Captain Bell laughed.

"It is not a matter for levity, Captain," Dr. Walker said. "If we surmise the situation correctly, that means that Dr. Fishbein was correct."

"This is your confession?" Captain Bell asked. "That you were wrong?"

"The authorities should be alerted at once," Dr. Walker said. "Before he escapes back to Del Rio. Before he performs more operations . . ."

Captain Bell sighed. "There isn't much I can do. I am just hoping we can get through the day here without any mishaps. Maybe you should write to the Texas Medical Association."

Dr. Walker huffed. "But surely—"

"Believe I will need to make another round," Captain Bell said. "If you will excuse me . . ."

"There is another matter of import that I would like to discuss."

"Not today," Captain Bell said.

"The categorization of my discharge . . ."

Captain Bell disappeared under the flap of the tent and found himself in a stream of people circling the pool. The end of the day couldn't come soon enough.

Joe was standing at a booth festooned with Texas flags and a large advertisement that said: "Vim Cola, for Vim and Vigor."

He was wearing a red-checkered flat cap, a blue shirt, and a pair of white pants. He handed Bell a Vim Cola. "It's free."

"Except for the sugar," Captain Bell said.

Joe frowned. Then he smiled and shook Captain Bell's hand heartily for at least a minute. "I am perfecting the Texas handshake. My clothes are the colors of the Texas flag."

"Thank you for donating the cola and the bread," Captain Bell said. "That was very generous of you."

"My family is known for its *karam*. That is generosity in our language," Joe said, smiling. "The day has been beautiful beyond my imagination."

"It's not over yet," Captain Bell said.

"Perhaps you would accept from me a gift. We drank it on Thanksgiving. That tastes of licorice," Joe said, brandishing an unmarked bottle with a clear liquid that looked like water. "My grandmother's recipe. From Zahle to Texas."

"Maybe later," Captain Bell said. "We agreed that there would be no alcohol at the event. I hope you are not selling that."

"*Tabaan*," Joe said. "Congratulations. *Sabah el-ward*. Like a morning or day full of roses."

But when Captain Bell looked back, he saw Dr. Brinkley handing Joe an envelope. So Joe was still selling Wonder Cure? Or other elixirs that made false promises?

He heard whistles and catcalls at the shallow end of the pool. The bathing suit contest had started, and a huge crowd had gathered. He had been against this contest because he felt it was divisive, but the ladies on the Balmorhea Celebrations Committee had insisted, and he had acquiesced.

He was standing next to one of the mothers, who said, "Why, Captain, you don't recognize me! I'm the Mrs. of the Postmaster. Mrs. Blankenship."

"Of course," Captain Bell said, shaking her hand. "How nice to . . ."

Her hair was tied into a tight bun at the back of her neck. She had a pleasant-looking face. She was wearing a blue-checkered dress with short sleeves, with a red belt.

"I expect you have a lot on your plate," Mrs. Blankenship said. "Barbecue was real tasty. My only criticism is the Negra cooks. Thought they were supposed to stay with their own kind."

"Glad you liked the food," Captain Bell said, ignoring her racist comments. He wished he could punch her in the nose. But you couldn't punch a lady in the nose!

"Can't understand why we have so many Latins here," Mrs. Blankenship said. "They're just taking over our country."

"They are American citizens," Captain Bell said.

"Bad enough that we got Latins and Negras, but now we got

A-rabs, too," Mrs. Blankenship said. "That Joe is from out of yonder Arabia. Pretty soon there won't be any Anglos left."

Captain Bell stared at the girls parading in front of the judges. There was not a single Mexican girl.

"That's my daughter, Charlotte," Mrs. Blankenship said. "Isn't she purty?"

A blonde with an attractive face beamed at the crowd. Her body was shaped like a pear.

"There are only four contestants!" Captain Bell said. "That's strange."

"No, it's not. There are only four Anglo girls in Brewster County who wanted to participate," Mrs. Blankenship said. "The committee decided Latin girls shouldn't be allowed."

This committee had gone rogue. How had that slipped through? A judge was shaking the blonde-haired girl's hand.

"Charlotte has won," Mrs. Blankenship said. "My baby has won! My baby has won!"

The girls were posing at the edge of the pool, while a photographer from the *Alpine Avalanche* snapped their picture. The girls were wearing red or blue one-piece bathing suits with a sash that said "Balmorhea." No cleavage was showing. It looked as if they were wearing shorts. As far as he could see, they were all attractive girls with nice figures. How could a winner really be chosen?

Suddenly, one of the girls screamed, "This contest is rigged! You're a bitch and you know it! You and your ma rigged the whole thing!" She pushed Charlotte's daughter into the pool.

"She can't swim!" her mother screeched.

Sam jumped into the water, although it was the shallow end. It wasn't necessary to pull her out because the water was only waist-deep. Sam held her hand and led her to the stairs of the pool. She was crying.

Mrs. Blankenship turned to Captain Bell. "That boy. I believe he was made for my Charlotte. If only he were Baptist. Told us he was Christian Science. Can't abide those people. Don't believe in doctors."

Captain Bell wasn't aware that Sam didn't believe in doctors. And he didn't know that he was a Christian Scientist. But maybe there was a good deal that he didn't know about Sam.

Sam squished and squelched when he walked because his uniform was soaked. Squish-squish-squish. The water oozed out of his leather shoes.

"Good job," Captain Bell said. "You better go change."

Mrs. Blankenship said, "You saved her life."

Sam smiled. "Well, it was the shallow end."

"You were made for each other," Mrs. Blankenship said. "Weren't they?" she said, turning to Captain Bell.

"Could be," Captain Bell said. He remembered the girl's face from the night of the dance, but Sam had never mentioned her again.

Soon, it would be dusk. The light was waning. Captain Bell could see the Davis Mountains in the distance. Clusters of visitors had started to walk toward their cars. Many thanked Captain Bell. "We haven't had this much fun in years."

"How could we ever thank you enough?"

"You have done so much for our community."

"It's not me," Captain Bell said. "Thank our president. It's the New Deal."

They had finally gotten to the end of the day. He was so relieved.

But here was E.O. and he was frowning. He pushed his thick glasses up on his nose. "There's a situation."

Captain Bell followed him. Suddenly, he was running.

At one of the food tents, Howard Perry and his two Pinkerton detectives were throwing chunks of watermelon at Dr. Brinkley.

"You ruined my marriage, Volkov," Howard Perry said, throwing another chunk of watermelon at Dr. Brinkley. "Now I can't . . ."

Dr. Brinkley ducked.

"I'm not Volkov," Dr. Brinkley shouted. "The name's John Romulus Brinkley. Don't know what you're talking about."

"I'm going to get you," Howard Perry said. "Fraud! Trickster! Swindler! Do you know what you've done to me?!"

As if he were a baseball pitcher, Brinkley hurled a chunk of watermelon that catapulted into Perry's face. Watermelon juice streamed down his face onto his expensive suit.

"Gentlemen, please," Captain Bell said, but neither paid any attention to him.

Sally and the little boy were at the corner of the tent, watching in amazement.

"I'm gonna kill you," Howard Perry said. "Don't you know who I am?"

Captain Bell wasn't interested in getting hit by a melon. Maybe it was better if they duked it out.

Dr. Brinkley smiled. "Never seen you in my whole life. The good Lord is my witness. But I heard you owned the Chisos Mine. Hasn't the price of mercury gone down?"

"Liar!" Howard Perry shouted. "We're coming to get you. Boys!"

But the two Pinkerton detectives didn't move. Captain Bell gave them a ferocious look.

Howard Perry continued to lob chunks of watermelon at Dr. Brinkley, but he wasn't a particularly good shot. Most of the watermelon hit the flap of the tent.

Dr. Brinkley dashed out of the tent. Sally and the little boy rushed after him.

Howard Perry and his two Pinkerton detectives ran after him. Captain Bell and E.O. followed them.

Dr. Brinkley was roaring out of the park in his maroon Cadillac in a cloud of red dust. All of them watched as he escaped. The hubcaps had a golden rim, with "B" in the middle.

Darlene's boy pressed his face against the back window. He waved.

"I'm taking you to court," Howard Perry shouted, waving his fist at Brinkley. "Fraud! Sue you for every penny! You'll be hearing from my lawyers in Chicago!"

"What?" E.O. asked. "He's madder than a wet hen."

Captain Bell was tired. He put his arm around E.O.'s shoulders as they walked back to camp. Howard Perry had gotten his just deserts, as far as he could see.

"Long story. Tell you tomorrow. Let's go for a swim before it gets dark."

CHAPTER 52.

# The Lost Letter, Arroyo Drive, Harlingen, Texas, 1980

Sam had worked his way through almost all the diaries, documents, and letters in the legal box marked "Balmorhea." But there was one letter at the bottom that had not been opened. It was postmarked June 26th, 1971. That was when they had taken the trip to Ireland so he could trace the family tree. How had it ended up in the box?

He had lost the use of his right arm now. Maggie read him the letter.

*June 26th, 1971*

*Dear Sam:*

*We had the 35th reunion of Balmorhea today in Fort Davis sponsored by the Texas State Parks. I was happy to hear that you went on to do graduate work in North Carolina. We were in touch when you returned to West Texas with your bride. You wrote to me that you had two sons and you had moved to Harlingen to practice law. The years have flown.*

*I hope you are in good health. I never would have guessed that I would live to be ninety. My mobility is not good and some of my injuries from the war bother me. My knees hurt. Like you, I found a bride after Balmorhea, to my surprise. Cecilia died last year. We had two children and now I have six grandchildren and two great-grandchildren. We finally sold the Menger Hotel.*

*The Texas State Parks interviewed all of us about our experiences at Balmorhea. I expect they would have liked to interview you. The oral interviews will be part of their archives to record the history of the CCC camps and the New Deal. I was disappointed that you weren't able to come. You were always my favorite. (Of course, I could never show it at the time.)*

*But I thought you might want to know what happened to your fellow enrollees and some of the folks we became acquainted with at the camp.*

***Chueco (Gonzalez):*** *He became a talker. Went to law school on the GI bill and became a leader in the Mexican American Legal Defense and Educational Fund. He sang "Cielito Lindo" for us with his guitar. He told us stories about his life in Terlingua and the mine there. He talked about "El Perrito" or Howard Perry. Did he tell you about how his uncle died? He is working for the rights of Mexican American workers.*

***Otto Kloss:*** *He told the story about the rattlesnake more than once. I didn't remember that he caught a cub, but he insists it happened. He has softened but is not charming, although he is now the President of the Rotary Club in Fredericksburg. Owns a schnitzel restaurant.*

***E.O. (Miller):*** *Didn't say more than ten words for the entire weekend, but we learned that he is head of an accounting firm in Houston. He lives in River Oaks and has a big house. He married Loretta, who he met when he was at Balmorhea.*

***Joe (Kafouri):*** *He was the life of the party. He brought homemade arak* *and Lebanese food. He has the largest clothing store in the state, Kafouri. He had us in stitches. Told us how you saved Mrs. Roosevelt from a bear on the camping trip. Told us about Jefferson Davis's experiment with camels—and about a character called Haji Ali (from Syria) who came to train them. Texans didn't listen to his advice about camels.*

*Sadly, there are many who are no longer with us.*

***Devilfish (Shines):*** *Toured with John Lomax and collected folk songs in prisons. But he also helped record the oral interviews of ex-slaves. Went to Chicago and played with some big names: Memphis Minnie, Big Bill Broonzy, and Sunnyland Sam. Cut one album. Sadly, he died in mysterious circumstances in his late thirties. I could not find any information about him, although I wrote to his mother in Dallas. No forwarding address.*

***Darlene (i.e., Minnie Brinkley):*** *You were aware that she was the wife of John Brinkley, the medical quack? We learned that she served in the Army Nurse Corps. Killed when a Japanese kamikaze hit the ship's operating room. Was serving on a ship in the Pacific. Awarded a medal posthumously.*

***Dr. Clyde Walker:*** *Returned to Tyler to practice as a G.P. He brought me a bottle of bourbon once when he was staying at the Menger. Wanted to wax lyrical about "the good old days" of Balmorhea. Heard a great deal about the genius of William Faulkner. Walker died in 1961. By the way, the War Department changed my decision and issued an "Honorable Discharge." (You typed the documents, as you must recall.)*

***Dr. John Brinkley:*** *Do you remember Dr. Fishbein? He was the one on the motorcycle with the sidecar. He took Brinkley to court and Brinkley was labeled "a charlatan." Brinkley appealed the decision, but the case was about defamation. His radio station was closed. He died in 1942. Never held accountable for his negligence or those who died by his hand. (With Darlene's assistance.) Or for those phony elixirs.*

***John Romulus Brinkley, Jr.:*** *He killed himself in Del Rio, I don't remember when. (This was what I read in the San Antonio Star. Few details were reported.)*

***Howard Perry:*** *Never filed a lawsuit against Volkov/Brinkley. Made a lot of money from his quicksilver mine, Chisos, during WWI. (This was converted to mercury.) But the company filed for bankruptcy in 1942. Esperado Mining Company bought the mine but couldn't make a go of it, so installations were sold for scrap. He died in his sleep in a hotel in Boston in 1944.*

*And finally,*

***Jack (Huley):*** *I went to the cemetery in Seagraves to visit Jack's grave. The gravestone must have been covered with dust from a storm. Cecilia and I could never find the grave so we left the white lilies under a nearby tree.*

*I would love to hear from you. Please don't hesitate to call:* ***512-555-0126****.*

*I always thought of you as a son. (I was blessed with two daughters.)*

*Sincerely,*

*Roy Bell*

• • •

Maggie held the letter. "Who's Jack?"

Sam blinked back tears. "He was a friend of mine from Sul Ross who drowned at Balmorhea."

"You never told me about that before," Maggie said, patting his arm.

"It was too painful," Sam said. "I just wanted to think about the future. Wanted to get as far away as I could from Balmorhea. Kept hitching until I got to North Carolina."

"You never mentioned any Darlene," Maggie said. "Minnie."

"Shoot. There's nothing to tell. She thought I was a greenhorn. It's a blessing I never got tangled up with her."

"It doesn't matter," Maggie said. "Would fried catfish make you feel better?"

"Why didn't you give me the letter when it came?" Sam asked.

"I don't remember that letter." Maggie said. "Maybe Alicia, our housekeeper, put it in the box."

"Could you call Captain Bell's number? Maybe . . ."

But when she returned to the bedroom, she shook her head. "He died in 1972. And the family sold the property to a flower shop called Morning Glory."

He didn't feel like talking anymore and turned his face to the wall.

CHAPTER 53.

# Buoyancy, November 1980

**The next day, he received a phone call from Chueco, but there was no way he could have known that Sam was reading Captain Bell's letter.** Sam remembered that Chueco had an intuitive gift that gave him an ability to connect with the universe.

Maggie held the cradle of the phone to his ear.

They laughed about "*Cielito Lindo.*" Reminisced about the camp. He still had Sam's sketch of himself with the guitar. How Balmorhea had given him confidence. "Jack was my first teacher," he said. "He encouraged me." You were *símpatico, amigo*. Chueco served in the war and after that he went to night school on the GI Bill. He was defending workers' rights so they weren't treated like "dead flies."

But when Chueo asked him how he was, he only said, "Fair." He did not feel like telling his medical story. There was no Wonder Cure, no magical elixir.

As if Chueco already knew, he said a prayer for the sick: "*Jesús, Hijo de Dios, a Ti que fuiste enviado por el Padre para asumir nuestra debilidad, te pedimos que nos acompañes en este momento de crisis. Salvador misericordioso, ayuda y consuela a los enfermos, para que al recobrar la salud puedan alabarte.*"

Then they said goodbye.

That night, he dreamed Jack was at the bottom of the pool at Balmorhea, pointing to the fissure in the earth, the source of the spring. Green algae covered the gravel bottom. Delilah was paddling above the surface, with her head bobbing. Sam was gesturing that he should go to the surface, but Jack kept gazing at the fissure, as if he were hypnotized. Jack gave a friendly wave as if he would follow. Sam kicked hard to get to the surface. The water was deep.

No more dreams, but a few memories bobbed up:

He had insisted that his children, Griffin and William, learn how to swim. He had taken them to the municipal pool in 1947 shortly after the war had ended. A cluster of Mexican girls from a volleyball team in La Feria were just sitting on the pool deck, looking glum. He asked one girl in Spanish why they weren't swimming, and she said: "*A los mexicanos no se les permite nadar en la piscina.* Can you believe it? I am mad."[1]

He'd dried off and had gone to talk to Earl, who was in charge of the pool.

But Earl, the head of the American Legion, shook his head and was implacable. "They're Mescans." Speculators in Iowa had told Earl he would get rich from citrus in the Rio Grande Valley,[2] yet he had taken losses on his groves several years in a row because of bad freezes.

"But Earl, that's not right. This is a public pool."

"Always has been this way," Earl said. "As far as I can remember."

"Texas was a part of Mexico, and we just took it," Sam said. "If you look at the history."

"Anyhow, this is our rodeo, and this is how we're gonna run it," Earl said.

The conversation had soured Sam's mood, and he had cut the outing with his boys short.

• • •

He remembers his two granddaughters, under the crux of his arms, as the waves surge forward at South Padre Island. Afterwards, he sprays the sand off them with a strong nozzle at the car wash. They are squealing with laughter.

He is hammering down a stake in the hard sand, and then he throws out the line—cheap twine with a chicken neck for bait. He takes a long pole with a looped net and scoops up the crabs.

He is showing his grandson, named after him, how to cast a line for a fish. How to bait the hook. "Patience, young fella. Wait for the right time. That's the secret."

He is twirling Maggie through the air. They are doing the foxtrot. Soon they will be married.

Gwyneth, his secretary, had finished typing up his oral reminiscences of his law practice, his early life in West Texas, and the oil-boom years. Maggie had corrected the grammar and typos with a pencil. But he remembered one story that he had not recorded when he was mayor of Harlingen in 1951.

He considered telling the story the next day, if Maggie would hold the microphone for him. He had never been one to toot his own horn. He might think it over for a day or two—it might seem like he was bragging on himself.

He had mulled over what to do about the American Legion gang and their hold on the Lon C. Hill swimming pool. One evening when he was watering his purple Crotons in the backyard, he watched two aggressive grackles duke it out. But then an emerald hummingbird sidled close to the feeder, full of syrup. When he turned around to turn off the hose, she had disappeared. He knew what he would do. There was no need to take the gang head-on. As the mayor, he took his proposal to the city council. "I propose that the pool be run by the city. The city will first lease and then buy the pool for this summer season." Not one single nay. Unanimous decision, June 1, 1951. He had watched Captain Bell handle these kinds of situations at Balmorhea—how he had sidestepped the directives on segregation. Was that the source that had inspired him? Was that why he kept circling back to those early years at Balmorhea?

Once the paperwork had gone through, he had taken a break from appointments at his law office and driven over to the pool. He wanted to make sure that city officials, not the American Legion, had opened up the gates to the pool. It was June in Harlingen and the air was muggy. The word had already gotten out. He stood at the wire fence, watching Anglo and Mexican children splashing in the Lon C. Hill pool. Retreating without any fanfare, he fired up the motor of his Oldsmobile and drove back to his office on Main Street in fine fettle. He thought of his pa, who never got his rights with ranch owners. He remembered Chueco's stories about Howard Perry: all of those workers who died in the mine because of poor conditions. He had not made a lot of money in his law practice, but he had helped many folks in trouble when he could.

That night in 1980, a few days before his seventy-first birthday, Sam McCabe at first drifted and then bobbed into a luminous, sapphire blue, like the water at Balmorhea, lighter and freer than he had felt in a long while. He never told the story of either swimming pool, but they surged to the surface many years later and floated, like the blossoms of a fuschia bougainvillea, on clear water.

# ACKNOWLEDGMENTS

**My grandfather left a few diaries about his early life, which were not very detailed.** Before he died in 1980, he recorded some oral interviews about his life, which later gave me the idea to write about him. Like the main character in the novel, Sam McCabe, he went to Sul Ross State Teachers' College (now Sul Ross University) in Alpine, which is in a remote part of Texas near the Big Bend National Park. Texas in the 1930s was rural and a very different place from my world as a teenager in the 1970s in Harlingen, Texas. There were many family stories about my grandfather, riding to a one-room schoolhouse on a pony with a compass!

When I was an adult, my father told me the story of my grandfather's role in the desegregation of the Lon C. Hill swimming pool when he was mayor of Harlingen in 1951. I found the documents that detail how the city of Harlingen under my grandfather's leadership took control of the public pool from the American Legion. I was unaware of this family story until much later in my life.

Originally, I was enamored with the idea of writing about Terlingua, a tiny town in West Texas with a mercury mine that was still operating in the 1930s. Kenneth Ragsdale's book *Quicksilver: Terlingua and the Chisos Mining Company* gives an extremely detailed picture of just how mistreated Mexican miners were. Many of the stories in Ragsdale's book were the inspiration for the characters Chueco and Howard Perry, the owner of the mine. I also became interested in the work of curanderas and the healing power of herbs.

I visited Sul Ross University in 2018 and am grateful to the librarians there at the archive, Lisa Zaharova and Melleta Bell, who directed my attention to countless oral interviews and other archival material that led me in another direction. I stumbled upon stories about the establishment of the Big Bend Park and the Balmorhea swimming pool as Civilian Conservation Corps projects under Roosevelt's New Deal. What I really wanted to write about was the wondrous pool at Balmorhea, which was built by the CCC. My grandfather never worked on a CCC project, but he was like many of the farm boys I read about who were eager for opportunity in the Great Depression.

I first swam in Balmorhea when I was twelve years old on a family vacation. However, on my first visit to Sul Ross in 2018, I had not visited the pool but had just gotten the idea to write about it. After I finished a draft of the novel, I visited the pool in the summer of 2023 to see if I needed to make changes to the manuscript. Many thanks to my friend Julie Kuglen, who accompanied me on this trip. I would also like to thank Torrey Bonham, the superintendent at Balmorhea State Park, who kindly gave us a tour of the pool and shared his archival information about it.

Another book that influenced the novel was Pope Brock's *Charlatan: America's Most Dangerous Huckster, The Man who Pursued Him and the Age of Flimflam.* He tells the story of Dr. John Brinkley, who was a con man, and the man who pursued him, Dr. Fishbein. The medical profession was not highly regulated at the time. Brinkley made the claim that he could improve male virility with goat testicle transplants. Many died from his experimental operations. Curiously enough, he set up shop in Texas in the thirties, using a radio station on the Mexican side of the border to evade authorities. I was interested in the line between medical experimentation and quackery, which often was not such a fine line in the early days of medicine. My grandfather's life was prolonged by radiation in the thirties, but sadly, it was also the cause of cancer later in his life.

I want to thank the American University in Cairo who granted me a professional development leave in the spring of 2023. Freed from academic duties and responsibilities, I was able to focus completely on the novel. The university also funded a trip to the Community of Writers' conference in 2019. Many thanks to Michelle Henry, who was the chair of the Rhetoric and Composition Department at the time.

I am grateful to many friends and writers who read the manuscript and offered helpful suggestions. Thanks to the Community of Writers, where I workshopped the first chapter. Thanks again to my dear friend Jennifer Horne, who has been such a loyal friend ever since I met her in Tuscaloosa in the nineties. Jeff Adams, a friend from Community of Writers, offered insightful comments. Thanks to William Melaney for his expansive knowledge of literature, Melanie Carter for her thoughtfulness and sensitivity, Raphael Cohen for his helpful feedback, and Julie Kuglen for her adventurous spirit and countless fruitful conversations.

Many thanks also to Jody Baboukis for her careful editing.

I would like to thank the entire team at TCU Press for shepherding this story into print: Dan Williams, Marco Roc, Adrienne Martinez, Tameko Spann, and Shannon Houchin. This is the right home for the book.

# BIBLIOGRAPHY


Alex, Thomas. *Big Bend Park and Vicinity.* Arcadia Publishing, 2011.

Alex, Thomas, and Robert Wirt. *Around Terlingua.* Arcadia Publishing, 2015.

Anaya, Rudolf. *Bless Me, Ultima.* Warner Books, 1994.

Anderson, John Q., ed. *Texas Folk Medicine: 1,333 Cures, Remedies, Preventatives and Health Practices.* University of North Texas Press, 1998.

Arnold, Catharine. *Pandemic 1918: Eyewitness Accounts for the Greatest Medical Holocaust in Modern History.* St. Martin's Press, 2020.

Beaumont, Sam. *Preaching the Blues: The Life and Times of Son House.* Chicago Review Press, 2010.

Boessenecker, John. *Texas Ranger: The Epic Life of Frank Hamer, the Man Who Killed Bonnie and Clyde.* Thomas Dunne Books, 2016.

Bowman, Timothy Paul. *Blood Oranges: Colonialism and Agriculture in the South Texas Borderlands.* Texas A & M University Press, 2016.

Boyd, Eva Jolene. *Noble Brutes: Camels on the American Frontier.* Wordware, 1994.

Brandemante, Cynthia, with Angela Reed. *Texas State Parks and the CCC: The Legacy of the Civilian Conservation Corps.* Texas A & M University Press, 2015.

Brock, Pope. *Charlatan: America's Most Dangerous Huckster, the Man who Pursued Him and the Age of Flimflam.* Three Rivers Press, 2009.

Cohen, Stan. *The Tree Army: A Pictorial History of the Civilian Conservation Corps, 1933–1942.* Pictorial Histories Publishing Company, 1980.

Cook-Wiesen, Blanche. *Eleanor Roosevelt.* Bloomsbury, 1993.

Cornebise, Alfred Emile. *The CCC Chronicle: Camp Newspapers of the Civilian Conservation Corps, 1933–1942.* McFarland, 2004.

Corrigan, William, and Clive Webb. *The Forgotten Dead: Mob Violence Against Mexicans in the United States, 1848–1928.* Oxford University Press, 2013.

Egan, Timothy. *The Worst Hard Time: The Untold Story of Those Who Survived the Great American Dust Bowl.* Houghton Mifflin, 2006.

Einhorn, Edward. "The Resistable Rise of J.R. Brinkley, Part III." Untitled Theater Company No. 61. Hosted by Apple Podcasts. October 25, 2020.

Fahrenthold, Stacy D. *Between the Ottomans and the Entente: The First World War in the Syrian and Lebanese Diaspora, 1908–1925*. Oxford University Press, 2019.

Fitzharris, Lindsey. *Facemaker: A Visionary Surgeon's Battle to Mend the Disfigured Soldiers of World War I*. Picador, 2023.

Govenar, Alan. *Lightnin' Hopkins, His Life and Blues*. Chicago Review Press, 2010.

Jacob, Linda. *Strangers No More: Syrians in the United States, 1880–1900*. Kalimah Press, 2019.

Johnson, Forrest Bryant. *The Last Camel Charge: The Untold Story of America's Desert Military Experiment*. Penguin, 2013.

Justin, John Kenneth. *Thirty Dollars a Day, One Day a Month: An Anecdotal History of the Civilian Conservation Corps, Volume II, Enrollee Memories*. Amazon Digital Services, 2019.

Keller, David. *Alpine*. Arcadia Publishing, 2011.

Lee, R. Alton. *The Bizarre Careers of John R. Brinkley*. University Press of Kentucky, 2022.

Leuchtenburg, William. *Franklin Roosevelt and the New Deal, 1932–1940*. Harper and Row, 1963.

Lomax, John. *Adventures of a Ballad Hunter*. University of Texas Press, 2017.

Lornell, Kip, Contributor. *The Blues Come to Texas: Paul Oliver and Mack McCormick's Unfinished Book*. Texas A & M University Press, 2019.

Maher, Neil M. *Nature's New Deal: The Civilian Conservation Corps and the Roots of the American Environmental Movement*. Oxford University Press, 2008.

Mann, Thomas. *The Magic Mountain*. Alfred Knopf, 1927.

Manning, Diane. *Hill Country Teachers: Oral Histories from the One-Room School and Beyond*. Twayne Publishers, 1990.

Miles, Elton. *Stray Tales of the Big Bend*. Texas A & M University Press, 1993.

Morgenthaler, Jefferson. *The German Settlement of the Texas Hill Country*. Mockingbird Books, 2011.

Najera, Jennifer R. *The Borderlands of Race*. University of Texas Press, 2015.

Paredes, Americo. *Folklore and Culture of the Texas-Mexican Border*. University of Texas Press, 1995.

Paredes, Americo, ed. and trans. *Folktales of Mexico*. University of Chicago Press, 1970.

Pastor, Camila. *The Mexican Mahjar: Transnational Maronites, Jews and Arabs under the French Mandate*. University of Texas Press, 2017.

Quinn, Susan. *Eleanor and Hick: The Love Affair That Shaped a First Lady.* Penguin Press, 2016.

Ragsdale, Kenneth Baxter. *Quicksilver: Terlingua and the Chisos Mining Company.* Texas A & M University Press, 2006.

Rivas-Rodriguez, Maggie. *Texas Mexican Americans and Postwar Civil Rights.* University of Texas Press, 2015.

Roberts, Ken. *The Cedar Choppers: Life at the Edge of Nothing.* Texas A & M University Press, 2018.

Robinson, Charles M. *The Men Who Wear the Star: The Story of the Texas Rangers.* Penguin, 2000.

Sitton, Thad, ed. *Harder than Hardscrabble: Oral Recollections of the Farming Life from the Edge of the Texas Hill Country.* University of Texas Press, 2004.

Smithers, W. D. *Chronicles of the Big Bend: A Photographic Memoir of the Border.* Texas State Historical Association, 1999.

Torres, Eliseo "Cheo," and Timothy Sawyer, Jr. *Curandero: A Life in Mexican Folk Healing.* University of Georgia Press, 1981.

Trotter, Robert II, and Juan Antonio Chavira. *Curandisimo: Mexican American Folk Healing.* University of Georgia Press, 1997.

Uzzel, Robert. *Blind Lemon Jefferson: His Life, His Death and His Legacy.* Eakin Press, 1994.

Velcamp-Alforo, Theresa. *So Far from Allah, So Close to Mexico: Middle Eastern Immigrants in Modern Mexico.* University of Texas Press, 2009.

Weber, John. *From South Texas to the Nation: The Exploitation of Mexican Labor in the Twentieth Century.* University of North Carolina Press, 2015.

Wooster, Ralph. *Texas and Texans in the Great War.* State House Press, 2010.

Worster, Donald. *Dust Bowl: The Southern Plains in the 1930s.* Oxford University Press, 1979.

# ENDNOTES

## CHAPTER 3

1. Many of the books I read about early blues in Texas inspired the character of Devilfish, especially the life of Lightnin' Hopkins. He played in juke joints in Deep Ellum, but also played for house parties and picked cotton. He had an itinerant lifestyle. But I also read a number of other books that were informative about the early blues in Texas and the lives of musicians. See Sam Beaumont, *Preaching the Blues: The Life and Times of Son House*; Robert Uzzel, *Blind Lemon Jefferson: His Life, His Death and His Legacy.* Especially helpful was Kip Lornell, *The Blues Comes to Texas: Paul Olivier and Mack McCormick's Unfinished Book.*
2. I wrote these lyrics. They were inspired by "Let Me Play with Your Poodle," a song made famous by Lightnin' Hopkins, an early blues guitarist, originally from Centerville, Texas. The lyrics are by Hudson Whittaker. Hopkins was friendly with Blind Lemon Jefferson, a pioneer in Texas blues. See *Lightnin' Hopkins: His Life and Blues*, by Alan Govenar.
3. This is a well-known nineteenth century spiritual, written by Wallace Willis. It is in the public domain.
4. Sotol is distilled from the *Dasylirian wheeleri* plant in the Chihuahuan desert in northern Mexico and West Texas.
5. "Purple flower" is a reference to echinacea. It was an herbal remedy used by Native-Americans and Mexican curanderos to treat bee stings, spider bites, and snake bites. See Robert Trotter and Juan Antonio Chavira, *Curandisimo: Mexican American Folk Healing*, and Eliseo Torres and Tim Sawyer, *Curandero: A Life in Mexican Folk Healing.*

## CHAPTER 5

1. I had read Rabea Jaber's novel, *Amereeka* in Arabic, about Syrians who immigrated to the United States, who became peddlers and then shopkeepers. However, I was unaware that many Syrians immigrated to Mexico during the breakup of

the Ottoman Empire, and then later immigrated to El Paso. They intermarried with Mexican Americans. These books were particularly helpful: Camila Pastor, *The Mexican Mahjar: Transnational Maronites, Jews and Arabs under the French Mandate*; Stacy Farhrenthold, *Between the Ottomans and the Entente: The First World War in the Syrian and Lebanese Diaspora, 1908–1926*; Linda Jacob, *Strangers No More: Syrians in the United States, 1880–1900; Theresa Velcamp-Alforo, So Far from Allah, So Close to Mexico: Middle Eastern Immigrants in Modern Mexico.*

2. This is a reference to Jefferson Davis's military camel project, when he was Secretary of War. From 1856 to 1861, camels were imported from the Middle East to haul supplies across the Southwest territories. This was before the establishment of railroads. The experiment was not a success. See Eva Boyd, *Noble Brute: Camels on the American Frontier*, and also Forrest Bryant Johnson, *The Last Camel Charge: The Untold Story of America's Desert Military Experiment.*

## CHAPTER 6

1. Robert Fechner, Director of the CCC: memo on segregation within the camps. In my research, I found that many Black Americans were digging trenches and working on the Big Bend National Park. In 1935, Robert Fechner ordered the "complete segregation of colored and white enrollees." I did not necessarily find any Black Americans who worked at Balmorhea, but it is plausible that the C.O. of the camp could ask for enrollees from Big Bend National Park for the kitchen. Many Black Americans worked in the kitchens.

## CHAPTER 8

1. The First Lady, Eleanor Roosevelt, did not visit Balmorhea in 1936. She visited Texas in 1939, which was what gave me the idea. (To my surprise, I found evidence from her column, "My Day," that she visited Harlingen, Texas, my hometown, in 1939, and took the train from there to San Antonio.) She was hoping that camps would also be established for women. By 1936, about 5,000 women were enrolled in "She-She-She" camps. She visited Camp Tera at Bear Mountain in New York, a camp for women, in 1933. There was resistance in the administration to the idea of camps for unemployed women. See Blanche Wiesen-Cook, *Eleanor Roosevelt.*

2. A new problem that arose during World War I was how to treat facial wounds caused by heavy artillery. Dr. Harold Gillies was a pioneer in plastic surgery who established Queen's Hospital in Sidcup in 1917. Soldiers with severe facial injuries were sent to

him from France. Soldiers' horrific injuries, Dr. Gillies's treatment of their wounds, and his relationships with his patients are described in Lindsey Fitzharris, *Facemaker: A Visionary Surgeon's Battle to Mend the Disfigured Soldiers of World War I.*

3. See Catharine Arnold, *Pandemic 1918: Eyewitness Accounts for the Greatest Medical Holocaust in Modern History.*

## CHAPTER 9

1. The treatment of Mexican miners at Terlingua is well documented by Ken Ragsdale in *Quicksilver: Terlingua and The Chisos Mining Company.*
2. The character of Chueco was inspired by Ragsdale's book. One *curandera* gained the trust of the miners, and they went to her for ailments, instead of the company doctor.

## CHAPTER 10

1. W. D. Smithers describes how he was cured from heatstroke by one of his Mexican neighbors who used a sunflower shampoo in his book, *Chronicles of the Big Bend, A Photographic Memoir of the Border.*
2. Pope Brock's book, *Charlatan:* America's *Most Dangerous Huckster, The Man who Pursued Him and the Age of Flimflam* was an invaluable source of information about Dr. John Brinkley, a quack who had a medical degree from a degree mill. Brinkley promised greater virility to men with goat transplant operations. Brinkley also sold elixirs and other products, "cure-alls." See also Lee Alton, *The Bizarre Careers of John R. Brinkley.*

## CHAPTER 13

1. John Boessenecker's biography of Frank Hamer, *Texas Ranger: The Epic Life of Frank Hamer: The Man Who Killed Bonnie and Clyde*, gave me a sense of Hamer's personality. He was a very reserved man.
2. Charles Robinson's book, *Texas Rangers: The Men Who Wear the Star*, is a comprehensive history of the Texas Rangers. Some of the Texas Ranger characters on the camping trip and their stories were derived from his book.
3. Eleanor Roosevelt and Lorena Hickok took trips together, but not to Texas. The trips were not official. See Susan Quinn's book, *Eleanor and Hick: The Love Affair that Shaped a First Lady.*

4. Apparently, there were a few wild camels left over in the Big Bend area from Jefferson Davis's Military Experiment, even in the 1930s. See Forrest Johnson, *The Last Camel Charge: The Untold Story of America's Military Experiment.*
5. There were many descriptions of Howard Perry in Ken Ragsdale's book, *Terlingua and the Chisos Mining Company*, from oral interviews with miners and other workers from the company.

## CHAPTER 14

1. Tuberculosis was a bacterial infection which attacked the lungs, often deadly in the 1930s. It was also called T.B. or "consumption." At that time, there was no antibiotic cure, so it was treated with rest, fresh air, and good food. Patients were isolated and sent to sanitoriums. One such sanitorium was sixteen miles from San Angelo, Texas. See Texas State Historical Association.

## CHAPTER 19

1. Dr. Morris Fishbein was a physician who was the editor of the *Journal of the American Medical Association* from 1924 to 1951. There was a series of articles in the *Kansas City Star* about Brinkley, but he was not the author. He wrote a two-part article called "Modern Medical Charlatans," which was published in *Hygeia* in 1938. Brinkley sued him for libel but lost the case. Fishbein was obsessed with exposing Brinkley. See Brock, *Charlatan: America's Most Dangerous Huckster.*
2. Pope Brock's book, *Charlatan: America's Most Dangerous Huckster*, gives details about Brinkley's marital history. He had a stormy marriage with Sally Wike. They pretended to be Quaker doctors. After the birth of their first child, Sally left him, but Brinkley kidnapped the daughter. They were reunited and had two more daughters. In 1913 he married Minerva Jones in Memphis, but was not divorced from Sally Wike. Sally confronted them in 1915, and they eventually divorced. They had a son, named John, who killed himself in the 1970s. Minerva assisted him in his operations in Milford, Kansas, where he set up a clinic and promised patients greater virility with his goat transplant operations. The couple later moved to Texas. Minerva Jones never worked in a Civilian Conservation Camp. That is my invention.

## CHAPTER 20

1. The case of the "Escanaba Fever Girl" is mentioned in Pope Brock's book.

2. The medical profession was not tightly regulated in the United States in the 1930s.

3. John Brinkley owned a radio station on the Mexican side of the border, XER. The advantage of this was that it was not regulated by the Federal Communications Commission. He could advertise his fraudulent pharmaceutical products and services. See Brock, *Charlatan: America's Most Dangerous Huckster.*

### CHAPTER 21

1. John Brinkley's house in Del Rio is described in Brock, *Charlatan: America's Most Dangerous Huckster.*

### CHAPTER 23

1. "The Resistible Rise of J. R. Brinkley, Part III." Untitled Theater Company No. 61. Written by Edward Einhorn. Hosted by Apple Podcasts. October 25, 2020. This is a radio play based on Brinkley's radio show. It gave me an idea of what their show was like.

### CHAPTER 26

1. In his book, *Quicksilver: Terlingua and the Chisos Mining Company*, Ken Ragsdale describes the lawsuits filed against Howard Perry, the owner of the Chisos Mining Company, by miners from the company. The logbook of the mine is also included, which shows the horrific injuries that miners suffered on a daily basis. Working conditions were very poor.

2. Howard Perry wanted the miners to buy only from his company store. But gradually, they began ordering from catalogs or buying from peddlers.

### CHAPTER 27

1. Dr. John Brinkley's medical license was revoked in Kansas and California.

2. Many workers lost their lawsuits against Perry because he had greater resources and influence in Brewster County.

### CHAPTER 29

1. I wrote the lyrics here. It was inspired by Li'l Johnson's song, "Just put my hot dog in your bun." He was active 1929–1937.

2. This is my invention. Inspired by the same song by Li'l Johnson.

## CHAPTER 30

1. The details about the Brinkleys' home and their Christmas parties in Del Rio are described in Brock, *Charlatan: America's Most Dangerous Huckster.*

## CHAPTER 34

1. Germans immigrated to central Texas from 1830 to 1900. As late as the 1950s, people still spoke German in the area. See Jefferson Morgenthaler, *The German Settlement of the Texas Hill Country.*

## CHAPTER 36

1. "The Prostate Plan" is described in Brock, *Charlatan: America's Most Dangerous Huckster.*

## CHAPTER 37

1. Eliseo Torres and Timothy Sawyer, *Curandero: A Life in Mexican Folk Healing*, and Robert Trotter II and Juan Antonio Chavira, *Curandisimo: Mexican American Folk Healing*, give details on remedies and the idea of "susto."

## CHAPTER 41

1. John Lomax and his son, Allen, traveled around the South collecting ballads and recording blues musicians. Their journey is described in John Lomax's book, *Adventures of a Ballad Hunter.* They were friendly with many Black musicians who introduced them to others. This was around the same time.

## CHAPTER 49

1. There were a few accidents in the CCC camps. In my research, I didn't find that there was a drowning at Balmorhea, but there were a few drownings at other camps.

## CHAPTER 51

1. Former Governor Neff attended the opening of Balmorhea. Some of this dialogue was taken from Neff's speeches. See Texas State Library and Archives Commission. There is no evidence that Dr. John Brinkley or Howard Perry attended. This is my invention.

## CHAPTER 53

1. In her book, *Borderlands of Race*, Jennifer Najera cites a number of oral interviews from South Texas about racism against Mexican Americans. This dialogue was inspired by one of her interviews. My grandfather spoke Spanish well and was interested in people. This encounter, though, is my invention.

2. Timothy Bowman describes the development of the Rio Grande Valley in his book, *Blood Oranges: Colonialism and Agriculture in the South Texas Borderlands*. Land speculators recruited buyers from Iowa and other northern states, promising them a "land of milk and honey" in the twenties thanks to "quick-rich" schemes with citrus. Many of the Anglos who came did not bother to learn Spanish. He mentions that many of the Anglos who were indigenous to the area knew Spanish.

## AUTHOR BIO

Originally from Harlingen, Texas, Gretchen McCullough's stories, essays, and reviews have appeared in *The Barcelona Review*, *World Literature Today*, *Story South*, *Guernica*, *The Millions*, *The Common*, and the *LA Review of Books*. She was awarded a BA from Brown University in 1984 and earned her MFA in Creative Writing from the University of Alabama in 1995. Her books include *Three Stories from Cairo* (2011), *Shahrazad's Tooth* (2013), *Confessions of a Knight Errant* (2022), and *Shahrazad's Gift* (2024). She also co-translated Mohamed Metwalli's poetry collection, *A Song by the Aegean Sea* (2022). Currently, she is on the faculty at the American University in Cairo. She lives with her husband, the Egyptian poet Mohamed Metwalli, in Cairo.

## DISCUSSION QUESTIONS FOR BOOK CLUBS

1. What did you learn about how the New Deal helped unemployed men during the Great Depression?
2. What was the role of Eleanor Roosevelt in promoting Roosevelt's New Deal?
3. Did the book feel "authentic" to you, historically? Did you learn anything new about the time period?
4. How were historical sources used in the novel? Did they give the novel credibility?
5. What did you learn about the challenges of running these "man-camps"? What challenges did Captain Bell face?
6. Medical quackery is still relevant. Does the healthcare profession do enough to hold doctors accountable for unethical behaviors or poor medical care?
7. When does the cure become the poison? For example, some medical treatment has severe side-effects, like chemotherapy, or medicine may cause other health problems. Can you give other examples?
8. Who was the most sympathetic character in the novel in your view? Most unsympathetic?
9. How did the expectations placed on women in Darlene's time affect her opportunities and decisions throughout the novel? Would she experience similar challenges today?
10. How was the use of discrimination against Black and Hispanic workers presented in the novel? Is this type of discrimination still present in our contemporary world?
11. How were workers abused at the mercury mine at Terlingua? Why were workers denied justice?
12. How were immigrants treated? How are their experiences similar to or different from how they are treated today?
13. What books or sources listed at the back of the book would you like to explore further? What topics would you like to learn more about?
14. What do you think were the novel's most important themes? Use examples from the book to support your answer.

www.ingramcontent.com/pod-product-compliance
Lightning Source LLC
LaVergne TN
LVHW092110101026
849885LV00030B/161